# THE HIKE

Landon Beach

Cover designed by Design for Writers

Landon Beach
Visit my website at landonbeachbooks.com

Printed in the United States of America

First Printing: May 2021
Landon Beach Books

ISBN-13 978-1-7322578-6-3

*For Eric (deity) and Jim (sui generis)*
*—friends who have hiked many miles of life with me.*

# THE HIKE

"You call that murder? Well, I see murder, too, not written on those drowned faces out there but on the faces of dead thousands! They are the assassins, the dealers in death, I am the avenger...Do you know the meaning of love, professor? What you fail to understand is the power of hate. It can fill the heart as surely as love can...But there is hope for the future. When the world is ready for a new and better life, all this will someday come to pass—in God's good time."

- Captain Nemo, *20,000 Leagues Under the Sea*


"If possible, you should always touch the body with your gun to make sure the man is dead. Man is the hardest animal to kill. If he gets away, he will come back to kill you."

- Salvatore Maranzano, First capo di tutti capi of the five New York Families


"When they come, they'll come at what you love."

- Michael Corleone, *The Godfather: Part III*


"Where is Good? In our reasoned choices. Where is Evil? In our reasoned choices. Where is that which is neither Good nor Evil? In things outside of our own reasoned choice."

- Epictetus, *Discourses*, 2.16.1

# PROLOGUE I

**Springer Mountain, Georgia, Saturday, April 4, 2015**

R ays of golden sunlight found their way easily through the bare, gray tree trunks rising toward the sky as Brad Cranston stood in front of the stone archway that marked the start of the Appalachian Approach Trail.

Last night, he had stayed at Amicalola Falls Lodge and been told by the front desk clerk that in a few months, the surrounding woods would be a lush green canopy of tree leaves. However, in April, it was as if nature refused to leave a deep winter depression and only a skeleton of the once vibrant woods remained with human beings hiking around her weathered-bark bones looking for flesh. Brad couldn't argue with the description, but he did see scattered patches of foliage, signifying that the forest was coming back to life and that spring was here, and summer was right around the corner. After a chilly morning with temperatures in the low forties, Brad's watch said the temperature was now in the upper fifties. Dressed in a red, long-sleeved, moisture-wicking Columbia shirt with tan Columbia pants and leather L.L. Bean Cresta hiking boots, he turned his forty-six-year-old body away from the stone archway, and a beam of sun shone

1

on his face. He enjoyed the momentary warmth and then took a couple of steps forward, then stopped and scanned the faces of the half-dozen hikers wearing bright-colored windbreakers and lugging huge backpacks, heading his way. They passed by him, stabbing the earth with their trekking poles, without offering any greetings and without much chatter between them, seemingly lost in their thoughts about the task that lay ahead. Some earlier hikers had been louder, cracking jokes and laughing to ease the tension, which he had settled on as a strategy to use with his own hiking partner. He looked at his watch. It was 1 p.m. They were supposed to meet near the arch at noon. Brad's hiking partner, his loveable screwup of a younger brother, Conrad, was still nowhere to be seen.

Brad pivoted and watched the hikers go under the arch. For a while, he could hear the sound of the group's boots cracking the scattered branches on the floor of the trail, but soon the cracks and snaps faded until all he could hear was the occasional buzzing of the few bugs that had dared to brave the cooler April temperatures. For the twentieth time today, Brad looked at the red sign with white letters next to the arch signifying the beginning of the approach trail. Eight and a half miles later was the official start of his 2,181-mile Appalachian Trail (AT) hike with Conrad. If all went well, they'd summit Mount Katahdin in Maine's Baxter State Park and hug the sign on Baxter Peak sometime in September or early October. Months had gone into their preparation, all leading to today—day one.

He had picked the approach trail as their start instead of being dropped off where Forest Service Road 42 intersected the trail less than a mile into the AT. If Conrad, the king of shortcuts, had known about this option, he would have demanded that they start there. Brad figured the 8.5-mile approach trail would be an easy test to see if Conrad was serious or not. Once Conrad started something he was interested in, he had a surprising amount of drive and resiliency, which had been a powerful advantage at a few brief points during his life and a debilitating liability during other stretches.

They were from Michigan, so a handful of Michigan state parks had been their training ground for day hikes to get them in shape and get them used to carrying the load they would hump with on the trail. They had scaled up to overnighters and performed equipment research and testing, read a dozen books about the trail, including Bryson's inspirational account, and, finally, tackled logistics planning. Their support person would be their sister, Heidi, and she had bump boxes, containing specific items to replenish their supplies, all addressed and ready to send to them as they reached certain towns. Brad reasoned that if they failed, it wouldn't be because of a lack of preparation. In fact, they were so prepared that he was seeing visions of toilet paper, duct tape, and half-toothbrushes on the wall at night, including his stay last night at the comfortable lodge. He'd invited Conrad to fly into Atlanta with him, ride to the lodge, and stay with him there so they could start hiking in the morning, but his brother had declined. *"Look, I'll be standing with you under the stone-arch at high noon, all right? Don't get all uptight on me. Let things flow,"* he had said. Like always, there had been no changing his mind.

Brad looked at his watch again. 1:15 p.m. Another group of hikers, louder than the one he had just seen disappear into the woods, passed by and stopped by the arch to have their pictures taken before embarking on their journeys. Thankfully, they did not ask for his help. He must have seen over fifty people already and helped most of them with their pictures. *"Hello, sir. Could you help us take a quick picture?"*

*Where in the hell was Conrad?* That was the most pressing question. Another question slithering around in Brad's mind was: Why am I doing this? He'd been divorced for five years, so this wasn't a knee-jerk escapist mission. He was relatively happy in his life, so this wasn't an "I've gotta go find myself" remedy. He had never been out of shape, and so this wasn't some crusade with echoes from a doctor's physical examination that said, "Lose the weight...*or else.*" He hadn't succumbed to materialism, so the hike was not to get away from the empty distractions and excesses that contemporary life in America offered at every turn. *Why am I here?* His best answer was that he had helped his brother turn his life around, they had both always been the outdoors type, they enjoyed each other's company, and, although Conrad was much more competitive than he was, they liked a challenge. Any other positive that this half-a-year provided would be welcomed but not required. *What will the rest of the world be doing for the next six months?* Standing here, pissed off waiting for Conrad, Brad Cranston decided that he didn't really care.

He moved away from the archway and took a seat far enough away to not be asked for any more picture assistance. He'd give Conrad another half-hour or so, then he'd hike back up to the lodge and start making phone calls.

*Don't start playing the 'What if?' game,* he told himself. He picked up a twig from the ground and started bending it, testing its pliability. On the third bend, it snapped in two. He threw the pieces down. *Okay, what have I missed here?* He searched his memory for any hints that Conrad would be a no-show.

All of the milestones that, if not taken care of, would have triggered Conrad's early exit from the adventure had been achieved. They had already paid for the necessary permits, had plenty of money for fees, bought the equipment, bought the airline tickets, and registered for the thru-hike. Their trail names were as different as they were: his—Sandusky, because of his love of Cedar Point and the happy memories of taking his daughter Noelle there when she was young; Conrad's—Proust, his brother's favorite author. Brad had wanted to leave earlier, late February, to avoid the crowds. With so many northbound hikers, shelters and tenting areas ran out of space quickly. Conrad had said no, and Brad had given in to the April start date. So, the schedule wasn't a show stopper. Then, there was the cash issue. The general rule of thumb was to budget one thousand dollars per month each on the hike. Since the hike took five to seven months, Brad had saved seven thousand dollars, and Conrad had shown him his bank account statement two days ago—the funds were there. As far as travel, Conrad's flight had taken off early this morning from Detroit Metro and had landed in Atlanta on time. He had called Conrad a half an hour after the plane had landed, but the call had gone straight to voicemail. Brad had called Heidi next, but she hadn't heard from Conrad either. There could have been an accident on the way from Atlanta. If that was the case, he would hear about it at some point.

He laughed to himself. *This is ridiculous.* Brad knew that Conrad was probably going to show up any minute now with some lame excuse, which would be forgiven, and then they'd hike the legendary Appalachian Trail. It sounded like he was relaxing, talking sense into himself, but something about the situation didn't feel right to Brad.

*Did Conrad try and bring a gun in his luggage?*

They had talked about bringing one on the trail, but Brad thought they had come to the agreement that it was not worth it. The gun could be taken and used against them, it was heavy to carry, and, with Conrad's luck, an accidental discharge was highly probable. There were risks hiking the trail. There were also risks getting behind the wheel of a car and driving ten miles down the road each day to work. In the past two decades, there had been two or three major crimes on the trail. Other than those, three million people had safely traveled its winding path. When he calculated the odds, Brad saw the three million safe passages; Conrad saw the handful of major crimes. *"Somebody could take us right out, Brad!"* he had yelled in one of their early arguments. Christ, he hoped he was wrong and that Conrad had not attempted to bring a weapon to the Detroit airport. *Did Conrad even own a gun?* He didn't want to know.

After waiting an extra ten minutes past the half-hour he had already waited, Brad made his way up to the lodge and called Heidi.

"It's Brad," he said.

"He already quit, didn't he?" Heidi said. "I knew it."

"No. He still hasn't shown up."

There was a pause. "What?"

5

"I've been waiting at the entrance to the approach trail since noon, and he's not here. Have you heard from him?"

"No. Since the plane landed on time and he didn't answer, I just figured he was on his way to you. You know how horrible he is with his cell phone, if he brought it at all," she said, an edge to her voice that seemed laced with both sadness and disappointment. He knew that rage was just around the bend.

"Yep." He tipped his head to the right, sandwiching the phone between his ear and right shoulder, while he lowered his pack to the lobby floor. He then told her all of the scenarios he had thought through. "Other than waiting here to see if he shows up, the only thing I can think of is to call and see if he even got on the plane in Detroit. Can you check for me?"

"Don't you have your cell phone?" she asked.

"No. I didn't want it on the trip with me."

Another pause. "Okay, I'll call," she said.

"Thanks, and, hey, let's not panic. He's put too much into this thing to back out now. That big-hearted oaf will be here any minute, wearing his toothy grin and armed with a ridiculous story about why he was late. And while he tells me the tale, he'll be slinging his backpack around with his thick, hairy arms because he can't stand still."

Heidi's tone was serious. "He may still have a touch of his old charisma, and he's smarter than he deserves to be, but, Brad, he's thirty-eight years old. I'll call."

Five minutes later, one of the phones behind the check-in counter rang. An attendant waved him over.

"Heidi?"

"He never got on the flight. Didn't even check in a bag," she said. Her voice was a whisper, half-concerned, half-enraged.

After all Conrad had put the family through, Brad knew this would be the fatal blow with Heidi. She would now join their parents in the 'Done with Conrad' Club. After dinner with his family a month ago, his father had pulled him aside, eyes narrowed and more serious than a retiree's should be, and said, *"Don't bring him on the hike."*

If he lost faith in Conrad now, he'd never forgive himself. There had to be some explanation. *Had* to be. Even Heidi knew that Conrad was overinvested in the hike, and Conrad was never invested in anything—spent too much time in his own head, or, when he was heavy into every drug on the market, spent too much time out of his head. "It doesn't add up," Brad said. "I—"

"Stop, Brad," she said. "Stop. This is it for me. I'm through. I've got a *whole* bedroom in my house stacked with packages ready to send to you two along the way." He heard her start to cry. "He's gone, and you know it."

"Heidi, I'm sorry. I know how much you've done to help us. We wouldn't even be able to attempt this thing without you." He paused, searching for something to say to keep her on board. "Look, I'm going to stay another night here and wait. We owe it to ourselves and to him. There has to be a reason," he said, wondering if he believed what he had just said. "You know how to reach me. I'll call you in the morning, okay?"

She sniffled. "Fine," she said.

The next morning, he awoke to no Conrad.

And the next morning.

And the next.

Nothing from Heidi.

On Wednesday, he left the lodge and headed home to Michigan. Conrad had disappeared.

# PROLOGUE II

## Location: CLASSIFIED, Winter 2016

C hief Petty Officer Allison Shannon could feel goosebumps on her brown skin underneath her drysuit as she kicked forty feet below the surface of the water. Her fin strokes were smooth as she swept her underwater light from side to side, searching for anyone and anything that was not supposed to be in the water at this time. Approximately ten feet above her was the hull of the most technologically advanced warship ever built, *USS Zumwalt* (DDG-1000). Costing approximately four billion dollars to construct, the destroyer was six hundred feet long, nearly eighty-one feet wide, and had been commissioned on the fifteenth of October in Baltimore's Inner Harbor during Fleet Week. Now, the ship was in another port, staying the night to refuel and to let a few select naval personnel at the base come aboard and tour the spectacular vessel. *Zumwalt*'s ultimate destination was San Diego, its new homeport. Before and after commissioning, there had been intelligence indicating that attempts would be made to destroy or damage the new pride of the American Navy before the ship ever reached the California coast. Hence, at each stop, security was tighter than a pair of spandex.

8

Chief Shannon had been a Search and Rescue (SAR) swimmer for most of her career. She was also a Master Diver, and when the Coast Guard established the diver (DV) rating in 2015, the commanding officer (CO) of the new program selected her to switch rates and help him develop and lead it. The maximum age for entry into the program was thirty-five; at thirty-four, she had outperformed over ninety percent of the new recruits—who were just over half of her age—in the physical fitness test. Now, she was a member of a Maritime Safety and Security Team (MSST), which provided anti-terrorism security for high-value vessels like *Zumwalt*. Her team had provided underwater security during the commissioning and for the two port visits so far as the destroyer made its way south from Baltimore. They were embarked until the ship made it through the Panama Canal; then, a west coast team would embark and take over security until the ship was safely moored in San Diego. Her CO thought that having the team embarked was a bit of an overkill—commissioning was one thing, but *every* port *and* when the *Zumwalt* was at sea? However, he saw the possible rewards of showcasing his top divers doing the job they had been trained to do, which was to make sure there were no divers in areas they shouldn't be—in this case, anywhere near the hull of *Zumwalt*.

Shannon checked the bright Luminox around her wrist: 2345, or 11:45 p.m. civilian time; fifteen minutes until her watch was over. Her pressure gauge indicated that she still had around twenty minutes of air left. *Take it nice and easy.* She rose a few feet and aimed her light at the hull. *Zumwalt*'s motto was *Pax Propter Vim*: Peace Through Power. From what she had observed the past month and a half in the Atlantic Ocean, this ship had power and then some. Up forward, she could see the light of her diving partner, Petty Officer First Class Matt Keller.

She pushed the button to talk on the full face mask she was wearing. "Fifteen minutes, Matt. See anything?"

Keller's voice came across crystal clear in Shannon's wet speaker that sat against her left ear. "Nothing, Chief. Cold, quiet, and dark."

9

*Zumwalt*'s command duty officer (CDO), the engineering duty officer (EDO), and the quarterdeck watch also had communications with the two divers via a net set up on a surface station that had a transducer cable lowered into the water. The CDO broke in, "All quiet up here."

The quarterdeck watch radioed in, "Your reliefs are on deck suiting up as we speak."

Shannon said, "Good to hear. Didn't have to pull them out of their racks this time." She turned in a slow circle away from the hull and pointed her light into the middle of the basin's dark water. From the outer reach of her light's beam, a shadow passed by. *What was that?* She kicked away from the ship, her light in one hand, her spear gun in the other.

"See something, Chief?" Keller asked.

She brought the hand that held the light to her face mask and pushed the talk button. "Saw a shadow at the edge of my light's range. Checking it out."

"Roger that," Keller said.

Shannon appreciated his brevity. During the commissioning, she had been paired with Scroggins, who wouldn't shut the hell up. Plus, Keller was thorough and smart—a pleasure to work with. She stole a glance back at the ship and saw Keller's light moving aft along the hull.

She went to aim her light in the direction where she had seen the shadow but felt a surge of water from her right. Turning just in time, she ducked and saw an enormous white underbelly pass overhead. She raised her light and focused the beam on the creature as it swam past her. Perhaps twelve feet long, there was no mistaking the conical snout, large dorsal fin, wide pectoral fins, and huge crescent-shaped tail: This was a great white shark. Having never seen one underwater before, the length was not what impressed her the most—it was the girth. She watched as the large fish turned and headed toward the middle of the basin and perhaps out to sea. *Had it been circling her, waiting to attack, or was it just searching the port's waters out of curiosity?* There was no barrier to prevent sea life from entering the basin, but she had never seen a shark, let alone a great white, in the U.S. ports where she provided security. Dolphins and the occasional sea turtle? Yes.

She keyed her microphone. "We've got a great white shark down here with us."

"Where? I've got to see it!" Keller said.

She could see Keller's light change direction and start heading toward her. "Too late, sport," Shannon said. "I think he or she is headed back to sea."

"Damn," Keller said, arriving next to Shannon. "Think it will come back?"

She looked in his faceplate. "I hope not. Beast's enormous. It's one thing to see it from a distance and watch its beauty and grace. It's another thing to have that sucker come out of the gloom of this shitty-visibility water."

"How big?" Asked *Zumwalt*'s CDO.

"Around twelve feet—big enough. You should let *Carney* and *Hué City* know, sir," she said. "They have divers working who would appreciate the heads up."

"Roger that, Chief," the CDO said.

"Hey, at least you've got another check on your bucket list now," Keller said.

They had been talking for the past few weeks about all of the underwater sea creatures they had seen throughout their years of diving: blue sharks, bull sharks, mako sharks, oceanic whitetip sharks, tiger sharks, grouper, moray eels, stingrays, sea turtles, manta rays, etc. But neither of them had seen a great white. "Helluva way to do it," Shannon said. "I had envisioned checking that one off in the clear blue water off of South Africa or Australia, both of which I plan to visit when I retire." She smiled, her eyes betraying a slight hint of greed. "Now that I've seen one, though, I've *got* to see another one."

"Okay, stop rubbing it in," Keller said.

They both aimed their lights into the basin and moved them together, first up and down and then side to side. The shark was nowhere to be seen. "Let's do our last sweep," she said. Their lights were now pointing up at their masks, and they could see each other while they spoke. "You move forward to aft, and I'll move aft to forward."

Keller nodded, and she gave him a wink. Then, she put her spear gun under her arm and, with her free hand, made a fin and moved it toward Keller's mask. "You'll get your chance."

"Yeah, right," Keller said.

They kicked back toward the ship.

Standard procedure for turning over the watch meant that the reliefs would start a walk-through about thirty minutes before assuming the watch and then meet up with the off-going watch approximately fifteen minutes later. However, for underwater security watches, the reliefs only needed to be in the water with the off-going watch for a few minutes. There were either enemy divers in the water, or there weren't, and any other piece of information that the on-coming watch might need could be learned from the quarterdeck watch. If they were further south in warmer water, then the watches could be as long as three hours, but, thankfully, Shannon thought, because of the current water temperature, their watches had been reduced to two hours with a tank change at the one-hour point. The MSST had enough divers to ensure that they would get a solid seven hours in the rack before their next two-hour dive at 8 a.m.

Shannon spoke to the quarterdeck watch. "Making our final run. Except for the shark, everything has been quiet," she said. "We are ready to be relieved."

"And ready for a mug of hot chocolate and some sleep," Keller added.

On the quarterdeck, the two divers taking the next watch were almost suited up. Hearing the report, they gave a thumbs up to the officer of the watch, who said, "Quarterdeck, aye. Next watch getting wet in five minutes."

Shannon and Keller acknowledged.

The cool night air stung Lieutenant Marissa Avery's face as she jogged along the base's white strip of beach. The rest of her body was covered in cold-weather running gear, including a watch cap and a thin pair of gloves. Since she had been running for nearly forty minutes to clear her mind after having trouble falling asleep, her sweat seemed like it was starting to freeze between her skin and the tight outer garments she had on.

*Twenty more minutes to go*, she told herself. *C'mon legs. Don't abandon me now.*

The nearly full moon slid behind a cluster of clouds, and, to her right, the ocean water darkened from slate gray to black. She looked ahead. There was approximately a half-mile of beach left before she'd have to turn left, follow the seawall along the river that branched off into the basin, and then complete her loop around the perimeter before arriving at the base's Bachelor Officer Quarters, the BOQ, where she had a room. One more week of training left, and she'd be headed back to Norfolk Naval Station, where her ship was homeported. She'd checked in after dinner with her husband and toddler, who were back home in Virginia. It had been a trying three weeks away from them. Beyond the physical and emotional separation—no, the Navy had not and would never be able to bridge that gap—her training school schedule had been demanding. Up at 0500 and not returning to her BOQ room until dinner, day after day, was starting to wear on her. In fact, as good as the training had been, it was getting repetitive. But that was an area of Navy pride: repeating everything a million times in the name of safety and training. Her word to describe this philosophy? Overkill. However, she was in the home stretch now, and her spirits were rising. What had kept her awake tonight was worrying about what would happen two weeks after she arrived home. Her ship was leaving on a six-month deployment; it would be mid-summer when she saw her family again. *How much do two-year-old boys grow in six months?* She pushed the thought away and focused on her breathing as each footstep patted the sand.

About two hundred yards from the seawall, she noticed something moving irregularly in the waves off to her right. She slowed, eventually jogging in place, and focused on the spot of ocean that had caught her attention. She squinted.

*Was that a boat out there?* She stopped jogging. Yes, it was a boat. A cabin cruiser, painted jet black and around forty feet with no running lights on, bobbed at anchor about fifty yards offshore. There was nothing unusual about a boat anchoring close to shore. However, there was something strange about one that did it and *didn't* display anchor lights. *Maybe the boat was having electrical problems?* She could see no one topside, but the cruiser's dinghy was still secured up forward, so whoever was on board had a way to reach the shore for help.

After a minute, she started to walk, still keeping her eyes on the craft. Maybe there was nothing wrong. Perhaps they had a little too much beer, or, tired after a day of cruising, they simply nodded off and forgot to turn on their anchor lights. It had happened before. She started to jog. After a half-a-dozen strides, a little voice inside her head told her to report it when she got back to her BOQ room. *If you see something, say something.* It had become a cliché since 9/11. The wind started to chill her as she picked up her pace, but her body still felt healthy and strong as she welcomed the cold air into her lungs and then exhaled loudly through her nose.

She neared her turn and jogged backward for a few seconds. The boat was still there, no lights on. She turned and kept going. She'd call base security when she finished her run and make a report. It would clear her conscience even though—she snuck one last look—there were probably just a couple of yo-yos out there passed out below deck.

She turned and ran along the massive seawall. Up ahead, the basin full of ships loomed in the darkness.

The two men kicked slowly along the mucky bottom. They neither used nor carried dive lights. According to their dive computers, which had backlighting and integrated compasses, they should be in the center of the basin by now, where the depth was just above fifty feet. The man on the right had taken on the name of Bill Johnson, according to his forged passport, and the man on the left, Henry

14

Peterson. He, Bill, was the underwater demolition expert. Henry was there to make sure that he was able to complete the mission—Henry was expendable, but he was not. Tonight's target: the Americans' newest machine of death, the *USS Zumwalt.*

A man whom they had never met before, known only as Marcus, was on board a cabin cruiser, anchored off the coast, waiting to pick them up once the explosives had been placed on the hull and the timer had been set for an hour. This would give them plenty of time to climb aboard, weigh anchor, and travel down the coast for thirty minutes until they were directly offshore the beach house that had been purchased a year ago for the mission. Marcus would drop them off close to the beach, and they would swim ashore in just bathing trunks while Marcus headed out to sea to sink the boat in deep water. Then, Marcus would motor back in the dinghy, sink it in water approximately one hundred yards from shore, and swim in. They would all stay the night in the beach house, and in the morning, Marcus would take them by car to an airport. Twenty-four hours later, they would be back home across the Atlantic Ocean. Where would Marcus go after that? Perhaps back to the beach house. Perhaps elsewhere. Bill didn't know.

They approached using closed-circuit rebreathers, which reused the gas that the divers exhaled, enabling them to use the replenished air for their next breath. This gave them three advantages. One, because of the increased efficiency, they could dive longer. Two, because the rebreathers recycled all of the gas they used, there would be only a few bubbles that escaped, meaning their approach would be very quiet, and the lack of bubbles rising would not give away their position to someone looking at the water from above the surface. Three, because they were breathing gas that had already been warmed by themselves, the rebreather would keep them warmer, which was perfect for this cold-weather dive tonight. They had drysuits available on the boat but had decided to go with wetsuits since they wouldn't be in the water that long. Plus, Marcus had explained that if they were a little colder, then they would concentrate harder and be more efficient. Bill thought the logic was sort of sound, but now he wished they had chosen the drysuits.

There was nothing ahead, and, for a moment, Bill started to second guess himself. *Were they headed in the wrong direction? Was the compass not working?* His doubts vanished after a few more kicks. In the distance, two yellow beams swept along the hull of their target. He reached down and felt the bag with the explosive charges and timer. Everything was perfect. As he brought his hand up, he felt a pinch in his thumb. He tried to pull his hand up, but it was caught on something sticking up from the bottom. He grabbed Henry's arm, and they stopped. As soon as he got in position to see what he was stuck on, his hand popped free. At first, there was a kind of pulsating relief, and he rubbed his thumb with his other fingers. Then, he could feel warm fluid ooze from just below the knuckle. Blood. If he had a light to shine on his thumb, at this depth, the blood would appear green. *How bad was the cut?* He straightened and bent his thumb a few times with minimal pain. He'd be fine. *What in the hell had been on the bottom?* He looked down and saw nothing but darkness.

A foot away to his left, he could see Henry's right arm, the hand holding a spear gun. He couldn't see but knew that in Henry's other hand was a stainless-steel dive knife. He gave the right arm a squeeze, and they began to fin toward the ship again. Bill looked at his watch. If everything went as planned, they would have a few moments when the two security divers would swim together and exit the water behind the stern just after the next team entered. Hence, with all four security divers aft, this would give them the opportunity to quickly affix the explosives and timer to the hull near one of the seawater intakes located amidships. It would still be visible, but placed right next to the intake, it would take a slow, detailed inspection to see it. And from what they had observed on a dive earlier in the evening, the security divers didn't go slowly enough all of the time to see everything. The odds of success were good. They continued toward the ship, the golden yellow dive light beams of the security divers growing larger and larger. Meanwhile, green liquid slowly left his thumb, leaving a trail behind them.

"You ready to head up?" Shannon asked Keller.

"All good on my end," Keller said. He was at the stern, looking up at *Zumwalt*'s two enormous shafts and propellers. Shannon was forward, past the bow, turning around.

"I'm headed to you," she said. "Quarterdeck, we're coming up."

The officer of the watch acknowledged and then notified the two divers waiting on the pier. They gave a thumbs up and walked down, fins and dive lights in hand, to the sea ladder at the end of the pier.

Shannon finned up to a depth of twenty feet, and her dive light's lemon beam bloomed against the port-side hull. All of the appropriate equipment aboard *Zumwalt* that would pose a threat to divers had been tagged out after the ship had entered the port and switched from ship to shore power. Still, she kept her distance from any intakes, not wanting to get a part of her body sucked up into the hull. Even though she and Keller had verified the tags prior to diving, accidents had happened before. She descended back down to forty feet and swam toward Keller's beam.

The mammoth shark appeared on the edge of her beam's reach. "Keller! The white is back! Swim toward me." Shannon watched as the large fish ignored her and swam past, heading toward the bow of the ship.

Keller arrived next to her and aimed his light in the same direction as Shannon's. "I see it!" he said. "Let's follow it forwa—wait a minute, what's it doing?"

Suddenly, the shark bolted toward the bottom. Shannon and Keller followed, continuing to shine their lights in the direction the shark had gone. A few kicks later, they witnessed horror as the shark had snapped its jaws around a diver and was shaking its head from side to side as blood billowed out from its mouth.

"Jesus Christ!" yelled Keller.

"What's going on?" shouted the CDO.

Shannon swam down toward the shark. The diver's head and one arm hung out the right side of the fish's mouth, and out the left side was...nothing. She aimed her light and saw two legs with fins, bitten off just above the knees, lying on the basin floor—a cloud of blood rising from them. A spear entered the shark's snout, and Keller's beam found a second diver, a few yards away from the great white. The diver let his used spear gun fall as he swam up to the fish and started to bang on its skin with one hand and repeatedly puncture it with his knife in the other. The shark opened its mouth, and the diver's corpse slipped out—a bloody hulk of shredded neoprene, bone, and gore. The diver with the knife kicked backward, avoiding the agape mouth packed with white, serrated teeth. The shark made a few strong strokes with its crescent tail, cruised by him, and left.

Shannon said, "CDO! We've got two divers down here. One has just been attacked by the shark, and one is—what's he doing?"

She watched as he swam down to what remained of the other diver and started cutting a bag away that was attached to the corpse's midsection. She aimed her speargun at him and approached. Keller was holding his position in the water, approximately ten feet above and behind the man, his spear gun also trained on the diver. "Matt, I don't like it. Whatever he's cutting away is important. He'd be outta here by now if it wasn't," she said. "I'm going to get a closer look."

The CDO came on the net. "There are no other divers who are supposed to be in the basin right now. All divers working on *Carney* and *Hué City* have been accounted for. Bring this guy up, Chief. Your reliefs are on their way to help."

At that moment, both divers sitting on the edge of the pier put on their fins and jumped in.

18

Keller watched as the diver freed the bag. Holding it in one hand and his dive knife in the other, the man turned and looked up at Keller and Shannon.

Using her spear gun, Shannon motioned for him to surface. The man's head turned slightly to the right as if to get a look at something behind her.

Two lights were making their way down toward them.

The man opened the bag and reached inside.

"Is that a...it's an explosive charge!" Keller yelled.

Shannon aimed her speargun at the diver's center of mass and fired. The spear found its mark, and the diver threw his head back in agony. "Get that bag!" Shannon commanded.

She watched as Keller swam down to grab it, but the man stuck his hand inside one more time before Keller could get there.

An explosion erupted from the bag.


"Chief? Chief, can you hear me?"

Shannon's eyes opened. Both of her ears were ringing, and her right leg felt as if the blood inside had been set on fire and a million pins were stabbing her flesh. There was someone on top of her; her mask was off, but the image was blurry. The rest of her body felt cold and clammy.

*Where was she?*

Her left arm was lifted up. A wrapping had been placed around her biceps. *A tourniquet? Please, no.* She felt a squeeze and started to cry out.

Her vision returned to her, and she could see that it was not a tourniquet around her arm, but the black canvas wrapping used to take a patient's blood pressure. A navy corpsman was squeezing the rubber ball at the end of the tube while studying the gauge. She exhaled and looked up into the face of the CDO.

"Chief? Can you hear me?"

Her ears continued to ring, but she could make out what he was saying. She said, "Yes, sir, barely."

He gave a thankful smile.

"My ears—"

"You're going to be okay," he said. "We've got the base ambulance on its way."

"My leg," she moaned.

"Our ship's doc has got it stabilized," he said. "It'll need surgery, but you shouldn't lose it."

She tilted her head left and saw other *Zumwalt* crew members huddled around her. She looked for Keller. Not locating him, she turned her head to the right. Two rigid-hulled inflatable boats were speeding out the mouth of the river and into the Atlantic. The basin's water lay flat with moonlight shining down, making a silver-mirrored strip across the center. She was on the pier. There had been an explosion. Underwater. *Was everyone okay?* She locked eyes with the CDO. "The other divers?"

"They're in the water, making a sweep. Basically, every available diver in the basin is getting wet, searching."

"Keller?" she asked.

His eyes became moist, and he dropped his head.

"No," Shannon said, tearing up.

He lifted his head back up. "I'm sorry, Chief."

She closed her eyes, and the noises around her disappeared as the ringing got louder.

At the first sound of the base sirens, Marcus had weighed anchor and sped down the coast, leaving the two divers. Clumsy fools were on their own now. *Probably fucked it up because they were cold,* he thought. *Should've used some of my local boys.* He knew that if they had been the ones diving, then there would not have been any problems. As for him, he was too old to dive now and had survived too long to be caught. If the wealthy men overseas wanted better results, then they needed to start sending him better soldiers.

Throttling down after ten minutes, he raised a pair of night-vision goggles and scanned the water aft of him. There were two small boats motoring back and forth along the coast just offshore of the base. He was certain that he had not been spotted because they would be giving chase if he had been. However, it didn't mean that they wouldn't head this way soon, or that another more powerful vessel wouldn't emerge from the basin and chase him down. Following the original plan was too risky now. He checked his depth. Almost seventy feet. It would have to do. Cabin cruiser, dinghy, the whole thing was going to the bottom. Of course, this meant a longer swim, but he couldn't chance getting caught in the dinghy. He shut off the engine and looked down at his round tummy putting a strain on the front of the black wetsuit he was wearing. Even this adult girdle couldn't fully suck in his fat. He raised a hand to his heart and massaged his chest while looking at the shore dotted with lights, far off in the distance. He felt tightness in his left arm and pulled it away from his chest. Then, he shook his arm up and down to see if the tightness would loosen up. It didn't. He swallowed.

*Stop it*, he told himself. *You can make it. Going to get to the beach, take off this body-sized diabetic sock and be at the beach house before dawn. Gonna rest up, fork out some serious cash on a couple of whores tomorrow night, do some blow, and then watch as the two lovelies work their magic on me. Hell. Yeah.* Delivering the bad news could wait. Striking their adversary was a virtue, but so was relaxing after putting your ass on the line.

He went below, set the charges, and quickly emerged from the cabin carrying a pair of fins, a mask, and a hood. Taking one more look with the night-vision goggles, he saw no craft approaching from any direction. He threw the goggles into the sea.

The hood took some effort to put on as he pulled the neoprene sleeve down over his large head full of thick, curly, gray hair. Once it was on, he felt an annoying pain underneath, and he struggled to reach in and pull both of his ears up as they had folded over on the final yank to get the hood down. Putting the mask over his face, he could now hear his heart beating in his ears and decided that he did not like it one bit. Everything was calm topside as he walked toward the stern. A nagging feeling washed over him. *What am I forgetting?* A moment later, it finally hit him. *Oh, right, the cabin!* He turned around and padded back across the deck to the opening next to the helm. He shook his head in annoyance as he closed the fiberglass cabin doors, slid a Master Lock through the metal eyes, and snapped the lock shut. The timer had been set for two minutes.

*Get going already.*

Marcus stepped through the open stern gate and sat on the swim step, putting his fins on. A quick dip of his hand in the ocean told him that this was not going to be a pleasant swim. *Fuck it.* He stood up, said a prayer, and jumped in.

The cold water engulfed him, and he thought that this was how it must feel when you are buried alive under an avalanche. His arms and legs felt clumsy, like dead weights that would not listen to the signals his brain was giving them. He turned over onto his back and started kicking to warm up his body. This way, he could also keep an eye on the boat. *Smart*, he thought. Thirty seconds later, he felt vibrations in the water and watched as the cabin cruiser slowly slipped below the surface. He kicked and watched for another minute and then turned over and started a lazy crawl toward shore.

He didn't get far. As if a bolt of lightning entered his left thumb and traveled down an inner expressway to his heart, Marcus jolted upright in the water. Reaching for the heavy and tightening fist-sized section of his chest, as if his touch would relieve the pressure, his eyes became wide behind the tempered glass of his mask. He gasped and then died.

A month later, a morning jogger would slow to a trot as he approached what he thought was a large clump of seaweed. A minute later, he would be on his knees, vomiting in the sand. Behind him, half-hidden by an entangled mass of seaweed and feeding crabs, would be the hooded head, shoulders, left arm, and upper torso of a diver.

Chief Petty Officer Allison Shannon blinked her eyes at the roof of the ambulance as it sped toward the base hospital. A female paramedic sat next to her, rubbing her shoulder.

"You're going to be fine, Chief. Hang in there. Just a few more turns, and we're there."

Shannon tried to give a smile, but the tears coming out of her eyes betrayed the attempt at positivity and hope. All she could think about was Keller and the fact that he was gone forever.

*I'll never get in the water again. I swear it.*

Little did she know that the water would call her back...

# I

## Shelter Harbor, Michigan

## *Present Day*

Remington Bradshaw Cranston Jr., the man deemed "Mr. Ordinary" in his senior yearbook, exited the front door of Sunrise-Side Press on a perfect June day, descended two concrete steps, and walked across the dirt parking lot toward the only thing he had left in life that he could count on: his 2010 Ford F-150, nicknamed "Rusty."

He'd never previously nicknamed a vehicle in his life, but when one gets divorced at forty-one, one tends to do stupid things like buy a brand-new truck and give it a nickname. And so, he'd taken out a car loan—cash to purchase it? Ha! No way—and settled on a regular cab because Brad Cranston didn't foresee anyone sitting in the passenger seat, let alone anyone sitting behind him in the extended cab section. His only child had just turned eighteen when he bought Rusty and was on her way to the University of Southern California to study film.

A year prior, he had protested, telling her that in four years she would have a fine arts degree that was basically useless. Then, the marriage had tanked, and he had changed his mind: Who in the hell was he to tell her the pathway to success in life? Four years later, she did graduate with a degree and had been accepted to film school to get a graduate degree in screenwriting. Well, she was now twenty-eight, and the current count was three spec scripts sold totaling over a million dollars and two more scripts under consideration. And where was he? A fifty-one-year-old divorcee, walking across a dirt lot toward a ten-year-old pickup, the color of rust, after working for eight hours as an underpaid cover artist for a small Michigan press.

"Hey, Brad! Hold on a minute."

*Not now.*

Brad stopped and turned around to see the director of the Sunrise-Side Press, J. Michael Preston, lumbering down the steps, tie bouncing off his gargantuan gut. If there was ever a body type that announced "heart attack imminent," it was J. Michael Preston's. Three hundred pounds of pure lard, maintained by a rotating schedule of fast food takeout for lunch and at least a twelve-pack of Miller Lite tallboys each night before going to bed, which Preston bragged about from behind his office throne. His ass crack showed every time he bent over to pick something up from the floor in the office, and he demanded that he be called J. Michael when he was promoted to director after going by his first name, Jerry, for the previous fifteen years.

Brad had no problem with him. In fact, when Preston was the managing editor at the press and the head of the editorial, design, and production department, he had fought to keep Brad on as the press's cover artist when the budget had thinned. Behind closed doors, Brad was the only one who could still call Preston "Jerry."

Preston arrived at the spot where Brad was standing, halfway across the dirt parking lot. "Jesus Christ, that walk gets longer every day, I swear," Preston said.

It was early June, and the temperature still hung around the seventies during the day—hot enough to celebrate the end of another wet, gray Michigan spring but still cold enough to keep most people out of Lake Huron. Sweat beaded on Preston's large forehead, and the underarm portions of his expensive shirt had massive sweat stains.

"What can I do for you, Jerry?" Brad said.

"That's what I like about you. Always to the point. Always to the," he pushed a meaty index finger into Brad's chest, "point."

Brad stared at him, then raised both eyebrows.

"Right," Preston said. He edged closer as if they were in a crowded room and he wanted to tell Brad something that no one else should hear. "They don't like the cover for the new book."

He knew who *they* were, the sales and marketing department. Same old small-town press political bullshit. His entire department recognized the limitations of the project. An author named Jody DeWaters from East Lansing had just penned his third novel, completing a trilogy about a fictitious state senator who had been a closet pothead for his two unremarkable terms before rising to power. In book one, *The Pot is Boiling*, Senator Tiger Aiken shocks the chamber and introduces legislation to legalize marijuana. In book two, *Rise of the Memory Eraser*, Tiger endures the wrath of Michigan's governor, but at a heated press conference outside the entrance to his favorite Lansing bar, Tiger says, "If you're going to kick the tiger in his ass, you better have a plan for dealing with his teeth." Brad had told Preston that DeWaters had stolen the line from the back cover of Clancy's *Teeth of the Tiger*, but Preston let it stand. Eventually, Tiger Aiken strong-arms and bullies other senators into an alliance to get the necessary votes to legalize. And now, in book three, *The King of Weed*, Tiger celebrates his legislative triumph and then retires to private life. Considering how horrible the books were—Preston mandated that every book the press was publishing be read by each of the press's thirteen employees—Brad had done all he could with the cover: a smirking Tiger Aiken wearing a dark suit, sitting on a beach chair with a joint in one hand and a book with the Michigan State Seal on its cover in his other hand—cannabis plants sprouting from the jeweled golden crown that Tiger wore over his greasy silver hair. On the back, a polished Jody DeWaters stared out at the hopeful purchaser from behind a mahogany desk in a darkened law office, wearing a suit exactly like his main character's and sporting a heavy brown beard trimmed to perfection. Brad hated Tiger, but Brad hated Jody more.

The editorial, design, and production department had been at war with the sales and marketing department since *The Pot is Boiling* had been acquired by the press's acquisitions editor five years ago, who had been fired last year after being busted for dealing crystal meth. Why sales and marketing liked the trilogy so much, he didn't know, and neither did his book design manager, Larry Eckstein. *"It's a dumbass book about some sleazy senator who gets laid at will, smokes up in his Lansing townhouse, and carries a fuckin' Glock 22 in a shoulder harness under his Brooks Brothers suit jacket,"* Larry had said. But Preston had pushed and wanted the three books to be the same high quality as the press's other acquisitions.

"Jerry, they're awful books," Brad said. "The cover's fine."

Jerry gave his eyes-wide-open shrug that he always offered when he was caught between two disagreeing departments. It said nothing and everything. "They don't think they can market the book."

"Neither does Larry," said Brad. "Neither do I—no matter what cover we give it. The first two books were flops, and this one will be too." Brad turned to leave. "Let it die, Jerry."

"The books sold well, and you know it," Preston said.

Relatively speaking, yes, they had made the press money—a minor miracle in itself. If they hadn't, there wouldn't even be a third book. The problem was the competition with the rise of independent authors publishing their books on Amazon. The press had acquired some real talent a few years back—*stories* with complex characters, a beginning, middle, and end, and some length—at least

27

eighty thousand words. But, with little to no marketing budget and the cost of printing, the books had died a slow death and had not even attained the respectable rank of mid-list. Brad had compared the books to the books published by indies on Amazon. There was no comparison because the indies priced their books so goddamned low. The press was charging $27.95 for the hardcover on its website—there was no e-book or audiobook available, and the paperback wouldn't be printed for another year. Other than a simple press release that went out to other small presses across the country, the press had arranged for one book signing at the local library and one in the author's hometown. Both were disasters. No one was paying $27.95 for a hardcover book, and the people who showed up to the library thought that there would be free pizza.

Additionally, the patrons weren't there to *buy* the book, they were there to reserve the library's only copy. In the end, the author had signed two books: one for his mother—his father didn't even show up—and one for Brad, who was proud of the cover he had designed. Well, like everything about the book industry, rarely were there answers that made sense. People are people, and they have different tastes and purchasing patterns. And, quite evidently, the modern consumer was not interested in small press authors, which was why the pompous sonofabitch Jody DeWaters was an anomaly. Why the Michigan faithful had lined up behind Jody was beyond him. Preston had even waved fan letters in front of the entire press and read snippets like, *"Reading Jody DeWaters is like catching up with an old friend by the fire in the midst of a Michigan snowstorm,"* and, *"I don't trust many authors, but I trust Jody. His stewardship of Tiger Akins's career is an unparalleled literary feat."* Then, Preston had shown a video of master storyteller Jody at a book talk prior to a signing: *"Tiger is my ethical compass—"* (sympathetic nods of deep understanding from attendees) *"—and sometimes—"* (self-deprecatory grin) *"—he gets into trouble,"* (laughter from the audience and a few coffee cups raised in salute). *"Actually, I've been throwing around the idea of taking that old warhorse all the way to 1600 Pennsylvania Avenue and ploppin' his ass behind the Resolute desk—"* (crowd cheers)—

*"Maybe even have President Aiken—"* (raises eyebrows) *"—God, that's got a nice sound to it—give that famous Howard Dean yell from 2004 the first time he signs an executive order,"* (room explodes in laughter, and one brave soul does his best Dean scream, *"Yeeaaaaa!"*). *"Remember, my friends, Michigan was the last state he mentioned before he talked about going to D.C. to—"* (raises voice) *"—take back The White House!"* (awestruck audience claps in recognition of his genius). Brad and Larry couldn't get to the bar fast enough that afternoon. Pitchers had been consumed, and expletives had been slung across the pool table in reference to trusted and valued author Jody DeWaters.

"They don't like—"

"What?" Brad said, turning back around.

"The crown," Preston said.

"For crying out loud, the title is The *King* of Weed!"

"Okay, okay," Preston said, taking a step back. "All I'm asking is that you take a look at it when you get back in on Monday."

Brad started to walk away again.

"Listen, I need some assurance that you're going to look at it on Monday. I don't want to have to— "

Brad pivoted and closed the gap between them in seconds, his Teva sandals kicking up dust and sending small stones flying. "Don't want to have to do *what*, Jerry?" He was eyeball to eyeball with Preston now.

"I need something to go back in there with, Brad," he said, motioning to the building with his eyes.

*Retreat. Don't lose your job over a stupid cover—there will be plenty more of them.* "I'll take a look on Monday," Brad said.

"You know I'm a bulldog," Preston said.

*No, you're not.* "Of course," Brad said.

Preston relaxed and put his hand on Brad's right shoulder. "Sounds good, boss," he said, which was what he said any time he got his way. *"Gotchya, boss,"*

*"You got it, boss," "Agreed, boss." Enough already.* Preston lowered his arm. "Have a good weekend," he said and headed back toward the fifty-year-old press building.

The drive north along US-23 helped Brad calm down as the majestic blue hues of Lake Huron, and bright green lawns ruled the landscape outside of his truck's passenger window. Perhaps his only win in the divorce proceedings was the beach cottage that he had retained ownership of. Three miles north of Shelter Harbor and tucked away on a point of land that was perhaps a quarter of a mile from 23, his 1,200-square foot cottage was the fifth in line down Fathom Point Road. He knew Ivy hated the drive up to the cottage from their home in Alpena, but he was certain that she would want to sell it and split the money. However, her lawyer had surprised his lawyer when she had stated that Ivy would give Brad full ownership of the cottage if she could get 75% of the money from the sale of their main house. In terms of numbers, she got the better deal. In terms of peace of mind, he was happy to offload the 3,500-square foot house in the uppity, gated neighborhood where he'd never been comfortable to begin with. The family home was Ivy's identity: modern, flashy, and expensive. The cottage was his: old-school, functional, and quiet. Well, last he had heard, she was living with some Hollywood producer in his mansion in Pacific Palisades—introduced to the mogul by her one and only daughter after he had turned one of her screenplays into an Oscar contender.

*Snap out of it,* he thought. *You're thinking about this because you just had your job threatened, and you need the income.* The truck was paid off, and so was the cottage, but the roof needed to be replaced next year—at the latest. He also had no pension, the condition brought on by yet another string of mistakes in his twenties—the decade where fortunes aren't necessarily made, but they sure as shit are lost. Mistake one: entering Central Michigan's Pre-Law program, a program he had no desire to be in. Mistake two: dropping out. Mistake three:

moving back home to Alpena, a small town south of Shelter Harbor. The following flow of milestones weren't necessarily mistakes, but they certainly had set him on his current path: attend Alpena Community College and achieve a degree in Fine Arts, find employment at North East Michigan Pottery and Paint and teach art classes while also being a cashier, somehow marry Ivy Dawn Tanner, whose family was loaded, help to conceive Noelle Rene Cranston and be a decent father, live a quiet life in Alpena, send your daughter off to college in California, arrive home one day from work to find your wife sitting at the dining room table with a glass of wine and divorce papers, then find out that the pottery and paint store, where you have worked for almost twenty years, is closing its doors, then, by a miracle, have your artwork get discovered by the previous owner of Sunrise-Side Press and get offered a job as a cover design artist. And, mistake four: buying a brand-new F-150, draining most of your savings in the process.

Brad ran his right hand over the smooth leather steering wheel and then turned on his blinker and slowed Rusty as the sign for Fathom Point Road appeared. The quarter-mile stretch of paved road ran perpendicular to US-23 and cut through the middle of a quiet patch of woods. Then, the road curved and ran parallel to Lake Huron, with only the lakefront lots separating the road from the beach and water. Beyond Brad's cottage, Fathom Point Road continued on another mile and a half and ended in a cul-de-sac. His daily morning run was from the driveway down to the cul-de-sac and back. He didn't touch any weights but did one hundred push-ups, one hundred sit-ups, a minute-long plank, and one hundred squats before each run. Again, ordinary. Six-foot-zero and 175 pounds ordinary. Brown hair, brown eyes ordinary. Teva sandals, cut-off jean shorts, white Hanes t-shirt with a pocket ordinary. Detroit Tigers home baseball cap...semi-ordinary.

His mailbox, black plastic labeled with the gold stickers 1715, came into view on the right-hand side of the road. He slowed but then turned into his long gravel driveway. He'd walk down to check the mail later. Needed to get his steps in.

31

The grocery bags on his passenger seat contained his provisions for the weekend: enough spaghetti for two nights, grapes, crackers, cheese, and bread to snack on, eggs and bacon for breakfast, a new tin of Maxwell House that would last a month, and one bottle of Merlot to spread out over two nights with the spaghetti. On Monday, he'd pick up the groceries for the week. Two trips. That was it. That was his system.

The trees opened up, and his unattached garage emerged on the left. When parked, Rusty barely fit on the concrete pad in front of the garage. He'd considered expanding the pad, but that would cost money that he didn't have. To the right of the garage was a concrete sidewalk that led to the front door, perhaps twenty yards away from the back corner of the garage. The garage's siding and trim matched the cottage's exactly. This was one of the upgrades that Ivy had made when they bought the place. She wanted it to resemble a Nantucket beach house: cedar shake siding, white trim, and black shingles. The crimson-colored door was her own touch, as were the navy curtains inside, the wicker chairs on the back deck—for some reason, she had left them—and the Tahiti breeze fans mounted on the deck's ceiling. Inside, she had removed the expensive furniture and décor when they had split, and he had been forced to start over. Now, the inside was the definition of minimalism: a small back bedroom with a twin bed, used dresser and nightstand; a kitchen with a round wooden table and four chairs, a living room with a wooden-framed couch and a Morris Chair with its accompanying footstool—two barrels serving as end tables—and underneath the windows that provided a spectacular view of the lake was a long desk with his art supplies scattered on top of it; a laundry room; and the master bedroom that had a queen bed, rocking chair, and dresser. The only bathroom was down the hallway—toilet, sink, shower, no tub.

He parked the truck and took the groceries inside.

When the food and drinks were put away, he poured himself a glass of ice water and sat on the couch. The wind had picked up, and whitecaps were rolling

32

in toward the beach. About to take a sip from his glass, he spotted the blinking red '1' on his cordless phone's display. When was the last time anyone had left him a message on the house phone? He had forgotten his cell phone when he had left for work this morning; sitting at his desk, trying to avoid any conversation about *The King of Weed*, he had felt his pockets and then remembered that he left his cell plugged into the charging cord on his nightstand. He didn't miss it, just felt weird without it in his pocket.

Brad slid over and picked up the phone. This had better not be Jerry Preston wanting him to come back in. Suddenly, he felt powerless. If Preston wanted him back in, he'd have to go. *Stop overthinking everything. Maybe Larry wants to grab a beer and commiserate.*

He accessed his voicemail and listened.

*"Hey, Brad. It's Conrad."*

It was his younger brother, and he sounded out of breath and nervous.

*"Look, man, I'm in deep here. They're on their way. I'm at a campsite at Sterling State Park in Monr—um, yeah, I think it's Monroe. They'll take or destroy my cell if I have it on me, so I'm putting it in a plastic bag and leaving it in the tank of the left-most toilet stall in the men's restroom, code's my birthday—month then year. Look at the pict—"*

There was a loud blast from what he thought was a car's horn followed by silence. Then, Conrad's voice again:

*"I think that's them. Shit, I hope she got away. Look, just bring a boat. They might be taking me back to—"*

This time his brother was interrupted by the sound of car doors slamming. Conrad got out:

*"God, I hope this is still your home number. Don't involve the police. Bigtime money."*

Brad's breathing almost came to a stop, and he felt drops of sweat slip down his back as he squeezed the cordless phone.

*What in the hell?*

# 2

Shelter Harbor, Michigan

## *Present Day*

The voicemail message ended, and Brad put the phone back on the receiver. He looked at his Ironman watch. 5:47 p.m. *When did Conrad call?* He checked the phone. 4:03 p.m. Had he left another message on Brad's cell phone? He dashed into his bedroom and unplugged his cell. One missed call at 4:02 p.m. but no voice message. He thought he knew why. He had opted for the robotic message that said the phone number followed by "is not available right now. Please leave a message." Perhaps Conrad heard that and didn't know if it was Brad's cell phone number anymore. He didn't know.

Brad left the bedroom and went into the living room, where he started to pace. What kind of trouble was Conrad in? Who was *she?* Why did he want him to bring a boat? Why in the hell was he at Sterling State Park? *Don't call the police.* Why? Taking him *where?* And who were *they?*

He pulled out his laptop from a backpack leaning against the far end of the couch. He Googled 'Sterling State Park Monroe,' hoping to God that it was a park in Michigan and not in Alaska. The search results posted, and he saw that Sterling State Park was indeed a park located in Monroe, Michigan, right on Lake Erie. In fact, the only Michigan State Park located on Lake Erie. Next, he checked the distance. It would be around a six-hour drive. If he left soon, he could be there by midnight.

*Anything else? Yeah, a boat. What kind?* He had his twelve-foot aluminum utility boat with a small outboard on a trailer in the garage. But Conrad didn't know about it. That's what happens when you cut yourself off from your family for the past six years, like Conrad had. However, sadly, his family wasn't complaining. Even if Brad called his parents or younger sister, they'd say, *"Conrad who?"* *"He's a forty-six-year-old delinquent who already sucked up a quarter of our retirement in rehab fees,"* were his father's latest words on the subject. A tortured, misguided soul would be Brad's way to describe his brother, but he just could not bring himself to cut ties.

*No time for those thoughts now.*

Brad presumed that he would be putting the boat in Lake Erie, but how far out or how far down the coastline would he be traveling? He couldn't sail, so a sailboat was out of the question. Leave it to Conrad to not disclose vital pieces of information even when his life was apparently on the line. *Okay, how to play this safe?* His mind scrolled through the friends he had who owned boats. The list was short, and they had all put their boats in at Hanratty's Marina before Memorial Day Weekend. Even though the water was still cooler, the Michigander boating crowd put their boats in at that time and left them in until at least late September. He frowned. It looked like he would be hauling his small all-purpose craft. *Wait a minute.* He snapped his fingers. Larry hadn't put in his twenty-five-foot Stingray, *Reminiscing*, yet. He had been out of state at a wedding in Florida last weekend—someplace called Steinhatchee—and was going wine tasting over

36

in Traverse City tomorrow and Sunday. *That's right.* He needed Brad's help putting the boat in *next* weekend. It was still on the trailer in Larry's driveway, which was starting to annoy Larry's wife.

He gave him a call, explained what he could of the situation, and Larry told him to swing by his place and hook up the trailer to his truck. No questions asked. The man was a saint, and, like Brad, had a soft spot for Conrad. *"Just don't get my boat shot up,"* Larry had joked. *"Remember, I know where you live and work."* Brad had laughed. The whole thing was ridiculous; his brother was probably tripped out somewhere. Perhaps this would be the final straw. But, on the slight chance that the situation was real, he proceeded.

Next, law enforcement. Conrad had said to not contact the police. Well, his brother had said a lot of things over the years. Still, maybe he should wait. He tapped the keyboard as he thought. *What about a private investigator?* There were two that he knew of in Shelter Harbor, but what good would that do? They weren't going to travel to Monroe with him, and he wasn't going to pay them to. He searched private investigators in Monroe and started to scroll through the five that it listed: Scully Services, Private "I" Inc., Shadow Security, LLC, Cozy Mitten Private Investigations & Consulting Firm, LLC, and Finding Secrets Investigations Inc.

*You have got to be kidding me,* he thought. He went back to the fourth one, Cozy Mitten Private Investigations & Consulting Firm, LLC. The artist in him imagined a hand-made mitten representing Michigan's Lower Peninsula being placed on a child's hand before sending her out to play in the snow. *Catchy.* He clicked on the link.

On the screen was a two-story home—tan siding, crimson shutters, large windows, brick chimney, and a big front porch. Below the picture was a phone number. He dialed it.

"Good evening, Cozy Mitten P.I. and Consulting," a woman's voice answered.

*What in the hell am I doing?* "Um, yeah. Hi. My name is—"

*Hmmm. Should I give her my real name?*

She answered for him. "You don't have to give me your name right now if you don't want to," she said in a calming tone. "Tell me how we can help you, and I'll let you know if it is a service that we offer. Deal?"

He relaxed. "Deal," said Brad. "I'm heading your way from about five hours north of you. My brother," he paused to search for the right words, "may be missing, and I need some help finding him."

"How long has he been missing, sir?"

"Maybe just a few hours. He left me a voice message saying that he was in danger." Christ, he sounded like an idiot.

"So, is he missing or in danger?" The woman said evenly.

"I think both," Brad said. "He may have been kidnapped."

"Now he's kidnapped too? Sir, if this is a prank call, then—"

"It's not, dammit!" he said. "Look, he left a message for me and said that his phone is in a toilet's water tank in Sterling State Park."

The woman laughed. "His phone is in a toilet tank? Sir, I'm going to have to let you—"

His voice became desperate. "Please, don't hang up. My name is Brad Cranston, and my brother's name is Conrad. He left me a message earlier today, and it sounds like he's in real trouble. I'm leaving my home in five minutes to travel down to the park." He thought for a moment. "How far is the park from your office?"

There were a few beats of silence followed by, "About twenty minutes."

"Fine. Twenty minutes. Tell you what, have one of your investigators go over there, check the tank, and call me back. If the phone is there, then I will hire one of your P.I.s, and you'll get my business. If the phone isn't there, then I'll pay you for one day of services at your daily rate when I arrive and apologize for wasting your time."

He gave her his cell phone number and home address. She gave him her name: Larissa.

"Okay, Mr. Cranston," she said. "I'll send someone over to the park, and then we'll call you."

"I'm sorry this is so weird," he said. "I—"

"Honey, you don't even know what weird is until you've sat in this chair for a year. Something tells me that you aren't full of it, and I just ran a check of your name and address. Book cover illustrator, huh?"

*That was quick*, he thought. "That's me," he said.

"I've never heard of any of these books, though."

He imagined her scrolling through the absolutely ridiculous titles that he had illustrated covers for over the years: *Smackdown, Double Lips: Double Trouble, The Lost Chronicles of Reginald Loomis, M.D., Treasure Palace, Predictably Ironic, The Grayling Secret,* and, of course, the cannabis volumes by Jody DeWaters. "Well, now you know who I am. Just give me a call when you find the phone. I'm heading out."

She agreed, and the call ended. Then, he realized that he hadn't told her about the 'she' mentioned in Conrad's voicemail or the boat or 'bigtime money.' He thought about calling her back but decided against it.

*Let's see if there even is a phone at Sterling State Park.*

He went into his bedroom and pulled out his twenty-year-old Kelty backpack from underneath the bed. He threw in underwear, a swimsuit, two pair of jean shorts, two white t-shirts, a pair of trousers, and a hooded sweatshirt with the Shelter Harbor Lighthouse on the front. From the bottom drawer of his dresser, he took out a flashlight, binoculars, and a leather pouch that held his Swiss Army knife. He put the flashlight and binoculars in his bag and threaded his belt through the openings in the back of the leather pouch, securing the knife to his waist. After a trip to the bathroom to collect his toiletries, he grabbed his phone charger and a pad of paper and pen from the drawer in his nightstand and put them in the bag.

In the living room, he took a recording of Conrad's voicemail on his cell phone and placed his laptop and charger in the backpack, then snapped the bag shut. He set it on the kitchen counter and then ran to the garage and back. In his hand was a small Igloo cooler. He grabbed both trays of ice cubes from the freezer and emptied the cubes into the cooler. Then, he placed the cheese and grapes inside along with a knife from the knife block. From the laundry room's recycling bin, he brought in a paper grocery bag and placed the bottle of wine, crackers, and bread in it. Lastly, he filled up his Yeti water bottle. Placing the backpack over his shoulder, he put on his Detroit Tigers baseball cap and sunglasses, and then picked up the cooler and grocery bag and headed out.

A few minutes later, he was in his truck heading to Larry's to hook up the boat.

Larissa Crawford rose from her desk at Cozy Mitten Private Investigations & Consulting Firm, LLC, and headed upstairs. The building was quiet. The phone call she had just received was the first in over a week. The firm only had three agents. One was out of the office working a divorce case. Another was on a week-long vacation to Mackinac Island. The third and newest member to the team was upstairs, moving into her office. Larissa had wanted to switch the phones at 5:50, which would send any incoming calls directly to voicemail for the weekend, but she knew the new P.I. would unpack until at least six, when Larissa planned to go home, and so she kept the phones on only to hear Brad somethin' or other and his crazy story about a toilet phone and missing/kidnapped/in-danger brother. Well, at least she didn't have to drive her ass out to Sterling State Park. That would be a little mission for the newbie.

She arrived on the second floor, and at the far end of the hallway, the newest private investigator to the team, Allison Shannon, bent over to pick up the second-to-last box left in the hallway.

*Girl has an ass on her,* Larissa thought, as Allison's skirt hugged her round behind. *Gotta warn her to leave those clothes at home, or the two boys won't get any investigating done—and I might miss a few phone calls because I'll be up here checking her out.* It was nice to have another female in the office.

"Almost in," Allison said to Larissa as she picked up the box and headed into her office.

Larissa arrived at the door and leaned against the frame. The room was already starting to take on some personality. The desk shined of Pledge, and Allison's computer was set up in a smart configuration to maximize the desktop space, which only had a legal pad, pen, and phone on it. Three pictures were already hanging on the wall over her small couch. Larissa's eyes stopped at the middle picture. It was of a younger Allison in a Coast Guard uniform having a medal pinned on. The gears in her mind turned until she located Allison's resumé. Right, Allison was a retired Coast Guard senior chief petty officer who had specialized in search and rescue. She was also a master diver. Larissa remembered the details because Allison was only thirty-nine—had enlisted right out of high school at eighteen—and when Larissa met her for the first time, she thought that Allison could pass for mid-twenties—the benefits, she thought, from taking care of your body. She admitted to herself that there was a hint of jealousy because whereas Allison was trim and energetic, Larissa had started to spread. If she had children, she could lay partial blame on the fact that once you gave birth, your body never returned to what it was before, but Larissa had no children. She *was* a year older than Allison, and, at this age, one bad year of health—injury, falling off the healthy food wagon, etc.—could erase a decade of eating right and hitting the gym every other day. And once the weight came on, it was twice as hard to get off. Well, instead of spending her time being jealous, she had decided to go the other way and would try to pick up some good habits from the new private investigator. Still, if it involved anything in the water, then *hell no.* Hot tub? Yup. Gym? Yes. Weights? Okay. Running? Pain in the ass,

41

but she'd do it. Swimming? Unh-uh. In fact, that was the other item that stood out to her in regard to Allison's Coast Guard career. A master diver? What good would that do her as a private investigator? Domestic violence, fraud, and arson investigations were handled on dry land. And why did she want to be a private investigator? Girl had it made being retired before forty with no kids or spouse. Take some time and disappear on an island for a year or two. Keep a champagne company in business. Get a massage every morning, maybe have sex with the masseuse if he or she is hot. She stopped herself, realizing that she was projecting what *she* really wanted onto Allison. "Looks like you're gettin' moved in," she said.

Allison turned toward her, and Larissa noticed that the top button to her blouse was undone. *Yeah, definitely gotta get my girl in jeans and a collared shirt from now on.* Now, if it were only the two of them in the office, then Ms. Allison Shannon could walk around in whatever she pleased.

"Is it okay if I stay late and finish up tonight?" Allison asked and then went back to unpacking.

"You can wear whatever you like."

"What?" Allison said, stopping to look at her.

Shit. *Get your mind off your fantasies.* Larissa smiled. "I'm sorry. My mind's shot. Friday. You know?"

Allison went back to work.

*Thank God.* That was close. "You don't have to get my permission to work after hours. You're an employee now and can stay as late as you want. You got your key, right?"

Allison pulled open a desk drawer and took out a key. "Got it."

"Good. Just hit 'away' on the alarm panel when you finally leave for the night. I'm heading out soon."

Allison nodded.

"However, there's one thing I need you to take care of before you head out for the weekend," she said and started to chuckle.

Allison grinned. "What?"

"We got a call a few minutes ago."

"New case?" Allison asked.

"Ha! Probably not. You'll be laughing too when I tell you what I need you to do, but I promised this guy that we would check it out for him."

"Let's hear it," Allison said. "Anything to get out of the office. I hate unpacking."

"Girl, you might regret what you just said."

# 3

## Grosse Pointe Shores, Michigan

### *1 Week Ago...*

The driver, Gino Gregorio "GiGi" Rizzo, turned off of Lake Shore Road, and the black luxury sedan rolled down a long asphalt driveway toward an enormous Tudor-style home. Neatly trimmed privacy hedges rose on both sides of the rectangular-shaped property, giving the narrow driveway a tunnel-like feeling.

In the soft, tan-colored, leather back seat of the Cadillac CT6-V sat the second in command of the entire Detroit Mafia—The Association—Underboss Fabio De Luca, who went by the name Fabian. He spoke to his driver and bodyguard. "Slower, GiGi. I haven't been here for a very long time."

GiGi obeyed, and the car crept, wheel turn by wheel turn, down the driveway—the silver-plated rims glittering in the sunlight. Fabian watched as the high, green hedge passed down his side of the car. Only the roof of the mansion next door was visible.

The visit had been coordinated and leaked to make it look like a friendly call to his aging uncle. This was, of course, true. But there were other things to discuss. Matters that no one else could know about. Matters that, if known, could make him disappear into the depths of Lake St. Clair. He remembered accompanying his father to the house when the construction had finally finished in 1982. His uncle had just been promoted to Fabian's current title of Underboss at that time, and his father was serving as the Street Boss. Fabian was eighteen and heading off to college to study business so that he could one day come back and help The Association. It had been a glorious evening full of cheer, hope, and love for his family. Now, almost forty years later, his uncle was semi-retired, and his father had died in prison, serving a sentence for racketeering. He peered out the front windshield. The house, growing larger by the second as the car approached, was the last place Fabian had spent time with his father before he was convicted and put in prison, where Fabian would observe him wither away for two decades before succumbing to throat cancer.

The pavement ended in a circle before the house with a fountain in the middle of a carpet of green grass. The home's stucco exterior was complemented by two stone sections, and the windows were tall and narrow with dark trim. There was a half-circle picture window above the arched doorway. The rest of the front windows had standard grids and fit within the pattern of exposed timbers. A dormer window halfway up the steep, multi-gabled roof stood out and called attention to the asymmetrical layout. Most multi-million-dollar lakefront homes in Grosse Pointe Shores were a mix of colonial and modern. The eight-thousand-square-foot Tudor home spoke of old money and had been built in the tradition of the Country Club of Detroit, a few miles away, where his uncle had been a member for twenty years now. He had also helped finance the club's nine-million-dollar renovation a few years back. Membership was by invitation only, and Fabian had eventually been approached when the renovation was completed. A gross oversight, one of the board members had explained. Naturally, the membership had its costs: thirty-five thousand dollars a year to be a golfing member plus eight hundred dollars a month in dues or five thousand dollars a year to be a social member plus five hundred dollars a month in dues. The golfing membership would have been pocket change, but he hated golf— chasing a palm-sized projectile around immaculately manicured grass while attempting to control his temper. Not a chance. Why not skip to the nineteenth hole and start there? So, he had opted for the five-grand social membership and witnessed the concierge staff frown, realizing they had failed to lure an insanely obese cat compared to the fat cats who were already golfing members. In a final move of desperation, the club manager had invited him to lunch and said, *"I hate the game too. It doesn't make any sense to call it a sport."* His voice had lowered to a whisper at this point. *"To be honest, I mostly ride around in the cart, waiting for my opportunity to screw one of the beer girls I hire."* Fabian had politely grinned, finished lunch, and said, *"No thank you,"* when the club owner paid the bill and said, *"So, what do you say? Let's play a couple of rounds and get some top-shelf pussy on the back nine?"*

The Cadillac traveled halfway around the circle and stopped in front of the brick sidewalk that led straight to the front door. GiGi opened the car door for him, and he emerged to feel the summer heat against his face, neck, and arms. The trickle of the circle's fountain soothed his nerves as he walked around the front of the sedan. The house was still majestic, quiet, and well-kept. At seventy-four and in tremendous physical shape from his daily workout regimen of swimming at the country club's lap pool followed by a set of tennis, Fabian figured that his uncle, Pietro De Luca, whose sobriquet was "Papa Pete," had at least twenty more years of good health left in him. Whereas his father had started smoking the cancer sticks as a teenager and never quit, Papa Pete had cut them out early and was not a heavy drinker or a drug user. Expensive scotch and wine were to be experienced, savored, not downed. But business meetings were another matter. The purple lilacs lining the front landscaping bed mixed with the smell of freshly cut grass gave him a jolt of energy and helped put his mind at ease as he approached the door. When he was a young boy, he would visit his uncle for a week every summer. Papa Pete would purchase a model car for him to put together, paint, and affix car-detail stickers to. Thinking back, one of those models may very well have been a Cadillac. *Maybe they all were*, he thought. At family gatherings, he could tell his uncle was respected. Everyone got quiet when he spoke, and people waited on him, always offering him coffee or homemade wine. Papa Pete was a devoted Roman Catholic who prayed every night. Fabian did too—even right after plotting a murder or beating. His uncle had been the voice of reason for The Association for nearly as long as Fabian had been alive. Now, Fabian needed that sage guidance, and he needed to ask his uncle a favor.

The men walked across the backyard toward the pool house, which stood half-way between the main house and Lake St. Clair. Pietro De Luca put a reassuring hand on Fabian's shoulder. "Let's walk to the water while Aldo tidies up."

Fabian nodded. The statement meant that his uncle's head of security, Aldo Mantegna, would sweep the pool house for any listening devices before the meeting. The majority of meetings held between members of The Association now took place in public places, selected at random, to avoid surveillance. However, his uncle trusted the old ways, and he trusted his compound. No doubt, the main house was still swept daily, but ensuring that eight thousand square feet were completely secure was no longer realistic. The pool house was where business had been and was still, on occasion, conducted. They passed it, and Fabian glanced back and saw his uncle's housekeeper, Vanni Palazzo, exit the main house and head toward the small building with Aldo. No doubt, there would be fresh bruschetta, antipasto salad, porchetta, sandwiches, and probably bottles of Chianti or Barbaresco.

The men arrived at the seawall that ran the entire width of the property. There were two recliners near the edge, stools around the bar underneath a large cabana, and a fire pit with benches around it at one end; the rest of the deck was empty except for an aluminum dock ladder and deck box that held towels on the far end. It was here that Fabian had taken his high school sweetheart for an evening swim and fucked her in the water as she faced the ladder and gripped the poles while he thrashed back and forth behind her. It was also where he had watched a former Association member held underwater and drowned by Aldo, a permanent punishment for skimming money.

They sat on the chairs looking out at the lake's cobalt blue surface while GiGi and his uncle's bodyguard, Aldo's son Marcello, stood by the cabana—high-powered guns within an arm's reach behind the cabana's bar if trouble arose.

Fabian started the chit-chat with innocuous updates about the family. His son, Leo, was doing well running the family restaurant, De Luca Pizza & Pasta, and getting larger around the waist from sampling too much of the cook's daily specials. Fabian's wife, Caterina, was content with life but hoping that Leo would soon make her a grandmother. However, Fabian knew, this would require Leo to enter into a long-term relationship, and, at present, Leo's wandering eyes changed direction as often as the women in his bed. *"What was with this generation and postponing having children or not having them at all?"* Caterina had said. Perhaps, he thought, she was still insecure with the fact that they had only been able to have one child. This had caused her to avoid large gatherings with the other Association members and their families when those gatherings were still possible. Arrests, raids, and other crackdowns by the feds and police had changed all that. Fabian ended with a few forgettable updates about himself and added, "The summers are getting shorter, and the winters are getting longer, it seems."

Papa Pete gave a weak grin and then took his turn, adding to the conversation. He was enjoying watching summer baseball from his suite at Comerica Park. He valued his hour-long swims at the country club's pool. He still missed his ex-wife, even though she had taken his two daughters away from him when they were young; the last time Fabian had seen them was at his fifth birthday when they were six and seven. And, finally, his uncle gave a delicate wink and then confided to him that he had lost all of his lust for women and was happy spending his afternoons writing his memoirs and reading the great Italian authors—his latest book was *Arturo's Island* by Elsa Morante. "I was a bat flying alone in a pitch-dark cave until I traded sex for books. I now know how Langella felt. How I miss watching him on the stage…the trips to New York…the—"

They both spotted a yacht motoring slowly past his property, perhaps fifty yards offshore—the feds taking pictures and trying to listen—and he imparted two pieces of forgettable wisdom: "Give most of your money to the church, Fabian," and, "A strong mind equals a strong body."

When the boat was nearly out of sight, Aldo jogged across the lawn to them. "A snack has been prepared, gentlemen," he said. This meant that the pool house was ready.

The bodyguards remained outside, sitting at a patio table with an umbrella extended overhead. A bucket of four Forst Premium beers on ice, a plate full of sandwiches, and two plates sat on the table between the men. They began to eat as Vanni exited the pool house and cracked open two of the beers and poured them into separate glasses for the men. They each gave her a kiss on the cheek, and she headed back to the main house.

Inside the pool house, Fabian and his uncle sat in leather chairs at a glass table in the middle of the room. Before leaving, Vanni had poured them each a glass of Chianti and served them a plate loaded with appetizers. The woman had the routine down to perfection. Next to the chiller holding the Chianti was a bottle of Strega—his uncle's favorite—and two small glasses. The Strega was significant. If they drank it at some point, then he knew that his uncle would be considering the offer; if the bottle stayed put, and the glasses stayed dry, then he knew he would be on his own.

A mahogany bar ran along one wall, ending in a small corner kitchen. There was a large leather couch, that matched the chairs they were seated in, against another wall with an oak coffee table in front of it. An enormous family portrait, taken in the late 60s before Papa Pete's wife and children had left him, hung on the wall behind Fabian. The wall ended in a hallway that led to a bathroom and a small bedroom in the back corner.

They toasted, and his uncle spoke first. "What can I do for you, my nephew?"

Fabian took a sip and set down his wine. "Don Russo has chosen his successor." He watched the old man for any sign that his uncle already knew.

A sip of wine. A pat of his lips with the napkin. A disarming smile. His uncle spoke, "I admit that I have heard the choice has been made. But as to who it is, I am afraid that I have long since left the circle whose members would know." His face became serious, the kind of serious that, for decades, had made grown men go pale before him. "Since you are here, I assume you know who it is. And I assume it is not *you*."

He didn't know, and that was a relief. If he had, the conversation might have ended here. Fabian picked up his wine glass. "It's Ciro." He took a long drink.

His uncle sat back and crossed his legs, folding his smooth olive-colored hands. "I expected this," he said. "Not because I believe his son is the right choice—*you* are the much wiser option—but because Don Russo is dying prematurely and sees his son as a way to fulfill his contribution to The Association. From what I hear, he will pass any day now."

"It should be thought of as a contribution, but Don Russo sees it more as a legacy. And leaving legacies is dangerous in our business." His uncle already knew this, which is why he had been such a stabilizing force within the Detroit family. The family was not made up of just one family, but many. The 'family' was a true association, and that is why it had been so successful. Its members intermarried, keeping the familial bonds strong and making it almost impossible for undercover agents to penetrate. If anyone could speak to the word legacy, it

50

was the man sitting in front of him now; in fact, his uncle's legacy was to condition members of The Association to not think of legacy.

Don Ilario "The Smile" Russo was currently on his deathbed at home—stomach cancer, the man had immense appetites—and hadn't been seen in public for almost a year. As Underboss, Fabian had handled almost all of The Association's business, and the machine had been running smoothly—until recently. Don Ilario, backed up by his longtime Consigliere Silvio Verratti and the Don's son Ciro "Ace" Russo, had broken with the tradition of taking ten percent of the total take and had demanded fifteen percent. Ciro was contemplating upping it to twenty percent when he became the boss. Fabian let his uncle know this.

Papa Pete sat forward and poured them both more Chianti. "Silvio...my old fellow capo, he knows better than to allow this. They won't be able to keep the necessary number of soldiers on the payroll." His uncle's eyes became glassy pools. "We had it all in front of us in those days. Liquor. Pockets bursting with cash. Women." He glanced up at the ceiling, and his face said that he was in tremendous emotional pain. Pain that Fabian thought accompanied remembering how you once were. "I never slept back in those days, unless it was with one of God's beautiful creations. Vanni is still with me. Now that lady, my dear nephew, is God's art."

"There's more," Fabian said.

His uncle put the wine bottle back inside the chiller and frowned.

"I'm being demoted."

The move was uncommon but not unheard of. However, when it had happened in the past, it meant that there had been either a pattern of careless behavior that had jeopardized the institution or a mistake so unforgivable that power had to be stripped. Careless behavior usually came from escalating drug use, which is why in the Detroit Association, it was discouraged. Absolutely, sell the hell out of pot, cocaine, and heroin—just don't *use it*. Unforgivable mistakes included sleeping with another made man's wife, cutting a deal with the feds and becoming a snitch, or screwing up a business opportunity beyond repair. Fabian had deduced that his upcoming demotion had nothing to do with any of these reasons. A week ago, in private with only Consigliere Verratti as witness, Don Russo had held Fabian's hand from the comfort of a hospital bed that had been wheeled into the bedroom of his home and told Fabian that he had been a superb Underboss, a man of honor, and that he should retire early and live the rest of his days in luxury and peace just like his Uncle, Papa Pete. *"Of course, you will be given a substantial cut of money because of your service, and men will continue to respect you,"* the Don had said. The sentiment was heartfelt—he had been an excellent Underboss—but the masking of the real reason behind an 'enjoy the rest of your life' gift made his heart knock against his ribs. The real reason was...

"They see you as a threat, Fabio," his uncle said, finishing Fabian's thought. "From what I hear, the narrative that has been established behind your back is that you have not moved with the times—that you are inferior when it comes to running the family through more technologically advanced means. A Don for the future is needed, and you would represent a leader who is stuck in the past like Don Ilario. We both know the propaganda is false. You have moved with the times and are just as in-step with today's gadgets as Ciro is." If the family business was a basketball game, then his uncle saw the court from the rafters above—seeing every player, every movement, the open lanes, the closed lanes, the slimmest of opportunities to take advantage of or hide a player's weakness or capitalize on a team or player's strength. He always appeared to have lightning-quick reflexes; he could sniff out or sense a threat before anyone else. He was also the most organized man that Fabian had ever met. His planning and foresight took care of potential problems before they became problems. This, and many other reasons, was why his advice was so sought after.

"True," Fabian said. "And they also don't want to give up their percentage."

"They're used to it now," said Papa Pete. His eyes drifted away from the table, settling on the window that looked out at the calm lake water. "Silvio...Silvio...oh, what have you done, my old friend?"

Silvio Verratti had been a close friend of his uncle since childhood. Together, they had made their bones four houses down from his current home. In 1965, a member of the family had made an unpardonable mistake out in Las Vegas, where The Association was expanding its territory. Silvio and Pietro were called to the legendary Don Giovanni Russo's mansion on a warm July night. Both boys were eighteen, about to head off to college in the fall. They entered the Don's house, where they were greeted warmly by his butler and then taken out back to the pool. There they saw the great Don, who would rule The Association from 1946 until 1978, seated at a pool lounger. In front of him, on his knees and held by two large men, was the Las Vegas traitor. The two boys were brought around the side of the pool to the Don, where he explained what the man on his knees had done. They saw the man's hands tied behind his back with heavy rope; his feet were also bound. Then, the Don told them that it was time for them to make their bones before going off to be educated by a bunch of soft bellies at the university. The boys nodded, and the two men holding the traitor picked him up and threw him into the pool. The Don simply said to the boys, *"Kill him."* For the next few minutes, they took turns holding the man underwater until he was dead. After that, Silvio and Pietro had a brother-like bond. Now Silvio was being complicit in Pietro's nephew's demotion—an unfair demotion at that. Fabian hoped to rouse his uncle's anger even though he knew he would never see it—only feel it.

"Who do you command loyalty from?" Papa Pete said.

Fabian exhaled. The real business was about to be discussed. From this point forward, there was no turning back. "GiGi, of course—"

"Of course," his uncle said.

"The Street Boss is not happy with the fifteen percent; I know that for certain. He will go with me."

His uncle started to eat again. He always ate heartily when difficult business was being discussed. After chewing on a bite of sandwich and washing it down with wine, he said, "That's an important man to have." He took another bite of the sandwich.

"The Caporegimes are a bit tricky. My son has put out some feelers, and the Abruzzi brothers will go along with us. Casale and Scala are a tough call. They don't like the situation, but they are close with Ciro—more so than they are with Leo."

"So, three and three. What about Florida, Canada, Ohio, and California?"

Papa Pete didn't miss a detail, for he was a man of numbers. In addition to his organizational mastery, he had turned The Association's gambling operation into a quarter-of-a-billion-dollar-a-year business in the 1980s. He who controls the numbers controls the business. The out-of-state members were important to have, but letting them in on the possible power move was too risky. And his uncle knew that. What his uncle wanted to know was which way Fabian *thought* they would tilt if Fabian moved. What were the numbers? The players were all key members in the family's machine: Dante "Miami" Marino in Florida, Nico "River Nicky" Colombo in Canada, Michael "Buckeye Mike" Romano from Toledo, and Paolo "Sunshine Paulie" Esposito out in California. As Underboss, Fabian had met with all of them, but the two with whom he had worked more closely with were River Nicky and Buckeye Mike.

"Miami Marino and Sunshine Paulie will accept whoever is in charge. They just need to know who to send their product to, and, more importantly, who is providing security for the transfer. I've never had a problem with them. They won't stick their necks out to help, but they'll accept me. River Nicky and I are tight, which makes my demotion a difficult move for Don Ilario. We've never lost a shipment of heroin, and Nicky is the best in the biz." He took a piece of Bruschetta and bit it in half, the *crunch* highlighting the end of his sentence. "Mike grew up two houses down from me—he's with us," Fabian added, his mouth half-full, as an afterthought.

"Us?" His uncle asked.

The moment of the meeting had arrived. Fabian took a drink of wine to help swallow the Bruschetta. "Uncle Pete, no one knows the business better than you do, which is one reason you are so respected." He leaned forward. "And you are both liked *and* feared."

His uncle's eyes narrowed, an intensity in them he had not seen today, but his body was in a relaxed posture that made him all the more intimidating.

"I should be the next Don, and I have the means to achieve this. If I succeed, I want you to come out of retirement for a few years and serve as my consigliere." Fabian let the offer hang in the air. Then, he leaned back and said, "Naturally, one of your jobs would be to help me select my long-term consigliere, and when this is done, you could go back to being semi-retired."

His uncle did not move but eventually said, "More."

"The details would have to be fine-tuned," he said, pausing to let the statement find its mark, "and there is no one better at doing that than you." Fabian took a controlled breath and exhaled. *Be direct.* "Four hits: the Don, Ciro, Ciro's driver Big Joey, and...Silvio."

His uncle motioned to the Strega and the two glasses. *Yes.* Fabian relaxed as he poured the yellow liquid into both glasses. He passed one to his uncle, and they drank. He shuddered as the liquid slid down his throat. He had forgotten the jolt that the liquor gave him.

His uncle grinned. "You need to drink more of this."

"Perhaps I will when I have your answer," he said—more bluntly than he had intended. Papa Pete's grin disappeared.

"Great danger, Fabio," his uncle said. "Many ways it could go wrong." He took another sip of Strega. "And only one where it goes right."

*And the one where it goes right is if I have you helping me.* Without his uncle, he would not be able to make the move—his uncle knew this because Fabian would have already moved if it weren't so.

His uncle sat, seeming to measure him. "There appears to be something you're not telling me. How can I advise if I cannot see all of the numbers?"

There was something, but he had hoped to persuade him without having to discuss the topic. Now, he had to talk about it. He needed Uncle Pete. "I have said that the Don is taking fifteen percent."

Papa Pete nodded in agreement.

"But I believe it to be more. The revenue has been too high the past few years compared to the profits being paid out. I have methodically narrowed it down to one wing of the family business, and you're not going to like it." The information would be his best chance to persuade him now because it would hit his uncle where it hurt the most: the numbers. "At first, I didn't notice because the amount was so small, but when Don Russo appointed Ciro to oversee the majority of the illegal numbers business, I noticed the profit start to shrink. Finally, I was able to get a member of his crew to let slip what was going on." He now looked directly into his uncle's eyes and, for the first time, matched the cold stare. "All of your hard work running the figures and managing a system you had built to last has been eroded—the skeleton is still there, but the organs are dying one by one. I need you back. I believe that Don Russo, with Silvio and Ciro's help, has stashed away an immense amount of money somewhere. Money that should have been distributed to me and the rest of the family. I intend to find it, and I intend to give you whatever you need to rebuild and modernize our gambling operation. If Ciro becomes Don, then soon there will be nothing left to distribute."

Papa Pete took a drawn-out breath, but instead of exhaling through his mouth, he blew the air out of his nostrils as if he was a dragon flame-spraying an enemy to death without mercy in that popular TV series he had been obsessed with. *What was it called?* Ah yes, *Game of Thrones*. A title that described his present predicament perfectly.

*I may have him.*

"What are your plans for Angela and Stansie?"

Angela Russo was the now rarely-seen wife of Don Russo. Beloved by the members of The Association, she was not only a friend of Fabian's but also a close friend of Papa Pete's. The Don's nickname may have been "The Smile" for his welcoming hard-to-say-no-to grin, but it was Angela's smile of approval that family members longed to receive. Fabian knew that with the Don's declining health, Angela had been meeting Papa Pete to play bridge every Friday afternoon for the past two months. Seeing her husband's decline was too much, and his uncle had provided a sanctuary for her to escape the misery for a few hours. The Don had approved.

Stansie Russo was the family's black sheep, who, against all odds, had recently become the golden child. She was young, spoiled, and a former drug addict, and Fabian had hoped that her situation would work itself out. It did work out, just the other way. To everyone's—mostly his—amazement, she had met a tall Anglo-Saxon who had helped her get and stay clean. As a reward for rescuing his daughter, the Don had made the man his head groundskeeper and allowed him to live in a room down the hallway from Stansie. Only if they were married could they share a room, which in Fabian's mind was ridiculous, as a maid had confided to him that the pair were sharing Stansie's room and each other's bodies from sunset to sunrise. A part of him was happy because her turnaround meant that he would no longer have to manage the payments to the rehab facility. She had turned her life around, matured, and, unfortunately for her, become a silent force behind Ciro's rise to power. Fabian wouldn't kill her immediately. By now, she had to know where the money was hidden. He would get the location out of her first and then orchestrate the vanishing of her and her gardener boyfriend. But there was another reason behind his disgust for Stansie Russo. There had been an agreement between the two families that Stansie and his son, Leonardo, would marry—the wedding one day taking place in the Don's back yard like all of the other Association weddings. The relationship had started well, with Stansie being the first and best piece of ass that his son had ever had. But then, in high school, they had drifted—Stansie to marijuana, Leo to bathroom blowjobs from pretty underclassmen who knew about his family. Fabian had not been concerned. He had been young once. The families always thought the couple would reunite, and all would be well. And it almost happened. One day in college, after sharing his bed with two co-eds at the same time, Leo claimed to have an epiphany: He still wanted Stansie as his bride. The problem was that by the time he realized this, she had graduated college and graduated to LSD, cocaine, and eventually heroin. Then, Don Russo had done something no other Don in The Association had ever done: He called Fabian and Leonardo into his office, apologized to them, and then broke the arrangement. Leonardo was free to marry someone else because the Don's daughter was forever lost to a more powerful suitor. Yes, rehab would be arranged, but in the Don's eyes, it would not matter. His little girl was gone. Fabian had never forgiven the Don for this slight.

He told his uncle all of this.

"We should have Marino arrange for Angie to have a nice quiet place on the beach in Florida. There, she can live out the rest of her days in peace," his uncle said.

He had figured this would be his uncle's position—had a soft spot for family members not involved in the family business. *They should remain untouchable,"* had been his firm stance. Well, let the old man think she would be safe. In time, she might find out who was responsible for killing her husband and children, and then no human could suspend the lust for revenge. He would let "Miami" Marino get her settled in and then take care of her quietly a few months after. Papa Pete would not need to know about it. The story he would hear is that she died of a broken heart.

"That's what I was thinking as well," Fabian said.

His uncle took a drink of water. "Shall we finish lunch?"

Fabian watched as he dipped the end of his sandwich in a pool of olive oil and then took a bite. This signaled that nothing more needed to be discussed. His uncle would think it over and give him his decision before Fabian left. He picked up another piece of Bruschetta, smiled, and took a bite.

*The killing would start soon.*

## Grosse Pointe Shores, Michigan

## *1 Week Ago...*

It was nearly 4 p.m., and Conrad Cranston stood naked beneath the outdoor shower by the Russo's pool house.  Only his head and feet could be seen as the rest was hidden behind the bamboo cube.  The cool water needled his hot skin, and he took cavernous breaths as his tight muscles felt the relief.  He had a deep tan from the never-ending mowing, edging, trimming, planting, and maintenance of the lawn and mammoth landscaping beds that surrounded the house and property.  His blonde hair was professionally cut to just above one of his dress shirt's collar and was even lighter now after the long hours outside.  He rubbed coconut oil shampoo through his thick locks, enjoying the sweet smell, and then massaged his scalp.  He had nowhere near the talent of their hairdresser's healing hands, but he had learned enough to now believe that the de-stressing process began with the head and ended with the toes.  He rinsed the foam from his hands and squirted a blue glob of body wash into one palm and then began to rub it all over his thin, taut body. His belly fat had disappeared after a month of morning workouts with Stansie, conducted by a trainer her mother had hired for them. Because of that, he was arguably in the best shape and best health of his life. He owed it all to his sweetheart. They had found each other at a low point, well, the *lowest* point; she was hooked on heroin, him on cocaine. Usually, this familiar American story ended in death: When two addicts got together, it just accelerated the process—sometimes by the drugs, sometimes by the addicts killing each other for money to get another fix. If they hadn't found each other, one of these scenarios would probably have led to two more casualties in the cesspool of drugs. But, in the ever-present unpredictability of life, Conrad Richard Cranston had found luck and the light out of the darkness once again. Instead of heading toward an inevitable outcome, they pulled each other out of the black hole.

Completely refreshed, he turned off the shower and put on his light blue swim trunks that had been hanging on a hook inside the wooden enclosure. *Time to relax.* He latched the bamboo door shut behind him and walked across the warm concrete pool deck. In a metal lounge chair with bright green cushions rested Stansie's five-foot-ten wiry frame. Her ebony-colored hair was pulled back in a ponytail, and her smooth brown skin was covered only in a tiny black bikini. What a difference the past few months had made. Her hair was rich and full again—cut and maintained by the hairstylist that visited the house every two weeks—and she had put on a healthy ten pounds. The heroin tracks on her left forearm had been reduced to three tiny scars, mostly hidden by her dark tan.

To think that he had almost left her after their first night on the street together when she passed him a naloxone kit right before shooting up and said, "If I overdose, load one of the syringes inside with a one-milliliter vial and inject it into a vein. I should respond in two to three minutes; if I don't, repeat the process every couple of minutes until I come back. If you can't get the needle into a vein, then go for muscle, but it will take longer, like five minutes. There's also nasal spray in the kit, but word is that it doesn't work as well. Give it a shot if nothing else works. Okay, here I go." He did not have to use the kit, but her attention to detail gave him the impression that behind this stick-skinny woman with unkempt hair was an intelligent person. What was her story? What had led her to this moment? How had she been introduced to drugs? Was it the gateway path, or did she take a dare and try brown sugar, thinking one time was no big deal? So, instead of walking away, he postponed his snort and stayed with her all night. In the morning, they started to talk, and talk eventually led them back to her parent's house a week later, both of them clean but needing help; Stansie was sick. Her mother had cried, seeing Stansie remorseful and coherent for the first time in months. She had attempted a polite thank you and then dismissal of Conrad, but Stansie was adamant that he was the only reason she was standing in front of her now. Her mother reversed course, and the road to freedom began. First, they were taken to separate rooms where they removed their smelly and torn clothes and took long showers. When they emerged from their respective bathrooms, there were terrycloth robes and slippers for them to put on. Stansie's mother, shocked at Stansie's weight loss, had her measured, and a house staff member was sent out to purchase clothes. Conrad also gave his sizes and, within a few hours, both closets were filled with new wardrobes. High-end toiletries of brand names that Conrad had never heard of before were stocked in his bathroom closet and drawers. Then, the family doctor and nurse were called to the house, and Stansie and Conrad were given thorough examinations. They were both suffering from malnutrition and sleep deprivation. Conrad had a staph infection, and Stansie had a cough that she couldn't remember how long she had had. The doctor gave them each multiple injections and wrote prescriptions for the local pharmacy. A staff member was sent out to pick them up. After the examination, they each changed into a sweatsuit and came downstairs to a banquet. At the meal, Stansie mentioned that a few of her teeth were sensitive.

The next day, they both had dentist appointments where multiple cavities were filled and caps ordered for teeth that were beyond repair. Her mother called her hairstylist, and they were each given a haircut at the house. Then, a barber was brought in to give Conrad a straight razor shave. In the late afternoon, Stansie and Conrad had their dirty, destroyed nails repaired during a manicure and pedicure that lasted almost three hours. Then, they were both sat down and told by Stansie's mother that instead of pouring more money into rehab, she had hired a nutritionist, chef, physical trainer, and masseuse.

Over the next month, three rooms on the mansion's lower floor were converted into a gym and wellness center—mirrored walls, free weights, pull-up bars, treadmills, ellipticals, spinning bikes, a yoga corner, massage tables, a stainless-steel cold bath, an enormous whirlpool, a healthy snack bar, and his and her locker rooms with mahogany lockers and brass fittings. Systematically, a routine was built to keep them clean, healthy, and, hopefully, happy. A psychologist had been hired to meet with them twice a week; a support system was one thing, getting underneath the reasons for the addiction was another. Session after session, they cried, laughed, and suffered the trauma of working through repressed memories. His breakthroughs were like sitting in the middle of a dark empty room and having lamps turned on at different times, one by one illuminating separate corners of the room until he could see the entire space. It was then he had finally discovered what had set him on this path so long ago.

Now, over a year from when they had shown up on the doorstep, the routine had become their lifestyle. On the pool deck by Stansie's lounger were two glass bottles of Evian water lined up perfectly next to each other with the labels facing in the exact same direction. On the other side of the pool lounger next to hers were two bottles lined up for him. He exhaled in relief, and it gave him comfort. Their workout and water system was a key component of the routine that had saved them from the nightmare cycle of shooting up, snorting, passing out, and then starting all over again to avoid the dreaded withdrawal symptoms—mood changes, anxiety, sweaty skin, nausea, vomiting, diarrhea, twitching muscles, goosebumps, and a constantly running nose. At all times, they needed to have two fresh Evian bottles with them. Conrad looked around. No doubt, Don Ilario Russo's housekeeper, Carlotta, was lurking nearby ready to replace a finished bottle with an ice-cold new one.

Astrud Gilberto's Greatest Hits played from the pool speakers as he continued to pad across the pool deck toward his lounger. That was the other component of their routine: Bossa Nova music during the day while they lounged by the pool. The beat spoke of endless white-sand beaches, sunshine, aquamarine water, waves, palm trees, and bliss. Conrad sat down in his chair and felt the warm afternoon sun start to work on the drips of water spread across his skin from the shower.

"Hello, my angel," Stansie said.

He reached over and gave her arm a slow rub, careful to avoid touching her scars. "Hello."

He opened one of his bottles of water and chugged until a third of it was gone. She heard him gulping and picked up one of her bottles and did the same. Together, they set their bottles down, lining them back up.

"Papa has taken a turn for the worse," she said. "It could be any day now."

"I know," he replied. "Is there anything I can do?"

She gave him a smile—one he knew the meaning of.

*Are you serious? We're talking about your father dying.* He knew that she was, and that was some twisted shit that he couldn't quite comprehend. When she was stressed or needed to forget about the world around her, she turned into a certified nymphomaniac. How they hadn't woken the rest of the house during their sessions this past year was beyond him. The psychologist had said that drugs had been their escape, and now they needed to replace that habit with another, more positive, one. He had chosen swimming extra laps; she had chosen marathon sessions of exploring every conceivable aspect of the Kama Sutra—

Conrad sitting on a chair, while she faced away from him and slid up and down on his phallus; Conrad going down on her for an hour straight; Stansie kneeling and sucking him off while he stood naked and held on to the wrought iron bars of the bed's canopy. Him initially feigning modesty and deference to the philosophy that they were in her parents' house, *"I really want to respect your family's rules and not play around while we're living under their roof."* And then she had pulled his pants down and grabbed his cock. *"Please, Stansie."* Two minutes later: *"Oh my God. No, no, no. Don't stop."* *Enough.* He was becoming aroused. "I meant besides that," he said, managing a half-smile.

She brought his hand to her lips and kissed it. "I just don't want to think about it. When I do, I feel guilty for the time I was away. And now—" She released his hand. "Conrad, I'm pregnant."

They both reached for their water bottles. As he tipped his Evian back, the chugs were like chain links being added one by one to a collar around his neck. He'd spent his entire life avoiding responsibility, letting others take care of him. Sometimes this had been to his advantage because family members and other people would underestimate him. He liked it when he was able to provide a surprise or two. However, his lack of self-reliance had also been to his disadvantage because no one could count on him, and because no one could count on him, he had decided that he couldn't count on himself. He was absolutely certain that he had never uttered the phrase 'I will figure it out,' in respect to anything. He felt free because he was still alive after being on his own and avoiding responsibility for the majority of his life. He felt restricted because his comebacks were never self-initiated. They had always involved charity from someone. He thought of Brad. *Jesus. What would his brother think of him right now, living in a mansion, surrounded by luxury that had been gained illegally, and living with a knockout who was now...pregnant with his child?* Conrad Cranston, a father? Conrad Cranston, a husband? Conrad Cranston, a...*success?* There were at least a thousand things he was not ready for in life. Being a father seemed to be connected to every item on the list. The symbolic collar around his neck and the chain extending away toward Stansie now had him spooked. They were just mastering rehab. *What kind of stress would raising a child entail?* A puffy cloud, high in the sky, dissolved into three lines of cocaine. He looked away and stopped chugging—not because he wanted to, but because his bottle was empty. Placing the cap back on top, he began to set it on the ground when Carlotta appeared behind him and took the bottle out of his hands. She placed a fresh bottle on the concrete next to his other one and was gone before he could thank her.

He turned to Stansie. *For heaven's sake, speak!* "I—I can't believe it," he said. "Does anyone else know?"

She began to sniffle, and soon tears were streaming down her cheeks. "I thought you would be happy. You're not."

*Get it together. Now.* "No, no, no. I am so happy for us, baby. I just—*"Go ahead and say it. Don't lie.* "I'm just...overwhelmed." He reached over for her arm, but she pulled it out of reach like a toddler keeping a toy away from another greedy child. He brought his hand back and started to rub his chest hair. *Okay. No Co-Co. Find a compromise. Wine. Yes, wine. Wine was healthy.* Wine made him feel young. Maybe a glass or two, or even a bottle. Well, sharing two or three bottles of wine sounded good right about now. *No. That's where it all begins.* One drink. Two drinks. A little weed. Then the white powder. One line. Two lines. And you're right back where you were before.

She reached her hand out and swept it down his arm from the shoulder to the elbow. "I am too," she said. "I can't go back."

His eyes started to well up. "Neither can I."

"Mamma knows, and she's worried, of course. I am sure Carlotta knows. Mamma tells her everything."

"When did you find out?"

"This morning."

"How far along are you?"

"Six weeks."

He had no idea what that meant. He nodded as if he did. "What made you think to take a test?"

"I don't know," she said. "I had a feeling."

He reached for his water bottle, but the opening of the back door to the main house broke his concentration. Ciro Russo exited and walked across the lawn toward the pool deck. "Do we say anything to him?" Conrad asked.

She eased up onto her elbows and saw her brother approaching. "Not right now."

Ciro gave them both the same smile of greeting that he had given them since they showed up in rags. Even though they were oceans away from their former condition, Conrad was convinced that the smile continued to be a sign of patronizing pity, not one of genuine pleasure to be in another's company. He also always directed the smile at Conrad first and then swiveled to Stansie, where he held it for an extended beat. The smile disappeared. "Father would like to see the two of you right now."

"Okay," was all Stansie said back.

Conrad gave a nod, but he was too late. Ciro had turned around and was headed back to the house.

They rose and followed him.

# 5

## Grosse Pointe Shores, Michigan

## *1 Week Ago...*

As the door to Don Ilario Russo's bedroom opened, Conrad Cranston felt a shiver of fear travel down his spine. The question: *Why does he need to see me?* had been nagging at him all the way across the back yard, across the patio, and down the long dark hallway to the Don's master suite. Stansie squeezed his hand, which momentarily took him out of his paranoia. He was sweating, though, and the urge to bolt out of the house and never return came on strong. But he quickly dismissed it, remembering his love for Stansie, and, well, their unborn child too. The doorway was now clear, and Conrad and Stansie were led in by Ciro. The Don's driver and bodyguard, Giuseppe "Big Joey" Manetti, entered after them.

The Don's immense bedroom had been transformed into a hospice suite. Where the king bed had once stood as the centerpiece of the twelve-footceilinged room was a hospital bed. Where the matching nightstands once stood were stands with EKG readouts, coat hanger-like stands with bags of saline solution hanging, and a few other machines that beeped and chirped. The drapes had been closed for weeks now, and soft lighting from lamps in two of the room's corners cast extended shadows across the wooden floor. There were no lights on near the bed, just the blue glow from the machines. The Don rested—the mattress adjusted, so he lay at a thirty-degree angle. His large, nearly elliptically-shaped head disappeared into a gigantic, soft pillow, and his favorite wool blanket covered his legs and torso and was neatly folded so that it stopped underneath his armpits.

Three chairs were set near the foot of the Don's bed.

Ciro walked over and gave his father a kiss on the forehead while Stansie and Conrad sat down.

Don Russo opened his eyes.

"Stansie is here, papa," Ciro said. He pushed a button, and the mechanism controlling the bed's position hummed as Ciro raised the Don until he was virtually sitting straight up. The bed stopped, and the room was silent.

"Thank you," Don Russo said. His voice was weak but clear.

Ciro took his seat next to Stansie.

The Don's eyes moved to Conrad first, which surprised him. He felt the cold stare and wondered if someone was about to sling a garrote over his head and tighten it around his neck. Unable to maintain discipline, he broke eye contact with the Don and looked behind him.

There was no one there.

Embarrassed, he turned his head slowly back around and met eyes with Don Russo again. He should have gone to the bathroom before entering the Don's room because the water from the bottles of Evian was now pushing against his bladder like water against a dam. He crossed his legs.

Stansie put a reassuring hand on his left leg, which was shaking.

The Don's stare became a polite smile, and Conrad exhaled.

"I will forever be grateful to you for what you have done for my daughter," the Don said. "Your work on my grounds and gardens has brought life back to this estate, and an old man such as myself appreciates these things. Soon, I will leave this earth, and I want you to know that you will continue to be given a living as long as you bring joy to my Stansie."

Conrad gave a nod of thanks and relief. When the Don had started to convey his thanks, Conrad had thought that he was about to be asked to leave the estate for good. He smiled at Stansie, who had tears of joy streaming down her cheeks.

The Don started once again, and their attention returned to him. "And now, I must ask you to leave us for a few minutes so that I may address my remaining children alone."

The request did not bother him—just a dying father wanting to speak with his heir and heiress. It was the phrase *remaining children* that spooked him. Stansie had told him that when she was nine and Ciro was thirteen, their older brother, nineteen-year-old Giovanni Russo, had been shot and killed. When Conrad had carefully pressed for more information, Stansie had told him that she knew nothing else. *"My mamma cried for days, and suddenly there were many men carrying guns stationed in and around our house. I never got to see Giovanni again; it was a closed casket at the funeral,"* Stansie had said. *"For many months, Ciro and I were homeschooled, while papa went away on business."* Conrad had never heard the Don talk about his oldest child; this was the closest he had ever come.

Stansie's pinch of his leg brought him out of his thoughts, and he became aware of his excruciating need to urinate. He rose and gave a slight bow. "Of course," Conrad said to the Don before exiting the room.

After the Don watched his daughter's boyfriend leave through the doorway, he motioned for Big Joey to leave too.

When the large wooden door's latch clicked in place, he knew they were now alone. The nurse had been instructed to come back in an hour, plenty of time to deliver his final directive. He had chosen today because everything that his father and grandfather before him had said about death was true. When you feel the angel of death sitting on your chest, smelling his foul breath as you struggle to breathe, you don't have long to live. And for Don Ilario "The Smile" Russo, he wanted to beat the angel of death to the last smile and, perhaps, have the last laugh. He would die this week, but he needed to give his children strict instructions now because Ciro's power was about to be challenged, and the survival of the Russo family depended on what he was about to say.

"Fabian is not happy with our arrangement."

"Excuse me, father, but why is *she* still here?" Ciro said.

Stansie's look said that she was angry at being marginalized once again by her brother.

He hadn't expected this. True enough, his wife had never been let in on his dealings or inner thoughts, but perhaps that had been a mistake. No, he would never admit it to anyone, but he wasn't so sure about keeping her shielded from the family business for their entire marriage. After all, it hadn't kept Giovanni alive, had it? And he had been his favorite, the boy who should have grown up to be a man and a Don. Angela would never forgive him for that—and shouldn't. He had failed to protect his child. Then, he had failed to protect Stansie from a different kind of threat. There was the rub. A great deal of his fortune had come from the trafficking of drugs. When she had become addicted with no rescue in sight, he started to believe that he would outlive his daughter, which made him feel heartless and cruel. That she was sitting in front of him right now was a miracle. But he had long sworn off miracles, and his relationship with God had taken a turn for the worse when, on the night Stansie had returned clean, he had asked Father Mattie to explain the mysterious ways in which the Lord worked. Father Mattie did not speak, choosing to hold his rosary and smile. And so, they

71

had lit two candles together and prayed for her soul. Then the good priest had entered her room later that night, disrobed at the foot of her bed, and said, *"This will be a night you'll never forget. Today, I blessed you with holy water; tonight, I shall bless you with my rod and staff."* Stansie had screamed, and twenty minutes later, Big Joey had chopped off the good Father's legs, just above the knee, with an ax. Before he could bleed out, Joey had finished him by strangling Father Mattie with his own rosary. With Joey by his side, Ciro could outfight Fabian; the Don was certain of this. But what about his daughter? Did she need to be here right now?

"Perhaps Ciro is right," he said.

"I'm not leaving, papa," she said.

It was a weakness to not include her. She had every right to know about the money. It was also a weakness to back down from his position. However, he had softened it with his trademark *perhaps*; he had tried to mentor Ciro in the benefits of using the word when making a decision. It gave the impression of asking for an opinion in the form of a verification, a rebuttal, or a probe for more information. The word 'perhaps' could also be used to convey that he was leaning in a particular direction. It was also one of the few words that allowed you to reverse course if you sensed heavy opposition. 'Perhaps I will' could turn into 'Perhaps I won't' depending on the advice or consensus of your advisors. He'd read a book years ago about how President Eisenhower would announce in front of his cabinet or group of advisors, *"I'm thinking about doing..."* and then sit back and listen to them debate. Ike had found it to be superior to the usual, *"What do you think about...?"* And so, as Don, he had adopted Ike's philosophy. Ciro had been open to both suggestions, but something inside the Don did not believe his son was thoroughly convinced of his father's tried and true phrases of statesmanship.

He glanced at Ciro, a gesture meant to prod his son into a decision—yet another one of his tools of negotiation. Or were all negotiations manipulations masquerading as compromises? He now, weakly—but clearly noticeably—raised an eyebrow at his son.

His daughter beat Ciro to the response. She was always a quicker thinker. Excusing her drug use, if she had been a man, she would have been named his successor—even if she was younger.

"I'm staying," she said. "Say what you need to, papa."

The Don watched Ciro's eyes squint in frustration, but he remained silent. The situation had appeared to work itself out, which was another leadership lesson in patience that he had failed to pass on to Ciro. Well, better get on with it. He pointed at Ciro. "Fabian may try to move against you the moment I'm gone, if not before." He let this settle in. Then he added, motioning at first to Stansie and then making a sweeping gesture to encompass the entire house, "You are all in danger and must be prepared to act with strength."

"But he has given us his word," Ciro said.

*And this is why you'll be dead before you know what hit you.* "What a man says and what a man does are rarely the same thing." The Don gathered a breath and exhaled. He had hoped to have at least six more months to mentor his son and smooth over the transition. But the cancer had spread too fast, and now he was down to days...maybe one day. "Yes, there is a slight chance he will retire and cause you no trouble."

Ciro seemed to sit up straighter—a show of confidence and vindication.

"But," the Don whispered. He took a sip of water and swallowed. The room was quiet enough for his swallow and lip-smacking to be heard. "Fabian is more likely to come after you. When I pass away, he'll call a meeting to swear his loyalty to you and to celebrate your leadership. A private dinner to commemorate your friendship. But that meeting will never take place. You'll be killed on the way to it, and your caporegimes, your consigliere, your bodyguard, and—" he paused to look at Stansie, "—your family will also embrace that same fate."

Ciro now leaned forward, putting his elbows on his knees and his chin on his knuckles. "We have to move first," he said.

Stansie put a hand on her brother's shoulder.

He shook it off.

"What should we do, papa?" she asked.

"We'll get to that. First, there is something you both need to know. And then there is something I need you both to do. Come closer."

The Don's children rose and joined him at his bedside—one on each side. He opened his hands, and they each took one in their own. Then, he told them.

As the words left his mouth, he saw his son's eyes open wide with surprise and greed.

# 6

## *Present Day*

The twenty-five-foot Stingray tracked steadily along behind Rusty on US-23 south as Brad Cranston picked up his cell phone. He had left Larry's house less than five minutes ago.

"Mr. Cranston?"

"Yes?" he answered.

"This is Private Investigator Allison Shannon from Cozy Mitten Private Investigations & Consulting Firm."

*God, that's a mouthful.* "Good evening," Brad said. "Let me guess, there was no cell phone."

"That would make it easier for both of us," she said, "but there was a phone. I've got it and am heading back to my office."

He thought about this development. Conrad had always been a master of deception and misdirection—some lies masquerading as truths and some truths masquerading as lies. Additionally, he excelled at half-truths—especially when he needed help. Hence, it had always been difficult to sort out what was actually happening in his brother's life. *But what about now? What if Conrad was telling the whole truth and really was in grave danger?* Brad felt a hint of anxiety well up in his stomach, like finding out your spouse *may* be cheating on you. "Well, at least my brother's voicemail wasn't a complete lie."

"True," she said.

He couldn't place her age. It was a game he played when an author would call him to discuss his or her vision for the book cover that Brad would be illustrating. He'd gotten pretty good at it over the years. His guess: early thirties. "Thanks for going over and checking for me," he said. "Does the phone still work?"

"Yes. I haven't taken it out of the Ziploc bag yet, but I pushed the 'on' button. Still has power."

*Take this one step at a time.* "Ms. Shannon, I'd like to hire you for a few days to help me find my brother. I'll pay you for a full day today. Are you available?"

"Tell me what you know so far," she said.

For the next ten minutes, he filled her in.

"And you haven't seen him for..."

"It's been over two years," Brad said. "Always been a pariah of sorts. He was pretty heavy into the drug scene about a decade ago. Our family got him to a rehab clinic. He cleaned up but then had a relapse about six years ago. We were supposed to hike the Appalachian Trail together; he never showed up. Hasn't had contact with anyone else in the family but me since then, and I haven't heard from him in over six months, which is not unusual. He sounded better, heard some sort of music in the background and voices, then the call suddenly ended. I called him right back. He never picked up."

"What happened the last time you saw him?"

"Well, when he didn't show up for the hike, I spent all of my free time from work searching for him for about a year. After that, I thought he was most likely dead or in a place where I'd never find him. Two years after that, I heard a knock on my door one winter evening, and it was him—smelly, hair down to his shoulders, beard down to the bottom of his neck. Thin, hungry, but, and I am still amazed at this, not strung out. Not a trace on either arm and no pills in his backpack, which I made him empty once he came inside."

"Interesting," Allison said. "Go on."

"So, I chewed him out for skipping the hike, and he apologized. That's one thing I'll give him credit for, he always owns up to his mistakes. The problem has always been that he keeps making them. Anyway, I tried to get out of him what he's been up to for the past three years, and he clammed up. And when he doesn't want to talk about something, there is no getting it out of him. It drove my parents crazy. In his backpack, he only had three things: a ratty Guns-n-Roses t-shirt, a tattered copy of *Swann's Way*—Proust's first volume in his *In Search of Lost Time* epic—and a pack of Wrigley's chewing gum.

"So, I gave him my robe and told him to take a shower. Meanwhile, I headed out and bought him some fresh clothes since he's north of six-four, about five inches taller than I am. I also bought him a warm winter coat, hat, gloves, and a scarf because I anticipated that he was going to bounce at some point, and I didn't want him out in a Michigan winter without them. I also got him a new backpack. We're the same shoe size, so, ironically, I went into my garage when I got back from the store and pulled out my L.L. Bean Cresta hiking boots that I had purchased for the Appalachian Trail hike, which I hadn't worn since. I took all of his nasty clothes and old backpack and threw them away. He borrowed my clippers and buzzed off all of his hair. He also shaved. Within two hours, he was sitting with me at my kitchen table, clean, and wolfing down sandwiches, soup, potato chips, along with guzzling a two-liter bottle of Coke. We made small talk, and he said that he needed to rest. So, I got him settled into the guest room and turned on a box fan—one of his safeties growing up. He crashed hard. The next day, I picked up vitamins and toiletries for him, and he ate heartily at both lunch and dinner. He also used almost an entire roll of clear packing tape to repair his book. During a bathroom break—I admit, we had a few beers watching football—I snuck into his room and put two hundred dollars in cash, a pre-paid calling card with one hundred dollars credit on it, a Swiss army knife, and a new sports watch, in the front pocket of his backpack and zipped it up." Brad sighed. "The next morning, he was gone."

"Did he steal anything from you?"

"When I woke up and found his bedroom empty—the bed was even made—I had that hollow feeling course through my body. I didn't want to start looking around to see what he might have swiped from me, but curiosity and sadness got the best of me, so I went through everything. He didn't take a thing—not even any food." There was a long pause.

"You have a good memory," she said.

"Well," Brad said, "it was the last time I saw him, and I miss him."

"But you've talked with him since then, right?"

"Just that one time six months ago."

"No idea where he goes?"

"I find the fact that he was in Sterling State Park a bit strange. Doesn't make sense to me, if anything does make sense where Conrad is concerned."

"Why is that?"

"Because before when he would drift, he would disappear into the Upper Peninsula for months, doing odd jobs and staying in cheap hotels, making just enough to pay his bar tab. Then, I'd usually get a call that his 1990 Volkswagen Beetle had been parked in some diner's parking lot for over a month, and I'd have to have it towed to my house. After the second time this happened, I sold the sonofabitch. Of course, this all took place before his stint in rehab. I don't know where he was before he showed up at my house or where he went after.

Homelessness is different in Michigan during the winter because of the weather. You can't sleep outside. So, he had to be someplace warm during those months."

"You're right," she said. "It's been so long since I've been in Michigan, I have to reorient myself to the seasons again."

"Where are you from?" Brad asked.

"Originally? Saginaw. But I've been away for over twenty years because of my service in the Coast Guard."

"What brings you back to *Pure Michigan?*" he said.

"My mom. She lives in Monroe, and I wanted to be closer." There was silence for a few beats. "So, you're on your way down with the boat and will be here a little past midnight. That right?"

"Yes. I called and made a reservation at Sterling State Park. Got lucky. They had one of their RV spots open up after a cancellation. I'm going to pull in and then sleep in the boat's cabin. Oh, I almost forgot. I made a recording of the voice message on my cell phone. Do you want it?"

"Yes. Text it to me at your next stop. This reminds me, any idea who the 'she' in the message is?"

"No clue. He was hoping that she got away, so he cared for her on some level."

"And the money?"

"Puzzling. Conrad has always been a moocher. My bet is that if there is money in the equation, it isn't his."

"And you think he's in danger?" Allison said.

"Wish I could give you a definite answer, but the truth is...I don't know. You know as much as I do now."

There was silence for a moment again. *She's not going to take this on*, he thought. *Hell, I wouldn't.*

"Consider me hired," she said. "But I've got to warn you, when I start something, I go all in. It's just the way I work."

He raised his eyes, surprised by her decision, and couldn't think of how to respond.

"You still there, Mr. Cranston?" she said.

"Yes," he finally got out. "I just didn't think you were going to take the case."

"We don't have much, but something seems to be going on. Agreed?"

"Yes," Brad said. He liked her approach. Straight up. No bullshit. "So, I guess I'll be seeing you soon."

"Tonight."

"Tonight? But I just told you that—"

"We don't have any time to waste if he really is in trouble. Look, I'm heading to my office. With your permission, I'll see if I can get any fingerprints from the phone and then check the pictures he took on it and run all of the incoming and outgoing calls. It'll take some time, but right now, we have time while you're traveling to me."

"Permission granted," Brad got in.

"I'll also see if listening to the message gives me anything else to work on. Call me when you get to the park, and I'll come over with what I have."

"Anything else you can think of for me to bring?" Brad asked.

"No. You're bringing the boat and…oh, never mind."

"What?"

"Well, I was just thinking about your brother telling you to bring a boat, and I have no idea what we're getting into. It made me think of dive gear."

"Don't you think that's a bit of an overkill?"

"Maybe, but I want to be prepared just in case. Do you dive?"

"Yes, although it's been a few years." He thought back. The last time he had been diving was with Conrad, when his brother had emerged from rehab a new man—his gauntness replaced by twenty pounds of muscle, a fresh haircut, and he was reading again. The key was to keep him busy, replacing idle time and old habits with a robust schedule and new habits. So, they took scuba classes together

80

and started to wreck dive in Lake Huron over the summer. Conrad was clean, happy, motivated, and they became closer than they had been since growing up. There had been talk of Conrad going back to school to finish his Ph.D. in History—at that point, he was still A.B.D. (all but dissertation)—and possibly joining the professorial ranks once he had the alphabet of armor after his name. Brad had even told him, *"And once you get your doctorate, don't be like most of the enlightened and feel the need to tell someone you have a Ph.D. within the first half hour of meeting him or her."* Conrad had smirked—his way of telling people that he heard them but was not committing to agreeing or disagreeing with them. They continued to dive, talk about life, and watch old films at night. It would be summer forever… But that was the thing with Michigan summers: They never lasted. Without diving to keep him busy, Conrad began to drift…

Her words brought him out of his recollection.

"It's been a few years for me too," she said, almost at a whisper, "but I think I know where my gear is."

"Anything I could use?" he said.

"I might have my old BCD, weight belt, and regulator assembly, but," she paused, "unfortunately, I don't have a wetsuit, mask, snorkel, or set of fins for you. You'd have to stop somewhere on the way down and pick those up."

Her confident, get-down-to-business manner had disappeared. There seemed to be uncertainty or a measure of uncomfortableness. *What was it? Diving?* Or, perhaps, her mind was already starting to piece together the case, and his question had distracted her. Whatever it was, he decided not to ask about her change in tone. "I'm guessing we won't need any of the gear, but I think you're right. We'd hate it if we did and didn't have it."

At first, she said nothing, then, "I agree."

"The mask, snorkel, and fins shouldn't be a problem, but the wetsuit might."

"See what you can do. If we have to get in the water for any extended amount of time, we don't want to freeze our asses off in Lake Erie. I'll check around down here because we'll need tanks too. Call me when you get to the park."

"Will, do, Ms.—"

She cut him off. "Allison," she said. Her confident tone was back.

"Good," said Brad.

"Why good?"

"I live by myself and am pretty informal. I just prefer using first names with people."

"Okay," she said. "I'll be standing by."

The call ended. He picked up his Speedway travel mug and took a long pull on his coffee. He'd call Larry and see if there was any dive gear in the boat; if not, he'd try to pick some up in Alpena.

# 7

## *Present Day*

I t was just past 8 p.m. when Brad pulled Rusty into a large parking lot that ended at a seawall right on Lake Huron. He had struck out in Alpena, but a family friend had told him about a hardware store in Hampstead that carried dive gear. His friend knew the owner and had called ahead for him; the store closed at eight, but the friend said that the owner would keep the store open for him. When he had called Larry, he had found out that Larry did have dive gear but that, unfortunately, it was inside a cabinet in Larry's garage.

The truck and trailer rolled to a halt a few yards from the end of the asphalt, and Brad shut off the engine. The lowering sun behind him cast a warm glow onto the lake, and the shadow from the hardware store made the water just offshore look dark gray. There was only one other car in the parking lot—a shiny black Mustang parked near the back of the store.

83

The Friday traffic had thinned out, and 23 was quiet as he walked to the entrance of—he looked up at the sign above the door—Beecher Hardware. The sound of waves striking the seawall drew his attention, and he saw a dock that stretched out the back of the hardware store. Near the end of the dock, there was a platform that extended out over the water on the left-hand side. Enough two-by-fours were still in place for Brad to make out the rough framing of what he guessed had once been a shed or something—one side still had a sheet of plywood up but the other sides, minus the two-by-fours, were bare. He heard laughing, and his attention was drawn to a boy and girl, teenagers he deduced, who were exiting the lake by climbing up the swim ladder that had rounded aluminum bars like grappling hooks bolted to the end of the dock. When they were both on the dock, they lined up next to each other, counted to three, and then dove back into the water. Seconds later, two heads appeared ten or fifteen yards away from the dock, and the boy and girl trod water. Brad grinned, remembering swimming and splashing with Conrad and Heidi in the lake while his mom and dad read paperbacks on an Alpena beach. He let the memories clear out as the two kids made it back to the swim ladder, climbed up, and dove in again. He continued across the parking lot.

The bells on the door chimed as he entered, and he immediately smelled fresh lumber mixed with some flowery scent of Febreze. Off to the right, behind the counter, a stately Native American woman with silver hair pulled back into a ponytail sat on a chair reading a hardcover book that she had removed the dust jacket from.

She set the book down. "Brad?" she said.

"Yes," he said back, walking toward the counter.

She extended her hand, "Levana Norris."

"Brad Cranston," he replied and shook. Her hand felt delicate, and yet there was a warmth and sense of reserved strength behind her grasp as if she could turn a dial and out-squeeze him if she wanted to. "Thanks for staying open."

"No problem," Levana said. "The owner, Marty Leif, is on vacation with his family for a week. I'm covering for him."

"Oh, I thought you were the owner."

"No, my brother used to run the store before Marty. I'm retired now, so I don't mind covering for him now and then. Keeps me busy."

"Does the dock out back belong to the hardware store?" Brad asked.

There was a noticeable pause, but her face remained the same—kind and welcoming. However, her eyes stared past him for an instant, giving him the impression that she was in another time, if not another place. And like that, she returned her attention to him. "Technically, yes," she said, "but the store doesn't really use it anymore. Why do you ask?"

"I saw a couple of kids diving off of it on my walk across the lot," he said.

She smiled. "Well, it is still good for that," she said. "Those are my twin grandkids, Lucien and Nina. I brought them in to help me out today, and since they did a good job, they are enjoying some time off now."

"Good to see their faces not buried in a screen, if you don't mind me saying," Brad said.

"Don't mind at all," she said. "So, I hear you need some dive gear."

He was about to answer when the door to the store chimed open, and an older man with closely cropped white hair and a full white five o'clock shadow entered.

"Everything okay, Levana?" the man asked and approached the counter.

She gave him the kind of knowing smile of appreciation reserved only for those people in life that you trust and have known for a long time. It was unmistakable and endearing. Brad knew because he had just had a similar exchange with Larry over an hour ago.

"Everything is fine, Abner. Just helping out a final customer, then we're heading home." She turned to Brad. "Brad, this is an old friend of mine, Abner Hutch."

Brad put out his hand, and Hutch gave it a quick, tight shake. "Nice to meet you," Hutch said, and then his eyes swiveled to Levana. "Saw the truck and trailer outside and knew it was past closing time. Thought I would poke my head in and see what was cookin'."

"I appreciate it," Levana said. "Kind of late for you to be in town, isn't it?" she teased him.

"Nonsense. Lucille's got me on a mission to pick up a bottle of wine to have on the porch tonight." He looked around the store. "Those two little rascals still around here?" Hutch asked.

"Out on the dock, doing what we used to do half a century ago."

"Ahem," he said. "I'm still doin' it." Hutch walked past them and stood at the back door, looking out the small window. "There they are." He lowered his voice and said, "Good on ya, kids," almost as if saying it only to himself. "Trist and Jill still out at the house?" he said louder.

"Yeah, they're staying for another week and then all heading home."

"Good," Hutch said. "You sure Marty doesn't want me to rebuild that shed? I could have that thing up in no-time."

"You're going to keep at it until he lets you, aren't you?"

"Yep. Don't like change," he said. He turned back toward them. "I'm gonna go out and say hi to these squirts. Nice to have met you, Brad."

"You too," Brad said. Levana waved.

Hutch opened the door and was gone.

"Sorry about that," she said to Brad. "I know you're kind of in a hurry."

"No need to apologize," he said. "I'm a bit old school and like to see people who can carry on a conversation for more than thirty seconds without looking at their phones."

She nodded in agreement. "We're trading conversation for what we think is connection." She paused. "And we don't have much time left to reverse course."

"Agreed."

"Now, what can I get for you?"

"I need a mask, snorkel, fins, and..." he surveyed the store, "you wouldn't happen to have any wetsuits, would you?"

"Oh, that's easy," she said. "We've got it all." She started to move around the counter. "You should also have a dive knife," she said, patting him on the shoulder. "Follow me."

Ten minutes later, he was back on the road headed south—his new gear neatly stowed in the Stingray's cabin. At the checkout counter, Levana Norris had pulled out a piece of paper—he swore it had nothing written on it—and told him that it was a fifty percent off coupon. She did that all on her own; he hadn't told her why he needed the gear or any details about his trip. It was a simple act of kindness—still some decent people left in the world. He gripped the leather steering wheel with his left hand and sat back as cool air came in through the window and ran through the brown hairs on his arm. To the left, the woods that had been hiding his view of the water opened up as US-23 curved by an old lakefront inn that had been leveled for construction to start on a block of condominiums. Lake Huron had darkened to a blue-black—choppy, powerful, and yet indifferent. And as quickly as the wall of trees had disappeared, giving him a view of the endless horizon of water, it reappeared, and the lake was gone again—a ten-second portal. As he took a sip of coffee, his thoughts shifted to his brother. A question emerged: How much of Conrad was still decent? A part of him didn't want to know. He wanted to go back to when they were young— climbing trees, drinking water from the hose, and playing basketball in their driveway—before things changed. Before Conrad changed.

*Don't do this to yourself. You can't change him,* he told himself.

Brad stepped on the accelerator, and the needle on Rusty's speedometer nudged past seventy.

*Present Day*

It was just after 9 p.m., and Allison Shannon sat at her desk and sipped on a cup of tea, waiting for the results of who Conrad Cranston had talked to and texted with in the past month. Dionne Warwick's "Déjà vu" was playing loud enough from her computer's speakers for her to hear it from her desk chair but not loud enough to fill the room. Through the room's only window, she saw that it was now dark outside, and the array of red, blue, green, and yellow city lights blinked in the distance. She knew that beyond the lights, the mighty Interstate 75 ran north like a circuit cable through Michigan, passing through cities like Detroit, Flint, Saginaw, and Bay City, eventually going over the Mackinac Bridge into the Upper Peninsula and running all the way up to Sault Ste. Marie on the Michigan-Canadian border. She estimated that by now Brad Cranston was southbound on I-75 and would pick up US-23 again in Flint, taking it straight down to state highway 50. Once on 50, it was around twenty minutes to Monroe and another fifteen or so to Sterling State Park.

Allison's eyes left the window and surveyed her office, which was now finished due to the downtime she had had waiting for information about the phone. The only light came from a corner lamp, illuminating the wall with her four pictures—one of Allison with her family at a reunion, one of Allison with just her mother and father, one of Allison in uniform at an awards ceremony…and then there was the fourth picture, which she had pulled from the bottom of her last box while unpacking and decided to add to the wall around an hour ago. The photograph was of her and Keller.

She fought back the memories and continued her scan. The pictures hung neatly over the cozy black leather couch that had her Detroit Tigers throw blanket draped over one of the armrests. The lamp's light also cast shadows against the far wall, which had a small bookshelf filled with manuals and her growing collection of crime-thriller paperbacks penned by a variety of her favorite authors. Above the bookshelf hung a shadowbox with an American Flag inside, which had been presented to her when she retired from the Coast Guard. A rectangular purple area rug was centered on the room's wooden floor, and there was a closet on the wall next to the lone window.

Her eyes returned to her desk, and she wondered how much time she would actually spend in this room. If she was busy with cases, then probably not much. If she wasn't, then at least the space felt comfortable. Plus, Larissa seemed like someone she could lose a few hours with, shooting the breeze about work and life. Perhaps the other two P.I.'s were also personable, and the group would start to feel like a family after a while.

The lamp and the glow from her computer screen provided enough light to work by but were also soft enough to allow her to relax and enjoy her cup of tea while she waited for Conrad Cranston's phone and text log. Hopefully, she wouldn't have to go back any farther than a month to get what she needed. In fact, she had never reviewed a month full of texts before. She wondered if he wrote in some sort of shorthand fashion or if he texted in grammatically correct sentences. Was he pro-emoji, anti-emoji, or uncaring? She was mostly pro-emoji but hated when friends overdid it. *One heart is all you need to post—not seven.* Her texts were written in the same manner as if she was composing a business letter. Her friends said she came across as ice-cold—maybe that was why they overused emojis—but she refused to alter her messages. This might be why her friends rarely texted her now. She didn't mind. Most of the messages were unnecessary anyway—distractions camouflaged as matters of importance and immediacy.

Larissa was gone when she had returned, but the scent of her perfume still lingered in the hallways and in her office. The building was quiet, and it made her uneasy. She didn't like a lot of noise—just enough to know that other people were around and going about their own routines. She was somewhat embarrassed that this gave her comfort. She should be able to be alone and work alone, but sometime in the past few months, she had realized that when she stripped away many of the other layers of life—family gatherings, working out, watching college sports, sleeping, coffee and books, the Sunday paper—she was lonely. And what disturbed her more than being lonely was that she was doing next to nothing to stop being lonely.

Warwick's smooth tune ended and a pitter-patter sound from behind the wall next to her desk jolted her from her thoughts. Larissa had warned her of the mice problem the company was working on; every once in a while, she would hear tiny feet scurrying behind the walls and sometimes a thump when a rodent would bump into one. This time, it sounded like an entire family was on the move, evading a predator. She listened for a few more seconds, and the sounds of the miniature stampede faded.

*Hope they made it home*, she thought.

She pulled a cream-colored shawl over her shoulders and then took a sip of hot tea. *What in the hell am I doing?* The tea warmed her, and she shook off the thought. "Concentrate," she said out loud to herself.

On her computer screen was a private investigator checklist and notes she had entered. Since this was her first official case, she was reviewing the list to ensure that she would be prepared. Private investigators were known as professional investigators in Michigan, and the average yearly salary for a professional investigator working in the mitten was $43,000. But she knew that to achieve that salary, she would need referrals, and to get referrals, she would have to establish a good record of delivering results to her clients. When she looked at the distribution of P.I.s in Michigan, she shook her head. Over two hundred were employed in the state, with *half of them* located in the Detroit area.

*Sweet Lord.*

She looked at her self-typed notes on the screen and laughed to herself, remembering when she typed it up months ago at her mother's kitchen table.

-**Car**: comfortable, nothing flashy—use landscape colors, no license plate frames or stickers, no identifiable marks—have dents and paint smudges fixed, mid-size SUV best (can see over smaller cars and yet blends in well)...go with *new* instead of *used*, use limo tint on all windows—can still sit in front seat while conducting surveillance, economical—need good gas mileage (don't pass on cost to client!), 4-wheel drive—God damn Michigan winters!, GPS is a must.

-**DC to AC Power Inverter**: at least two outlets and a USB port.

-**Binoculars**: Dad's Bushnell's?

-**Battery Jump Starter**

-**Compressor**

-**Tire Repair System**: Can of Fix a Flat & Universal Tire Repair Kit

-**Tri-Pod**: Compact?

-**Video Camera**: Hand-held & Covert (pen camera?), charger, backup battery, backup/secondary video camera

-**Toilet Paper**: Duh. Wipes and tampons too. Sometimes I hate being a woman.

*Ain't that the truth.*

-**Money**: Cash—$200.00 in 20s, 10s, 5s, and 1s. Change: $10.00 in Quarters

-**Overnight Bag**: Evening dress, heels, flats, sweater, scarf, earrings, matching purse, jeans, sweatshirt—definitely overthinking this shit, oh well—t-shirt, running shoes, hiking boots, underwear, socks, nylons, shorts, swimsuit, winter hat, ballcap, winter gloves, winter scarf, toiletries. Well, Allison, you'll definitely be ready. Sure you want to do this?

*Guess so.*

-**Food and Water**: Use Hurricane prep list—also, don't move to Florida!

-**Portable Camping Toilet**: Why am I doing this?

-**Flashlight**

-**Tools**: Basic, and a socket wrench set

-**Window Shades**

-**Laptop**

-**Pen and Paper**: Old school...like me

*Definitely. Got my legal pad and pen right here, baby.*

-**Cell Phone**: Get iPhone app that masks my number

*Yeah, yeah, yeah...cell phones can be evil, but sometimes I love them.*

-**Gas**: Never let your tank get below half-a-tank! Gas can in back?

-**Trash bags**: Obvious.

The next page contained her checklist for becoming a Professional investigator.

-**Must be licensed by the Michigan Department of Licensing and Regulatory Affairs (LARA)**. Requirements:

-**25 years of age or older**: check

-**U.S. Citizen and earned at least a high school degree**: check

-**Provide 5 character references from Michigan citizens who have known you for at least 5 years and are not family members and earn a Certificate of Corporation**: check—what a pain in the ass.

-**Military History**: no dishonorable discharge: check—I'm a highly decorated veteran, bitch.

-**Personal Finances**: won't be examined: score! Got a little bit of a credit card problem…

*Workin' on it…but still packin' plastic everywhere I go.*

-**Mental Disease or Defect**: no restrictions based on mental health: check—thank God they aren't checking into my dysfunctional family. Does thinking a lot about Keller count?

*Don't look at the wall.*

-**Bonding**: must have $10,000 bond or insurance policy: check.

-**Disqualifications**: DQ'd if I have committed a felony or misdemeanor involving impersonating a government official, assault, illegal possession or use of a firearm, fraud, selling information or evidence, controlled substances or two or more alcohol-based offenses: check—only one alcohol offense.

*Next!*

-**Education and Experience**: must have an accredited bachelor's degree in a field related to professional investigation: check—investigation and security management.

-**Written Exam**: No examination required in Michigan: Hell, yeah! Standardized tests can burn there, too.

*Yeah, screw exams.*

-Forms:

-Application Fees: 750 bones for a license—total bullshit

-Maintenance: $350 renewal fee—the bastards!

*Go me. I was one sassy lady when I filled this out—oh, right, mom was looking over my shoulder every chance she had. I don't do nosey!*

93

-**Fingerprinting**: have to have it done to be hired by any agency: check, no big deal.

*Done and done.*

Well, whatever the initial reasons were for pursuing a career as a professional investigator, the final and decisive reason was still clear in her mind: She needed to keep busy. An idle mind is the devil's workshop or some such ridiculousness she had heard in church eons ago. After struggling with establishing a routine when she had retired from the Coast Guard last year, she realized that the saying was a cliché for a reason, the reason being, it was true. She did not do well without structure. After the first week, which felt good because it was similar to vacation—sleeping in, cup after cup of coffee while lounging on the couch in her robe, losing a few mornings and afternoons to the binge-watching of a Netflix show that had been popular while she was still on active duty when she had no time to watch, lunches at a corner café, ordering pizza and wings for a few dinners and washing it down with a good amount of beer, and taking long, hot baths with Epsom salt added—she closed herself off from the outside world—no cable news, newspapers, internet browsing on her laptop, or smartphone use. Her mother did not believe her until Allison added that she had accidentally spilled coffee on her laptop keyboard the first morning of retirement and that her new smartphone had still not arrived, forcing Allison to set up a landline, which, after three telemarketing calls, she unplugged except to give her mother a morning and nightly check-in call. The week had been liberating. It felt good to have no superior to report to, no 4:30 a.m. wake-up time in order to be at morning physical training (P.T.) by 5:30 a.m., no mission to complete, no training cycle to endure, no dive equipment to check, no travel plans obliging her to coordinate bills, yard maintenance, and other details ahead of time, no enlisted personnel or junior officers to mentor and keep in line, and no errands to run—which had always eaten up most of her precious free time. However, she had been shocked at how fast the week had passed by.

The second week had passed by even faster, forcing her to confront the fact that she was losing weeks to her new sedentary lifestyle. Then, she had stepped on the scale. The eight-pound weight gain was enough to make her abandon her aimless routine and refocus. Additionally, her leg had started to stiffen from not working out. The doctors had warned her that she would need to stretch and exercise the leg at least every other day for the rest of her life or suffer the consequences of immobility and the evils of arthritis. She now believed them. Of course, none of these reasons were the primary reason why she could not afford to remain idle, having days and nights blur together. Those two weeks had brought back thoughts of Keller, which had turned into nightmares involving Keller. She would be back underwater, seeing him look at her wide-open eyes from behind his mask's tempered glass in the moments before his body blew apart, the great white circling...then she would be awake, screaming, the sheets drenched in her sweat and vanilla-scented perfume.

She looked up from the screen and over at the picture wall above her couch. Her eyes were watering but not enough to prevent her from making out the dark frame around the photo that, if the overhead light was on, showed her and Keller in full dive gear standing on a dock, ready to jump into the aquamarine water below them. *Why keep punishing yourself? Take the photo down and move on.* She could not. Her eyes made their way back to her screen, and she dabbed the tears with a tissue as she continued to remember.

The next morning, she had placed the bedding in the washing machine, set the water temperature to hot, poured in a full cup of Tide Plus Febreze Spring & Renewal laundry detergent, and pushed start. Wearing sweat pants, a windbreaker, and running shoes, she had then exited her house and run a thirty-minute loop, returning home to do push-ups and crunches on the cold grass of her front lawn. That afternoon, she had bought a new laptop and started researching how to become a professional investigator, which was when she had started the list she was now looking at.

Her cell phone vibrated. *Good.* She hoped it was some news about her case, but frowned when she saw the number. It was a case all right—the ever-evolving case of her family.

"Hi," she said with the slightest hint of annoyance.

The weathered voice of her sixty-seven-year-old mother, Kathy Rae Shannon, replied, "You comin' over tonight?"

"I won't be able to make it, mom." *Please let this be enough. No third degree, no guilt trip, no smoke and mirrors.* "Everything okay?"

There was a pause. This usually meant some level of disapproval. "You promised."

Allison held the phone away from her at arm's length and exhaled. She counted to three and then brought the phone back to her ear. "I know, but I have good news. I started my first case today."

"You just moved in," her mother said.

"Yeah, but I work here now, mom." She swiveled in her chair. "Plus, it's good that I finally have a case."

"Maw-Maw is here, said she wants to see her muffin."

*Great. The loaded guilt trip.*

Grace Wilson O'Connor, Maw-Maw, was her mother's mom and the glue that had held their family together through too many unfortunate turns over the years: her older sister Danielle's pregnancy at sixteen and Danielle's defiance when she moved into her boyfriend's apartment, which had driven her father crazy; the loss of her grandfather, Gracie's husband, a week before Allison graduated high school; the loss of *her* father when she was twenty-four while on a classified deployment—she found out a week after he had passed away—and, perhaps the most painful, the falling out between her and Danielle after their father passed away. Danielle was twenty-seven at the time and living with a different boyfriend by then, who, out of all of the losers Danielle had been with, deserved his own special all-star loser category. After continually spending most of Danielle's monthly paychecks on weed, booze, pizza, and the occasional hooker, he had convinced Danielle to angle in for more than her share of her father's inheritance. When Allison and her mother said no, Danielle stopped speaking to them. Now, she was married to a salesman named Donnie Marvin, and they lived in Toledo and never visited.

And so, for these and other reasons, Allison was Gracie's favorite.

"You'll have to give Maw-Maw a hug and a smooch for me," Allison said.

"She's worried about you, child. Doesn't think you're getting out enough. Gotta find you a man, she says."

Allison rolled her eyes. She was doing just dandy without a man, thank you very much. "You tell her I'm fine—been gettin' out a lot lately." One half-truth and one lie. Half-truth: She was fine, except when she thought about Keller. Lie: She had not been getting out much. Her only social events in the past few months were the occasional dinner with her best friend and one gathering to play a version of Monopoly where you collected experiences instead of property—and always returned home. No player actually won the game; it just went on until all of the experiences had been collected. Then, the spirited debate would commence about the experiences that the game had left out. There had been coffee—mixed with Bailey's—and two trays of weed brownies. The coffee had been good; she had passed on the brownies and had won the game. Promises of a rematch had been made, and, surprisingly, she had been invited to play again last week. She had passed.

Her mother sighed, loud enough for her to hear, and said, "Okay. But you best be here next Friday for my ribs. You're still too thin."

She had won tonight's tilt. No sense in handling next week's business yet. "I will," she lied, and the phone call ended.

Allison sat back and exhaled. *Clear your mind and focus.*

She took in a breath, held it for five seconds, and then exhaled for five seconds. *The case. Concentrate on the case.* She sat back up and wheeled the chair to her desk where three color pictures sat, retrieved from Conrad Cranston's phone, that she had enlarged and printed on 8 ½" x 11" paper. She had tried to reach Brad earlier to tell him about the photos, but he hadn't picked up, and she had left a short voice message. So far, he hadn't called back.

She had scanned the pictures earlier but had not been able to study them in detail. Her first impression had been that they were from a vacation Conrad had taken with a current/former girlfriend and were not of much use. Wherever they had traveled to was warm, beautiful, and she wished that she was there right now and not in her new office. The irony of her thoughts made her chuckle. She had just told her mother that she couldn't join her tonight because of the case, and yet here she was wishing to be anywhere doing anything but working on the case. Shrugging, she turned on her desk lamp and spread the pictures out on the table, then picked up the first picture. It was a close up of a beautiful woman, perhaps in her thirties, with a building that looked like a round American flag rising behind her. She was slender, had silky black hair, and wore a light blue summer dress with sandals. Because of the angle—the photographer must have shot it from on one knee—her head was covering up everything on the establishment's name after the letter 'R.' Whatever the name was, chances were that it was a bar. There were dozens of people holding drinks in the background, standing around or sitting at tables arranged on a porch. Combinations flooded her brain again as they had before: Rudolph's Bar, Rhianna's Bar, Rip Roarin' Bar, Rest Stop Bar, and so on. Pointless. She put the picture down.

Picture two was of the woman again, but this time she had sunglasses on and was seated on the starboard side cockpit bench of a beautiful sailboat cruising through cobalt-blue water. The woman's hair was blowing away from her face, and in her hand was a large bottle of Evian. Again, not much to go on. The yacht had to be over forty feet, however, because the angle that the picture had been taken from revealed the sizable distance from the cockpit to the bow.

98

Picture three was the same as picture two except that the woman was now seated next to a shirtless man—lean, tanned, blonde hair—wearing sunglasses and red-colored swimming trunks. A pair of black fins lay on the deck next to his bare feet. Was this Conrad or someone else? Either way, there was a third person present who had taken the picture.

Allison studied picture three for a few moments more. There were no tattoos that could help identify the two people in the sailboat and no markings on the boat that would give her something to search.

Staring at the woman in the photographs, she played the recording Brad had sent her.

*"Hey, Brad. It's Conrad. Look, man, I'm in deep here. They're on their way. I'm at a campsite at Sterling State Park in Monr—um, yeah, I think it's Monroe. They'll take or destroy my cell if I have it on me, so I'm putting it in a plastic bag and leaving it in the tank of the left-most toilet stall in the men's restroom, code's my birthday—month then year. Look at the pict—"*

Conrad was cut off momentarily by the sound of what, earlier, she and Brad had agreed was an automobile's horn.

*"I think that's them. Shit, I hope she got away. Look, just bring a boat. They might be taking me back to—"*

Then came the sound of car doors slamming; again, she had agreed with Brad.

*"God, I hope this is still your home number. Don't involve the police. Bigtime money."*

Allison's eyes flicked back to the picture. "Are you the 'she' he's talking about?" she said aloud, looking at the woman in the photograph.

Her thoughts were interrupted by the ring of her cell phone. It was Mike Martinson, the agency's cell phone tracking guru, who was a Google software engineer but helped out Michigan professional investigators on the side.

"Hi, Mike," she answered, while putting the three pictures back into a manilla envelope.

"Hey, Allison," he said. "I'm going to e-mail the file to you with all of this stuff but wanted to call first. Reason is, there's not much at all. The phone was only activated last week, and there have been exactly three calls and one text message. Two calls were to Brad Cranston—one to his cell phone, one to his house phone. The other was made yesterday to a number that I'll need more time to track down."

"Why?" she asked. "Has this ever happened before?"

"Usually not," he said. "I mean, I'm good, but on some investigations, phones and phone owners are harder to track. Like when someone does not want to be located." He paused. "The one text that was sent from the phone you gave me was to a different number, which is giving me the same problems."

"What did the text say?"

"Three words: Done and safe. Sent at two a.m. three days ago."

"Any guesses?"

"I'd say that the three phones were to be used only for a short time and then destroyed. You see this thing now and again for drug deals or murders. The only reason we're talking about it right now is because something didn't go right, and instead of getting rid of his phone, your missing man got desperate."

"But why would he take pictures on it?"

"I never said he was smart," Mike snickered.

"True," Allison said. She wondered if Conrad's brother Brad would be any smarter. He had sounded somewhat competent on the phone, but the hell with phones. She needed to meet him in person to get a real measure. "His brother is on his way down, and I'm meeting him tonight."

"Are you asking me if I'm going to keep working on the numbers this weekend?"

"Guilty," she said.

"Tell you what," Mike said. "I wasn't planning on it, but I also don't like taking a break from a challenge like these other two phones present. I'll keep at it for a few more hours tonight, and if I can't crack them, then I'll pick back up again tomorrow morning."

"Thanks," she said. "Whoever Conrad Cranston is, I have a feeling he's in trouble."

"Understood," Mike said.

They were about to hang up when he added, "Hey, those photos might not be as useless as you think."

"Why?" she asked.

"Didn't you tell me that Conrad told Brad to bring a boat?"

"Yes."

"Well, it might be worth your time, while you wait for Brad, to see if there are any bars within boating distance of Sterling State Park that match the one in your photo. A long shot, but something to do, I guess."

Of course, she thought, wondering why she hadn't made that connection herself. She knew why. *Boats and scuba diving. Keller.* She had put Conrad's request for his brother to bring a boat in the back of her mind and left it there. *Get over it. You might have to face the water again.* "There are worse ways to kill time," she said. "Thanks."

"Call you when I have something," he said and hung up.

She took a drink of her tea and thought about calling Brad again. *No, give him a chance to call you back.* She also reasoned that there was nothing about the pictures or text message that he could help with while driving down to her. If Mike had provided information that made the situation more immediate, then, of course, she would have called Brad right away. She decided that if Brad called back, she'd fill him in; if he didn't, then she'd update him when they met at Sterling State Park.

She set her cup of tea down. *Now, about this bar.* Allison opened up Google Chrome on her computer—didn't mind searching for things on her phone but felt more in control with a larger screen. The Google search bar came up, and the great red, white, and blue 'R' Bar search commenced. As she began pressing keys, she thought that the odds of identifying and locating the bar were slim.

She had no idea that the odds would be in her favor.

# 9

## St. Clair Shores, Michigan

### *4 Days Ago . . .*

FBI Special Agent Patrick Bruno sat in his beloved Irving leather armchair—molasses-colored with bronze nailheads—which had been a present from his wife, Tara, when they had moved back to their hometown of St. Clair Shores, Michigan a month ago from Nashville. He stretched his tired legs—they felt like wet logs—and turned off the lamp next to his chair. The room became an orange and black blur, and he closed his eyes and counted to ten. When he reopened them, he could see out the second-story window into the back yard below. It was after nine, and the sprinklers were twitching away, giving his thick, half-acre carpet of grass an evening drink. He wished he could sit here, watching forever, instead of turning the lamp back on and opening the file folder. It was one thing to fight the mafia on the East coast where he would be taking down men and women he didn't know. It was another to be in his home town, trying to put away people he *did* know.

*What if I have to kill one of them?*

Tara's father was not well, and they had decided to come back home to help her mother. Patrick had been in no rush to ever return to the Detroit area. In fact, the first eighteen years of his life had been dedicated to getting *out of* Detroit. Why his own parents had decided to remain there was a question that mystified him. However, he had yet to ask them the question. It was nice for his two boys to get to see their grandparents more often, but he had his own reasons for not wanting to return to Detroit. And one of those reasons was in his hand.

He turned the lamp back on and opened the manila folder slowly, hoping it would be a different picture inside from the one he had glanced at earlier. It wasn't. The face of his childhood best friend commanded his entire attention. His breathing quickened, and his sweating palms stuck to the folder. Feeling lightheaded, he broke eye contact with the man in the picture and looked at his bookshelf, trying to slow down his breathing.

*The situation isn't going to change. He chose his path; you chose yours.* He took in a quick breath and then attempted to perform an extended exhale. He ended up coughing instead. *But why did their paths have to cross now?* Thomas Wolfe had written about situations like this in his masterpiece, *You Can't Go Home Again.* You cannot return home to your childhood, your family, and your old friends to escape the world. For the things that seemed everlasting and eternal in your mind ended up changing no matter how much you wanted them to stay the same. It was one of life's crueler lessons, and it happened to every optimistic traveler who returned to the idealistic realms of his youth, only to be disappointed and wish that he'd never come back. Every glory of the past could not escape becoming diminished in stature when revisited in the present.

In Nashville, he had been assigned to the money laundering division. After serving there for over a decade, he had come to the conclusion that there were better jobs but also worse jobs. The better jobs were in the field—more challenging and dangerous; the worse jobs were almost all sedentary oases of long hours behind a desk, staring into a monitor that both wore your eyes out and tricked your brain into thinking that consuming a daily six-pack of Diet Pepsi and a large bag of Cheetos was normal. Bruno didn't mind busting the bad guys in the heartland of country music, but he had been ready for a change and was pleased when the Bureau approved his transfer request from Nashville to Boston. His job would be fighting organized crime, which he considered one of the better jobs. Then, three weeks before they started their move, Tara's father had blood in his stool, and the transfer destination switched from Boston to Detroit.

He looked back at the picture. Could he kill Gino Rizzo, the driver and bodyguard of the second-highest ranked Detroit mafia member, Fabio "Fabian" De Luca? *"Had he and I but met..."* The line of poetry sprung out of a distant memory as an unwelcome visitor. He tried to dodge it, but his attempt failed. He closed the file and grabbed his well-thumbed volume of Thomas Hardy's poems from his knotty pine bookcase. Finding the earmarked page, he read the first four stanzas of "The Man He Killed." Then, after exhaling, he read the fifth and final stanza:

*Yes; quaint and curious war is!*
*You shoot a fellow down*
*You'd treat, if met where any bar is,*
*Or help to half a crown.*

The concept of two unknown soldiers trying to kill each other only due to the fact that their countries were at war resonated with Patrick. Except he knew some of the people he was now going up against, which made it more difficult than if he hadn't known them at all. He recalled his white-bearded high school English teacher saying, *"The speaker in the poem explains that if these two men had met under different circumstances, then they may have sat down in an 'ancient inn' and enjoyed a few drinks together. Instead, they both shoot at each other. One misses, and one doesn't. They could have been friends! Heartbreaking, my young scholars. Heartbreaking."*

Patrick took a sip of the scotch that he had been nursing for the past half-hour. As he lowered the glass, his eyes closed once again, and he saw himself with Gino, both twelve, playing baseball at a park with a dozen other neighborhood kids. *"Patrizio!"* yelled Gino as Patrick rounded third base, heading for home. Then, he remembered going to a different high school than Gino and choosing from that point forward to go by Patrick. He saw Gino for the last time during his senior year. Patrick was up to bat against Gino's high school team, but his friend was no longer playing. Gino was there but spent the majority of his time talking to a man wearing a driver's cap and a leather jacket; he missed Patrick's at-bat and was gone by the end of the game.

The door to the office opened, and Tara entered. She had on pink running shorts and a white tank top that was soaked with sweat, and her blonde hair was pulled back into a high ponytail. *Must have just returned from her nightly run.* He hadn't heard the front door open and close when she had left, and he hadn't heard it open and close when she had returned—too obsessed with his work.

"The boys are heading to bed and want to say goodnight," she said.

The boys. What friends were they going to make this summer and in school next year? Would they go to school with any of the organized crime family's children? Probably. What would happen when those kids found out that he was trying to put their parents behind bars?

"Patrick?"

He watched as she approached the chair across the burgundy carpet. "I'll be down in a minute," he finally got out.

She sat down on one of the huge armrests and ran her right hand through the thick black hair on the top of his head—the sides were almost all gray now. "Can you take the gun off before you come down?"

106

She knew his reservations about taking the job and had given him space since they had moved in, but now the actual work was starting, and he knew she was scared for him. He had never carried a weapon in his time at the Nashville office. Now, he had a .40 caliber Glock 22 in his waist holster while he was at work—and for most of the time when he was home. The boys had asked about it, but he had assured them that he forgot to take it off when he returned home. They were four and six years old, and his story elicited no further questions, just harmless joking. That was the key to extending any lie: making it a joke. *"Dad, you forgot your gun again."* A smile followed by, *"Got me again, buddy. Daddy's losin' his mind."* The last statement was not a joke, which was also a key to maintaining a lie—there had to be some truth attached. "Sure," he said to Tara.

"You okay?"

He stood and started to remove the holster. "Yeah," he lied. The Godfather, Don Ilario "The Smile" Russo was on his deathbed and had named his son, Ciro, to inherit the throne. However, an undercover agent had reported that something was not right. The agent was currently working in the caporegime headed by the underboss's son, Leo De Luca, and had been given instructions from Leo himself to change his entire routine—deliveries, pick-ups, driving routes, etc.—for the past few days and to tell no one about it. Bruno's boss, Special Agent in Charge of the Detroit Field Office Terrance Nolan, had word that the Detroit Association's second-in-command, Fabian De Luca, was not happy with being passed over. There hadn't been a succession war in almost a hundred years, and the Bureau wasn't sure that there would be one. In New York? Maybe. But Detroit? They couldn't see it happening. Besides, Nolan was still running his Top Echelon Informant—had been running him now for over a decade. Nolan's predecessor had run him for ten years before that, and Patrick knew that this was why Nolan had stayed so long in Detroit; he was the only agent that the informant felt comfortable with. Because the informant was the most valuable Detroit mob informant ever, the Bureau kept extending Nolan. The information had been worth it, and the informant had never been caught talking with Nolan. More importantly, for twenty years, the informant had avoided suspicion of being a rat from the members of The Association.

But Nolan was retiring in less than a month, and the Bureau needed someone to transfer the Top Echelon Informant to. Last week, Nolan had pulled Patrick aside and told him that it was going to be him. The turnover process would be thorough. They would start this week. Patrick had told Tara none of this, just that he might be late a few nights this week.

He set the holster on the table next to his chair.

She kissed him. "I just got off the phone with Liz. Dari tried to run away from rehab last night."

He gave her a hug.

"She didn't get far. They lock up their shoes at night and make them wear flip flops. She ran barefoot and was caught a mile and a half away trying to break into someone's house to get at their liquor. She nearly got shot by the homeowner."

"Where is she now?"

"In a different juvenile detention center for the time being. Liz wants to get her back into Wolverine immediately, but it's not looking good." Tara started to sniffle. "This was supposed to be the fix, Patrick. She's fourteen."

If working to bring down his former friend made him a bit uneasy, then Dari's tragic story steeled him to continue his work. Organized crime was heavily involved in sports gambling, which could be considered a harmless vice—until you gambled away a month's salary in a few hours—but drugs were a different animal. He couldn't care less whether some dumbass OB-GYN, making $400,000 a year, lost $50,000 on the Super Bowl, but he did give a shit about innocent civilians getting caught up in addictive drugs. His niece, Dari Williams, had been serving a nine-month sentence at Wolverine Growth and Recovery Center in the small farming town of Vassar, which was almost three hours away from their house, two hours away from his sister-in-law Liz's. Wolverine treated twelve- to seventeen-year-olds and tried to get them off drugs—mostly alcohol, pills, and weed—before they moved on to heroin and overdosed. Dari's story was atypical from most of the kids at Wolverine. She came from a good family, had friends, lived in a nice neighborhood, and went to a nationally recognized public school. Furthermore, the family did not have a history of addiction. Both Liz and her husband, Jack, were light drinkers. All of these were reasons why the sweet, innocent Dari Williams was the least likely to ever start down the path she was now fighting to get off of. Unfortunately, she had become the poster child for the saying: One time is all it takes.

A year ago, she had attended a sleepover at a friend's house—a campout in the back yard. Liz and Jack knew the parents but did not know that Dari's friend had an older sister who was already hooked on pills. After the parents went to sleep, the older sister brought weed out to the tents. A month later, Dari was smoking up every weekend at her friend's house and had tried alcohol. Two months later, she tried pills. Then, the phone calls from school started. Dari had been tardy to first period two times that week. Dari had lied and said she was being there for a friend. Her parents scolded her but believed her. The next week, her attendance was fine. A month later, her teachers called. Dari's grades were slipping. The following weekend, she went to an adult party with her friend's older sister and tried heroin for the first time. Two weeks later, Liz noticed some of her jewelry was missing. A week later, Dari had sex for the first time to pay for heroin. Two weeks later, the older sister died from an overdose, and Dari woke up in a hospital bed after being brought back to life by the same paramedics who had failed to revive the older sister. Her parents sat by her bed, sobbing. Then, a doctor came in and told them what the blood and urine tests had revealed about what was in their daughter's system. He also mentioned that she had chlamydia and wrote a prescription for antibiotics. And so, the journey had begun to get Dari cured, which, after weeks of trauma filled with unimaginable stress, failed counseling visits, and a relapse after Dari escaped one night, had finally led to Dari ending up in Wolverine.

And where had the drugs come from that had entered Dari's body and poisoned his sweet niece who used to go to the movies with him to watch *Star Wars*? Dealers owned by the Detroit Association, which was in business with the cartels. And now Michigan had voted to legalize marijuana. Well, he knew that law enforcement was in a tough spot, always had been. The war on drugs would never be won by law enforcement alone. The war on drugs would not be won by fighting the cartels down in Mexico; he'd read that ninety percent of all heroin came from America's neighbor to the south. No, the war on drugs would be won in America, and it would be won by Americans no longer dishing out twenty-five billion dollars a year to the cartels for their products. Stop the money going south, and you win the war on drugs. However, to stop Americans from taking drugs would require Americans to face why they took drugs in the first place. Which...led him back full circle to his job: the stopgap measure, the everlasting Band-Aid on the wound, the best of a list of bad options to maintain societal stability. Law enforcement couldn't walk away, and law enforcement couldn't win—an ongoing draw with a host of casualties like little Dari Williams along the way was the best it would ever be until Americans stood in front of the mirror long enough or there were enough Daris to prompt different action.

He felt Tara pull away from him and thought he heard her say something, but his mind was still racing.

And now, with the majority of his home state about to be high on a regular basis, Patrick Bruno felt a hint of defeat. The tie would become a loss, but it was now his job to make that loss as slow as possible. But if legal pot became the gateway drug it had been rumored to be for decades as an illegal drug, then the addictive drug explosion was now on the horizon. And if that explosion was anything like cell phone addiction, then the loss would be quicker. If society felt pills, cocaine, and heroin use was bad now, just wait.

"Patrick?" she said.

He snapped out of it. "Mind took off again."

"You were starting to mouth words and mumble. You're far away when you do that."

"Thinking about Dari and wanting to get my hands on the fucks." He had said it louder than he meant.

"Shhh," she said, frowning. "The boys."

"Sorry," he said. "And sorry about Dari."

Tara's eyes started to well up. "I'm not sure Liz and Jack are going to make it through this. It's starting to tear them apart. You know, blaming each other for missing the early signs and second-guessing the past few years. They always seemed to be so put together. My sister was like super mom." She wiped her eyes. "They are arguing about everything now."

Patrick looked over her head and out the window. "Yeah, but stuff like this exposes cracks in relationships." He looked back down at her.

She nodded.

He hugged her. "Let's go down and see the boys," he said.

"Okay."

He turned the lamp off and followed her out the office door and down the stairs.

# 10

## Greektown Historic District, Downtown Detroit

## *4 Days Ago...*

It had been three days since Fabian De Luca had met with his uncle, Papa Pete. Their plan to seize control of The Association was now set, and it was time to start executing it. Flanked by GiGi Rizzo and three other family soldiers, Fabian entered Saint Anthony's Mission through the back-alley door. Just inside, he was met by both the familiar musty smell and Father Antonio Ferraro, the overweight and charismatic head priest of Saint Anthony's church, which Fabian had been baptized in and attended ever since. Father Tony, as Fabian called him, had been a friend for over twenty years and was preparing to host an afternoon meal for some of the city's homeless. Fabian was there to help dish out the food but not before another matter was settled.

The men embraced.

"And how is my favorite son of God today?" Father Tony said.

"Ready to feed some of his lost sheep," Fabian replied.

The old priest laughed. "There are many who need saving."

Indeed, there were. The money Fabian had generously donated over the years had helped put some of them back on their feet. And, ironically, the family business, which he was soon to take over, kept a steady stream of them pouring into the church and mission looking for redemption, forgiveness, or just enough sustenance to keep them alive. He didn't deny his role in wrecking a number of lives, breaking up families, or ending other lives. In its simplest form, life was one large cycle. A virtue was always counterbalanced with a vice. Power would never be and could never be eliminated. It could only be shifted. He had experienced both, and he had decided that the evils that accompanied power were much easier to live with than living with no power. Anyone who denied this was either a liar or someone who had never known power. And so, Fabian De Luca would continue to be charitable: feed the poor, donate to the local hospital, buy presents for a host of families at Christmas, donate to the local school, keep Father Tony's mission funded, his belly full, and his sexual voraciousness satiated, and do his part to keep fans filling Detroit's professional sports' stadiums by donating money and gifts for new arenas and the required upkeep of those arenas. And no one could talk him out of the money he diverted to keep the local YMCA and YWCA running. To him, a healthy body led to a healthy mind, and the two facilities were an important part of the community. Was it the ideal location to lure new people into the world of drugs? Of course. But the Detroit Association forbade it. The two centers existed to get people away from drugs. There would always be enough buyers, but some deserved the chance to escape that world. He felt a particular amount of pride in engineering a portion of those who would make it out and have a chance at a full life. There would also be those who were not strong enough, but the key to understanding power was to admit that you could not save them all. On this point, he had always justified the family business when compared to the other businesses that society labeled as legitimate. They did the exact same thing, played the numbers.

The men ended their hug, and Fabian's eyes took in the room. The back parlor, where the men stood, looked like a Catholic church's flea market—a stack of dusty hymnals on a rickety table, splintered pews with broken kneeling bars standing on end and rising to the ceiling in a corner, a rack of old coats against one wall, and old missals strewn across tables and the floor. There were large water spots on the ceiling, and water dripped into a bucket near a light bulb that hung from a cord coming out of the ceiling.

Fabian motioned toward the coats on the rack. "Still the same ones from when I was here last year?"

Father Tony rested his plump palms on top of his sizable belly. There was a sparkle of pride in his eyes. "Of course not." His eyes led Fabian's back to the rack. "These will keep our lost souls from freezing this coming winter."

Fabian walked toward the hodgepodge of coats jammed close together, and GiGi locked the door that opened into the alley. Then, one soldier stationed himself in front of it. The other two soldiers covered the entrance to the mission's main room, where the food would be served. GiGi drew apace with Fabian, and soon Father Tony had dropped his hands from his gut and was waddling toward them, whistling "How Great Thou Art." A few steps later, he stopped next to Fabian and GiGi at the coat rack.

"I'd like to take a further look at this one," Fabian said, pointing to a charcoal covered overcoat.

"I thought you might," Father Tony said. He glanced around as if there were security cameras watching his every move. There weren't. The fat priest ushered the two men to the side of the coat rack and then reached behind a light blue down-filled child's coat and pulled a lever. The priest's eyes had narrowed.

The coat rack and wall behind it swung open, exposing a doorway that was only five feet high. Father Tony took the large crucifix that hung from a gold chain around his neck and, after fiddling with it for a moment, popped the crucifix open. He withdrew a key and opened the small door.

Fabian inclined his head to say thanks, and GiGi led the way into a darkened soundproof room. The priest brought up the rear, and, after one of the soldiers had closed the coat rack and wall, he closed the small door behind them.

Seated at a stainless-steel chair that was bolted to the floor was Don Russo's Consigliere, Silvio Verratti. The old man's once immaculately combed white hair now looked like the aftermath of a thousand noogies. One of his eyes was swollen shut, and his mouth was gagged with his own pink handkerchief. The other eye nervously cycled, looking at each man entering the room. The expensive cream-colored linen suit jacket hung off one shoulder and was splattered with blood that had erupted from Silvio's nose. On the floor in front of him was the body of his twenty-six-year-old mistress. The distinct garrote line showed on her neck like a red pen line drawn across the middle of a piece of copy paper that was turning more purple by the minute. She was still dressed in her white blouse and orange skirt.

Father Tony made the sign of the cross over his face and chest and then rested up against the wall. "He wouldn't tell me where it was," said the old priest.

Fabian stood in front of Silvio. "The money that you, Don Russo, and Ciro stole. Where is it?"

Silvio let out an angry exhale from his nose, blowing snot and dried blood onto his upper lip. His open eye burned into Fabian's.

For whatever else that could be said about the old man, Silvio Verratti was stone-faced old-school. He would not plead for mercy, would not cry, would not beg for forgiveness. He knew he was dead. But, with enough *persuasion*, would he give them the location of the millions that had been hoarded by him, the Don, and the Don's son? Fabian motioned to GiGi, who took out a dagger. Then, the bodyguard took out a lighter and began to heat the blade.

Silvio may have been tough, but he wasn't stupid. He immediately started trying to say something behind his pink handkerchief. GiGi continued to move the blade across the lighter's flame.

Fabian spoke to Silvio. "Do you know where the money is?"

Silvio shook his head no.

"I don't believe you," Fabian said. He met eyes with GiGi and then moved his eyes to Silvio's shaking legs. "Either one," Fabian commanded.

GiGi turned the lighter off and then plunged the hot blade into Silvio's right thigh. The bodyguard's eyes opened in what appeared to be surprise at how easily the knife entered the meaty portion of the consigliere's leg.

Silvio screamed, but all that came out was a muffled moan through the pink piece of cloth in his mouth.

Fabian waved his hand, and GiGi removed the dagger, bringing blood and gristle with it.

Fabian approached Silvio and pulled the old man's hair back. "Where. Is. The. Money?" He let go of his hair.

With a final surge of strength, Silvio shook his head violently back and forth.

Fabian paused and then said to GiGi, who was warming the blade again, "Give me that."

His bodyguard handed it over, and, in one quick motion, Fabian sliced through the pink handkerchief.

Silvio gasped for air and then began to cough.

Father Tony grasped his crucifix and brought it to his lips while closing his eyes. Then he let the heavy cross drop down and rest against his bursting belly. He picked up a wine bottle that was resting on a table next to him. After removing the cork, he poured the red liquid into a golden chalice. "I do not believe that he knows," he said and then took a long drink.

Silvio stopped coughing and managed to get out, "I do not know!"

116

Fabian passed the dagger back to GiGi and then studied the old advisor. Was he telling the truth? He wanted to believe him. "But you know *about* the money?" he asked.

Silvio sat back. "A drink of wine."

Fabian turned to Father Tony and pointed to the chalice. "Give it to him."

Father Tony gave a small bow and did as he was told.

Silvio gulped as the priest tipped the cup back until it was empty. "Thank you," Silvio said.

GiGi watched while heating the blade, the small bits of flesh still clinging to the edge blazing up and then turning black.

The smell reminded Fabian of a visit to the dentist when he was a teenager. One adult canine tooth was refusing to come down and fill in the open space on the left side of his smile. So, he had undergone surgery to have the tooth exposed and a bracket and wire run through it to pull it down. Numbed, he could not feel the pain, only smell his burning flesh as the dentist cut away at the roof of his mouth to find the tooth. Fabian pulled a handgun with a silencer attached to it from the inside of his own linen blazer. Holding the weapon in his right hand, he gently dragged the silencer across Silvio's forehead, then over the top of his head and then down his neck. "Do you know about the money?" he asked again.

Silvio hesitated.

Fabian grabbed a handful of the old man's hair and then forced the silencer into his mouth. He motioned to GiGi, who took the dagger's blade out from over the flame and, with a quick downward jab, inserted it into Silvio's other thigh. The old man bit down on the silencer as he tried to yell. Fabian held the weapon firmly in place, making the old man gag. "Out," Fabian said.

GiGi pulled the blade out of Silvio's thigh.

With a forceful push, Fabian pushed the end of the silencer into the man's throat, and then pulled it out and stepped back.

Silvio Verratti vomited the red wine he had just consumed all over his pants, some of it going into the burning holes in his thighs.

Fabian walked over and poured himself a glass of wine and drank. GiGi was back to heating the blade. The smell of charred flesh was stronger now.

After he swallowed a sip, Fabian said, "The money, Silvio?"

Silvio's head bobbed up and down before he raised it enough to eye the family's underboss. "I know about it," he said, and then tried to clean his nose cavities of the vomit in them by blowing as hard as he could. "But I do not know where it is." He paused. "That is all I know."

GiGi stopped heating the blade.

Fabian gave Silvio a nod of validation at first but then frowned, knowing that the family was about to be forever changed. The peaceful transition of power that had taken place ever since the 1920s would end with the elimination of Silvio Verratti. There would be no turning back. Previous Dons had died due to natural causes like pneumonia, and for others, it had been the lure of semi-retirement. Never had the throne been usurped through assassination. That only happened in New York and in the works of William Shakespeare—works he had read at the behest of Father Tony. In fact, 1934 was the last time a family member had gone to prison for murder. One hundred years of diplomatic, seamless transitions through depressions, world wars, impeachments, inflation, space disasters, stock market crashes, excesses, and recessions. Papa Pete's father and Don Russo's father had both served in World War II, most notably Operation Market Garden, and had told the family when they returned that they would never put on a parachute again and that any dispute within The Association would and must be handled diplomatically. No future generation should ever have to see the things that they had seen. This maxim did not, however, apply to anyone outside of the family. Rivals and traitors must be handled with a show of unwavering strength. And if that meant killing, then so be it. Papa Pete had told him that the faces would change, but that the game would remain the same. Again, his uncle was referring to numbers. And it was numbers that drove the family to allow the post-World War II heroin boom in Detroit. If The Association had not, then there would have been someone else who would have, and when those people had gained enough money, they would have become a threat to the family's power. There was nothing *good* about heroin except the number of dollars its sales brought in. The family had even become strange bedfellows with the CIA at one point, helping the U.S. government stop the spread of communism in Italy in exchange for the agency looking the other way as heroin, or 'babania' as it was referred to by Cosa Nostra, traveled the pipeline from Sicily to France to Canada and then poured into Detroit via trafficking boats across the Detroit river via the grandfather of Nico Colombo—The Association's current runner from Canada to Detroit. This was back in the days of Cosa Nostra's network called "The Pizza Connection," where loads of China White Heroin were smuggled into the United States and distributed via pizza parlors from the mid-1970s until the Feds broke it up in the mid-1980s. His uncle had owned two parlors in Detroit, which had been converted from Papa Pete's favorite pool halls that he had played at in his youth. The pizza was the best in town, and the China White had come in and left the building as often as the customers. The national pipeline's profits were around two billion, and New York had taken a hefty cut, which was only fair since they controlled the docks and the labor unions that worked the docks where the ships carrying the drugs arrived. An astounding ninety-five percent of the heroin coming into the United States was brought in by the five New York Families.

Speaking of New York...if they were one of the five New York Families, then they would have to get The Commission's approval to rub out a boss. Charles "Lucky" Luciano had formed The Commission for decisions like these, and he had also created the position of consigliere so that each family had a skilled advisor. And Fabian's future consigliere, Papa Pete, had diplomatically told him that because they were taking out a major city's Godfather, Fabian should grease the skids to ensure a quick and peaceful transition after the hit. Ultimately, blood was bad for business. Ever since the 1970 Racketeer-Influenced and Corrupt Organizations (RICO) Act had been passed as a part of Congress's Organized Crime Control Act, avoiding large wars had been essential to keeping the Feds off their backs. Things had gotten even worse in 1983 when Rudolph Giuliani had formed his version of *Butch Cassidy and the Sundance Kid*'s super posse by joining elements of the FBI, DEA, Justice Department federal attorneys, INS, IRS, and local and state cops to destroy Cosa Nostra. Twelve Task Forces, fully funded and equipped, were formed and sent to major U.S. cities. The results had been devastating for organized crime. Hence, there had been a retreat to the shadows, and wars were to be avoided. So, on Papa Pete's advice, Fabian had sent a trusted made man to secretly meet with one of Papa Pete's oldest friends: Don Vito Padovano, who just happened to be the capo di tutti capi—boss of bosses—of the five New York Families. At Don Padovano's mansion on Staten Island, Papa Pete's man had waited in a living room for three hours, while being served an elaborate lunch, until the Don's consigliere entered the room and passed a sealed envelope to him. The man had returned to Detroit that evening and delivered it to Papa Pete. The coded letter had said that if Don Russo was removed, then The Commission would accept Fabian as the new Godfather of Detroit. Fabian had watched as Papa Pete walked to the fireplace in Fabian's study and tossed the envelope and note into the fire, both men witnessing it burn to a crisp like Silvio's thigh flesh on the dagger.

Fabian looked at the consigliere's tired eyes, which were focused on the body of the top advisor's dead mistress. Silvio's confirmation of the money signaled a point of no return, but a prolonged war for power would only ultimately weaken The Association. Fabian's stroke must be swift and absolute.

With tears in his eyes, Father Tony came over and gave the old man a loving yet fatalistic pat on the back. "I will pray with you, my old friend."

As the priest delivered the last rites, Fabian watched as GiGi bent down and, using the dead mistress's blouse, wiped the dagger's blade clean. He then pulled GiGi aside.

"Are we ready to move on Ciro?"

"Everything is in place," GiGi replied. "Papa Pete is heading over to meet with Don Russo as we speak."

"Have two of our men help Father Tony dispose of these bodies."

"Further south? Or should the good Father take a nighttime fishing trip out in Lake St. Clair? Or," he said, eyes gleaming, "Can I get my set of carving knives and saws out of the trunk of the car?"

"Further south" meant that the bodies would be taken to the funeral parlor that Papa Pete still owned. There, many bodies had been quietly disposed of through an old trick. In a hidden room in the parlor's basement, the undertaker stored special two-tiered coffins that had a secret compartment underneath the main one for the recorded corpse. That way, two bodies could be buried simultaneously. How many graveyard ceremonies had been conducted where the grieving family circled around the coffin had no idea that underneath their beloved was the body of a person whom The Association needed to disappear? He'd lost count after fifty.

"Fishing trip" meant that the bodies would be weighted down and dumped over the deepest point in Lake St. Clair.

GiGi's set of knives and saws were a gift that Fabian had given him years ago. Since then, GiGi had studied books on dissection and had perfected the art and science of cutting up a victim and making the parts vanish. It had become his obsession, which Fabian had to now keep in check. If he gave permission, GiGi would stab Silvio in the heart multiple times to stop the blood flow and then wait for approximately forty-five minutes for Silvio's blood to harden before GiGi cut him up.

Fabian looked around GiGi's head at the chubby priest praying with Silvio Verratti. "Fishing trip," he said.

"Understood."

"We move tomorrow morning on Ciro, Stansie," he said, looking back into the black eyes of his driver and bodyguard, "all of them."

"I am finished," Father Tony announced and headed for the table with the wine.

Fabian calmly walked over, raised his gun, and fired two shots into Silvio's skull from behind. He placed the weapon back inside his coat. "Let's go feed our lost brothers and sisters, Father," Fabian said.

"Amen," Father Tony replied.

# 11

## Grosse Pointe Shores

### *4 Days Ago...*

"Has anyone heard from Silvio?" asked Ciro Russo, who was pacing the floor of his father's study. It was 7 p.m., and no one in the family had heard from the Don's consigliere since breakfast.

"Not a peep," said his father's driver and bodyguard, Giuseppe "Big Joey" Manetti. "He was shacking up with that waitress again, but as far as our men can tell, they never left his house." Big Joey paused, and Ciro could sense his discomfort. "They might be making their move, kid."

He did not want to believe it. This is not how the Don had predicted Fabian would come at them. He shook his head. "No, Papa Pete just left here an hour ago. His cheeks were wet when he embraced me, and he spoke with mamma for almost an hour in the library. They have always been close. No, he would not have come if Fabian was moving on us. Fabian would not put his own uncle in that kind of danger."

Big Joey regarded the young man. "That is the logical conclusion," he finally said. "But Papa Pete has always had a silver tongue, and his charm is what disarms people. Then he strikes like a coiled snake."

The statement made Ciro's stomach feel like a hollow cave that had suddenly been flooded with bats. *Was it happening right now?* He thought he would have more time. After all, his father was still alive.

The money.

He was sure it was still safe.

Three days ago, his father had told them of the secret room in the estate. Even being his son, a made member of the family business, and the heir apparent had not qualified him to know about the existence of the room until that point. This was yet another lesson to him in the ways of running an empire. At the top, you still need to keep secrets. When his father told him where the room was and how to access it, Ciro had lowered his head for a moment and shook it side to side in disbelief. Before the fitness center had been constructed for Stansie and Conrad, the main family exercise room had been located on the second story. It was rarely used now but still had old school charm: free weights, a massage table, a sauna, an exercise bike, stacked towels with the family crest on them, a wet bar—only his father could appreciate the irony of working up a sweat and then hydrating with a Bloody Mary—and a small boxing ring with a variety of headgear and gloves hanging on the wall. One wall was dominated by a mirror where the Don and his bodyguards could study their form while lifting. Ciro had never used the gym for fitness. He was a runner and a basketball player. However, he had used the gym over the years for quickies with his high school girlfriends, cleaning staff, and other guests. In those situations, the mirrored wall was indispensable. So, he was surprised when his father told him that once the main doors to the gym were deadbolted, a sensor in the lock allowed for a piece of flooring behind the bar to be removed by a special key. Underneath the removed section was a lever that, when pulled, engaged the hydraulic mechanism that slid a portion of the mirror into the wall, exposing a circular staircase that led down into darkness. While the mirror was retracting into the wall, speakers automatically blared music—America's Greatest Hits—to mask the sound of the sliding door. At the bottom of the staircase was a door. Using the same key he had used to remove the flooring behind the bar, he had opened the door and saw what his father had described to him: the millions skimmed off the family's business, kept in a dozen black duffle bags on a u-shaped stainless-steel counter that ran along three walls of the small room. When Ciro asked his father who else knew about the room, his father had said that other than himself, only Big Joey, whose job it had been to take the stolen cash and stow it in the room's bags at the end of each month— for years.

Yesterday, the family plumber arrived just before lunch to unclog a toilet. All vehicles that visited Don Russo's mansion were required to park inside the garage to be swept for listening devices, explosives, etc. before the occupant was allowed to enter the house. After the inspection, the plumber went inside and waited in a guest bathroom on the first floor, never touching the toilet but flushing it a few times to appear that he was working. Meanwhile, Ciro had the bags loaded inside the plumber's van, and Stansie and Conrad climbed in and hid in the back with the bags. Half an hour later, the plumber left and, after making sure that he was not being followed, drove to a garage where the bags were transferred to a green pickup, which already had twenty-four bottles of Evian water loaded in the bed. Then, Stansie and Conrad took off in the truck for their destination: Sterling State Park. If all had gone well, Nico "River Nicky" Colombo would have picked them up along with the bags in his fifty-foot sloop, *Apollonia's Ashes*, and sailed to his house on the island.

"Have we heard from Nicky?" he asked.

"The delivery was successful. They should be to the island by now," Big Joey said. "It'll take them some time to stuff the dry boxes and then hide them in the underwater cave." He looked at his watch. "If the weather is good, they'll probably do it tonight."

"Will the dry boxes keep all that cash from getting wet?" He had asked this before but wanted reassurance once again. It was a legitimate concern. How embarrassing would it be to go through this elaborate plan just to find a bunch of mush inside the boxes in a few months when he thought the danger had passed? He had wanted to simply keep the money at River Nicky's house, but his father had insisted upon this extra measure. Nicky's house would eventually be searched if his adversaries wanted to find the cash badly enough. No one would know about the cave.

"Yes. They're all good for one hundred feet. The cave opening is at around forty feet deep, and the deepest point in the cave is no more than sixty feet deep. No worries."

"When should they be back to the park?"

"Tomorrow or the next day. You want me to call and make sure it's tomorrow? I can have some of our people there waiting for them."

Ciro thought. *If Silvio's disappearance is the start of the war, it's better if they're not around.* But *was* Fabian starting a war? What if Silvio showed up in twenty minutes with his young woman on his arm and a belly full of wine? The Don was hanging onto life, and Papa Pete had paid a respectful and emotional visit. No, Fabian would not move on him while his father was still alive. "No," he said. "We're in no rush for them to come back, especially because no one knows where they are."

Big Joey nodded.


Ciro Russo sat in a leather chair by the fireplace in his father's study. He had been in his father's room for most of the night after the meeting with Big Joey, waiting for his father to take his last breath. However, the old Don had refused to go, and Ciro had retired to the study to rest. He guessed that he had dozed off around eleven but was now awakened by the grandfather clock striking two o'clock in the morning. Big Joey remained asleep, sprawled out on the leather couch and snoring like a grizzly bear. Before falling asleep, Ciro had noticed that Big Joey would stop breathing for periods while he slept. He remembered hearing that a former girlfriend had told the large driver and bodyguard that she thought he had sleep apnea and needed to get it checked out. After constant nagging, he had seen a sleep specialist, who recommended that Joey shave off his beard and wear an oxygen mask to sleep at night for the rest of his life. The Don had said that it might not be a bad idea, although he had never heard of anything like it before. Big Joey had shaved and tried it for a week. It was a disaster; he hated the mask and broke up with the girl. His trademark Dan Fouts beard was back within a few weeks, and he had kept it ever since.

The cell phone on the chair's armrest beeped, and Ciro looked at the text message.

Done and safe.

It was from the phone he had given Stansie and Conrad. The money was now hidden in the cave. Good. He thought about waking Big Joey but decided that he could tell him in the morning. Ciro stood up and stretched. Time to head up to bed. He rubbed his eyes and then suddenly shivered. Cool air from the overhead vent was blowing directly on his head. He grabbed a blanket from the back of his leather chair and walked over to the couch, where he covered up as much of Big Joey as the blanket would allow.

The door to the library opened, and his father's nurse entered. Suspicious that there had been no knock, Ciro went to speak.

But before he could get a word out, the nurse said, "Your father is gone."

# 12

## Sterling State Park, Michigan

## *Present Day*

Brad Cranston pulled Rusty along with the trailer carrying Larry's twenty-five-foot Stingray into a camping lot normally reserved for an RV. It was almost midnight, four hours since he had picked up his dive gear at the hardware store in Hampstead, and he lowered his windows, hearing the sound of gravel popping as the tires rolled until the truck and boat were centered in the lot. A light breeze brought in the wonderful smell of campfires, which made him wonder what delicious things had been cooked above or directly in their flames earlier that night—hot dogs, bratwurst, baked beans with bacon, smores… He turned off his headlights, and the area around his lot came into focus. There was a soft glow emanating from inside the RV in the lot to his right; perhaps, someone inside was lost in an unputdownable summer read, or it could be that a couple was making love by candlelight and feeling a connection they hadn't felt in years because of the pace of life at home, or maybe someone just forgot to turn off a light. To his left, he saw a litter of warm orange flickers from campfires that were attempting to close their eyes for the night. All around, the patches of woods were dark and seemingly impenetrable. He heard a burst of laughter and, like all sounds human beings hear in the darkness, wanted to know what had caused the noise. A joke? Someone falling over after one-too-many cold ones? At that precise moment, Brad realized that he could use some humor, but then he remembered why, and it brought him out of his survey of the campsite. He rolled up the windows and turned Rusty off.

He'd touched base with Allison Shannon when he arrived at the park ten minutes ago, and she was on her way to meet him—nothing immediate to fill him in on, but she'd tell him what she did have when they met. In fact, right before he called her, he saw that he had missed a call and voicemail from her. Why it hadn't shown up earlier on his phone, he didn't know—just another failure of the machine that was supposed to take communication to a whole new level.

He got out of the truck and stretched. As he reached his fingertips toward his toes, he became aware of his bladder. Standing up, he located the building that housed the showers and restroom—the green glow from the building's lights peeking through a less-dense bunch of trees. He locked the truck and headed out.

As he hiked down the path that split two patches of woods, he felt close to Conrad. His brother had been here and presumably hidden a cell phone in the building he was heading toward. The creative part of his mind that allowed him to illustrate book covers had been burning on the entire trip down. What had Conrad gotten into? He had been at this park, yes. But where did his brother *live*? A twig snapped underneath his sandals, and he remembered the failed thru-hike of the Appalachian Trail. Why had Conrad missed the hike? And did that disappearance have anything to do with this one?

He reached the building's entrance and opened the door for the men's restroom. He was both thrown off and impressed with the inside. The place was *clean* and well-lit, not your usual campground restroom. By curiosity or falling prey to his creative side and the romance of playing detective, he went down to the last stall, closed the door behind him, and then opened the tank cover. Nothing but rust-colored water inside. *What had Conrad been thinking?* He went to put the ceramic tank lid back on, but his right hand slipped and the tank cover hit the front edge with a clang. He caught it before it fell to the floor and was in the process of putting it back on when he heard a man's voice from the adjacent stall.

"Just what do you think yer doin' in there?"

Brad set the tank top back on and then crouched down to see underneath the side of the stall. There were a pair of worn sneakers pointed away from the stall with a pair of jeans pulled down and resting on them.

"Hey! You tryin' to look at me?" the voice shouted. Then, the man lowered his hand and made a fist. "What are you up to?"

Brad immediately stood, cleared his throat, and said, "Ah, nothing."

"Sure sounds like somethin'," the man said. "Gonna report you."

Brad left the stall and exited the restroom door just as he heard the toilet flush from the stall that had been next to him.

Outside, he jogged down the path and, when he saw no one coming in either direction, unzipped his pants and urinated. Going to the bathroom was not supposed to be this complicated, but, upon further examination, the root cause traced back to one person, the same person of his family's consternation: Conrad Cranston. As his stream started to slow, he said aloud, "Where in the hell are you?"

Five minutes later, he was grabbing a heavy-duty yellow extension cord from the boat when he heard tires rolling over his lot's gravel drive. A pair of lemon-colored beams illuminated him from behind, making the white hull of the Stingray glow like a ghost in the middle of a pitch-black night.

He turned around.

# 13

## Sterling State Park, Michigan

## *Present Day*

Allison Shannon pulled her Ford Explorer into the lone lot that had a trailered boat behind a truck. A man using a flashlight was pulling a yellow extension cord out from an open compartment in the boat's stern. The name *Reminiscing* was spelled in large black letters across the transom. She pulled in behind the boat, and the man looked back at her as she turned off the lights and engine.

The night air felt good as she emerged from the vehicle, and the smell of burning wood was a welcome change from the cinnamon-scented potpourri fixture hanging from her rearview mirror in the Explorer. "Brad Cranston?" she asked, closing the door.

"Hi," Brad said. "Allison Shannon?"

She walked toward him, and they shook hands. "What are you up to?"

He aimed his light at the black RV pedestal and then at a water spigot nearby. "Hooking up some electricity and water for the boat. My home for the evening."

She watched as he plugged the power cord into the pedestal's thirty-amp receptacle. He then jogged back to the stern and returned with a hose that he attached to the spigot.

"Follow me," he said. "Bring your stuff."

She opened the door to her vehicle and removed a large bag that had her laptop, notebook, and the manilla envelope that held the three pictures. She also had a can of mace in her jeans' front pocket in case this guy tried anything. Inside the bag was also her Glock 22, hidden in a zippered case that looked like a toiletries bag.

Allison put the bag on her shoulder and closed her car door.

Brad hopped up on the boat's swim platform and then helped her onboard. He was not who she had expected. Like her, he was trim, toned…athletic. Handsome might be another word she would use to describe him to friends. He wasn't gorgeous, but he was someone who moved with a purpose. She liked that.

They stood in the cockpit, and he said, "I'll be right back."

She watched as he disappeared into the boat's cabin. Soon, she heard the sound of switches clicking, and then the lights came on below.

"All right," he said. "C'mon down."

She descended the companionway steps and felt cool air entering the compartment. Brad motioned to the port bench, and she slid in behind a small table. On the galley's countertop, she saw a bottle of red wine, a cooler, and a bag of groceries. On the bunk to her left was a backpack.

He walked to the galley's sink and said, "Okay, we've got electricity. So, the air conditioning is on. The batteries should be charging, so we'll have hot water soon...as long as we have—"

She wasn't sure if he was reporting this to her or just talking out loud to himself, but either way, he kept right on going.

133

A turn of the nozzle at the sink was followed by a steady stream of water. "Water's working." He shut the water off. "Going to check the head," he stated as he opened a hatch, exposing a small sink and commode next to it. He moved inside the room, blocking her view of the sink.

The sound of running water was followed by a flush of the commode. "Head's up and running." She heard the water stop flowing, followed by, "Good."

Brad closed the hatch and smiled at her. "Thanks for waiting. Wanted to make sure everything was working before I spent the night on her."

"No problem. You work fast," she said.

He sat down across the table from her. "Sorry again for not returning your call. Don't know what happened with my phone."

She waved it off as fine. He was polite, and she liked that.

"I'm excited to see the pictures and hear what you've got so far," he said.

For the next twenty minutes, they filled each other in on what they knew. She started out by asking him the same questions as before to check for consistency. His answers were the same and delivered in a thorough yet not lengthy way, which she found encouraging. She had heard of elaborate schemes devised by former criminals, con men, and other horrible human beings to trap people like herself and then do unspeakable things to them. It was one of the first lessons she had learned when joining the agency: Don't trust anyone, especially your client and especially when you first meet them. So far, Brad was coming across as genuine. She didn't fully trust him yet, but his credentials had checked out; Larissa had filled her in on his background as an illustrator, and he had just made a six-hour drive trailering a boat. Those facts had her leaning against the possibility that he was a psychopath, but one could never be sure. What gave her the most comfort was the news Mike had delivered about the phone. If Mike couldn't trace the calls right off the bat, then chances were something was going on that someone did not want others to know about. And, Brad did seem concerned.

After her questions had been answered, he didn't have much to offer other than he had successfully been able to acquire some dive gear, which she was in no hurry to have him use. She had been able to locate her gear—which included an extra BCD, regulator, and weight belt for him—and had it loaded up along with four fully topped-off tanks in the back of her Explorer, but she hadn't told him any of this yet. She *had* told him more about the phone, though. The calls, text message, and, again, the pictures.

After further explaining that her friend Mike was working on tracking down the numbers that Conrad had contacted, she showed him the printouts of the photographs.

"Definitely Conrad," he said. He concentrated on them for a minute more and slid them back across the table to her. "No idea who he's with. She's beautiful. But…"

"But what?" she asked.

"He just looks so good and happy." He pulled one of the pictures back to him. "Look at his hair. Clean. And his tan and muscle definition. His arms have always been huge, but check out his chest and shoulders. He hasn't looked this good since the summer I told you about when we basically went scuba diving every day. Reminds me—were you successful locating your gear?"

Allison pointed at the woman next to Conrad in the picture. "What about her?"

"What does she have to do with the gear?" Brad said.

*Fine. He's stubborn.* "I've got everything we need," she said.

He nodded.

"Now, what about her?"

He focused on the picture again. "Well, either she," he said, pointing at the woman, "or the person taking this picture has been taking care of him."

"Are you sure it's not the other way around?"

He scoffed. "No way. He can't even take care of himself."

She had no reason to doubt him but decided to push for a little bit more information about the boat and the woman. "And you've never seen her or this sailboat before?"

"No," Brad said.

"Sure?" she asked.

"Sure," Brad said. "But I think we have to assume that the woman is the 'she' that Conrad was referring to in the message. But who would they be running from? And why were they separated when he made this last-ditch phone call?"

He seemed genuine, and she also appreciated that he was attentive and focused on the case. The last thing she wanted was some deadbeat who had the attitude of 'Just solve the damn case already. That's what I'm payin' ya for, and I ain't doin' shit to help either.' She had now ruled Brad out of that category. "All good questions," she said. "We don't have any answers, but I think I found out where this picture was taken. It could also be the place he thought they were going to take him." Her use of 'we' was calculated. If he stayed interested, then she would consider them more of a team in this. If he shut down, then it would be a sign that something with the whole thing could be rotten and would be more guarded with him.

Brad picked up the photograph she had her hand on. It was the one where the woman took up most of the frame with the red, white, and blue building looming in the background. He quickly said, "Looks like a place he'd be at—full of people drinking." Then, she thought his expression turned to a mix of sorrow and disappointment. He studied the picture from every angle. "What are you mixed up in?" he said to the photograph and then passed it back to her.

The way he stared at the photo—the way he *reacted*—told her that he was onboard and concerned. *He might illustrate covers for fictional accounts of life, but his body language and emotions were anything but an act*, she thought. Additionally, he didn't seem to pretend that he was living in a land of make-believe; rather, he projected a man who had accepted the fact that there was no guarantee that his brother would be found. She opened her laptop and brought up a web page. Then, she took the picture back from Brad and held it up next to the screen.

His eyes swiveled back and forth between the photo and screen. "The Round House Bar, huh?" Brad said. He then eyed the bag of groceries and bottle of wine. "Unless you tell me otherwise, we're not going anywhere tonight, right?"

She placed the picture back on the table. "It's a famous bar located on South Bass Island in Lake Erie. Once I identified the place, I did a little research. Most people take the fifteen-minute ride on Miller Ferry from Catawba Island Ferry Terminal, but boaters can get a slip in Miller Marina or one of the other docks at Put-in-Bay. From what I've read, it gets pretty rowdy there. Locals call themselves North Coast Parrotheads and refer to South Bass as the Key West of the North. And no, we aren't going anywhere tonight."

"A heaven-sent location for Conrad," Brad said as he got up and stood at the boat's small galley. "I'm starved. Since we're not leaving, want some food and wine?"

She had two principles that she had tried to adhere to in the Coast Guard. One: Don't drink on the job. Two: Don't become involved with anyone in your profession. The first principle had been easy to follow. The second principle had been as well—until she had met Keller. Look where that had gotten her. But now, she did not have the constraints of the armed services restricting her choices. She had just met Brad Cranston but was at ease with him—almost too at ease. A glass of wine couldn't hurt, and she had skipped dinner too.

"Okay," she said and watched as he opened the bottle, poured two glasses, and prepared a plate of cheese, bread, crackers, and grapes.

He sat back down, and they each took a sip of wine. He ran a hand through his hair and exhaled. "So, where does that leave us?"

137

She explained to him that other than the phone and the information that Mike was trying to run down, The Round House Bar in Put-in-Bay was the only lead they had. From her study earlier, it was a seventy-mile drive from where they were to the Catawba Island Ferry Terminal in Port Clinton, Ohio. There, they could each purchase a round trip ticket to Put-in-Bay and back for around $15.00. The earliest ferry left the terminal at 6:30 a.m., and the last ferry of the day left Put-in-Bay at 9:00 p.m., which was why they couldn't go tonight. They could leave early tomorrow morning and have the entire day to investigate.

"Conrad said to bring a boat though," Brad said. "Could we put the boat in here tomorrow morning and zip straight over to Put-in-Bay?"

She told him that she had thought about that too. It was an option, but the weather forecast for tomorrow did not look good—thunderstorms and high winds in their area and offshore. This meant heavy seas, and a small craft advisory had already been issued. She was not comfortable trying to cross a large stretch of open water in Lake Erie in the twenty-five-foot Stingray.

He said, "Agreed," and popped a grape in his mouth. "What about trailering the boat to Catawba?"

She rubbed her left hand along the top of the v-berth's navy-colored cushions. "Pretty determined to put this thing in the water, aren't you?"

"Seems like a waste to bring it all the way down here and not use it. Maybe Conrad was out of his mind when he called me, but if there is a chance that he wasn't, and was serious about the boat, then I think we have to try it." He picked up the picture of the woman and Conrad on the sailboat. "He's in swimming trunks and has a pair of fins by his feet."

Allison rested her back against the cushions and took a long drink. The wine was going down too fast. She needed to pace herself, but when was the last time she had sat and talked with someone like Brad over wine and cheese? Eons ago. Of course, he was right. They had to bring the boat. "Can't talk you out of it?"

He gave her a tired grin and tapped her laptop's screen. "Let's look at where we can launch." He glanced at her near-empty wine glass. "More?" he asked.

She knew that she shouldn't. "Please," she said, holding out her glass.

He refilled their glasses. This time, he raised his in a toast. After they both had swallowed, he gave her a grin.

"What?" she asked.

"Just getting a kick out of life. I apologize in advance if I seem a bit awkward, but I haven't had a drink with someone in private for a long time." He let out a peal of laughter. "I never would have guessed that working with a professional investigator would be the occasion that led me back."

He was self-deprecating in an honest way, and she liked that. She had to be careful, though. Two glasses of wine were it. Still had to drive back to her house, which was over half-an-hour away.

She closed the laptop.

"Not going to show me where we can launch *Reminiscing?*"

She gave her first grin. "Did your friend name it after the song by Little River Band?"

"You know, I never asked him, but I do like that song." He cleared his throat then quietly sang, "*Friday night, it was late, I was walkin' you home, we got down to the gate, and I was dreaming about the night. Would it turn out right?*"

*Smooth voice.* She swirled the wine in her glass and picked up the lyrics. "*How to tell you girl...I wanna build my world around you. Tell you that's it truuuueee.*" She drank.

"Well, we're both off the hook for awkwardness now," he said.

She picked up a piece of cheese, loaded it on a cracker, and bit down, enjoying the *crunch* of her teeth severing the combination in two. After washing it down with a sip, she said, "I thought you might be stubborn about launching the boat. We can put her in at West Harbor Public Boat Launch on Catawba. As long as the weather tomorrow doesn't swing that far east, then we should have a decent ride out to Put-in-Bay. From there, we can poke around The Round House Bar and see if anyone recognizes the woman or Conrad."

"We could also check on the sailboat. The photographer could be the owner."

She nodded and picked up the other picture. "I wish we had something more in these shots that could help us identify the boat. We know that it is well-kept, white-hulled, and probably over forty feet. However, I looked at some online pictures of Put-in-Bay's various docks, and there are probably over a dozen boats that fit this description. Plus, boats are arriving and departing every day. I read that over a million tourists visit South Bass Island every summer." She shrugged and passed him the picture.

"Sorry I asked," Brad said.

"No. We have to check it out. It's just a long shot."

He set the picture down. "You don't have to keep lowering my expectations," he said. "This whole thing is a long shot. But he is my brother, and I'm all the family he has left."

"Pardon me, but it sounds like you're the one who is lowering expectations."

He didn't reply, and the hum of the cabin's air conditioner was the only noise present, giving her enough time to regret what she had said. It wasn't Brad that was making her edgy. She was enjoying his company and found herself attracted to his easygoing manner, and, perhaps, even attracted to him. And he wasn't disinterested in finding his brother; he was being realistic about the prospects of finding him, which is what she was trying to be. Was there some insecurity in feeling like her first case would be a failure? Yes. *That is what he thinks he's picking up on—my lack of confidence.* But she knew that what he had really discovered was her hesitation to commit. The guilt of telling him earlier that the way she works is to *go all-in* on a project was making her uncomfortable. Her entire career in the Coast Guard had been spent in and underneath the water, and now she was afraid of it. And tomorrow, she would have to face that fear. The odds were that they would not be doing any diving, but traveling on a boat was enough to make her heart beat faster.

"I'm sorry," she said. "My lack of optimism isn't helping."

"I came out a little strong there, myself," he said. "It's late, and we don't have much to go on."

"We'll see what we can do tomorrow." At least that sounded a little optimistic.

"Yeah, I suppose we should get your gear loaded up when we're done with this," he said, gesturing to the wine and food, "and then get you on your way."

She gave a weak nod, not wanting the night to be over yet.

"There is another option," he said.

Her spirits picked back up. "And what is that?"

"Well, there's a bunk right behind that privacy curtain if you want to stay on board tonight. I'd sleep up here, and that way we could get an early start together."

*Sounds good to me,* she thought. But she couldn't agree that easily. "I don't know," she said, looking at her watch.

"Just an idea," he said. "Sorry if that was a bit forward, but when you've been divorced for ten years, your formality filter disappears. Not that I meant anything more than just staying on the boat for the sake of convenience."

Now she could proceed. "No offense taken. It would make it easier to get an early start." She looked around the cabin. "I'm game if you are." She eyed him. "However, just so you know, I'm a light sleeper and am going to text Larissa with the plan."

"Point taken," Brad said. "I promise you that the only thing I have in mind for the rest of the evening is sleeping. However, if I snore and keep you up, you have permission to wake me up, and I'll go conk out in the truck. Feel free to bill me for the extra time."

"I planned to," she smirked. *Okay, I'm starting to like this man.*

Fifteen minutes later, all of Allison's gear had been transferred from her vehicle to the boat and was neatly stowed. They stood in the cockpit, and Brad threw a blanket over the four scuba tanks that he had secured to the deck, just aft of the captain's chair. It was now past one in the morning.

"Go ahead and make yourself at home below," he said. "Just call up to me when I can come down."

"Thanks," she said. "What time do you want to get up?"

"We don't need to leave too early. The Round House won't be open until around noon. Let's both set an alarm for seven. That will give us time to get there and check out the marina and docks before heading to the bar."

"Got it," she said and headed below.

Later, as she drifted off to sleep, she felt secure that they would start to get answers tomorrow.

However, if she had known what those answers would be, she wouldn't have slept a minute.

# 14

## FBI Detroit Field Office, Michigan

## *3 Days Ago . . .*

P atrick Bruno got off the elevator on the twenty-sixth floor in the building located at 477 Michigan Avenue in Detroit. Walking down the hallway, he said hi to a fellow assistant special agent in charge, smiled at the young receptionist, and then entered the FBI Detroit Field Office's small breakroom. There was no time for small talk this morning, not that he liked shooting the shit to begin with. He had a few minutes before the meeting and needed sustenance.

The room was empty, but the smell of fresh coffee restored him. He grabbed his mug from the rung underneath the cabinet, which housed the coffee essentials, and then poured himself a fresh cup from the large Krups pot by the sink. A tray full of donuts, muffins, and bagels sat next to the coffee maker. He grabbed a napkin and a chocolate cake donut. He'd start the diet tomorrow. He was carrying 235 pounds and needed to be carrying two hundred. *"You've got bowlegs, and the cartilage is almost gone from the area underneath and to the right of your left knee, bubba,"* his doctor had told him. *"Now, I can fit you with a brace to try and shift the wear to the other side, which could postpone surgery."* He had paused and looked at Patrick's chart. *"Losing weight would also reduce pressure on your joints."* Reluctantly, he'd left the office with a brace...and gained five more pounds over the next week.

About to turn and head out, his hand holding the mug bumped the side of the coffee maker, and some of the hot, life-saving liquid splashed over the side and onto his hand. He set the mug and napkin with the donut down and pivoted toward the sink. The dirty dishes from last week were still piled so high that he couldn't get his hand underneath the faucet. There had been an annoying string of internal e-mails sent telling employees to please wash their dishes and take them home. In his two months here, the situation had not improved. Still feeling the pain from the burning coffee, he decided that he had had enough. He pulled the garbage can over and then threw every dish, cup, and piece of silverware that was in the sink into the trash. Time for the adults to start acting like adults. Satisfied, he washed his hands, wiped his mug, and left the break room.

When he arrived at the end of the hallway, the door to his boss's corner office was open. He peeked in and saw fifty-eight-year-old Terrance Nolan seated behind the enormous desk on the far side of the room. Nolan's feet rested on the desktop, and he was flipping through a sheaf of papers. Patrick tapped the door with his knuckles.

Nolan looked up from the papers and invited him in.

He wasn't an intimidating man, but Patrick sensed an undercurrent in Nolan that bred uneasiness. At first, he had thought that Nolan was like a coiled spring, waiting to extend at any moment and attack. But after a month of observation, he had backed away from that theory and now thought that Nolan was simply solitary, preferring his own company. Staff meetings were rare, and, when they happened, more of a case study on keeping your own counsel than collaboration.

He wasn't antisocial—he could bend an elbow at a bar on a Friday afternoon—but he made no attempt to form relationships with his co-workers beyond the mandatory meetings or the office's impromptu let-off-steam gatherings.

Patrick shut the door and walked across the newly carpeted office. For being stationed here for over ten years, Nolan's quarters were bare—the very definition of a space maintained by someone who worshiped minimalism. Navy carpet, walls painted tan with no pictures or artwork hanging on them, a wet bar, a couch, and six black file cabinets in a row against the wall opposite the desk. More than likely, this would become his office when Nolan retired, and even though he considered himself organized and appreciated a person who could keep his area clean and uncluttered, Nolan's spartan room came off as cold and too quiet. The four other assistant special agents in charge and the senior supervisory intelligence analyst had all been here for at least a year and would not be happy that the new guy was getting promoted or getting the coveted and high-profile job of running a Top Echelon Informant. Had Nolan already told them? Patrick had felt a few stares—some envious, others disbelieving—at the end of last week but didn't think that Nolan would make the announcement informally. It would probably be this week. He thought perhaps yesterday, but Nolan had been out of the office all day.

The job would also entail coordinating with the eleven satellite offices in Ann Arbor, Bay City, Flint, Grand Rapids, Kalamazoo, Lansing, Macomb, Marquette, Oakland, St. Joseph, and Traverse City. He'd traveled up to Flint for a great uncle's funeral when he was a kid, dated a girl who was from Oakland while he was in college, and been to one football game in Ann Arbor after the joys and disillusionments of college, but the rest of the cities were foreign to him. He didn't care for traveling, but if he had to meet the agents at these satellite offices, then he preferred to do it in person. All the rave about virtual meetings was mystifying. If you're going to meet someone, then meet them face-to-face. Don't do it behind a screen.

He sat down on one of the two leather chairs in front of the vast oak desk.

Nolan threw the sheaf of paper onto the desk. "Not a fan of paperwork," he said.

Patrick nodded, and for the next few minutes, Nolan discussed how he would systematically destroy the Bureau's massive tentacles of bureaucracy.

"But that's for someone else to tackle now," Nolan said. He eased back and folded his hands behind his head.

"So, we've got a new Don?"

Nolan smirked. "Yes. We. Do. Ciro 'Ace' Russo. Little shit isn't ready for it...and doesn't deserve it either."

"You had someone else in mind?"

"Doesn't matter now," Nolan said.

*What was that about?* He thought about asking more but decided to switch topics. He wasn't here to talk about the new Don today. "I'm ready to start discussing Nineteen," Patrick said.

Nolan laughed. "Right to the point. I should take my own advice and stop flapping my lips."

"Does anyone else here know that I'm being promoted to your position or that I'll be handling Nineteen?"

Nolan remained motionless. Then, he raised his eyebrows. "Nope. Never been discussed." He looked out the window for a few seconds, seeming to search for the next words. His eyes swiveled back toward Patrick. "I figure we'll make the announcement at the end of the week. They know I'm due to retire soon. Another few days won't hurt. That way, we can get a couple of days of turnover done in peace without the rest of the bastards snooping around." He paused. "You look worried about something."

"Never handled a Top Echelon Informant."

Nolan brought his hands down in a smooth motion, eventually interlocking his fingers and then resting his bearded chin on them. "It takes some getting used to. But you won't be alone. Every confidential informant has to interface with two contacting agents. Whenever you meet with Nineteen, you have to have another agent from our branch with you. Good old MIOG rules, you know? Don't want a single agent getting too comfortable with his informant."

The MIOG was the FBI's Manual of Investigative and Operational Guidelines—a rule book that outlined the conduct of special agents. Nolan's admission of adhering to the rules relaxed Patrick. There were some agents who had long since abandoned reading, let alone knowing, the MIOG. And a few of those agents were now dead or no longer with the FBI. *Who will I get paired with?* He got along fine with three of the agents, but the other two were megalomaniacs—climbers who thought they were the reincarnation of J. Edgar Hoover. *Relax, boys and girls. We're in Detroit. New York City is where the career escalator is.* He tensed back up. Should he ask? More questions at this point could make him seem weak.

*Just let him do the talking.*

"Brittenhoff and I had been meeting with Nineteen, but now that he's been transferred, it will be the two of us until I leave. Then, you'll be able to pick whomever you want." He swung his beefy legs over the side of the desk and walked toward the wet bar. "Got anybody in mind?"

Of the three agents that he was comfortable with, Maggie Schiff seemed the most competent and the toughest. And, he was sure that none of the dishes in the sink that he had thrown away were hers. "I think Schiff would be up for it."

Nolan opened a bottle of Kahlúa and brought it over to Patrick. "A little eye-opener in your coffee?"

Patrick took a gulp to clear some room, and then Nolan poured in a finger.

"I think Schiff's a wise choice," Nolan said, returning to his desk. He poured a finger in his own coffee and screwed the cap back on the bottle. After stirring the mixture with a Bic pen, he took a pull and then started in on Detroit's—and quite possibly the entire United States'—most valuable organized crime informant.

He was officially known to the Bureau as DET 1989-C-TE, a man known only to other members of the Detroit FBI Field Office as "19." Nolan's predecessor, James Carr, had been approached by Nineteen in the fall of 2000 when the informant was a capo in The Detroit Association. It had been a surprise because Nineteen was a made man and high up in the organization, but, as Carr learned, it was becoming more and more popular for organized crime members to break the law of Omerta—the law of silence or code of secrecy. Omerta's literal translation meant "to be a man," and part of being a man in organized crime meant that one did not talk *at all* if one was arrested. However, when faced with never leaving a cell for the rest of one's life, some members had chosen to cut a deal and spill their guts. Some had been relocated via the Witness Protection Program, and some had decided to return to their cities and live out the rest of their lives as respectable citizens. And then there were some like Nineteen who became informants as an insurance policy.

When an informant did this—switched over before being arrested—it opened up interesting possibilities but also necessitated strict rules. For instance, the informant could be authorized by the FBI to still participate in criminal activities. The first type fell under the ordinary category—crimes of the misdemeanor variety that could be authorized by the Detroit office. The second type fell under the extraordinary category, meaning a heightened risk of violence or significant financial loss to a potential victim. These could only be sanctioned by the special agent in charge, who had to also have the approval of the relevant U.S. attorney. In either case, homicide was never authorized. If the informant ever crossed this line, then the deal would be off, and the special agent in charge could be charged with murder.

"Thankfully, Nineteen has stayed in his lane the entire time I've been running him," Nolan said.

"Who is he?" Patrick asked.

Nolan took a sip. "He's one of the highest-placed informants this nation has ever had in an organized crime family, including New York."

*And I'm about to be working with this guy. Great.* Patrick then thought about the risks he would be taking. He thought about his family.

"At one time, I thought he might climb to the head of the family, which would have made him the *highest* placed informant ever. Yes, we did have 'Little Al' D'Arco, who was the acting boss of the Lucchesse Family, and Joseph 'the Ear' Massino, who was the boss of the Bonanno Family, switch sides, but they turned informant after their reigns were effectively over. *No one* has been an informant while still running the family. Could you imagine having a major city's godfather as an informant? We could learn so much more about how Cosa Nostra operates on a national and international level."

"Didn't make the cut?" Patrick said.

"Technically, he could still be named, but I think it's a long shot now."

"That's why you're not happy with Ciro Russo being head boy."

"Yeah, I suppose. Thought Nineteen would have been the one named." Nolan opened a drawer and pulled out a file folder. "But, even with a Top Echelon Informant, there is still a lot that is out of our control." He rubbed his hand down the spine of the folder. "You finished with the file on your childhood friend yet?"

After putting the boys to sleep last evening, he had disguised his half-hearted motivation to make love to his wife with a full-hearted effort. Finally getting somewhere, his knee had made a strange click, and his erection had vanished like a polar bear in a snow storm. With a bag of ice wrapped around his knee by an Ace bandage, he had hobbled up the stairs and finished going over the file on his one-time friend, GiGi Rizzo.

"Yes," Patrick replied.

Nolan handed him the manilla folder, and he opened it.

149

"Who's this?"

"A lost drug runner."

"What you mean *lost?*"

"Can't find him."

Patrick pulled out a small color photograph that was paperclipped to a larger black and white photograph. He crossed his legs and propped the photo up against his leg.

"The smaller photo is him, and the larger one behind it is his grandfather."

Patrick slipped off the paperclip and set it on Nolan's desk. The smaller photo was of a man wearing Ray-Ban clubmaster sunglasses with a reedy face, dimpled chin with black whiskers, and a head full of black wavy hair. The mouth was neither in a smile nor a frown. He flipped the photograph over and saw a name written in pen. Nico Colombo. Below it was a date. 11-5-2016.

The larger photograph looked like the same person except the hair had streaks of gray in it and a cigarette was hanging from the person's mouth. He flipped it over. 'Anthony Colombo'—written in cursive—followed by '1976'.

"The five families in New York City used to import around ninety-five percent of the heroin coming into the United States," Nolan said. "Anthony Colombo was in charge of transporting Detroit's cut. In the early days, he would wait in a marina on the Canadian side of the Detroit River, receive the shipment, and then motor across to a Detroit marina and offload it to The Association's members for transfer to the local pizza parlors for distribution. Later, when the operation got too big for just him, he was promoted to a leadership position where he oversaw multiple boats that would make the river run. That picture you have of him was when he was at the height of his career and went by the name 'River Tony.' Later, he made the fatal mistake of trying the product. Became an addict, jeopardized the entire operation, and overdosed around 1980."

"I heard that's what gets a lot of these guys," Patrick said, taking in the pictures.

"It is. Dealing drugs is high risk, high reward. Even if you have status and are getting rich, you can't quite escape the operation. For one, you're always around traffickers who are usually the low men on the totem pole. Because of that, they'd usually make any deal with law enforcement to reduce their time, so you can't trust any of them. And then, like you just noted, you're around the stuff so much that your guard goes down, and because the money is good, you decide to just take a small sample or someone who works for you decides to. Then, you or he becomes undependable, like 'River Tony' did. I asked Nineteen about it and was told that when a guy starts using drugs, he's immediately seen as a liability. They become weak and don't usually hold up. Problem is, there's someone right underneath him—an unlimited supply of low-life bums—waiting to take his spot."

Patrick picked up the smaller picture. "And this is his grandson."

"Yeah. He's picked up his grandfather's old sobriquet and is referred to as 'River Nicky' in the Detroit wing of Cosa Nostra."

"What happened to the phrase *La* Cosa Nostra? You shorten it." He'd never heard it referred to as just Cosa Nostra before.

"You don't know? Hoover added 'la' because he loved abbreviations. But it's stupid."

"Why?"

"Because 'la' means 'the.' Cosa Nostra means 'our thing.' So, La Cosa Nostra translates to 'the our thing.' Ridiculous, right?"

Patrick gave an embarrassed laugh.

"Not the only thing that Hoover did that didn't make sense."

"Oh?"

"Yeah, just when we were starting to make progress, he put us at a disadvantage. In the early sixties, he authorized the illegal placement of bugs, and, man, did they start giving us *tons* of information that we could use to fight crime. But, a lot of the information was embarrassing because we had so many

151

of our elected officials tied up with organized crime, bribery, you name it. They could have made a monument to the unethical behavior that was going on. So, LBJ cut it off in 1965, and the Bureau got clobbered. Who knows what could have been done or prevented had we remained serious about taking the fight to the criminals back then? Hell, that move by LBJ set us back twenty, thirty years."

"I've never heard that story before," Patrick said. In fact, all he remembered about Hoover was from his initial training at the FBI Academy in Quantico, Virginia—the sixteen-week course that transformed him from a civilian to an FBI agent.

In 1934, Hoover had demanded that the Bureau of Investigation, BI, be given a new name. And so, his third-highest Bureau official Special Agent Edward Tamm came up with the Federal Bureau of Investigation (FBI). Patrick had additionally been told in Quantico that the initials also stood for Fidelity, Bravery, and Integrity. When he had taken the oath and sworn to protect and defend the Constitution of the United States, he had wondered, for just a moment, how many FBI special agents would embody those traits. He had been optimistic that many would since only one in twenty applications to be a special agent was accepted. When he joined, approximately one-third of the Bureau's thirty thousand personnel were SAs. His experience had now taught him that every SA had at least one of the traits, some had two, but very few had all three. From what he had observed of Nolan, he surmised that Nolan was one of those few.

"I'm not surprised. We don't necessarily lead with all of our vulnerabilities and mistakes." Nolan took a gulp of coffee. "Nowadays, CN has different names in different areas of the country. Detroit, 'The Association.' In Chicago, it's 'The Outfit.' In New England, it's 'The Office.' Buffalo, 'The Arm.'"

Patrick flicked the picture with his right middle finger. "So why is this guy lost?"

# 15

## FBI Detroit Field Office, Michigan

### *3 Days Ago...*

Patrick watched as Nolan took a watch out of his top desk drawer and started to fiddle with the dial instead of answering the question. After watching the senior agent for a few seconds, he realized that he had never seen Nolan with a watch on. A guy usually picks up on what type of watch another guy has on, or at least the guys he knew did—probably due to thousands of years of conditioning that prompted a male to measure himself against all other males. *Cut the psychological eat or be eaten bullshit already.* He went back to observing Nolan work on the watch and wondered if Nolan would ever answer his question.

He'd been fascinated with watches since he was a boy and had dreamed of owning an expensive one to pass on to the upcoming generations of Bruno men. Last Christmas, he had approached Tara with the idea. *"Sure, babe,"* she had said. *"But how much are we talking?"* When he had replied that he wanted a Rolex Sea-

Dweller—44mm, oystersteel, black ceramic bezel with luminescent display, D-blue dial, oyster bracelet, waterproof up to twelve thousand eight hundred feet, *thirteen* grand—she had turned ghost white. The conversation had ended there, and instead of the best dive watch in history, Santa had brought him a two-hundred-dollar Casio, which was water resistant up to 660 feet. *"Maybe when you retire,"* she had whispered in his ear as the boys opened the rest of their presents.

Nolan turned his wrist and Patrick got a clear look at his mentor's watch. A Rolex Submariner. Not in the Sea-Dweller stratosphere but a close second.

"Like it?" Nolan asked.

Patrick laughed. "Was I drooling?"

"Naw, just staring," Nolan said. He put the watch on and admired the look of it on his wrist. "Got it from my dad when he passed away."

"Looks brand new," Patrick said.

Nolan paused, then looked at Patrick and said, "Only had it for about five years. The old boy had the longevity gene in spades—ninety-three. And he only purchased it with five years left on his timeline. Never understood why he bought it then." He took one more look at it. "Anyways, just got it back from being serviced for the first time. Rolex service center crooks. Talk about a price tag! Eight hundred big ones, gone like that," he said, snapping his fingers.

*Four Casios*, Patrick thought, looking down at his wrist. *And that's just the cost of a tune-up.* When he looked up, he noticed that Nolan had caught him assessing his own timepiece.

"Where were we?" Nolan asked. "Oh right, our missing drug runner. He inherited the business from his father a few years ago, but he's shifty. Hard to find. Been looking for him for the past year. We had some intel he had a sailboat that he was using to run special shipments across the river, but we've never seen him, let alone caught him. That picture came from Nineteen."

"And Nineteen didn't know where to locate him?" Patrick asked.

Nolan exhaled. Not a gesture of annoyance at the question, Patrick guessed, but, perhaps, rather an admission of limitations. "Nineteen doesn't know everything."

Pleased that he had read Nolan correctly, he added, "Or tell everything."

"True. All part of the Top Echelon Informant game. Sometimes Nineteen gives us a gold mine, and sometimes it's silence." Nolan pointed at the photograph. "If we can find *him*, though, we might get a better glimpse at how they're currently transporting the junk from Canada to Detroit. I think the fleet of boats days are over, but you never know because the stuff is still flowing in."

"Crime is fluid."

"Ha! You bet your ass it is. Always mutating to exploit some other loophole, and, unfortunately, new demographics."

"Or take advantage of new technology."

The room was quiet for a moment. They stared at each other.

"Indeed," Nolan finally said. "Probably why it's time for me to get out of the game—seen the writing on the wall for a while now. A lot of the work nowadays is done by bureau computer nerds who sit behind screens and try to hack the mafia's computers, which are used to run gambling online through foreign countries. I guess we're making a dent in their armor, but to me, the action will always be in the field." He paused. "A lesser man wouldn't admit to this, but my field work in running Nineteen is probably the only reason I've been able to stay on as long as I have. Don't regret one day of it. Besides, gambling isn't where the real fight is. In Detroit and the other major U.S. cities, CN is still an integrated member of the power hierarchy—law enforcement, politics, business, philanthropy, you name it. But the mafia still has *strength* because of its unparalleled drug infrastructure. Easy to crack some of the networks and distribution systems." He lifted the mug to his mouth. "Hard to crack 'em all."

155

"I once read that on one side of the morality spectrum, you have what the law forbids. On the other side, you have what a portion of our citizens crave. And in between those is organized crime."

"Couldn't have said it better. Sicilians are like libertarians; they distrust government and loath its interference in their own lives. But, when the public wants something bad enough, they'll go wherever they need to go to get it."

"And even if it sabotages their fellow human beings. Drugs destabilize neighborhoods in a hurry." He stopped, now realizing that he had leaned forward and was starting to raise his voice.

Nolan drank and then smacked his lips. "Personal experience?"

Patrick thought of his niece. The day she was born, her first steps, her phone calls to him about Corduroy the Bear. The way her smile melted him when she had lost her two front teeth at the same time. Then, there were the frantic calls from his sister-in-law. The crying. "Yeah," Patrick said, lowering his voice.

"Sorry," said Nolan.

Patrick took a sip. There was nothing else to say on the topic. He felt exposed because of the personal connection, but there was no denying it or trying to explain it away. "I'm sure 'River Nicky' is also running cocaine."

"Assuredly. When it gets here, Nineteen told me that it gets sold in usually three ways: weight, eight balls, or pieces."

He was familiar with the terms from his Nashville days. 'Weight' meant that the coke was sold on the streets in quarter, half, or full kilo amounts. An 'eight ball' was one-eighth of an ounce—around 3.5 grams of coke. When the cocaine had been broken down into smaller quantities, it was considered to be in 'pieces,' normally a gram, which were sold in individual packets for around twenty bucks. "And the Detroit Police?"

"Angels," Nolan said. "They know what they're up against and do the cold bastard work that needs to be done. I've never had a problem. The men and women in blue in this town are tough as nails. Wake up every day and have to deal with their fellow human beings' shortcomings, which, even after thousands of years of recorded human history and so-called *progress*, are never in short supply."

In his brief time here, he'd seen it too. But it felt good to hear it from a veteran like Nolan.

"There is one thing that appeals to me about Cosa Nostra, though, that I can't separate myself from—even after all of these years trying to bring it down." Nolan gazed out the window and became distant again. It wouldn't be too much of a stretch to think that he was replaying his twenty-year career in his head right now. "I guess that's why it still appeals to some people."

"What is it?" asked Patrick.

"Just the concept of being a man. Taking care of your own problems and not having to run to someone else for protection. No spineless tattletales or calling the police for irrelevant matters. Domestic violence is real and a problem, but a buddy in the Detroit PD said that he now gets calls to go visit homes where he's met at the door by a husband who says that his wife won't stop nagging him to lose the twenty pounds he's put on." Nolan jeered. "Seriously, what the fuck?"

Patrick shrugged.

"Maybe I'm just getting old, but there is a part of me that—from a purely Darwinian perspective—envies the fact that if an ex-boyfriend cokehead won't stop stalking the daughter of one of The Association's members, they bypass all the restraining order, court-appointed counseling baloney and just go fuck the guy up, so he doesn't come around again. When the punishment for stealing is getting your hand cut off with a meat cleaver, suddenly, you don't have a lot of thieves, right?"

Patrick gave a nod—not one of agreement, but a slow one of the 'let's wrap up this conversation' variety. Nolan's point fit his age. When you were either young or old, patience had a way of waning, and more drastic solutions seemed to become appealing. What always kept those solutions in check was the large middle-aged cohort, whose sense and level-headedness about the demoralization and chaos that would ensue if these extreme measures were ever enacted prevented the youth and elders from winning out. In a way, it was like raising kids: The older generation wanted to spank, the youngsters didn't like the spank but were glad that at least it was over quickly, and in between those extremes you had the middle-aged legion who valued emotional intelligence and used sit-down discussions first and spanking as only a last resort.

Nolan drained his cup and once again pointed at the small color photograph. "Well, anyway, we've got to try and locate him."

"Maybe Nineteen will come through for us."

"If we play it right." He paused. "As the new SA running Nineteen, you'll have access to all of my 302s and 209s. I think they'll give you a sense of the relationship and how it operates—the kind of information you're likely to get and when you're likely to get it. After you review them, I'd be happy to answer any questions you have. They're pretty standard."

One of his questions had just been answered. He knew that a 302 was a document that a Special Agent created to detail a meeting with an informant. A 209 was a report that also detailed communication with an informant and any information that had been acquired. But, one of his superiors at the Nashville station had warned him about 209s and 302s. In the past, agents had compromised themselves by sanitizing the reports to protect their informants—and themselves. When caught, the investigation always concluded that the agents had lost their objectivity. They had gotten too close. *"By all means, read them and ask questions,"* the supervisor had said. *"But don't fully trust what is said in them or the conclusions drawn from them."* He was glad that the subject had come up because he wanted to read the documents concerning Nineteen.

"Thanks. I think I'll start reading them today as long as nothing else comes our way."

"Thought you might say that. I pulled the files yesterday and have 'em ready for you. You can read in here or in your own office if you like. In here might be easier if you have any immediate questions. However you want to work it is fine with me."

"In here works," Patrick said. "When do you think we'll meet with Nineteen?"

"Probably next week. You'll be through the 302s and 209s by then, and I'll have had a chance to drive you around to our favorite spots to meet. It's a good idea to pick out a few new locations, but I'll show you how I get to each of the current places undetected. I'll even run you through Nineteen's routine. He's a master. As you know, if he ever got caught, he'd be executed immediately. The last two guys we flipped were not as good. The one we found in a back-alley dumpster had been shot execution style and had also been shot five times around the mouth—a message to us that he had been silenced to keep him from snitching any more. It also sent a message to other members of The Association: If we find out you have been talking to the Feds, you're dead. The other one was found in a floating fifty-gallon metal drum in Lake St. Clair. The top had been welded shut. A fisherman hauled it on board his boat and when it was opened on the dock, inside was our man. He had been strangled to death, and his body had been cut in half at the belly button so that the body would fit in the drum." Nolan raised his eyebrows. "These are the people we're dealing with. Never forget it."

"I won't."

"Anyway, my last meeting with him was pretty boring. He knew that I'd be turning things over soon and didn't reveal much. Sure didn't waste time taking his payment, though."

"How much have we paid him?"

"You don't want to know."

Patrick waited.

Nolan looked at the ceiling. "Over a million dollars."

"Jesus. And The Association is still operating?"

"That particular million has done a ton of damage to them over the years. But let me be clear. In a game that involves *billions* of dollars, one million barely gets you a seat at the gambling table. Look, I know it's ridiculous."

Patrick shook his head. And there was the answer that all things came down to: money. Strip down the altruistic missions, the worthy causes, the good fights, the movements, the activism, and the solemn vows, and you discovered the language that human beings responded to the most was not found in any dictionary—it was found in currency. "What did our millionaire have to say the last time you spoke with him?"

"Just that one of the capos, Leonardo "Leo" De Luca, the underboss's son, had finally accomplished the long-awaited goal of unionizing the bouncers in all of the Detroit night clubs."

"Unionize?"

"Leo set it up so that each club now has two bouncers working every night. The head bouncer gets two hundred a night, but fifty of it goes to The Association. The second bouncer gets one twenty-five a night, and twenty-five of that goes to The Association. So, you figure ten Detroit clubs—"

Patrick's eyes opened a little more.

"Yeah," Nolan said. "That's more than two-hundred and seventy grand a year in cold cash profit. Nothing unusual, though. You see it in all of the major cities."

"Have we done anything about it?"

Nolan waved his hand. "Nah. Not enough time or manpower. Our main focus is the narcotics."

"The legalization of marijuana will throw a little bit of a wrench in their operation."

"Not much. Pot is like potatoes now. The real money is still in heroin—coke and pills after that. And right now, we've got an emerging problem: Cocaine being sold that has been laced with an opioid. Bad, bad news. We've had five people overdose in Grosse Pointe in under a week. My money is that when the toxicology reports come back, the snowstorms of cocaine floating around—and heroin that they're selling for people to shove in their veins—is laced with fentanyl, which is around ninety times more powerful than morphine. Shit's cheaper to buy than coco, so dealers mix it in to give them more product to sell. They're also lacing oxycodone pills with it. Users don't know until it's too late."

"How long until the toxicology reports come back?"

"Maybe a month. I know, I know, ridiculous, right? Anyways, I saw an article the other day that showed just how small of an amount of fentanyl can send you on an early trip to the pearly gates. Ready for this?" Nolan pulled a penny out of his pocket. "Cover Lincoln's ear and you've got your lethal amount. Insane."

And all at once, he felt the momentary reprieve from his melancholic outlook the other night slipping. Running a Top Echelon Informant had given him hope. He'd now be at the tip of the spear in the fight, but Nolan's sobering facts were more than a challenge to his heightened sense of right and wrong. The last five minutes had him reconsidering his career choice.

*What real good was being done if gangsters were making a million, while people were continuing to drop left and right to overdoses?*

"I know what you're thinking," Nolan said, frowning. "I was there too when I found out what the program was."

He needed answers. He needed them now. He had a problem, and he wanted to walk into the professor's office and have the mental giant explain the answer. "How did you keep going?"

"Like other first-time SAs, I thought of the job primarily in the short term. I wanted action. Let's get the bad guys. Let's get 'em now. I even told my mentor James Carr that when we started to meet with Nineteen together fifteen years ago." Nolan leaned forward. "I'm gonna bring down this whole motherfuckin' enterprise by myself if I have to. That kind of shit." He leaned back. "Hell, during the cold war, the FBI had four hundred agents in New York going after communists—only five after organized crime. Then, when we found out just how big of an organization Cosa Nostra was, we started upping the number of agents and, of course, the moolah. That's when the FBI came to be known by CN as Forever Bothering Italians." Nolan cracked his knuckles. "But, as time went on, I learned that you have to play the long game on this one—winning small battles on the road to winning the war. Carr was convinced of it, and so was I. CN knows that we don't run out of money or time—that's *actual* power. Believe me, we're going to win."

It could have come across as shop talk dreaming, but instead, Nolan's hard-won wisdom rang true. They didn't talk for a minute as the last word, *win*, hung in the air.

"Here's something else. We may have already gotten the best thing from him that we're ever gonna get, and it didn't have a Goddamned thing to do with the Mafia."

"I'm not following you."

"Through his street contacts, he had found out about a small terrorist cell setting up shop in the basement of a local house. He let me know, and in the summer of 2006, we prevented a major terrorist attack that would have crippled Detroit, maybe finished it. I admit that we were monitoring chat rooms a lot back then, and it helped out, but few know that it was Nineteen who gave us the critical information we needed for the raid. Carr was supposed to be transferring, but, after that triumph, they labeled us 'The Golden Team,' and Carr stayed on a few more years—mostly advising me and attending the meetings to satisfy the MIOG requirements. Truth was, I was basically running Nineteen at that point and have been ever since."

The irony. Sometimes he wondered if he could handle information like this. Was there a tipping point where he'd know too much and lose his nerve or become paralyzed with paranoia? He didn't want to find out, but taking on

Nineteen seemed like it would now be a possibility. "I never heard anything about it."

"And neither did the public." Nolan itched his nose. "Didn't come without its costs, though. I lost a friend, SA John Bautista, in the raid. Got blown—" Nolan's words trailed off. "I was the one who had to notify his wife. He had a small kid too." He looked away from Patrick. "Can still hear her screams some nights when I'm home alone."

"I haven't had to do that yet."

"And I hope you never have to," Nolan said. "What I've found out in this business is that, when you take a view of our world from the moon, everyone is in bed with everyone else. It's just one giant orgy down here."

The room went silent again.

"So, who is Nineteen?" Patrick finally asked.

Nolan's smile returned. "That's it. Right back in the fight."

Patrick let out a quick laugh of relief. "Guess I'm not ready to quit yet."

Nolan nodded in agreement. He pulled a single sheet of paper from his drawer and showed it to Patrick. "Here's the family structure that Nineteen helped me keep current over the years."

Patrick studied the paper.

## THE DETROIT ASSOCIATION

### BOSS
Ilario "The Smile" Russo

Driver/Bodyguard
Giuseppe "Big Joey" Manetti

### UNDERBOSS
Fabio "Fabian" De Luca

<u>Driver/Bodyguard</u>
Gino Gregorio "GiGi" Rizzo

## CONSIGLIERE
Silvio Verratti

## STREET BOSS
Salvatore "Street Sal" Gallo

## CAPOREGIMES
1. Ciro "Ace" Russo
2. Leonardo "Leo" De Luca
3. Andrea "Handy Andy" Casale
4. Anthony "Black Jack Tony" Scala
5. Roman Abruzzi
6. Giancarlo Abruzzi

## FLORIDA
Dante "Miami" Marino

## CANADA
Nico "River Nicky" Colombo

## OHIO
Michael "Buckeye Mike" Romano

## CALIFORNIA
Paolo "Sunshine Paulie" Esposito

"Only two things have changed—one we know, and one we don't. We know Ciro is the new Don, but we don't know who will be the Capo that takes his place." Nolan itched his nose again. "Speaking of capos, remember the one I was just talking about?"

Patrick ran his hand down the sheet until it stopped at Leonardo "Leo" De Luca. "Leo De Luca?"

"Yeah," said Nolan. "You ready for this? *Nineteen* is his dad, Underboss Fabian De Luca."

# 16

## Grosse Pointe Shores

### *3 Days Ago…*

Big Joey had waxed the shit out of the big black Mercedes, and the sun's reflection on the surface was so bright that the car looked like an aerodynamic rectangle of ebony glass with sparks of orange moving down the street toward I-94, the Edsel Ford Expressway. Normally, they'd take a more scenic route to Greektown, but he had insisted that they take the Interstate to change up the routine. There would be increased security when they got closer to Monroe Street, but since ambush was always a possibility, they had decided not to take Don Ilario's quieter route to Greektown. It was almost 1 p.m., and he felt excitement rise in his stomach as if he was having one of those "falling" dreams where he plummeted toward the earth from the puffy clouds high above.

The Edsel Ford Expressway was named after Henry Ford's only son and had made urban expansion possible after its construction was completed in the mid-

1950s. However, Big Joey knew that so-called progress always came at a cost, and one of the major costs of the Edsel Ford Expressway was that nearly three thousand buildings were demolished to accommodate its construction. What came along with the loss of the buildings was the catastrophic displacement of urban neighborhoods—mostly African-American ones. Maybe this was why Don Ilario had always avoided I-94 whenever he could.

But Big Joey couldn't think of this today as he palmed the wheel and turned, entering the expressway. They'd take the Edsel down to Exit 219 and then take Gratiot southwest. They'd make a left onto Randolph and then the final left onto The Association's beloved Monroe Street, where business had been conducted for almost ninety years. It was a momentous day for the new Detroit Godfather, Ciro Russo, who sat in the back seat in a double-breasted tailor-made midnight blue suit, white shirt, and crimson tie. His black hair was combed in a pompadour, and an Omega was around his left wrist. The pompadour was a nice touch, stick it right back at the police for what they did to Rollie Mazza. Damned pork chops had shaved Rollie's pomp into a mohawk before they released him. Shit wasn't right. Let 'em try and do it to Ciro.

*Over my two-hundred-and-fifty-pound ass.*

On Ciro's right hand was his father's gold pinkie ring that had a cursive 'R' on the face. The man looked sharp. Joey wished that everything else looked sharp. The family consigliere, Silvio Verratti, was still missing. Ciro's men had checked his home to find his wife just as curious as to her husband's whereabouts as Ciro was. The trip to Silvio's gumar's apartment had yielded nothing; no one was home. The final trip was to his girlfriend's house, and it ended up being a waste of time. The door had been forced open, and two Soldati had found the girlfriend in bed with her housekeeper—the housekeeper whom Silvio had hired to not only clean the house but to keep an eye on his girlfriend who had recently experienced a cocaine relapse. On the nightstand next to the bed were two empty packets and a straw. Sweaty from destroying each other's pussy, both women had sat on the edge of the small bed, speaking at lightning speed trying to explain that they didn't know where Silvio was, and that, of course, they meant no disrespect to him by sleeping together. The girlfriend had finished with, *"He's my silver teddy bear."*

Big Joey knew that Don Ciro was a little worried about the disappearance of his consigliere, but not worried enough to cancel his first official lunch at the Red Robin Lounge in Greektown. Don Ilario had wanted it that way. *"We've known my end was coming for a long time, and I have said my goodbyes,"* the old Don had said to his son. *"Take control immediately, show that there has been an unmistakable and peaceful transition of power, and then bury me."* The Don's final orders were being followed to the letter by Ciro, who had spent a few of the early morning hours moping around, saddened by the loss of his father. However, the young Don had made a good comeback and was now ready to keep the appointment that Big Joey had arranged, per Don Ilario's orders, moments after Ciro had woken him up with the news that the wise old man had gone off to meet his maker. After the calls had been placed, the hefty driver had helped the undertaker load Don Ilario's diminished body into the hearse for his journey to the funeral home. The showing would be in two days followed by a massive funeral. But, first, The Association needed to gather at The Red Robin Lounge and meet the new Don— and ensure that the family business stayed on track. Then, within the next few weeks, Ciro would be able to issue his own directives and vision for The Association. Don Ilario had scripted it all.

The street boss and all of the other caporegimes had checked in and were due to show up as a sign of respect for the new Don. In regards to Consigliere Verratti, the street boss, Salvatore Gallo, had said, *"I'll find the silver fox and bring him home."* Most importantly, the family underboss, Fabian De Luca, and his uncle, the legendary Papa Pete, would be there to validate Ciro's position. Hell, Buckeye Mike was even coming up from Cincinnati to kiss Ciro's cheeks and bring an envelope with cash wrapped in rubber bands like all of the others. Big

Joey's nose always twitched when something was afoot. He trusted his instincts. And right now, his nose wasn't twitchin' a fuckin' millimeter.

He relaxed as his huge, chunky hands gripped the leather steering wheel. A handicapped parking permit hung from the rearview mirror that would give them premium parking anywhere—a small perk that Don Ilario had secured years ago. Another quick look into the mirror showed him a content Ciro, examining his manicured fingernails. He let a prideful grin show and went back to concentrating on the road. He was looking forward to seeing his new boss take over. A younger generation would now be in charge, and he hoped it would mean a new era of peace and prosperity for The Association. His calm demeanor did not last long as he thought about the charge Don Ilario had given to him in private. Not only was he Ciro's driver, he was the only one on the new Don's innermost ring of trust. If all other defenses were penetrated, then he was the solitary person who would stand between the threat and Ciro. His job was to give his life so that Ciro would live on. His job was also to have the ear of the capos in case a soldier was thinking about becoming a snitch. It had been a while since an underling had 'found God' and become an informant. The Association's rules were simple regarding informers: If The Association could get to a snitch who had found God, then they made sure that the snitch got to join God. In a shoulder harness underneath his suit was a .40 caliber Glock 22. He wore a special belt that had ten extra magazines of fifteen rounds each. On the passenger seat, underneath a Detroit Tigers sweatshirt, was his Uzi if there was big trouble. He was right to have it with him—would make Don Ilario's dick stand straight up in his twenty-five thousand-dollar Promethean coffin at the funeral home—there could always be trouble, but Big Joey had thought it all through and didn't expect any this day. He also had a lupara in a specially built compartment above his head.

He looked back at Ciro once more. The new Don had pulled out his phone and was smiling as he punched away at the screen. *Probably playing that ridiculous game again.* He even knew that Ciro had chosen the name "Sarcastic Panda" for the character Ciro controlled in the game. Joey sighed. Ciro's father had been old school, never using a phone. Now, a technology addict would be The Association's top man. However, in retrospect, Joey thought that the Don had made the right choice in choosing his son—said it came to him a month prior while reading Jim Collins's book *How the Mighty Fall* in his hospital bed. *"Our hubris of success will be our downfall if we don't adapt"* the Don had lectured. As solid a leader as Fabian De Luca was, the Don had believed that Ciro would do a better job of moving certain sectors of the family business into the virtual arena. However, even though the Don and Ciro feared a possible move by Fabian, Ciro needed to be seen as embracing the long-time underboss for his knowledge of loan sharking and prostitution—at least at the initial gathering. Fabian knew that he had been ordered by Don Ilario to step down once Ciro took over, but the fact that he would be at the Red Robin had put Big Joey's and Ciro's minds at ease for the time being. The family underboss had a calming effect, and that was what was needed right now. Ciro still hadn't made up his mind about who would be the new underboss, but perhaps he was playing his cards close to his vest like his father and would announce it at the Red Robin. Joey knew that Don Ilario had given his son a set of prepared remarks to make when he announced the celebration of Fabian's retirement. This might be the perfect opportunity. But if a threat from Fabian emerged over the coming weeks when Ciro asserted his power, then the underboss could be quietly taken care of. And Big Joey knew just how to do it.

Ciro laughed at his phone's screen and did a little dance as he continued to push buttons. For Cosa Nostra to thrive in the future, it needed personnel who were tech savvy—starting with the Don. Ciro had smart friends who were not only college educated but also computer whizzes. They would be needed to run the family's gambling operations online through another country. Big Joey had already set up a meeting with them for tomorrow afternoon. After that, in private, he would talk to Ciro about getting the dry boxes out of the cave as soon as possible. They had respected the Don's wishes, but an underwater cave was no place for that amount of money. His deceased boss was too old-school and too paranoid. And Big Joey had his doubts about River Nicky—and the gardener following Stansie Russo around like a lost puppy. He also wanted to speak with Ciro about how long the new Don planned on keeping the gardener around.

Details, details.

He got off at Exit 219, and the car began its journey down Gratiot Street toward Greektown—and a new beginning.

Greektown Historic District

Fabian De Luca sat alone in the back seat of a rented Lincoln MKZ— *"Get us one of those cars that McConaughey does the commercials for,"* he had said to his driver and bodyguard GiGi Rizzo. The MKZ was parked in front of the Underground Railroad Reading Station Bookstore just before the intersection of Beaubien and Monroe Streets. If his calculations were correct, Don Russo's Mercedes would pass by any minute now, cross over Beaubien, and pull over on the left-hand side of Monroe in front of the Red Robin Lounge. And when it did, he would witness the execution of Don Ciro and his pain-in-the-ass, overweight driver Big Joey Manetti. His teeth began to grind. He wanted Stansie Russo dead today too, but she was nowhere to be found along with her idiot gardener boyfriend. He opened his mouth, enjoying the cool air running over his teeth as he inhaled. This relaxed him, and he took comfort in the fact that Stansie Russo, wherever she was, would be easy to find. A drug addict who leaves the sanctuary of her home is like a baby without a diaper.

The car's tinted windows would make it difficult for anyone to see him from the sidewalk. From the entrance of the Red Robin, it looked like no one was in the MKZ. He looked at his watch—1:03 p.m. The Don was supposed to arrive three minutes ago. The rest of The Association members were to have shown up at noon. The tradition of keeping subordinates waiting was started decades ago by Don Ilario. He reasoned that it would remind them just who was in charge without having to tell them so. It appeared that Ciro would be continuing the tradition, but not for long.

The Red Robin had a back entrance, and earlier, GiGi Rizzo had left him in the car and entered the lounge from that entrance. Here, they would use another one of Don Ilario's traditions to their advantage. The upstairs bar was off-limits to everyone except for the Don, the underboss, the consigliere, and their bodyguards. The upstairs bar also had a secret stairway that led to a hallway and out another back entrance. His son Leo was inside the main bar area downstairs, waiting to pay his respects to Don Ciro, as was Papa Pete. When the assassination took place, Fabian would exit the vehicle, take a left down Beaubien Street and then cross the street and head down the back alley until he reached the back entrance. Leo would slip to the back entrance and let his father in and guide him to the hallway and secret staircase. Fabian would head upstairs and meet GiGi, who would then usher him down the regular staircase to see what all the commotion was about. Papa Pete would be playing his role as the emotional elder who had seen too much but vowed The Association would avenge Ciro's death. This would allow Fabian to be a level-headed calming force for the organization at that moment. And, because of Papa Pete's urging to everyone present, Fabian would be named Don later that afternoon.

The three men he had recruited for the hit were drug dealers that he had sprung from jail. They were each given ten thousand dollars and told that they would be paid a hundred thousand more upon completion of the hit. They had no idea who was hiring them or who had gotten them out of jail. In fact, the person who had arranged it and met with them was already dead, his body feeding the fishes along with Silvio Verratti's in Lake St. Clair.

They were given an escape route to follow from the lounge and a time and place to meet later that day to collect the rest of the money. Fabian knew they would never make it to the meeting. Papa Pete had his men stationed outside the entrance to the Red Robin, and after the assassination, they would kill the three assassins. All bases were covered as Papa Pete's men had officially been hired as security consultants and were licensed to carry firearms. One of Fabian's contacts in the Detroit Police Department was making sure that there would be no officers within two blocks during the hit. Behind the Lincoln was a crash car, which was to be driven out into Monroe Street and hit any police car that came from behind them. This would give Papa Pete's men more time if they needed it and Fabian more time to get to the alley and up the staircase. There was another crash car stationed on Beaubien Street, north of the alley, to do the same if a police car came from that direction. Fabian looked at the phone on the seat next to him. It remained dark and silent. If there were any problems, GiGi or Leo would call. He looked down at his disguise: running shoes, sweatpants, a baggy Detroit Lions t-shirt, blonde wig, sunglasses, and a Detroit Lions hat. GiGi had his suit, shoes, watch, and rings waiting for him to change into behind the upstairs bar. Papa Pete and Leo had tried to talk him out of it. *"Just wait upstairs and have some wine,"* his uncle had said. *"No,"* he had replied. *"I have to see it."*

He waited patiently for the Mercedes. It was the last time he would wait for anything or anyone ever again. After today, he would be the one they were all waiting to see. From the left-hand pocket of his sweatpants, he pulled out a single playing card: the Ace of Spades, the death card. He rubbed the tip of his right index finger along the four edges, making a slow rectangle. He did it over and over and over again, while he watched the street.

Kelvin Murphy exited the Greektown Casino Hotel with his wife Lydia and their four-year-old daughter Nancy. Last night had been a merciless experience at the roulette wheel, the blackjack table, and every slot machine he had tried. Lydia had not fared much better. Drunk, tired, and depressed, they had both entered the elevator and decided on the ride up to their floor that saving up money to take a vacation just to gamble even more of it away didn't make any sense.

It had made sense when they made the reservation two months ago. They had recovered from his lousy stretch of unemployment, and it was time to celebrate and take a chance. The silver bullet of hitting the jackpot this week was just as appealing to the Murphys as it was to the other casino players who were donating their hard-earned bucks for a chance at glory. Now, after a peek at prosperity on night one and an epic disaster on night two, they were ready to cut their losses and skip the routine on night three. Lydia was also grumpy because of his outburst after losing two thousand dollars in one spin of the roulette wheel. He'd said, *"These Goddamn Native American casino owners are taking revenge on all of us for stealing their land all of those years ago!"* She had immediately pulled him aside and admonished him for his racist rant. Then he had said, *"But it's true!"* She had slapped his face and headed to the bar.

Right now, they were both hungover and hungry. Nancy had stayed in the room next door with Lydia's mother, who had accompanied them on the vacation but was growing more impatient by the minute. At this point, he agreed with her, which was one of only two times during his marriage when he had found common ground with his mother-in-law. The other was when Nancy wanted to wear a witch costume to pre-school every day. *"But we have all of these cute outfits that I want her to wear,"* Lydia had said. He had replied, *"Just let her wear the damned thing. She loves it."* His mother-in-law had agreed, and the topic had ruffled the marriage feathers for three months until the morning when Nancy couldn't find it in her dresser and had to wear something else to pre-school. He was convinced that Lydia had thrown the costume away but had decided not to ask.

When they knocked on her mother's door five minutes ago, they had been informed that Nancy had had breakfast a few hours ago but needed lunch—and that grandma needed some time alone. Now.

As they walked hand-in-hand down East Lafayette Street, Lydia started in on Kelvin. "I don't understand why we didn't use the exit on Monroe Street. We'd be to Five Guys by now."

Kelvin rolled his eyes behind his sunglasses. "Because I wanted to see Old St. Mary's Catholic Church."

"You're not even a practicing Catholic anymore," she shot back.

"I know, I just wanted to see it. Plus, we needed some fresh air."

"What I need is a greasy burger and then an afternoon nap."

"You slept all morning," he said.

"Ho, ho, ho. Look who's talking."

Before he could fire, Nancy broke the tension with, "Mommy, why are you talking like Santa?"

Kelvin burst out laughing, and then so did Lydia.

They turned and starting walking up St. Antoine Street.

"Look," he said, pointing at the massive church. "There it is. See? Not that far out of our way." He leaned over Nancy and gave Lydia a quick kiss on the side of the head. "We'll be inhaling burgers soon, team. But, wow, look at that architecture. Almost pretty enough to pull me back in."

"That'll be the day," Lydia said. "Although with what we donated last night, maybe we should go inside."

"What's 'donated' mean?" asked Nancy.

Kelvin ignored her for a moment, his eyes transfixed on the towering spires.

"It means to give, sweetie," Lydia said.

*How much did we lose last night?* The thoughts of losing his job returned, followed by the thoughts of how much he hated being on a bare-bones budget afterwards until he had landed his current job. Feeling queasy, he said, "Okay, team, let's get some burgers and fries."

They turned onto Monroe Street and soon saw Five Guys down at the end of the block, right before Beaubien Street. Across the street and toward them was the Red Robin Lounge. Maybe after the food had settled, he'd head in there and just start drinking again. He shook his head. *Don't be an adolescent.* Get the food, collect the mother-in-law, and get the hell out of Detroit. There were no silver bullets in life.

They walked past the Monroe Street entrance to the casino, and he was met with a patronizing look from Lydia. *Okay, okay, you win.* He dropped his chin to his chest and let it hang there for a few seconds.

Lydia triumphantly reached her hand over and lifted his chin.

*All was forgiven.*

Then, after a few more feet, Nancy said, "Daddy, I see the sign for Five Guys!"


The Mercedes traveled the final few car lengths down Randolph Street, past Buffalo Wild Wings on the left, and Big Joey made the final left of the journey onto Monroe Street. They passed by the Acropolis bakery, the Ham Shop Café, and the Deluxe Bar and Lounge on the right, while The Old Shillelagh passed down the left.

Ciro said, "I've been down this stretch my entire life, Giuseppe, but it all looks different today."

"There's been some turnover—different stores and restaurants. But I'm thinkin' it's mostly because you're big boss now," he replied and then tipped his driver's cap to the image of the young Don he saw in the rearview mirror. Ciro had put away his phone.

The car crossed over Brush Street, and more familiar places came into sight. Fishbones, Firebird Tavern, the International Banquet Center, Second Baptist Church, Sports Mania...The Underground Railroad Reading Station Bookstore.


Fabian watched as the Mercedes passed by. His breathing picked up, and his left hand closed around the Ace of Spades, crumpling the card. His eyes narrowed as he watched the Mercedes' crimson brake lights come on. The car wheeled to the left and pulled up in front of the Red Robin Lounge.

Perhaps five paces from the door to Five Guys, Kelvin Murphy watched as the door swung open and three men wearing ski masks, Hawaiian shirts, and jeans raced across the street and started firing handguns at the two men who had just emerged from a beautiful black Mercedes.

Ciro Russo felt the first sting in his right arm as a barrage of popping noises filled the air. Then, he heard Big Joey, who had opened the back door to the Mercedes for him, yell, "Get do—" but his speech was cut off as the side of his head exploded into a mess of goo. He fell to the ground, his hand stuck inside his jacket, reaching for his gun.

Then, as Ciro went to duck back into the car, his chest was hit by multiple rounds and pieces of his shirt, suit, and tie fluttered away into the air as blood erupted from the holes. He fell and felt pain as his back and then head smacked the sidewalk's concrete. The last thing he saw before he died was a figure in a ski mask standing over him, taking aim at his head with a gun.

Papa Pete's men opened up their Uzis on full automatic, and two of the assassins' bodies fell to the ground near Ciro and Big Joey, their corpses covered in bloody holes. But the last assassin, who had not yet made it around the side of the bullet-riddled Mercedes, was able to get off a few rounds at one of Papa Pete's men. The man staggered back in pain, and the arm holding the Uzi lifted and then swung wildly to the left. The other men aimed their weapons at the last assassin and finished him off. There was silence for a moment—and then screaming from directly across the street.

* * *

Kelvin Murphy applied pressure to little Nancy Murphy's chest, which had two holes in it—one two inches above the belly button and the other a few inches south of her throat in the center of her tiny chest. Lydia had been hit in the leg, and her blood dripped onto the sidewalk as she huddled over Nancy and wailed.

"Daddy," Nancy said. "I feel like I do when I'm gonna...get...sick." And she was gone.

FBI Detroit Field Office

Patrick Bruno was in the middle of studying a December 2009 302 from Nolan to FBI Headquarters when Nolan burst through the office door.

"We've got to go. Now," Nolan said.

Patrick rose quickly, watching the elder Special Agent sprint to his desk and bend down behind it. Nolan had left for the break room to snatch a donut ten minutes ago. What in the hell had happened in that time? "What's going on?" Patrick said.

He heard Nolan shut a drawer and saw him stand up with two extra magazines for his Glock. "Ciro Russo has just been killed along with his driver. Civilians have been injured." Nolan put the magazines in one of his jacket pockets. "Fuck! This is not gonna be pretty."

Patrick handed the stack of 302s to Nolan, who locked them back up in one of the filing cabinets. Then, Patrick put his hand underneath his jacket and felt his Glock there. *Are you ready to use this? You better be.* He pulled his hand back out.

Nolan turned around. "Ready?"

"Right behind you," Patrick said.

178

# 17

## Put-in-Bay, South Bass Island, Ohio

## *Present Day*

Brad Cranston walked down the C dock in Miller's Marina. It was noon, and he thought the temperature was around seventy, albeit a windy seventy. On the way over, the winds had been northerly, barely a knot, but had now shifted to SSE at around ten knots. After another stride, Allison Shannon drew even with him.

"Got the directions?" he asked.

"Right here," she said, holding a notepad in her hand.

"Not going to use your cell phone?"

"Not unless we have to," she replied, all business. "C'mon, let's pick up the pace."

Last night had been uncomplicated and a reminder that he missed the company of a woman. Just knowing that another human being was sleeping in close proximity to him had given him a sound night's sleep. Then, this morning, they had maneuvered around each other with ease. He was up before she was and had made coffee. When the aroma began to fill the cabin, he had heard movement from her berth, followed by a yawn, and then, *"Something smells good."* It was simple and unnoteworthy, but that was why it meant something to him. It was genuine human contact but without recognition of supposed rules of cohabitation. He was so out of practice from the morning rituals and routines followed by two adults living together that he was surprised the morning had proceeded like they had lived together for years. Did this mean something? He was attracted to her. Was this a start? Whether it was working with her on the case or just the chit chat on the boat ride over about safe, select details from each other's past, he appreciated her straightforward manner. There appeared to be no positioning, strategizing, or hedging present in her manner or words. There was only what he could see and hear, and he liked it. He had once read that on a first date *you* don't actually show up but rather send a representative of your best self. Well, he had been on too many first dates over the past decade that had been stuffy and filled with rote pleasantries, boring conversation, empty promises to call again soon, and lies that he had enjoyed the evenings. A few of the dinners had led to sexual encounters, momentarily satiating his physical needs, but he determined that without the emotional connection, the relationship was doomed. Surprisingly, when the subject of his divorce had come up, he had felt at ease sharing how he had been left by his wife for the glamor and vistas of the west coast. Allison had seen a few of the films produced by his ex-wife's partner and said that she liked them. Normally, even this slight nod of positivity toward the people that now populated his ex-wife's life would trigger bitterness, but this time it didn't. Perhaps it was Allison's indifferent and matter-of-fact way of talking about it. She felt no need to probe or make anything more of it than what it was. She didn't feel that she needed to understand him and his full story before breaching other topics. She had a reservoir of practicality and tough-mindedness, and yet there was still a sliver of vulnerability in her professional manner. For a few minutes on the ride over, the conversation had faded, and she had reclined on the cockpit bench and watched the sun glisten on the cobalt sheen of water as the Stingray cut the surface in two. Then, the conversation had shifted to some of her past. There had been someone once, but it had ended. She didn't provide details, and he hadn't pressed for any. What became clear, without overtly saying so, was that they were both single and both passing through life doing their respective jobs.

Brad snuck a quick peek back at the twenty-five-foot Stingray, which was berthed ten yards behind them. Larry's boat had run like a dream on the way up from West Harbor past Catawba Island and all along the eastern shore of South Bass Island, slicing the calm Great Lake with ease. When they had reached the northern tip of South Bass and rounded Buckeye Point, the seas had grown to two to four feet as they headed west before calming down as they turned south into the harbor. To their left, and in the distance, they had seen the legendary 352-foot Doric column rising from the island to commemorate Commodore Oliver Hazard Perry's victory over the British in the War of 1812. The column was officially named "Perry's Victory and International Peace Memorial," and Allison had told him the park was a major tourist attraction. It was the U.S.'s third-tallest monument after the St. Louis Arch and Washington Monument.

"Where else do you get to stand by a monument that honors both war and peace and yet stands only five miles from the longest undefended border on the planet?" she had asked him.

He had only replied with Perry's famous quote, "We have met the enemy, and they are ours."

"You a history buff?" she had asked.

"No. That would be my brother. And an author named Jody DeWaters had the quote inside one of his books. I did the cover art for it."

"A nautical adventure?"

"No, a book about weed."

They had called Park Place Boat Club on VHF Channel 79, hoping it had a cancellation, but its slips were full. So, they had called Miller's Marina on VHF 74 and hailed the dockmaster, who had been helpful and pleasant to work with and had slips available. The electricity and fresh water had been easy to hook up, and there was a pavilion, newly renovated restrooms and showers, Wi-Fi, and a dock shop. Since it was the weekend, they were supposed to rent the slip for two nights, but Allison had explained the situation to the dockmaster. It was $2.50 per foot, so fifty dollars a night for the Stingray. Brad had paid to top off the boat's fuel before they left in the morning, so she gave the dockmaster seventy-five dollars for one night. He had tipped his cap, and the slip was theirs.

Brad turned back around and watched as Allison strode with a purpose toward the end of the dock and Bayview Avenue. She had the three pictures tucked into her tan backpack along with a camera. He patted the leather case on his belt that held his trusty Swiss Army knife as they stepped off the dock and crossed over Bayview to the sidewalk. They turned left and headed toward the village of Put-In-Bay.

"Okay, we go down a block, take a right on Catawba Avenue, then a left on Delaware, go past a couple of golf cart rental places, past—" she looked at the notepad in her hand—"Mama Maria's Pizza, then Pasquale's. We cross over Loraine Avenue, and we're there." She put the pad down and met eyes with him. "Sure you don't want to rent one of those golf carts?"

"Not yet," Brad said. "No Siri, no golf cart."

She grinned. "Smart ass."

They arrived in front of The Round House Bar, and Allison unzipped her backpack, taking out her camera and the picture with the woman in front of the bar. She handed the camera to Brad.

"Step back, drop to one knee, and see if you can recreate the shot."

He stepped back as she positioned herself in the street like the woman in the picture.

Dropping to one knee, he brought the camera to his right eye and started to swivel the zoom. "Move a little to the right...there. Hold it." *Click. Click.*

He rose and they compared his pictures to the one taken from Conrad's cell phone. It was a close match—Allison's head blocked out all of the letters except for 'R'.

It felt eerie recreating the picture. It had been a long time since he had seen his brother, but now he felt closer to him knowing that his brother had recently stood about where he had just stood and snapped a picture of someone that appeared to mean something to him.

"Brad?"

He heard his name, but it had the soft and muffled quality like when his ex-wife would call for him while he was working on a book cover sketch and had on his Koss headphones. For a moment, the people milling about on the sidewalk were silent; the patrons lifting drinks to their mouths behind the red, white, and blue bunting of The Round House were silent, and the breeze rustling through the trees behind him was silent. He heard it again. "Brad?" *Where was he?* Now all he could see was Conrad, slim, stressed out, reaching out with his hands, pleading for help.

"Brad!" yelled Allison.

The noises around him flooded his ears, and Allison's hand was gripping his arm, pulling him off of the street.

His feet left the hard pavement and stepped back onto soft grass. A golf cart passed in front of him, the driver frowning and shaking his head, the passenger giving him the evil eye and then turning around and running her hands through her hair.

He felt Allison's grip release. "You okay?" she said.

"Yeah. Sorry about that. Not sure why my brain picked that moment to zone out."

"Thinking about your brother?"

"I guess recreating the picture affected me."

She gave a positive nod of acknowledgment. It wasn't fake, and it wasn't sympathetic. He sensed empathy, and that made him wonder what similar experience she had had.

"Let's head inside the bar."

Two more golf carts whizzed by, and they crossed Loraine Avenue and walked up to the bar's entrance.

The Round House Bar had been around for over one hundred and forty years on South Bass Island and was known for its live entertainment, buckets of beer, and rowdy summer crowds. The boats poured into Put-in-Bay, the boaters made their way to The Round House, the buckets of beer were filled, emptied, and refilled—and the volume rose as summer visitors partied deep into the night. If drinking was a graduate degree, then Put-in-Bay's population in June, July, and August had the largest concentration of PhDs in the world. Things started in April with a tradition that rose the collective spirits of the island faithful: the legendary turning on of the neon "WHISKEY" light above the front door. There was even a song to commemorate the occasion by a talented musician named Ray Fogg. And the song was played again in the waning days of October at the ceremony where the light was turned off until April when the weather began to warm again and the patrons got thirsty.

As Brad looked up at the WHISKEY light, Conrad passed through his mind again like a cab traveling down a road at night and then turning a corner toward a monstrous city's lights.

"Time to commence the siege of the Round-House, David Balfour," Brad said as he opened the door for Allison.

"What was that from?"

"*Kidnapped* by Robert Louis Stevenson. Ever read it?"

She shook her head no, and they entered the bar.

To say it was busy was an understatement. Boaters knew how to party, and they started early. What struck him was not the crowd dipping their plastic cups into their red buckets of beer but the absolute beauty of the wood inside. Round wooden bar stools, round wooden bar tables, and a round bar with a stage behind it. Murals adorned the walls, and an enormous red, white, and blue canopy hung from the ceiling. A banner on one portion of the wall had the phrase, 'Don't Give Up the Ship' on it.

As they maneuvered their way to the bar, he caught snippets of conversation, 'Mad Dog'll be on in an hour,' 'Dude's forty-first season, bro,' 'Go Bucks, Muck Fichigan.'

Allison asked for two waters and if the manager was available. The bartender filled two plastic cups and then disappeared into the crowd behind the bar to check.

"I like this place," Brad said. "Wouldn't mind coming back here when this is over."

"Yeah, the vibe in here is real. There's a reason this place has lasted over a hundred and forty years. You think Conrad and his lady went inside?"

"I wouldn't bet against it."

They listened to the music and sipped on their waters. After five minutes had passed, the bartender returned with a tall and slender balding man with a handlebar moustache. He wore a red t-shirt and khaki shorts. If Brad had to guess, the guy's gray hair and wrinkled forehead put him around sixty.

"Art Mackadoo," the man said, extending his hand.

Brad and Allison shook it and introduced themselves.

"What can I do for you?" Art shouted over the music.

Allison told him that she was a professional investigator and asked if they could speak with him in private. Art rubbed his moustache and looked as if he was pondering whether the world was flat or round. Then he shrugged and led the way back to his private office. Inside, he offered them two chairs and then sat on the edge of a weathered wooden desk that had a bucket of beer on it with a stack of plastic cups next to it. "Beer?"

They both shook their heads. He dipped a plastic cup into the bucket and then took a chug. His manner was relaxed, like 'it's summer in Put-in-Bay and nobody's countin' the number of beers you've had or are gonna have' type of relaxed. "What problem can I make go away for you today?" Art asked, using his shirt to wipe the excess beer off of the outside of the cup. His grin made the handlebar portions of his moustache more pronounced.

Allison showed him the photographs and explained the situation.

After a moment of thoughtful reflection, or feigned thoughtful reflection, Art handed the photographs back. "I've been workin' this here bar for thirty years, almost as long as Mad Dog's been playing here," he said, motioning to the muffled live music and crowd cheering just outside the closed door. "I know every local and season regular, and I'm being honest when I tell you that I've never seen this man or woman before."

"Any idea about the boat? Anything look familiar?"

Art shook with laughter. "Do you know how many boats visit South Bass in a summer? Thousands." He scooped out another cupful of beer and drank. Then, he followed the same routine by wiping the outside of the cup with his shirt. "I'm sorry, but I think you're shit out of luck."

Not ready to give up, Brad took the picture that had the woman in front of the bar and tapped it with the back of his right hand. "Any chance they came into the bar? You'd have video, right?"

Art ran his index finger around the rim of his beer cup. He gave a shrug. "Always a possibility." He raised his cup up and tipped it back.

Brad was about to get the well-then-let's-see-your-videos ball rolling and get Art away from the beer bucket, when something seemed to change in the old bar manager—like he had just had an epiphany about the whole situation during his drink, realizing that he was the sole holder of the most valuable information ever sought.

Art set his cup down. "Excuse me for a moment," he said, jogging to the door.

Allison and Brad exchanged looks of bewilderment.

When he returned, Art was followed by a male employee who was immaculately groomed and had fruity-scented cologne on. Brad thought the guy was in his mid-twenties. Brad also thought he had a cocky grin.

Art closed the door behind them. As if he were Senator Tiger Akin, pulled from the pages of a horrible Jody DeWaters novel, Art put his hands on his hips and set his jaw. His eyes swiveled to Mr. Perfect. "This is Christian Huer—"

*Of course it is*, thought Brad.

"—one of our summer bartenders." His eyes moved to Allison. "Your pictures had me convinced that our business was over for the day. But when the possibility of them entering the bar and video—well, you know, all that tech stuff got mentioned, it clicked."

"What does that mean?" Brad asked.

"Don't just stand there. Get me a beer," Art said to Christian.

Christian 'The Chiseled Model' frowned, embarrassment evident in his eyes as well, and then dipped a cup in the bucket for Art.

After a measured sip—this was serious business now—Art said, "What I mean, is that this grasshopper couldn't stop talking about 'The Goddess in Blue' the other day. It was one of my rare days off, and I come in the next afternoon, and it's all he can talk about. Says she stood him up, and that her tall boyfriend threatened to kick his ass."

"So, they did come in the bar," Brad said to Allison.

"I guess she didn't fall for his good looks," Art joked.

"Look, I can get any piece of ass I want—"

Art slammed his cup down, and beer erupted like a volcano, splashing all over the desktop. "Shut up, Christian!"

# 18

**Put-in-Bay, South Bass Island, Ohio**

*Present Day*

In a way that only a male who has been passed over or left by a beautiful woman for another male can know, Brad could see that old Art had been a victim, perhaps many times over, to Christian's youth and vitality. There had been silence in the room for almost thirty seconds when Brad, who didn't owe Art anything, decided to give him an empathetic nod.

Allison broke in. "Listen, can you tell us anything more, or should we just go study the video?"

Art was still fuming, but Christian was able to take his eyes off of his boss and meet Allison's. "Look, I never got her name. They sat at the bar for around a half-an-hour. When her boyfriend went to use the bathroom, I made my move. She wasn't interested. Then her boyfriend came back, and I overheard her telling

189

him what had happened while I was serving another customer. He waved me over and threw the piece of paper I had given her with my number on it at my face. He threatened me, and then they got up and left."

Art's rage had turned to jubilation. "He threw the paper at your face? Now, I've gotta see that video. You never told me that part."

Christian ignored him and continued. "They got about five feet away from the bar and were met by someone I know."

"Who?" Allison asked.

"Nick. Guy's a regular here."

She took out her notepad and pen. "Nick who?"

Christian donned his embarrassed look once more, but this time it also had the flair of him trying to flirt with Allison at the same time. "Nick's all I've ever known him by. Hung out a few times after work."

"Does he have a boat?" Allison asked, beating Brad once more to the question.

Meanwhile, seeing that his attempts to jump in with questions were always late, Art refilled his beer cup once more and studied everyone as if he were evaluating the entire situation and would give out grades when the conversation was over.

"Hell yeah, he does," Christian said. "A beautiful fifty-foot Hunter—center cockpit, the works. I've been on her too, glides through Lake Erie like a hot knife through warm butter." He paused, almost as if to congratulate himself on the overused simile.

Brad could not resist. "I'll bet it's a chick magnet."

Allison's eyes narrowed at him.

"Shit yeah, it is. We got *bizzzeee* onboard one night with a few ladi—" He tried to stop himself, but realized he had gone too far.

"Go ahead," Allison said. "You're not getting *bizzzeee* with me," she said, mocking him and seeming to enjoy it.

This proclamation also broke Art's serious veneer. "You are such an idiot," he said to Christian.

"Boat got a name, Christian?" Allison said.

His face's color was close to matching his shirt's cherry red shade. He began rubbing his hands together.

She tried again. "The boat, Christian. Does. It. Have. A. Name?"

He dropped his hands. "Yeah, it's called *Apollonia's Ashes*. Don't know what it means. Asked him about it once, and he said that if I didn't know what it meant then I really was a stupid millennial. I didn't appreciate that. Guess I never took the time to look it up on my phone, now that I think of it."

The name immediately registered with Brad. Apollonia. She was Michael Corleone's first wife in *The Godfather*. Yeah, Christian didn't seem like someone who would know anything about Coppola's masterpiece or about film for that matter.

Art looked away, apparently hoping not to make eye contact and possibly reveal that he too didn't know shit about *The Godfather*.

Allison stayed on point and showed Christian the photographs of the sailboat. "This his love machine?" she said, smirking.

"That's it. And there's that fox and her asshole boyfriend."

*Should I take this pretty boy outside and waste on him a bit?* No, too easy, and, he had to admit it, Conrad could be annoying. However, the fact that he might be in real trouble kept Brad's heart rate up. He had unknowingly made his right hand into a fist.

Allison patted his fist as if to say, 'Down boy.' Then, she put the pictures away and asked Christian, "He keep the boat in one of Put-in-Bay's marinas?"

"Yeah, he's got a slip at Park Place, but sometimes he uses the mooring ball offshore of his house."

"Where?" Brad said. His intensity was rising.

"It's on the other side of the island, north of Lighthouse Point, right on the water. Sweet pad. By road, you take Laura Drive to get there." Christian paused. "You got a boat?"

"We do," Allison said. "Docked at Miller's."

Christian snapped his fingers. "Easy, you just head out of the marina, hang a left, and then travel down the coast until you see the boat. Can't miss it."

Hang a left? Okay, Christian was not a boater. Nick probably told him that it was a Hunter Fifty Center Cockpit, and Christian was just repeating it, trying to impress them. Christian the parrot. "No other sailboats moored along the coast?"

Christian grinned. "Oh, there are, but no other Hunter Fifties."

*Don't know what we'd do without you, Christian.*

"Anything else you can tell us about this Nick?" Allison asked, scribbling more notes on her pad.

"Doesn't come around too often. I know I said he was a regular, but it's more like once every couple weeks. He's always alone. Told me he was retired and just wanted a nice quiet place to live out the rest of his years. Can't blame the player; he's got it made."

"How old is he?" Brad asked.

"Hovering around fifty I'd say."

"Early retiree."

"Beats me. Guy can still party, though."

"Weed or something stronger?" Allison said.

Christian eyed Art and then looked at the floor.

"Oh, for cryin' out loud, answer her," Art said.

"I've *seen* some cocaine at his place, but that's it."

They stayed for ten more minutes and learned that Nick had never given Christian a phone number, and Christian had never seen Nick use a phone. Furthermore, Christian had never seen anyone else at Nick's besides the girls they brought there. He admitted that he had helped to set up a few of the trysts with women he had bedded that still frequented The Round House. Nick also never let any of them stay over at his house after the romps; Christian had to drive a golf cart with the girls piled in next to him back to a bed and breakfast in the middle of the night—all while he was high or inebriated.

Before leaving the bar, they thanked Art, who had continued to down cups of beer and almost missed their hands when they went to shake, and lied by promising to drop by later. Allison reluctantly gave her cell phone number to Christian with instructions to call if he thought of anything else.

As they walked down Delaware, Allison asked, "Golf cart or boat?"

"Boat," Brad said.

Then, Allison's phone rang. It was Mike. He had tracked down the phone numbers.

# 19

**Grosse Pointe Shores, Michigan**

*3 Days Ago . . .*

Don Fabian De Luca entered his oak-paneled library wearing a five-thousand-dollar Ermenegildo Zegna charcoal-colored tailored suit. As Don Ilario had aged, so had his taste in good clothing. 'You act how you dress' Fabian believed the old adage went, or something close to it. And as the late Don Ilario's dress shoes had turned to slippers, so had his leadership gone soft and comfy. In the twilight years of his reign, he had rarely dressed in anything other than silk pajamas and a silk robe with his initials monogrammed on the breast pocket. The family consigliere, Silvio Verratti, had tried to compensate for the Don's appearance by wearing expensive suits, shoes, and jewelry that should have been worn by the Don. As underboss, Fabian had too. But even together, they could not overcome another one of America's favorite election-time philosophies: You still vote for the top of the ticket. However, the most appropriate description of Don Russo's final years at the helm were best summed up in a fairy tale by Hans Christian Anderson that he had read to Leo when he was young, *The Emperor's New Clothes.* Fabian would bring back a sense of class, respect, and legitimacy to the position. Gravitas. He would apply the lessons of his favorite Shakespearean play, *I Henry IV*—specifically, the wisdom that King Henry imparts to his son Hal about being seen less:

*By being seldom seen, I could not stir*
*But like a comet I was wondered at,*
*That men would tell their children, "This is he!"*
*...*
*Thus did I keep my person fresh and new,*
*My presence, like a robe pontifical,*
*Ne'er seen but wondered at; and so my state,*
*Seldom but sumptuous, showed like a feast*
*And won by rareness such solemnity.*

And the diminishing that occurs when you are seen too much:

*That, being daily swallowed by men's eyes,*
*They surfeited with honey and began*
*To loathe the taste of sweetness, whereof a little*
*More than a little is by much too much.*
*So, when he had occasion to be seen,*
*He was but as the cuckoo is in June,*
*Heard, not regarded; seen, but with such eyes*
*As, sick and blunted with community,*
*Afford no extraordinary gaze,*
*Such as is bent on sun-like majesty*

*When it shines seldom in admiring eyes,*
*But rather drowsed and hung their eyelids down,*
*Slept in his face, and rendered such aspect*
*As cloudy men use to their adversaries,*
*Being with his presence glutted, gorged, and full.*


GiGi Rizzo ushered in Don De Luca and then closed the heavy doors to the library. Inside the room were all the made men in The Association, for it was not only time for the new Don to give his directives but also to induct a new member of the family. He embraced his son, Leo, and could see the pride in his face. Fabian was curious to see how he would perform as the Family's street boss. As a capo, Leo had been average—ran his crew too tightly. Perhaps, Fabian thought, it was because he felt his father's shadow and did not want to disappoint him. He needed to loosen up and become his own man. Promoting him to street boss was one way to publicly show his confidence in his son's ability and also a way to give him some room to operate as Leo would now be dealing more directly with the Underboss than with the Don. The setup was in Leo's favor because the former street boss, Salvatore "Street Sal" Gallo, was the Family's new underboss and could mentor Leo. They broke their embrace, and Leo stepped over to chat with one of his capos while Don Fabian continued into the room.

The meeting would proceed according to tradition but also swiftly. That was another critique he had of Don Russo's gatherings: They took *forever* to get started and to finish. Additionally, his long-time gumar, Academy Award Nominee Solange Tomei, was waiting upstairs with champagne, caviar, and crackers to celebrate. His wife, Caterina, was on a secret trip to stay for a month in their chateau in the French Basque mountains—a precaution in case anything went wrong with the assassination. He had sent her best friend, Carmela, with her along with two Soldati to guard them. He was not worried about either Soldati making moves on his wife; if they did, they were dead. Now, Carmela? He admitted that their marriage bed had been cold—lukewarm at best over the years—and that his fascination with Solange and all the high-class Hollywood pizazz she brought to their affair had disinterested him in his wife's needs, both emotionally and behind closed doors in the bedroom. It was rumored that Carmela had been more than just a friend of Caterina's for some time. He'd never bothered to investigate, thinking that if Carmela kept his wife happy and her daggers away from him when he traveled to Vegas or L.A. to meet up with Solange, then that was fine.

Papa Pete, his new consigliere, who *because of extraordinary and tragic circumstances* had come out of retirement to help steady The Association during this time, rose and embraced him first with a hug and then a kiss on each cheek. His uncle had vowed to find out who was responsible for the murder of Don Ciro but had also warned The Association during the past twenty-four hours that blood, in the end analysis, was bad for business. A war of any kind, especially a war where the two sides were not clearly defined, would threaten The Association's earning power— from the Don all the way down to the button man. Again, *numbers.* He preached patience, situational awareness, and a reaffirmation to numbers, which over time, always told the whole story by filling in a puzzle one piece at a time. Last night, he had made a house call to Angela Russo and wept with her for Ciro. To ensure her safety, he had left the two remaining men who had been outside of the Red Robin Lounge to guard her. The third man had died before the ambulance arrived downtown yesterday afternoon.

Fabian's newly-appointed underboss, Salvatore "Street Sal" Gallo, welcomed him next, and soon every member of The Association had paid his respects and was seated in chairs facing the Don's enormous hand-made desk made out of oak and stained dark mahogany. Fabian delayed beginning his speech as he enjoyed observing Street Sal watch the seated men with the cold, disinterested pragmatism of a snowstorm that came on and would not go away. In The Association, he had mastered the loan-shark wing of the family business and had gotten his nickname because there was no one better at putting money on the street. Fabian predicted that he would make an effective underboss who could one day earn the appellation of Don. For one, his last name was not Russo or De Luca; there would be no nepotism, even though much of the Cosa Nostra structure relied on a certain amount of it to maintain stability or at least a sense of who is who. The position of Don was not inherited, and to be called Don was because one was a person of absolute honor—the respect led to the title, not the other way around. Ciro hadn't earned it. Street Sal probably would—even if this meant that Fabian's own son's rise to the position was delayed.

The Don spoke, "As I announced yesterday, until our beloved consigliere, Silvio Verratti, is located, my uncle Pietro 'Papa Pete' De Luca will serve as my consigliere. We are honored by his gesture to come out of retirement and help see us through this transition. There is not a better man in this room."

The room was briefly filled with polite applause and then silence.

"I want it made clear that I do not think Consigliere Verratti had anything to do with Don Ciro's death. He is older and should be enjoying the things that life should be giving back to him. He had no zest for power beyond his position, and him hiring the assassins that Papa Pete's men took care of seems out of the realm of possibility. I just pray that he is okay."

"We will find him," declared Father Tony, standing by the closed drapes on the far wall but inching closer and closer to the bar.

Fabian paused, hoping he would not say another word.

Father Tony bowed his head and grasped his rosary.

Fabian continued. "We will continue to search for him, and I want to know the moment that any contact is made." He paused longer this time, giving the statement room to breathe and widen the minds of those present. "But, for now, let us take a moment of silence to honor him."

Heads bowed, eyes closed, heavy breaths were held and then exhaled, and a few of the older Capos teared up. Papa Pete put his face in his hands, and GiGi gave him a soft pat on the shoulder. Father Tony had made it to the bar and snuck a quick sip of wine. The old priest would be on his way to Children's Hospital of Michigan after the ceremony to arrange a different ceremony—one at the hospital later in the week when Mr. Fabian De Luca, respectable Detroit businessman, would be donating one hundred thousand dollars to the hospital that had saved his infant son Leonardo many years ago. The plaque was already being made and would hang in the hospital lobby. The gesture was genuine; he cared for children and had witnessed a wife and husband run down the hallway screaming after they had been informed that their toddler son had just died. A four-year-old Leonardo had been fighting for his life two doors down. Fabian had set aside money every year to anonymously give to the hospital for research. Now, he would be able to give a greater amount and make it public. Let the police, Feds, and District Attorney try and take *that* money away. However, so as not to forget his Shakespeare, he would retreat to the shadows after the appearance. Less is more. Less *is* more.

The Association men continued their silence, lost in their memories of Silvio Verratti. Fabian waited. He never considered himself the master politician that Don Ilario was or a master charmer like Papa Pete, but if there was one thing he was a master of, it was lies. His skill set of secrecy and deception was more than enough to get him through this transition period. Confusion played into his hands because none of the men seated and standing in front of him were absolutely sure about what had happened over the past forty-eight hours. Now they needed leadership, certainty, and tradition to lean on.

As far as the authorities, he would maintain his relationship with agent Nolan, but he would also have the upper hand with the Detroit Police Department. Two high-ranking cops were on The Association's payroll—ten grand a month each. For that sum, Fabian received a steady flow of department secrets; one of the men had access to files where surveillance information was stored. They had even carried out hits for him in the past, and Fabian had given each man a giant bonus for the work. Everything would continue to be run professionally.

He spoke again, "And now, perhaps the best way to honor Consigliere Verratti is to proceed with one of his favorite traditions."

Street Sal motioned to GiGi, who opened the doors, admitting a short man named Paulie Gervasi. The longtime soldato, who was dressed in his best suit, was becoming a made man today. He had made his bones long ago, but his latest murder was done with the promise of the ceremony today. He had been the one to kill the man who had contacted the three guns-for-hire who had killed Ciro and Big Joey. His loyalty was unquestioned, and he would now enter a select group. After today, he would join the two-thousand-member fraternity of "connected" men. It wasn't the fifteen thousand Sicilian Mafia members, who made up one percent of Sicily's population, but it was still an imposing force across the land of the free and home of the brave.

Words were spoken, and Gervasi took them all in: You will kill one of your brothers if commanded by one of your bosses; you will keep omerta; you will not have relations with or desire another made member's wife or gumar; you will not physically assault or verbally insult another made man; the organization is supreme, parts like you are replaceable—a spoke in the wheel. Then, the final law was given: There is no retirement—you have a lifetime obligation. Don De Luca remembered when he had gone through this same ceremony. After the final directive had been given, his uncle had whispered to him the words of Lucky Luciano, "The only way out is in a box."

At this point, Gervasi's trigger finger was cut with a dagger, and he watched as his crimson blood dripped onto the picture of a saint he was holding. Then, the picture was set on fire, and Gervasi held it in his hand. While the blood, picture, and the tissue on the inside of his hand burned, he vowed to burn like the saint if he ever broke the commandments he had been given, betraying Cosa Nostra. Then, he took in more of the ceremony: You live by the gun and the knife and you die by the gun and the knife; this is your boss; this is your underboss; this is your capo; *this family* comes before *your family.*

Finally, he pressed his pin-pricked trigger finger to the trigger finger of Capo Andrea "Handy Andy" Casale, who would be his godfather.

Don De Luca embraced Gervasi and said, "You are born today."

As other members embraced Gervasi and the celebration started, GiGi Rizzo took the Don aside.

"We've got him downstairs," GiGi said.

Fabian looked over GiGi's shoulder at the crowd moving toward the bar and tables set up with hors d'oeuvres. "And?"

"He drove Stansie and her boyfriend to a garage where they loaded the bags of money into a green pickup truck. He didn't know where they were headed."

"Do you believe him?"

"We've already tried our usual methods of persuasion, and he would have told us by now. Yes, I believe him."

Fabian trusted his bodyguard. *Damn.* He had hoped for more information. *After Stansie and her boyfriend are taken care of, I'll be in the clear. What to do with the plumber? Kill him? No. Make him yours. How much of a goodwill payment? A nickel ($500.00)? A dime ($1000.00)?* He looked at the happy faces around the room, including his son Leo. *I'm feeling generous today.* He turned to GiGi and said, "Release him quietly, and give him a dime. He's *my* plumber now, if he wants to live."

GiGi said, "Understood."

"They would have checked in at some point," Fabian said.

"But we've already checked Ciro's and Big Joey's cell phones. There was nothing."

"There has to be another phone. My uncle is going to visit Angela again tonight to comfort her. Go with him. Search the house." Fabian thought for a moment. "Has everyone checked in who was not able to be at the Red Robin yesterday?"

"Yes. Miami Marino, Sunshine Paulie, and River Nicky all called."

This was crucial. If one of them had not checked in, then there would be a possible threat vector, forcing him to initiate inquiries. And that usually meant bodies were about to start piling up. However, he was still unsure about Nico because he had been close to the old Don. His special agent acquaintance was trying to find Nico at this moment. "I'm still a little worried about—"

"Nico," GiGi said, cutting him off.

"Yes. Who took the call yesterday?"

GiGi searched his memory. "It was Street Sal."

"I'm wondering if I should call him back at the number he called us from?"

GiGi shook his head. "You know he dumps those phones as soon as he uses them. He's always been shifty."

"Probably why he's stayed alive so long," Fabian said. "What about tracing the call? It would give us his location."

"He changes that immediately too. He's been very good at playing the game of, 'I'll check in with you; you don't check in with me.'"

"Then it is time for that game to change."

"It never bothered you when you were underboss."

His bodyguard was right. It was because Nico Colombo was one of the few old-school-mentality types left in The Association—did his job, avoided law enforcement, avoided the press, and, as far as he knew, wasn't hooked on the product they were pushing. That had been Nico's grandfather's mistake: falling in love with the white powder. "I know."

Papa Pete gave him a look from across the room that said, 'Everything all right?'

Fabian grinned his reply, and Papa Pete went back to his Strega. "What would *he* advise me to do right now?" Fabian said, motioning to his uncle.

"He'd tell you to focus on finding Stansie and her boyfriend. Worry about Nico later."

Fabian gave GiGi a kiss on the cheek. "That's exactly what he would tell me. Now, after a drink, I'm heading upstairs to see Solange." He became serious. "Find the phone."

Lake Erie

The fifty-foot Hunter, *Apollonia's Ashes*, glided through Lake Erie toward the eastern coast of Michigan. Nico "River Nicky" Colombo stood behind the helm as Conrad Cranston and Stansie Russo relaxed on the starboard cockpit bench, drinking from glass bottles of Evian. *What in the hell is up with those bottles anyway?* After they had loaded the bags of cash onboard a few days ago, they had brought onboard another bag full of Evians. He hadn't seen them without one since he had picked them up, which was where he was about to drop them back off at— not during the transit to South Bass, not during the loading of the cash into the fifty dry boxes at his house, not during the diving operation (each time their heads had broken the surface of the water aft of the swim step, Stansie had handed Conrad a bottle, and he had taken a few chugs before submerging with another large dry box) and not on the return trip. He had heard the rumors that she was a recovering drug addict and assumed Conrad was too, but Evian bottles? Weird. *Whatever works*, he thought. Out of respect, he had done his lines of coke in the privacy of his bedroom, while they stayed at his house overnight. He did not want to face the Don's wrath for causing a relapse.

He watched as they cuddled and sipped their water. Looking back, he shouldn't have let them go exploring on South Bass, but they had asked after he had sniffed a few morning lines and was making coffee in the kitchen. He was still surprised that he had made it to The Roundhouse on time. They were supposed to have lunch there, but the two had run into trouble with his favorite bartender, and they all decided to leave before their presence became more noticeable than they wanted it to be. Why in the hell had they had agreed to meet him in a bar was beyond him. *Well, who in the fuck knows why people do what they do? Humans are predictable and unpredictable. There. That was your philosopher moment of the day.* Anyhow, on the way back to his house in the golf cart, they had drunk from their Evian bottles and had snuggled like they were doing right now on his boat.

They had asked him nothing about events back home. He wouldn't have told them anyway. What good would it do to inform Stansie that her father and brother were both dead. She'd freak, probably shatter a few of her water bottles. His contact in Canada had called him with the news. Immediately, he initiated his emergency protocol for checking in. His contact, who sounded just like him, used a throwaway phone and placed a short call to Salvatore "Street Sal" Gallo, the new underboss, and pledged his loyalty to the new Don. As he had foreseen, Street Sal accepted his call with grace, told him he would pass on the news, but that he had a lot of business to attend to and had to end the short call. Nico's contact had then dumped the phone and called Nico back with the news. This is what Nico wanted to hear; he knew he would not be suspected of anything. He had maintained the routine for years, and it had worked because it had never been necessary for him to come in and meet anyone in person. As long as the product got delivered, then he was fine driving the ghost ship. Speaking of ghost ships, he was reminded of a complaint about the final years of Don Russo's leadership. One of his other contacts had said that the organization operated like a ghost ship; every now and then, you might see a crew member on deck, but no one knew who in the hell was actually steering the vessel. None of that mattered to him. He was fine being alone and preferred it that way. No one knew about his place on South Bass except for the now-deceased Don Ilario Russo, his now-deceased son Ciro, and these two posers seated in his cockpit.

He had a revolver tucked into his cut-off shorts that was hidden by his untucked Tommy Bahama collared shirt. Since there were now only three living people who knew about the cave, himself and the Evian twins there on the bench, he had contemplated killing them on the way over and dumping their bodies. The old saying, 'Three can keep a secret if two are dead,' had come to mind. Then it would only be him, and he could control the narrative if Don De Luca ever made a visit, which would mean that he would have to find Nico's place first. It wouldn't be because of his slip at Park Place because he'd registered under the name Nick Collins. But then again, there were holes in the overall theory. There were people who had seen him pick them up at the Sterling State dock, the truck was still there, and he figured the Don's men would be able to put two and two together and figure out one—that he had helped, and two—where he lived. When they found that out and didn't find Conrad and Stansie, they'd pin their disappearance on him and would either torture him to find out more, and, of course, he would break, and then the whole thing would come out. Hence, he had decided that the best option was to drop these two off, head back to South Bass and wait. He knew that Stansie and Conrad didn't have a prayer of living once they were found. So what if they talked? He'd explain that he was protecting the money for Don Fabian, and, of course, he would show the Don where it was. Better yet, a huge shipment of heroin was to arrive in Canada in a week, and he would pick it up on *Apollonia's Ashes* and show it to the Don at his house to prove how reliable he was. Then, he would help the Don's men bring the boxes up from the cave, probably take a small cut, and all would be well. He was willing to risk the location of his safe house being discovered if it meant staying alive— or at least staying alive long enough to enjoy some more of the wonderful white powder—stuff was insanely good! Plus, maybe he'd invite the Don to summer at his house. An A-plus idea. He'd show Don Fabian the best time he'd ever had. He might even get promoted. Yeah, then someone else could worry about getting the product from Canada to Detroit. He'd served his time in the trenches. Now, it was time to *par-tay*.

He smiled at his reflection in the stainless-steel wheel. He knew how to play both sides in the big game. In fact, he was pretty sure he had a trump card on Don Fabian that no one else knew about. Five years ago, he had taken his boat on a nighttime sail in Lake St. Clair after a delivery. And as he passed by Don Fabian De Luca's waterfront mansion, he'd seen the strangest thing through his night-vision goggles. Just before 2 a.m., a scuba diver emerged from the water and climbed up the ladder bolted to Fabian's sea wall. Nico had grabbed his cell phone, ready to call and say there was an intruder, but didn't get the chance as he saw Fabian's bodyguard, GiGi Rizzo, jog across the immaculately cut backyard grass and shake hands with the man as they both stood on the sea wall. Nico had focused his night-vision goggles on the man and saw his profile perfectly when the man turned toward Lake St. Clair and set the rest of his gear down on the sea wall. Then, he had watched as the men headed toward the pool house. After an hour of waiting for them to emerge, he had gotten bored and sailed away. He told no one what he had seen. That's a sure way to *lose* the big game. For months, he had no idea who the man was—definitely not a member of The Detroit Association. Then, while watching the news before making a delivery, which had become a superstition, he had seen the man on the television screen. Special Agent Terrance Nolan. A Fed. Why in the hell was The Association's underboss meeting with a federal agent? There had been no major arrests lately. And now he remembered how it had come to him halfway across the Detroit river later than night: Fabian De Luca was an informer who had bought himself some immunity if things ever got bad. He had thought of bringing it to the attention of Don Russo but decided that he had no proof, and, because of that, he would soon go *poof!* No, it was better to hang on to that information and use it when the time came. And now it had. He reached a hand in both of his shorts pockets and felt his own cell phone in one pocket and the one that Don Russo had given him in the other. No need to keep that one anymore. A few miles out, and he'd drop it into the depths of Lake Erie.

He lowered the mainsail and motored toward Sandy Creek, which would take them to the public boat launch.

"Almost there," he said to them. "Nice and easy like I said it would be."

Stansie twisted her head back and smiled at him.

*Damn, if I wasn't sure that Conrad could take me, I would have already been hittin' that.* When she had first turned away from him the other day, his mind had shouted, *Mamma Mia! Look at that upside-down heart of an ass!* He smiled back and shook his body as if he had just gotten a shiver.

*Banish those thoughts from your mind right now.*

Stansie had seen him shake. "Okay?" she asked.

"Yeah, just keepin' active. Easy to zone out when you've been at the helm for a while."

Her smile returned, and she turned around.

*Man, that was close.*

His passengers both finished off their bottles of water and headed below to use the head and change. Good. Would give him a chance to concentrate. Didn't need to see any more of her in that swimsuit.

A few minutes later, they emerged. Stansie was wearing a coverup, and Conrad had put his white t-shirt back on. They each had a fresh water bottle, and Conrad carried the bag with the rest of their stuff.

*Good. Let's get you two off to your death sentence.*

He swung the wheel to port, and they were soon at the dock.

There were no other boats waiting at the launch. In fact, the area was so quiet, all that could be heard was the water gently lapping against the hull and the occasional rubbing of the port rail against the two fenders he had thrown over to protect the boat from the dock. Perfect. They sat in the cockpit, and he went over the plan again.

"Now, go back to your tent, relax, stay a few days, and then head home. We're all set."

"Are you sure we shouldn't call my brother and check in?" Stansie said.

Nico raised his hands in a questioning gesture. "I am in no position to tell you what to do or what not to do, Madame Russo. I just know that I am responsible for your safety and that your brother has told me that you should have no contact with him while you wait here for a few days. As we know, he did say that if anything went wrong, he would contact *you* and let you know what to do. Having served your family for many years, I know enough not to go against those orders."

Conrad spoke to Stansie. "That sounds reasonable, sweetie."

She nodded. "I just wanted to make sure."

"Of course, of course," Nico said, patting her shoulder. "No one is getting to you or the family money."

Conrad turned to Nico and extended his hand. "Thanks for taking care of us. I liked working with you—good diver."

"It was a pleasure." He looked at Stansie. "I'll do anything for my godfather."

They disembarked, and Conrad cast off the lines. Nico motored aft and, when he had cleared the end of the dock by enough, put a starboard twist on and then headed back out to sea. He looked back and watched as they walked down the pier toward the campground and their unhappy destiny.

# 20

## FBI Detroit Field Office

## *3 Days Ago . . .*

S pecial Agents Terrance Nolan and Patrick Bruno were seated in Nolan's office as they had been yesterday—before everything went haywire. Patrick felt like he was in a crypt. The overhead light was off, and the drapes were half-closed, allowing a single shaft of bright sunlight into the room that hit the floor to the left of Nolan's desk. To the right, a small green-shaded lamp by the wet bar was turned on, which bathed the area around the bar in an emerald glow, like a traffic signal hanging over an intersection at night. Patrick could see the hard outline of Nolan's features, but the weathered veteran agent's clothes and face and hands all seemed to blend together into a dull gray color, similar to the late morning's mood. The initial musty smell of the office—like entering a back room of an ancient library or a confessional booth at church— had been replaced with the aroma from the coffee in the pot on the wet bar.

209

After sucking down a mug of coffee at home and a travel mug of it on the way in, Patrick had switched to a bottle of water and had been popping spearmint Tic Tacs for the last hour. Nolan's mug was on his desk, but he hadn't touched it since Patrick had entered the office. The greetings to each other had been short, and the men now sat in silence. Yesterday had been tough.

The scene Patrick had witnessed when they showed up outside the Red Robin Lounge had been unlike anything he had seen before. The forensics team was already taking pictures, taping off the area, collecting evidence, and making measurements. Blood was still pooled on the pavement where Ciro Russo and his driver Giuseppe Manetti had been mowed down. It was splattered all over the hood of the limousine from where John Conti had been shot by one of the rushing assassins; John had died of his wounds as had the three assassins, Jack Kurzweil, Billy Beadle, and Steve Cook. Cook had gotten close enough to wound Conti, which had made Conti's weapon jerk up and fire the rounds that had hit and killed poor Nancy Murphy. By the time they had arrived, the girl had been pronounced dead, and the mother and father had been taken away. The bloodstains on the sidewalk in front of Five Guys were like red tentacles extending out from a central blob. Nolan had flown into a rage, running across the street and kicking the limousine until he had put a huge dent in the middle of the rear passenger's side door. One of the forensics team members had yelled, *"Hey, get the hell out of here. You're tampering with the evidence!"* About to hit the man, Nolan had seen the front door to the lounge open up. He then walked into the Red Robin and threatened to arrest every one of the patrons. After being restrained by a host of Detroit police officers, he steamed out the front door and headed down Monroe Street. Patrick had thought of going after Nolan but decided to let him cool off. Then, the Detroit Police chief had arrived. He was shown the scene in front of the Red Robin Lounge and then escorted across the street. His special assistant couldn't catch him in time as the old veteran dropped to his knees by the bloodstain in front of Five Guys and wept.

"What do you think happened?" Patrick asked.

"I stayed up most of the night reviewing all of the 209s and 302s, trying to see if there was something I had missed along the way from Nineteen."

"You told me you were heading home. I wish you would have let me know that you had decided to stay. I could have helped."

"Sorry. Old workaholic habits die hard. Plus, as you've noticed, I'm not the best collaborator. Yet another reason why it's time for me to retire. All this cooperating, sharing, and groupthink bullshit is just another way for lazy agents to hide. 'Oh, I'll have to talk to my team about that,' and, 'I really couldn't say, we'll have to take a look at it together,' and, 'I might offend someone if I do a better job.' What a crock. I'm glad I'm leaving when I am."

"Well, if you're going to work on anything related to this, I want in, okay?" Patrick said. He had to assert himself now. After yesterday, there was no more waiting. Nancy Murphy could have been one of his own kids.

Nolan put up his hands. "Got it. 'Bout time someone stood up to me."

"I'm not challenging you. I just want to move on this. We lost a kid yesterday."

Nolan became somber and looked away from him. "I know." He settled his gaze on something outside his office window. "The costs," he said in a whisper, one that Patrick was not sure if Nolan meant Patrick to hear.

"What in the hell does that mean?"

Nolan's eyes swiveled over to him. "I mean the costs of letting Cosa Nostra exist. Usually, we take the attitude of, 'Let 'em just cannibalize each other.' And many times, it is that simple. But days like yesterday prove that it's never just those guys who get axed. And that's the toughest part of this whole business."

"And all of the families that are affected by the sale of illegal drugs."

"Still gotta play the long game. The short game will get you thinking that every loss is as big as yesterday's." Nolan leaned back, his face tilting up at the ceiling. "Our situation is like breaking the Japanese and German codes in World

War II. If the allies would have suddenly started to win every battle, our enemies would have known that the codes were broken and changed them. The allies had to engineer the wins and losses so that they always came out ahead—like winning six out of every ten times—but also so that the axis powers still felt like their codes were safe. Working with Nineteen has been like that. We have to protect his identity, and, unfortunately, that means losing some battles that we know we could win."

Patrick didn't like it but knew it was true. Lose some short-term battles in order to one day win the war. He wondered what battles Nolan had watched law enforcement lose over the years to maintain the overall winning percentage. He wondered which ones he would purposely have to lose in the coming years.

Nolan rocked his chair back up; the noise took Patrick out of his thought.

Patrick's eyes had now adjusted to the lack of light in the room, and he could make out Nolan's eyes, staring at him. "Looks like you got your wish, though," Patrick said.

For the first time, Nolan looked offended, like Patrick had just opened a private door that was private for a reason. "What do you mean?" His tone was stern and his eyes cold.

"Nineteen is now the boss, right?"

Nolan relaxed. "I guess if there is a silver lining to yesterday, then that is it."

"How do we know he didn't engineer it?"

"Not his style," he said, but then backtracked. "I mean anything is possible, but I just don't see it. Every time I have spoken with him recently, he hasn't been short on complaints about the situation, but I never got the sense that he wanted to do anything about it." Nolan swiveled in his chair, moving his thick legs from one corner of the desk to the other. "No, my money is on the old consigliere Silvio Verratti. He's disappeared."

"How long ago?"

Nolan took out a pack of cigarettes. Throw a cowboy hat on Nolan, and he could've been the Marlboro Man. Nolan shook out a cigarette then offered one to Patrick.

"Won't the smoke alarm go—"

"Took out the battery. Screw the regulations." He lit up.

The familiar scent reached Patrick's nostrils. His father had been a Marlboro customer, and it had eventually killed him. Emphysema. Like breathing through a restaurant straw every day. *No thanks.*

"He was last seen a few days before Ciro's assassination. He could be halfway to Tahiti by now for all we know."

*Did we talk about this yesterday?* He searched his memory. *No, we didn't. Why not?* "How come you didn't bring that up yesterday?"

Nolan took a long drag and then blew two smoke rings toward the ceiling. His dad had done this too, but Patrick had never figured out how to do it in his brief stint as a smoker. "I thought I did," Nolan said. "But maybe we got too caught up in the Nineteen business."

"Still, how would you know that he was last seen a few days ago? Do we have a surveillance operation going on?"

Nolan smirked. "I'm impressed. You work fast, but not too fast."

Patrick ignored the compliment, waiting for the answer.

"Nineteen called me last night."

"Last night!"

"Don't worry. I was going to tell you." He took another drag. "Truth is, he got spooked by the whole thing and wanted me to know that he had nothing to do with it. I might add that he's also a man of letters who is well-read. After all of our time together, we couldn't avoid discussing the irony of the situation and how many times something like this has happened throughout the history of the world. Then, he told me about Silvio Verratti."

Patrick's face started to get red, and he loosened his collar, which was wet with the sweat from his neck as he felt his body start to heat.

"Don't get all sore on me now," said Nolan. "I trust you, but we've only worked together on this for a single day. I've been running this guy for years. I called headquarters immediately after I got off the phone with him last night. They want to see where he leads."

"You should have told me first thing this morning."

"Yeah, I know. Sorry. Like I said...old habits. Got some good info from him, though."

His professionalism returned. *Don't be pissy right now. This guy's been on the front lines for a lot longer than you have. Cut him some slack.* "What did he have to say?"

"He said that even though the situation was not of his making, he intended to continue working with me. So, I pressed him for his organizational chart to see if he meant it or not." He opened up a desk drawer and took out a piece of paper. "Typed it up last night. Take a look."

Patrick took the paper from him as Nolan lit another cigarette. *Sonofabitch sucked the first one down fast.* He read.

## THE DETROIT ASSOCIATION

### BOSS

Fabian De Luca

<u>Driver/Bodyguard</u>
Gino Gregorio "GiGi" Rizzo

### UNDERBOSS

Salvatore "Street Sal" Gallo

## CONSIGLIERE

Pietro "Papa Pete" De Luca

## STREET BOSS

Leonardo "Leo" De Luca

## CAPOREGIMES

1. Marco Greco
2. Dino Roselli
3. Andrea "Handy Andy" Casale
4. Anthony "Black Jack Tony" Scala
5. Roman Abruzzi
6. Giancarlo Abruzzi

## FLORIDA

Dante "Miami" Marino

## CANADA

Nico "River Nicky" Colombo

## OHIO

Michael "Buckeye Mike" Romano

## CALIFORNIA

Paolo "Sunshine Paulie" Esposito

"Promoted his son?"

"Perks of being on top. You want some coffee? I love coffee when I'm smoking."

"No, thanks," Patrick said and continued to study the chart. Nineteen moved fast.

*Is Nolan absolutely sure that Fabian didn't order the hit on Ciro?*

Nolan grabbed his mug and went over to the wet bar, where a half-full coffee pot sat on a burner. His cigarette hung from his lips as he poured and then added cream from the wet bar's refrigerator. He finished the concoction by adding a heaping spoonful of sugar and stirred with the spoon. He toasted Patrick, "Here's to the breezes that blow through the treeses, that lift the skirt above the kneeses, that reveals the spot that teases and pleases, oh what a snatch…down the hatch." He drank; Patrick just stared at him.

Nolan was on his way back to the desk when Patrick asked, "But why would Silvio Verratti want to have Ciro killed?"

"Because maybe he thought he was getting passed over. I know one thing I did say yesterday was that many of these guys didn't think Ciro was ready. They take seniority pretty seriously."

"Except Nineteen, of course?"

Nolan coughed. "One giant shit soup. Trying to understand it all is like trying to separate the ingredients after it's already been made."

*It might help if we knew who made the soup,* Patrick thought. "Who is Pietro 'Papa Pete' De Luca?" Patrick asked.

"Fabian's uncle." Nolan inhaled; the end of his cigarette glowed crimson. Then, he exhaled a cloud of blue smoke. "The man is a legend in the Detroit mafia. Was semi-retired, but it's a wise choice by Fabian—steadies the ship so to speak. Don Russo's wife, Angela, is extremely close with him, so it will smooth the transition over. Papa Pete would never have taken the position if Fabian had ordered the execution of Ciro. Ilario, Pietro, Silvio, and Rudolpho Abruzzi—"

The last name rang a bell, and Patrick looked at the paper. Roman and Giancarlo Abruzzi were both capos for Fabian.

Nolan had seen him searching the document. "Yeah, Roman and Giancarlo are Rudolpho's sons."

"The old man still alive?"

"As far as I know," said Nolan. Then, he continued. "Anyway, Ilario, Pietro, Silvio, and Rudolpho were the best of friends in the glory days of the seventies and eighties, when, from what Nineteen told me along with my own research, The Association basically did whatever it wanted to do. However, Silvio always thought he was smarter than Ilario, and those decades of resentment could have spilled over when Ilario passed away. Ciro was fair game."

"Did Nineteen tell you that last bit?"

"That and also that Ciro had been badmouthing Silvio, which is tough to take because if you are the Don's son, you get to say whatever you want, and no one can do anything about it. From what I hear, Ciro was a spoiled brat who was not the sharpest knife in the drawer."

Patrick crossed his legs. "So, he makes his uncle consigliere, his son street boss, and," Patrick ran his hand down the paper, "Salvatore 'Street Sal' Gallo his underboss."

"Another solid move. Street Sal is universally respected by everyone. On one hand, he has no single loyalty to anyone, which is why everyone trusts him, and on the other hand, he is completely old school and devoted one hundred percent to The Association. He's like a hybrid—half independent operator, half company man."

"Does De Luca have any legitimate businesses?"

"For sure. Main one's a pizza parlor called De Luca Pizza & Pasta. It's a typical move by these guys. They have at least one legit biz so when they make a purchase, they can always say where the money came from. Also, if they're ever on parole, one of the conditions is that they have to show regular and acceptable employment. His pizza joint is his major cover. Other interests include bakeries, funeral parlors, roofing companies, concrete suppliers, construction unions, garment shops, car dealerships…the sonsabitches are everywhere."

He was beginning to see why the fight on organized crime had lasted so long. Taking out their gambling, loansharking, extortion, and theft would cripple them, but it was the mafia's reach into the businesses Nolan had just listed that made it difficult to win absolutely. They couldn't give the streets back to the criminals, but some of the criminals were legitimate business owners who didn't want the streets.

*Jesus. After Nolan retires and I shake the tree a little, what in the hell is going to fall out?*

"Wondering why Cosa Nostra still survives?" Nolan asked.

His head felt like it was being squished like a grape—everything they had gone over turning to mush. He rubbed his temples, then said, "Yeah."

"The main reason is because it mirrors American capitalism. It constantly adapts and finds new ways to make its business model work. It also has some guaranteed sources of revenue: gambling and construction. Always going to be people willing to risk their hard-earned dollars in an attempt to get more. Always going to have buildings going up." Nolan took a tissue from a box on his desk and blew his nose. "If people are gambling, chances are they're going to need a loan shark. You can almost hear the conversation now, can't you? Loan shark to prospective client: 'You know what you're committing to, right? You can walk away right now.' But we both know the gambler isn't walking away. And so the Ferris wheel goes round and round. Highs and lows and highs again. And, remember, with construction, you have to think of it like a mob tax. Developers and real estate tycoons in every major city have to deal with Cosa Nostra. But the way they avoid prosecution for any possible collusion is they always claim that they have nothing to do with the construction unions. There's never a direct connection. But the concrete, the windows—you name anything that goes into a building and, believe me, the mob is taking its cut."

Patrick felt even worse, but he could not sulk now. *Try to concentrate on the business at hand—figure out how to win later.* "I see your lost drug runner is still listed as the Canadian point of contact," he said.

Nolan tapped his cigarette, and the tip of ash fell onto a file folder on his desk. "What can I say, the guy must be getting the job done. We still need to find him, though, see what his routine is. No one's been able to crack it yet."

Patrick leaned back. "Well, now everyone in the building knows that I'm taking over for you."

"Life happens. Maybe it's better to get it out in front of everyone early. Talk to Maggie Schiff later today and see if she's interested in helping you run Nineteen. I thought about it some more last night, and I'm even more certain than I was yesterday about your choice. You're going to need a solid agent who is loyal going forward. Those parents are going to be out for blood after they put their daughter in the ground. We're gonna take some heat, but there was no way to predict this. The Detroit Association had done away with this type of power move almost a century ago. We've got headquarters behind us too. I called this morning and gave them a run down. We'll keep 'em posted if there are any developments. Naturally, they want to know where Silvio Verratti is too."

What little comfort he had with the turnover had evaporated after the shooting outside of the Red Robin Lounge. Now, he felt completely at the mercy of Nolan and how much the veteran agent decided to tell him. And even though Patrick thought that he had acquitted himself well in this meeting, he did not have an optimistic feeling going forward—at least not in the short term. "And me?" Patrick asked.

"I told them that we had started our turnover, but now that this has happened, I could see them extending me for another month until you've got a handle and the new regime is settled in. I'm actually envious of you."

*Great.* "Why?"

"Because I worked years with Nineteen, thinking that if we got him installed as Don that we'd finally be in a place to take down the whole show. But now it's going to be you who gets to pull the lever."

"Easier said than done."

Nolan was in stitches. "You see? That's what I like about you. Always realistic. Probably going to keep you sane and alive."

*Or fired.* "How about the press?"

"Ah, the fucking media. They'll probably interview me later today. Blew 'em off this morning, let the bigwigs at headquarters deal with those assholes."

"What are you going to give them?"

"They'll want some tough talk and probably start throwing around words from their Associated Press Style Guide," Nolan mocked. "They'll get all hot and bothered when I bring up *task force* and *manhunt* in regard to finding out who was responsible for the hit on Ciro Russo that, of course, led to the death of innocent little Nancy Murphy. I'll get all serious, maybe point a finger or something. Twenty bucks says that right after I end my interview, there will be a few politicians in the wings waiting to duke it out over gun control."

"I get that it's a show," Patrick said. "But yesterday...the kicking of the limousine and the threats inside the lounge...didn't seem like you were putting on a show then."

Nolan held his cigarette between his index finger and thumb. His hand was frozen a foot above the file folder he had been using as an ashtray, and, for a moment, they both watched the smoke rise.

Patrick had been wanting to talk about the episode since it had happened yesterday. He'd seen law enforcement officers come apart during a tragedy before, but Nolan's anger seemed to be pointed at some distant object that was out of view for everyone except him. Patrick had told his wife about what had happened to Nancy Murphy, and they had both immediately gone into their children's rooms and kissed them on the forehead while they slept. *What was eating at Nolan?* His answers and wisdom the previous day had seemed a bit curmudgeonly, but there had been nothing that even neared the intensity Patrick saw when Nolan arrived at the scene.

Nolan stubbed out his cigarette. He did not reach for another. "You never get used to seeing an innocent life taken."

Patrick was about to probe deeper when they were interrupted by frantic knocking at the door. He and Nolan were up in an instant, but before they could reach the handle, the head administrative assistant, Gabrielle Howe, rumbled through the doorway. She was out of breath, her normally smooth auburn hair looked like it had just survived a wind tunnel, and the armpits of her light blue blouse were soaked.

"Jesus, Gabby, what is it?" Nolan asked in a concerned tone.

She bent over to catch her breath. "The press is downstairs, and they want to talk *now*," she said. "I don't think I can hold them off any longer."

Nolan looked at his Rolex and shook his head in disgust. "Fuckin' bottom feeders." He turned to Patrick. "Well, you ready?"

# 21

## Sterling State Park, Michigan

## *2 Days Ago . . .*

The golden sun was barely over the horizon, and Conrad Cranston and Stansie Russo made their way along the six miles of the Sterling-Marsh Trail. They were now on the 2.9-mile loop that circled Hunt Club Marsh. Conrad was feeling relaxed, strong. There were a few interpretive areas and an observation deck coming up where they could stop to rest and enjoy the solitude of natural weeps, chirps, and buzzes. Much better than the human-made machines that honked, blared, and beeped. The peaceful yet vibrant energy of the morning's lush green surroundings, where everything was in focus and teeming with life, reminded him of his time with Brad on Lake Huron when they would sit in the stern of the boat, eating sandwiches and drinking ice-cold coke after a dive, feeling the sublime combination of the cool wind refreshing them while the sun warmed their bodies. Like those halcyon days on the water, there had been few words and much reflection on the trail so far today.

After a quick morning dip in Lake Erie to wake them up, they were now hiking with a purpose; working out was key to their physical and mental health— and to staying clean. Conrad had four Evian bottles in his backpack. Two were empty, and two had yet to be opened. They had started early because if they didn't start early, then they risked skipping a day, and skipping a day meant breaking routine. Breaking routine meant that other ideas would begin to form as to how they might spend the day. And, from painful experience, when it got to imagining the possibilities for an unstructured day, the schedule *always* narrowed to one devastating event.

He was impressed by Stansie's dedication, discipline, and focus. The moment they had left Don Russo's mansion, he had started to wonder about life outside of the protective grounds. But it was Stansie who held firm every time he had pursed his lips and tilted his head to one shoulder and then suggested something out of the routine to try, always ending with, *"Whaddya think?"* She made sure they always had water and that they started every morning with a workout. While waiting for Nico Colombo to pick them up at the park, they had set up their tent and then had a sex marathon inside it next to the pile of black duffel bags—partly fueled by the excitement of their mission and partly fueled by their need to be close to each other. They had done push-ups and sit-ups on the sailboat while en route to the island, and she had asked Nico to lower the sails a few times so that they could swim around the boat for a few minutes. He had complied, albeit with a somewhat mystified expression. They hadn't touched a single cold beer in the galley's refrigerator even though Nico kept offering every time he went below to fetch one for himself. At the island, it had been more push-ups, sit-ups, swimming, and a stroll to the village of Put-in-Bay. They had wanted to recline in Nico's sunroom that was built over the deck, but Nico had said that, unfortunately, they couldn't because the decking was being repaired and refinished. There was also a strange smell near the sliding glass door that led from the house to the deck, but Conrad had determined that it must be some of the stain Nico was using. Anyway, the sex had been better than ever in Nico's guest room, and they had followed the same exercise routine on the boat ride back to Sterling State Park.

She told him after the swim this morning that the baby she carried inside of her would be healthy, and nothing was going to stand in her way. Now that she had helped her father out, she would start making preparations for them to get their own place. Conrad had agreed in the way he always agreed with her: confident toothy smile on the outside, tornado of butterflies on the inside.

A few bikers whizzed by, and, as if Stansie was energized by the speed at which the bikes opened the distance between them, she picked up the pace. Lagging a few paces behind, he admired her strong legs and fit rear in her black stretch pants. He admitted that he drew strength from her determination, and that made him comfortable. His white t-shirt was wet under his armpits and underneath the backpack's straps. One of the interpretive areas was coming up. He picked up his pace, and his long legs enabled him to draw even in half-a-dozen strides. She gave him a quick smile of approval and then focused on the trail ahead.

They stopped at the interpretive area, and he pulled two energy bars and both fresh water bottles out of the backpack. For a few minutes, they quietly ate and drank and looked out over the marsh. Stansie's crinkling wrapper broke his attention away from a flock of birds that was flying low across the water.

He grabbed the wrapper and threw it in the open backpack that was at his feet. "You're moving well," he said, attempting to infuse a little athlete-speak into the conversation.

"Confession?"

"Please."

"I've never been hiking before this trip."

"Never?" he said, his voice flush with shock. "You must have gone camping sometime while growing up?"

She shook her head no. "We made trips all over the world to five-star hotels and beach bungalows but never any sort of hiking." She took a swig of water. "I have been missing out. This is fantastic."

"Always enjoyed the outdoors. Where I'm from, there wasn't a lot to do, so you spent most of your time as a kid running through the woods or playing in a park."

She took off her sunglasses and wiped them off with the bottom of her white tank-top. "My childhood was very controlled. As I got older, there was freedom, yes, but it was always with a few of my father's men following at a distance." She motioned to the trees, water, and trail. "I never had any of this."

"Ever cross-country skied before?"

"No," she said.

It amazed him. He felt closer to her than anyone he had ever met. But there was so much he didn't know about her that would have come out in the first few dates had they gone that route. The explosion of emotions he had experienced as they had navigated rehab together had postponed the superficial, trivia-like information like favorite foods, favorite movies, and favorite places to shop for clothes. He had been somewhat fearful that once these details started to come out, they would find that they had little in common. And, for him, having little in common was usually a recipe for a short, sex-filled courtship with no future.

Fortunately, as particulars about their lives—interests, curiosities, preferences—emerged the past few days, he had realized that his fear was unfounded. They had many interests in common, and now he could add hiking to the list. In terms of drugs, they had tried everything on the menu, well beyond what most people would ever risk trying over a lifetime, and so anything outside of that realm felt new and exciting and worth a try. They admitted in counseling sessions back at Don Russo's house that once drugs become the thing to do, all other options bow to the addiction first and then are eliminated by it.

"When this place is covered with snow in six months, we'll get skis and hit these trails."

"As good a workout as hiking?"

He exhaled in a laugh of defeat. "Yeah, just colder."

She took a long drink of water and then looked up and down the trail. "What's the name of that huge trail that ends in Maine? I'm drawing a blank. Starts with an A."

"The Appalachian Trail?"

"Yes." She pointed to her stomach. "After this one is born, do you want to hike it?"

He looked away and didn't answer.

"What is it?" Stansie asked.

He turned toward her. "Six years ago, I was supposed to hike the trail with my brother."

She put her water bottle back inside the backpack and then rubbed his shoulder. "What happened?"

He told her about his wandering, his initial struggle with drugs, all of the planning and preparation that had gone into the hike by his brother, Brad, and his sister, Heidi. Then, he got to the morning when he was supposed to board the plane from Detroit to Atlanta.

"I had my bag all packed, was in the best shape of my life—with the exception of right now—and was staying at a friend's house in Detroit who was going to take me to the airport in the morning. So, I'm in the guest bedroom bed, aiming my new flashlight at the ceiling and turning it on and off. My backpack is leaning against the small dresser in the corner, and my hiking boots and socks are lined up neatly in front of it. I think about how tomorrow is going to be a big step for me. I had been sober for about a year at that point, filling my time with hiking, camping, and working out with Brad to get ready for the trail. Not an ounce of fat on me. I turn on the light and do a survey of the room. Nothing moves. There are some old stuffed animals in a net above a corner dresser, and the light from the flashlight reflects off of their glass eyes back at me like they all have headlights shooting out of their eye sockets. I turn off my light, and my friend's house is absolutely quiet. I close my eyes and start to breathe.

"Then I hear this *BANG!*" he said, hitting his right fist into his open left hand. "And it's like the front door has been opened and ripped off of its hinges. I sit up, listening. Then, I hear the door shut. The hallway light comes on, and I can see the light outlining the door. I start to ease my legs out of bed so that I can get at the revolver in my backpack."

"You had a gun? What for?"

"The trail. I had read about some fatalities over the past few decades and got spooked. I wanted to be able to defend myself and Brad if we got into trouble. Looking back, it was stupid."

"What about your friend? Were you worried about him?"

Conrad paused and took a sip from his water bottle. It was a bit too planned, and she seemed to pick up on it.

"Oh, it wasn't a *he*, was it?"

He put the top back on the bottle. "No. We had dated before, but it was long over. She just offered me a place to stay for the night because she lived close to the airport. I wasn't worried about her because she said she was going out that night, and I hadn't heard her come in yet. I thought her place was about to be robbed, or it was the police doing a drug raid."

"A drug raid!" she said, looking to him. Her voice was full of shock and concern.

Conrad shook his head in embarrassment. "Her place was my party central for about a year. Strangers coming and going, you know the scene."

She took her eyes off him for a second, perhaps recalling a similar place in her own history, and then met his eyes and waited for him to continue.

"I should have just stayed in a hotel, but the truth is that I liked her company and hadn't seen her in so long that I wanted to catch up."

"Do you still have the gun?"

"I'll get to that. So, my knees are on the carpet in front of my bag, and I'm trying to unzip the top as quickly and quietly as I can. Then, I hear giggling outside my door. I relax a little, no longer feeling I'm in immediate danger. I get back to my bed, and the doorknob starts to twist, real slow, like in the movies. It opens, and she is standing there with a woman I've never seen before. When I asked them what they were doing, they said that they had been doing lines off of her patio table and, well..."

"You don't have to tell me this part," Stansie said. "What about the next morning?"

"I wake up alone, the sun shining in through the blinds. I know I've missed my flight. In fact, I'm so afraid to look at my watch that I take it off and sit with my head in my hands for I don't know how long. Finally, I look at my watch: It is *two* in the afternoon. I pick up my cell phone, and there are missed calls from my sister. I know that I could go to the airport, catch a later flight, make up some lame excuse, and that the hike could still happen. I'd take some shit from Brad and Heidi, but once we started, all would be forgiven. After all, they had invested so much in the adventure, they would trade a day for the damn thing to still happen."

"But you didn't go to the airport."

He shook his head no. "I went to the bank, withdrew my seven grand in cash—told them I was purchasing a used car and that I liked to use cash—and left two hundred dollars in the account. They give it to me in a half-an-inch stack of hundred-dollar bills, which fit right into the top zippered compartment of my backpack. I walk over to a rest stop, and the next thing I know, I'm traveling with a trucker named Roland on I-94 West."

"Did you ever say goodbye to the ladies?"

"They were still asleep in my friend's room when I left. Haven't seen 'em since."

"Where did you go?"

"At first, I had no idea where I wanted to go—just wanted to get as far away from Detroit, and Brad, and Heidi, and the Appalachian Trail as possible. In hindsight, I was doing what I always did: self-sabotaging. The first half-hour in the truck with Roland was quiet, but then we started to chat. Tells me he's been trucking for twenty straight years, working twenty-hour days and saving every dime, basically living out of the truck. Tells me he's forty-two and going to retire next year. Got a college degree from Central Michigan University, no debt, was going to go into grad school but said the hell with that, the open road is a-callin'. It gets comfortable. I tell him I have everything but my dissertation in History done and that I just need a break from the grind. He doesn't probe for information, and I don't probe any further. I can't explain it, but we realize that we both don't need anything from each other. Then, I remember I've got a gun and seven thousand dollars in cash in my backpack, and I get a little nervous. But he's got U2 in his disc changer, so I calm down. Says he's heading west, all the way to Omaha, Nebraska to deliver a shipment, load up, and then bring it back east. I tell him that's fine with me. Before we reach Battle Creek, we hit I-69 South and take it into Indiana, where we hit I-80 West. This is where Roland tells me, 'Now we just sit back and enjoy the ride. Only highway we'll need now.' I buy us lunch and coffee, and then we spend the night in Illinois." He took a swig of water. "Get an early start the next day. Well, we cross the Illinois-Iowa border, and he says to me, 'Got a surprise for you.' I start to sweat, not knowing what in the hell that means."

Conrad paused to wipe his forehead, both because he was sweating and because it served the need of his dramatic rendition of the story.

"I had nothing to worry about. I see his blinker go on, and the next thing I know, I'm in trucker's paradise: Iowa 80, Exit Two. Eight. Four, the largest trucker stop in the world. Good times, good times." He toasted her with his water bottle. "I mean, they've got everything: a barbershop, a library, fresh showers, a better food court than the mall, a laundromat, a shopping center, a movie theater, a dentist, a chiropractor." He smiled, remembering that this had been a good time in his life.

"So, what did you do there?"

"Ha. The better question is: How long did I do it? We have an incredible home-cooked meal at the Iowa 80 kitchen, then he says to me, 'You ready for a Hollywood shower?' So, I follow him into the gift store and we each purchase a shower ticket. I buy shaving cream and a razor—I hadn't planned on shaving during the hike—and we head to the third floor where the twenty-four private showers are. I come out of there a half-hour later, feeling like I've been born again. We catch a movie in the theater, Roland introduces me to a few of his old driver buddies in the driver den, and I sleep soundly in his cab."

"Where did he sleep? Wait a minute, where did *you* sleep the night before in Illinois?"

"In Illinois, I told him I was fine sleeping in my sleeping bag outside the truck. He protested, but I didn't want to be a burden. Now, the night I slept in the cab at Iowa 80, he was shacking up with his girlfriend in her cab. I guess they met there twice a week due to their schedules and made it work. The next morning, I hear the driver's side door open, and he asks me if I'm ready to get going. I tell him that I appreciate the offer, but just don't feel like leaving yet. We shake hands, and he says that he'll be back in a few days. I get my backpack, and he heads out." Conrad paused. "You know how long I stayed there?" Another pause. "Two months."

"How did you do that?" she asked, opening her eyes in wonder. Her voice had a beat to it that said, 'Tell me more!' Well, Brad had always said that he could spin a yarn. He agreed. Telling stories about past or even made-up events was sometimes more preferable than having to live in the present.

"I would just hang around, buy paperbacks at the gift store, take a hike during the day, stop and read, then come back, shower, and eat at my usual spot in the Iowa 80 Kitchen. Over dinner, I would scope out the diners, and after a week, I could spot who was hooking up with who, and I would follow them up to the driver den for a few nips of scotch. Then, I'd either get a recommendation of who to try and hook up with or one of them would offer me his or her empty truck cab for the night. Caught up with Roland at least once a week. Good dude. I met his girlfriend, Priscilla, and I've never laughed with anyone the way I laughed with them over dinners there. Even got invited to their wedding a few years after that. I never showed up." He looked away. "I regret that."

Stansie waited, and he started up again.

"They were going to settle down in Green Bay, Wisconsin. Roland was a huge Packers fan—always had a Packers hat on while he drove the truck."

"When we get settled, we should go see them," Stansie said.

"Seriously?"

"Yeah. Sounds like good people."

"They are. With the exception of scotch and Miller High Life, I was clean for my entire time in Iowa."

"And now you don't need those anymore, do you?"

Conrad exhaled and rubbed his hands together. "I still miss alcohol, all day every day. Remember, you're talking to a guy who, when it got really bad, used to celebrate sunrise and sunset with booze. Then, I moved on to days of the week. 'Wahoo! It's fuckin' Tuesday!' and stupid shit like that." He paused. "I just know now that I can't have it. Not even a sip."

"Maybe we should live in Green Bay."

"You wanna freeze your ass off?"

"C'mon, I'm from Michigan, and so are you."

"Well, there's Michigan freezin' your ass off, and then there's Green Bay freezin' your ass off. And I'll take the former anytime."

"Okay, what about Florida then?"

"Too hot. We'd spend half of our money on these," he said, lifting up his Evian water bottle."

"Okay, where then?"

"I haven't finished my Iowa story yet."

"I didn't think there was any more. You left after two months and headed back to Michigan, right?"

He looked across the marsh. "No, I stayed in Iowa..." his voice trailed off, "for almost three years."

"What?" she asked. "Where? I mean, *how?*"

He thought her tone had now escalated past 'Tell me more' to 'I *have* to know what happened. Right. Now.' Tears started to well up in his eyes, and the marsh's horizon started to resemble a corn field...and then a city...and then a building.

*I don't know if I can do this.*

She touched his face with her delicate hand. "Please, tell me the rest."

*What will she think of me?* He turned toward her, and she gave him a look that inspired him to risk because it was safe to do so with her; it had been since they had met. He wiped his eyes. "Okay, I'll tell you."

# 22

Iowa City, Iowa

## *September 2017 . . .*

Conrad Cranston, better known as Mr. C. to the children with cancer at The University of Iowa's Stead Family Children's Hospital, walked into the level eleven classroom and saw his reason for living. At one of the kidney-shaped tables was a five-year-old patient named Marcy Hart. As he put his portfolio on the tabletop and sat down, he thought that she looked smaller today, less upright. They hugged. *My God, there's nothing to her. She's lost weight again.* Her black Iowa Hawkeyes knit cap almost slid down over her eyes. Underneath the cap, he knew there was no hair at all, but he admired the girl's loyalty and devotion to her beloved Hawkeyes. *"You don't get it, Mr. C. In Iowa, we all love our Hawkeyes."* Her mother sat in a powder-blue-colored lounge chair nearby but out of hearing range to give Conrad and Marcy the privacy that the sweet but assertive little kindergartener demanded. Conrad grinned at the mother, and she gave a weak smile back. He thought he saw tears, but she looked down at her phone before he could confirm it. He had been Marcy's art teacher for two months now and knew that this time of the day was her favorite because she only got to have art every Friday when she and her parents traveled to the hospital for a round of treatment. He'd last seen her two weeks ago.

Back at Iowa 80, Priscilla had hooked him up with her laptop, and he had applied for a teaching license in K-12 art. Because of his distinguished undergraduate, graduate, and doctoral work in history, education, and a minor in art, he had miraculously qualified for a temporary certificate. Then, he had seen that the University of Iowa was located in Iowa City, only around forty more miles down Interstate 80. Not ready to return to Michigan, he had decided to give the academic game one last try. He'd rent a place, use some of his money to get a cheap laptop, and then make an appointment to meet with the History Department Chair. Roland had given him a lift, and he had rented an apartment in the plentiful sector of cheap student housing. Before Priscilla had driven off, she had helped him search for a job. There was a posting for an art teacher at the Stead Family Children's Hospital, and when he applied, he had found that his charm, easygoing manner with children, and temporary certificate were enough to get him to the final interview, where he taught a lesson with a group of young children who had cancer, while the staff watched. The kids loved him, and he won everyone over. The provisional teaching certificate was never checked to see if it had become a professional educator's license. He could draw, teach, and, most importantly, when the children saw Mr. C., their days got a little brighter. The parents also helped solidify his employment with their glowing reviews and positive word of mouth passed along to the hospital administrator in charge of the education program. He eventually moved into a nicer apartment away from campus, hosted Roland and Priscilla a few times, and was now dating a nurse named Tiffany who worked on his floor. He was sober, earning a good paycheck, dating someone who was going places in life, and helping kids endure something unimaginable. He was focused. Sometimes going to work, he laughed to himself about how it had all worked out so well for him. But he figured that life was a game of balance. With a lengthy record of self-sabotages behind him, he decided that it was time to *hit back*, whatever that meant. Now and again, he would think about the pain he had caused his family—especially Brad and Heidi because of the hike—but he was not ready to contact them. No, he needed a few more years to solidify his position, and then he would come home, apologize, and show them that he had turned things around. Then, he'd offer to hike the Appalachian Trail with Brad again and pay for the entire thing. As of right now, because of living a frugal and spartan existence since leaving Iowa 80, he had twenty-two thousand dollars saved up. After the hike, he would come back and live the rest of his days in Iowa City, perhaps marrying Tiffany, and then retire, going to Hawkeye sporting events and reading every book in the campus library—or maybe just re-reading Proust's *In Search of Lost Time* as many times as he could. For these and other reasons, Conrad Cranston never visited the University of Iowa's History Department Chair.

"And how are we today, young lady?" he said, untying the strings of his portfolio.

"Just fine, Mr. C."

He opened the portfolio and removed a sleeve of markers and white drawing paper. "Got a special assignment for us to work on."

After placing a piece of paper and a light blue marker in front of her, he said, "Any guesses?"

She twitched her nose and studied the marker. "Something fun?"

He smiled. "Have I ever told you what a good guesser you are?"

"No, Coach."

She had always alternated between calling him Mr. C. and Coach. His method was to give kids two options, which allowed for choice but also kept it simple. Every kid picked one and stayed with it, but not Marcy Hart. Sweet little Miss Independent used them interchangeably.

"Well..." he said, pausing to try and make eye contact with Marcy's mom. She was still zoned into her phone. "Someone told me that you got to see a pretty good movie this past weekend."

Her head lifted, and her eyes sparkled as if there was no hospital, no cancer, no problems in the world. "I did! I saw Frozen with mommy and daddy!"

"Guess who else saw it?" he said mischievously.

"Um...Mr. C!" she yelled, pointing at his chest.

Marcy's mother looked up from her phone, saw that there was nothing wrong, and returned her eyes to the screen.

"Yes, ma'am, I did," said Conrad. "So, you know what we're going to draw today? Anna and Elsa!"

"Oooh, oooh, can we make Elsa's snow castle too?"

Conrad pulled out a purple marker. "You bet we can. How about that tiny funny snowman too?"

"You mean Olaf, Coach?"

He snapped his fingers. "That's the one."

An hour later, Conrad had completed his drawings, and Marcy had her versions proudly displayed across the desk.

"Look at those," her mother said, standing behind her.

"It's just like the movie, mommy."

Marcy's mother started to cry. Something was different. Had they received bad news? Conrad reacted quickly. "Here, kiddo," he said, passing her one of his drawings. "Could you help color in the spots I missed for a minute?"

"Sure," she said and grabbed a handful of markers.

"I'll be right back. Gonna talk to your mom for a minute."

She had already started coloring and said, "Okay, Coach."

Mrs. Hart stood by one of the large windows that overlooked The University of Iowa's campus. She was dabbing her eyes with a tissue as Conrad arrived.

"Hi, Ashley," he said.

She turned toward him, eyes now puffy, and some of the makeup that had been hiding her wrinkles was gone. It was weird to notice, but he could tell that she had aged beyond what was apparent in her facial expressions. The way she moved was slower, and her immaculate way of dressing in expensive clothes two months ago had become jeans, a sweatshirt, and tennis shoes. "Conrad, they're giving her a month, maybe less."

His heart sank, and the inside of his mouth became like cotton. Then, his eyes started to get glossy, and, for a moment, he pondered taking the tears that were about to start dropping and putting them on his lips to make swallowing easier. "I thought—" His words trailed off because he *had not* thought about Marcy's condition. He had decided to not keep abreast of his patients' up-to-the-minute conditions, reasoning that if he knew, it would be too much for him to handle and make him a less effective art teacher. It had served him well for the past few years, but now, in this instance, he felt shallow—a fraud.

"After last month, we had hope," she said, "but she hasn't turned the corner. We got the news earlier this morning."

A tear bubbled on his right eye and then released. "I'm sorry. She's an incredible kid." He wiped his eye, but it was no use—they were coming too fast.

"My husband and I thought about taking her home after the news, but her class with you is one of the highlights of every visit. We couldn't take that away from her."

Conrad nodded, sniffling. "So, this will be it, huh?"

She rubbed his arm. "No, we've been invited to stay for the football game tomorrow night. As you know, one floor above us is the rooftop, and at the west end is the press box where families can view the home Hawkeye football games. We usually never stay for the game, but since Marcy has never seen a live game and this will be our last visit to the hospital, we've been invited to sit up there and watch the game." She wiped more tears from her face then handed Conrad a tissue. "We'd like you to be our guest in the press box with us tomorrow night."

His eyes had wandered back to the table. Marcy was bent over a drawing, concentrating, her little arm moving back and forth. "Where is Chad?"

She barely got out, "Downstairs, arranging hospice care for Marcy. We're going to try and make her as comfortable as we can at home."

He had a date with Tiffany planned, but there was no indecision in him. "I'll be there. What time?"

"Game starts at 7:30."

He motioned to Marcy. "Does she know?"

"About the game? Yes. About the news this morning? No."

"Does she know that you've invited *me* to the game?"

"I thought I would let you tell her."

"Okay."

They hugged.

"I'll wrap up the session," he said.

She nodded and then started tapping her fingers on the screen of her phone.

He would need to be strong, comforting, but not give anything away. Stay with routine. Routine is your ally. Routine gets you through. He gathered himself and walked over to Marcy.

"Got your picture colored, Mr. C.," she said with a wide smile that exposed her small mouth crowded with tiny white teeth.

"That you did," he said, sitting down next to her.

She slid the picture over to him. Elsa now had on a half-pink, half-red dress. "This is some of your best work, kiddo."

"Want me to do another one?" she asked.

"Well, I think our time is about up," he said.

She looked down at the table, the Hawkeyes cap starting to slide over her eyebrows. He nudged the cap back up her forehead.

"You know what, though? Your mom and I were talking about the big game tomorrow night, and guess what?" he said as joyfully as possible.

She titled her head up toward his. "What?"

"I have been invited to watch the game with you and your family."

Her eyes sparkled again. "Really?"

"Wouldn't miss it. We'll get to cheer your Hawkeyes on together."

"Yippee!" she yelled. Then, she looked at him, serious now. "But aren't they your Hawkeyes too?"

"Well, I'm from Michi...of course they are, ma'am. I'll be wearing my Hawkeye shirt tomorrow night."

She hugged him, and his eyes started to water again.

*Hold it together, Conrad. Just a few more minutes.*

Marcy's mother arrived at the table. "Time to go, sweetie. From your shout, I am guessing that you know that Mr. C. is going to watch the game with us tomorrow night?"

"Yes. I'm so excited."

Marcy rose from the table. Conrad pretended to be busy packing up. The truth was, he was just shuffling papers and markers around in no coherent way.

"See you tomorrow night, Coach," she said.

"Go Hawkeyes."

They left, and seeing that no one else was around, he broke down and sobbed at the desk.

A few hours later, he exited the hospital and began to walk home. His thoughts were on Marcy and her family and the impending loss they would soon experience. He had never lost a student yet, at least none that he had known of. When they stopped coming, he just assumed that they had been cured. Now, he realized how stupid that sounded. Marcy's mother was the first to ever tell him that he would be losing a student—*forever.*

He began crossing a street...and almost got hit by a car. The sidewalk appeared fuzzy, and the lights above each store on the strip were like a blur of the entire light spectrum. He leaned against the window of a store for a moment, trying to slow his breathing. He couldn't. The pressure was building. Now, he felt the weight of his other students who had not made it. Which ones were they? The situation was too much to handle.

The door to the store swung open, and he heard the sound of glass bottles clinking as a customer exited and walked down the street. Then, his vision came back, and another customer opened the door, holding a black, unmarked bag. He looked up at the sign above his head. Norman's Party Store.

His heart began to pick up pace, like a track athlete gaining speed during the final one hundred meters of a race. Tiffany would not be home tonight. He straightened his wobbly legs, and they began to move down the sidewalk, but his mind pulled them into the store.

The next evening, Marcy Hart and her family would witness, perhaps, the greatest tradition in all of sports. At the end of the first quarter, the packed crowd and both teams inside historic Kinnick Stadium turned in unison and waved up at the children and their families in the press box section of The University of Iowa's Stead Family Children's Hospital. From that point forward, it would be known as the 'Iowa Wave.'

Conrad Cranston never saw it. His previous night had consisted of watching almost a fifth of Jack Daniels disappear from the bottle and travel down his throat followed by the smoking of a joint with his neighbor, Irwin, a sociology professor whose favorite phrase was, 'America is a lie.' The first time they met, Irwin had told Conrad his view of what a true utopian society was and how the United States didn't have a chance in hell of ever becoming one. *"I've already been dragged across the empirical floor of evidence, kicking and screaming, and forced to admit that kids who grow up with two parents are statistically better off than those who grow up with only one parent. I'm not caving on anything else!"* Then, he had said that he sold weed and pills to his devotees, affectionately dubbed "Irwinians," for medicinal purposes. A bit wary of someone who overshared during a first encounter, Conrad had remained polite when they saw each other but had kept his distance. *"About time you took me up on my offer,"* Irwin had said when Conrad showed up at his door. *"I've told you a million times: We're both adults, and smoking a joint in the privacy of my backyard isn't going to hurt anyone. Ruh-laax. See you brought over a little Mr. Daniels for the occasion. Mind if I have a pull?"*

Tiffany had found Conrad on the bathroom floor, vomit everywhere. He stayed there until Sunday morning and did not see Marcy again. Nor did he see the new mandatory drug tests coming that the hospital instituted two weeks later. He failed, lost his job, lost Tiffany, and, two months later, was back in Michigan and well on his way to spending all of the money he had saved up.

Sterling State Park, Michigan

*2 Days Ago . . .*

Conrad wiped the corners of his eyes for about the tenth time and looked away from the marsh and back to Stansie. He said, "And that's what happened in Iowa, which eventually led me to you."

He had told the truth, which surprised him. There were a few places where he could have padded his position or drawn the attention away from his failure to try and start his listener's empathy IV, which was his usual procedure when manipulating a situation. But today, with Stansie by his side, he broke free from the ingrained routine. The words, "Still want to be with me?" slipped out of his mouth, and he realized that he actually meant them. Normally, his follow-up question was posed to put the spotlight back on himself and elicit an emotional response, usually pity, from his listener. Right now, it wasn't, and that made him feel good but also uneasy. For a man who had at many times over the course of his life wondered if he could get a doctoral degree in emotional hijacking instead of history, he felt the sorrow and relief that accompanied coming clean.

She was quick to hug him, but in no rush to let go. *Thank God.*

He took the gesture as part forgiveness, although he had nothing to be forgiven for from her. It was forgiveness from Marcy Hart that he needed but would never get. When he had shown up at Brad's house during the winter, three years after disappearing from the hike, he had used his brother's laptop to search for her obituary. A small part of himself held out hope that a miracle had occurred and that she was still alive. She was not. Marcy Hart had passed away two weeks after watching her beloved Iowa Hawkeyes play. Conrad had closed the door to Brad's guest room and wept.

Stansie eased herself away and gave a sympathetic look to his red eyes. She touched his face. "And now we have a chance to make things right for at least ourselves. I hurt people too. That's the way it goes in life, I suppose. We hurt people, we leave them, and then we never speak to them again. Months, years later, they enter our minds when we don't have a minute to think of something else, and we remember. We think about reaching out, but know it would be too out of place. Right now, you could contact Marcy's parents, but what good would it do for them? It might help you feel better, but then, once you had realized that you had hurt them again, you'd feel even worse." She grasped his elbow. "This is why it isn't always the right answer to atone with contact. Sometimes forgiveness is better at a distance."

He wiped his eyes with the bottom of his t-shirt and drank from his water bottle as if replenishing his tear supply for the next time he was moved by recalling another mistake he had made.

"That's all I can do at this point," he said. "Try to live a better life."

They packed up and started hiking again.

# 23

## St. Clair Shores, Michigan

## *2 Days Ago...*

FBI Special Agent Patrick Bruno reclined in his home office's leather chair. It was after nine in the evening, and a day had passed since his last meeting in Nolan's office. Three feet away, his wife, Tara, sat on the carpeted floor and leaned back against one of the bookshelves that lined the wall opposite the leather chair. Through the office's open window, he heard the sound of a car starting up and then driving off.

"And so that's everything I can tell you about what has happened and what I'll be doing for the next few years," Patrick said.

It was the first alone time they had had together over the past few days. Once things blew up downtown, he had spent the majority of his time at the office with Nolan. A meeting with Nineteen was being set up, but it would be a few weeks out, hopefully enough time for the mob hit and civilian girl fatality to leave the front page. Tara had not asked any questions about what he had presented to her. To him, she seemed all at once calm, realizing the demands of his work, but also distant as if whatever Patrick did over the next few years would do little to make life safer and better for the average citizen.

She crossed her legs and rubbed the toes of her right foot up and down her left foot, starting at the ankle, working them up to just beneath the toes, and then a retreat to the ankle. "I know you can't tell me what Nolan is turning over to you, but does he seem like a decent guy?"

Nolan had spent most of the past twenty-four hours doing exactly what he had told Patrick he would be doing: dealing with the media—issuing tough statements about justice, organizing a task force that wouldn't probably come together for at least another few days because of the bureaucratic nature of the District Attorney's office and the ineptitude of FBI Headquarters or so Nolan said. Patrick had to admit, however, that Nolan had been a magician with the press at the impromptu conference, using the perfect balance of charm and tough talk to satiate the reporters' thirst for information. He hadn't realized how quick Nolan was with misdirection or that his wit was sharp and calculated enough to both soothe and cut at the same time until he had heard Nolan perform live without a script. If it had been him giving the briefing...

And then there was the part that Patrick didn't like. Nolan's confidential calls with Nineteen. Why wasn't Patrick in on them? Nolan assured him that he would be soon, but that this was a delicate situation to maneuver and that Nolan had approval from headquarters to, and he quoted, *"leverage his extraordinary and delicate relationship with Nineteen to find out what happened and what the plan was to start collecting information now that the FBI had a Godfather as an informer."* Patrick had accepted this but hadn't stopped his review of Nolan's 302s and 209s.

Everything seemed to be in order, and he was starting to grasp the evolution of the relationship and the value of the information that Nineteen was producing. Then, just this afternoon, he had remembered what Nolan had said yesterday,

*"You never get used to seeing an innocent life taken."* And it was not so much the words that stuck out to him but the way that Nolan had lost his pompous demeanor about how he would handle the media and retreated inside himself—like a tortoise who had stuck his head out too far from the safety of his shell. This had prompted Patrick to go down the hallway to the workroom, where he began to dig through the database of innocent people killed by suspected mob action during the past twenty years. About to refill his coffee cup for the fourth time, he stopped on an article in the *Detroit Free Press* from 2007. A hit crew had apparently assassinated a capo at a downtown apartment complex. Forty-seven-year-old Vincent Trentino had been gunned down by four men in the hallway outside of his second-floor apartment on the morning of December 12th. Trentino had been wearing a Santa Claus outfit and had a bag full of presents that he was going to deliver to a hospital down the street. The article said that Trentino was one of The Association's top cocaine dealers and had previously served two prison sentences for possession and racketeering. He was survived by his wife and three young boys.

The tragedy, however, was that nine-year-old Debbie Archer, who lived in the adjacent apartment, had been struck and killed by a stray bullet. Patrick had checked the dates. Yes, Nolan was running Nineteen at the time, along with Carr. He went back and looked at the 302s and 209s from October 2006 to February 2007. There was no mention of Debbie Archer in any of the memos. Furthermore, the only mention of the incident was in a January 209, where Nolan had written, *"Spoke to Nineteen about the Trentino death. Nineteen assures me that he and The Association knew nothing about it and had nothing to do with it. Nineteen suspects east side gang hit because Trentino had recently raised the price on all products."* He searched the database and did not find any east side gang murders reported, and also the four assailants who had killed Vincent Trentino were never caught.

These items had raised some questions in Patrick's mind. Why didn't Nolan account for the civilian casualty in the 209? Did he lean on Nineteen to try and find out what had happened? There *had* to have been some retribution. What became of the east side gang? Why hadn't that been mentioned? After spending another few hours going through the records, he had found no civilian death that was similar to nine-year-old Debbie Archer's. Was this why Nolan had lost it at the downtown site the other day? He intended to get the answers to all of these questions.

"He's been a good source of information," Patrick said. "Had a lot of experience."

"Do you trust him?"

Mostly, but he needed to sit down and talk with him tomorrow. "Yeah, I do," he said.

She closed her eyes and started to breathe—in for eight counts, hold for four, and then out for eight more. For a minute, it was like he had a noise machine plugged in to protect a private meeting. They hadn't connected at all this week, emotionally or physically. Would she respond if he made his way across the floor and started in? Probably not. A year into their marriage, she had told him, *"Look, I'm a woman, Patrick. The puppy love and infatuation stage where eye contact would lead to disrobing and starting right in left us a while back. You've gotta warm me up first. Massage my shoulders, kiss my cheek, my forehead, my neck, then my lips. Rub on me, hold me. Talk nicely to me. Give me attention. Then, when I'm warmed up, proceed."* When he listened to this, it happened. When he didn't, it rarely did.

He dropped to the carpet and crawled over beside her. Her eyes opened. "Hey there," she said.

He began rubbing her shin bone, working his way up to her thigh. Then, he gave her arm a kiss. "The boys are in bed, right?"

Her cell phone rang.

"Leave it," he said, rubbing her shoulders now.

But her eyes had apparently caught sight of the caller, and she said, "It's Liz." She looked over at him, gave a smile that said she was sorry—he hated those—

and gave his leg a few quick pats. "I gotta take this. We'll pick back up in a minute."

Without giving him time to reply, she hopped up and left the room.

He rolled over onto his back and put his feet up on the ottoman. His lower back felt instant relief as he yawned and stretched his arms toward the ceiling. It was a good start. She'd be back, and they would finally get to connect. Everything was—

His wife's scream from the hallway jolted him upright, and he was at the office doorway in seconds. She was running down the hall toward him, tears streaming out of her eyes, wails leaving her mouth about every other bound.

"What in the hell is it?" he said.

She ran to his open arms and then sobbed into his shoulder. The cell phone dropped to the carpet.

He held her and then gently pulled her away, attempting to make eye contact. She was now hyperventilating.

"Calm down, sweetie. Calm down," he said, rubbing her back.

A door on the far end of the hallway creaked open, and his youngest poked his head out. "Daddy, what was that?"

In a calming voice, Patrick said, "Mommy just banged her foot on the banister again, and it really hurts. Sorry it scared you, buddy. Just head back to bed, and I'll check on you in a minute."

The little boy disappeared back into his room and shut the door.

He looked back down at Tara. "What is it, honey?"

"D-DD-DDUH-Dari," she finally got out. "Shhhh-shhhee-sheee's dead. Fffound her three miles from the detention center. Needle on the grass next to her. Heroin overdose."

He went to ask another question, but Tara just screamed into his shoulder, and he held her tightly against him. As she cried and cried, the shock turned to reality, and he found his insides empty and his throat with a lump that, when swallowed, would signify the start of his own hot tears.

His niece, fourteen, was gone forever.

# 24

## Sterling State Park

## *2 Days Ago...*

C onrad Cranston pulled the tent's door zipper all the way down until it touched the second zipper near the tent floor. The inside smelled mostly of Stansie's lotion and the campfire with just a hint of must left lingering from taking the rainfly off and airing the tent out earlier. He was still both emotionally and physically drained from the morning hike, but any burden he might have been carrying because of what he had revealed was gone. Hence, it was a different kind of tired that he felt, a good tired, and he projected that he was in for a night of deep sleep.

They had picked up dinner at a deli, showered, sat by the campfire for an hour and had smores, and were now in for the night. A small Coleman lantern hung from a loop of string woven into the highest point of the tent's domed ceiling. Two forest green sleeping bags lay side by side, each with a bottle of water next to it.

He stood up but then squatted down and checked the zipper again. When he turned around, Stansie was stretched out on her sleeping bag. He took off his shirt and threw it onto his backpack on the far side of the tent.

"Ready?" he said.

"Ready."

He switched on a flashlight and then turned off the Coleman lantern.

"You sore?" he asked while sitting down on his sleeping bag and rubbing his calves.

"A little," she said. "Feels good, though."

He rubbed each leg for another few seconds and then laid back. "Right on," he said.

The beam was focused on the tent's ceiling, and the light dissipated on the way down to the floor like the sea darkening the deeper one descended. He made a pair of rabbit ears with his fingers, got a brief giggle from Stansie, and then turned off the flashlight.

"So, no Florida and maybe no Green Bay. Where are we moving to?"

He'd forgotten that they hadn't continued that part of their conversation earlier. He put his hands behind his head. Laughter drifted over from another campsite and then died down. "I was thinking the Upper Peninsula."

"Isn't that just as cold as Green Bay?"

"Close, but if we're looking for peace and quiet, then the Upper Peninsula is where it's at."

"Never been there."

If she had said this earlier, he would have shown his astonishment. But after finding out that she had never been hiking before, the news did not surprise him. "It's a different way of life compared to the Lower Peninsula. People like to keep to themselves, but there are still strong communities. What I enjoy is the solitude—night and day from our life in Detroit."

"Do you want to live on the water or inland?"

"Well, that depends on what I decide to do with my life," he said. "After rehashing my time in Iowa today, I'm thinking that it might not be a bad idea for me to finish up my dissertation and become a professor. So, we'd have to initially move to a college town for me to finish up and then see where it takes us. There are some great schools up there. Good places to raise our little one." He reached over with his right hand and slid it under the bottom of her t-shirt. He began rubbing her stomach. "What do you think? Can you handle living with a stuffy old man that has his nose in a history book?"

"I could warm to that," she said.

For a moment, there was no talking, and they could hear crickets chirping. She took his hand. "If we have the chance, I think we should live on the water. Watching you dive off of South Bass Island was fun. I want to learn how to do it."

"No problem. What about a boat?"

"Sure. Sail or power?"

"After our trip with Nico, I'm leaning sail."

"Me too, but I also like the speed of a powerboat. Why not both?"

"I think a professor's salary could handle one of those. Which reminds me, what are you planning on doing for work?"

"Maybe I could go back to school too?"

He gave her hand a squeeze and then put his hand back behind his head. "What would you study?"

"I don't know. I graduated with a degree in communications. I hated it."

"What are you *interested* in?"

"Well, I like to read, always have." She gave a soft laugh. "I know, not much help. Let's see..." A stiff wind blew against the tent's nylon fabric, and the rainfly flapped like a sail that was luffing.

When the wind subsided, Conrad said, "Bet there are some big waves out on the lake right now."

251

"Bigger than when we were on the sailboat?"

"Yeah. Sorry, you were saying what you might be interested in."

"The truth is, I've never really considered it. If my family had its way, I'd have around three or four kids by now and be married to someone in The Association. But I didn't want that life. Unfortunately, there was only one way I knew how to escape it."

"Do you think your family will let you leave that easily?"

"Papa will be gone soon, and Ciro doesn't want us around; he'll get another gardener. My mamma will support my decision. We are simply leaving the life, not her. She will be welcome to come visit us, and we will promise to see her."

And now the question he had been thinking about for as long as they had been living at her house came out. "Do you think anyone would travel to wherever we were living and try and...you know, off us or something?"

"If someone had wanted to kill me to get back at my father, then I was never an easier target than when I was on the streets. No one bothered then, and they won't now. It's sexist as hell, but the women and small children in the family are off-limits, even with vendettas. Ciro will be the real target."

His breathing slowed, and he relaxed. Once he had found out what business Stansie's family was in, he had thought about leaving that night. But he had realized that he was in no condition to make it on his own at that point, and so he had stayed around. He soon came to grasp that, for the most part, the mafia aspect of the Russos' life was invisible. Business associates came and went. Business luncheons and meetings were held and adjourned. There were family dinners, family card parties, and even family movie nights. There were arguments and reconciliations, tears and laughter. It was not wise guys with machine guns patrolling the grounds, although he had seen some of the Don's *security consultants*, and they scared him. However, the secrecy of the business they were taking care of right now reminded him that living with the Russos was not like living a normal life. Some of the stuff in the mobster movies had to be true, or the movies wouldn't exist, right? And he did not want to be in his home office one day, grading term papers, when bullets starting whizzing through his house. He was not certain that Stansie was right. Even though she was a woman and would probably be left alone, and he *was* the most forgettable gardener on the planet. Still... "That's what I thought," he lied. "Just wanted to make sure that we would be left alone to do our own thing."

"We will, baby. And don't think that we won't be getting something from my parents to help us out. You saw what was in the boxes you took underwater."

He didn't want to be crass, but the words came out too easily. "How much do you think we would get?"

"Gold digger."

He turned on his side, facing her. "Shit, that came out wrong."

She giggled. "Don't worry. You're so cute."

He gave a nervous laugh back. "Glad I'm still that."

She found his face in the dark and gave him a kiss. He could feel the warmth of her body as she inched closer. Then, the kiss ended, and they were on their backs again. "We will be taken care of," she said. "Now, seeing how we were both addicts, I am sure that it will not be a lump sum. Probably a monthly allotment."

As if he were already a professor and had just heard a convincing opening argument in a classroom discussion, he said, "Your point is well taken."

"Ugh. Is that the kind of talk I'm going to get if you go back to school?"

"More than likely," he said. Then, a thought occurred to him. "We haven't heard from anyone back home yet. Does that worry you?"

"No. Remember, Ciro said that we wouldn't if everything was okay. And we should definitely not call them. That's what Nico said too."

"Right. It's just strange to me, that's all. If everything was good, then why wouldn't it be okay for them to call us and let us know or us call them to let them know *we're* okay?"

"It takes some getting used to. But I believe it is for our safety. They expect us to return tomorrow afternoon. Don't worry, they'll be ready for us, and then we can tell them all about our adventure. You just asked me about getting money, right? Well, when we show up clean and on time, having done exactly what they wanted, then the chances of us getting to leave to start our own life increases."

She was right. And yet, he couldn't help but think something was not right. The deli that they had gone to for lunch had no televisions inside, and he had never been much of a newspaper reader—that was Brad—so he had no idea about the world outside of the tent right now. This bothered him some because he was always anticipating something historical to happen, but he admitted that it was nice not getting caught up in the twenty-four-hour news cycle addiction. That kind of news was *not* history—and not how you *studied* history. What he felt, though, had nothing to do with that world. Ralph Waldo Emerson had once said, *"There is properly no history, only biography."*

*Maybe Emerson was right.*

"Conrad?"

The sound of his name brought his mind back inside the tent. *You're wasting your time worrying about things you don't even know about*, he told himself. "Sorry. You're right. Everything is fine. I guess I'm so used to having things go wrong, many times by my own hand, that I got carried away." He leaned over and kissed her. "We're good."

She put her hand on his muscular, hairy chest and started to move it slowly down his flat stomach. "Not yet," she said.

Grosse Pointe Shores

"Okay, well, we'll see about the payment," Don Fabian De Luca said into the phone. "I have to find where the money is first. Understand?"

254

The phone call ended, and Fabian handed the phone to a butler who would take the phone into the basement and destroy it. Then, he would bring Fabian a new disposable phone to use for any calls tomorrow.

As the butler left the study, Fabian sat back against the charcoal-colored couch cushions. On the ebony end table was a glass coaster and a snifter of brandy. He dipped his new cigar in the drink and then wrapped his lips around the end, tasting the heavenly sweetness mixed with the aroma of tobacco.

He looked at his watch. 9:30 p.m. Where were they? The search of Angela's house for the phone yesterday had proven to be a challenge. Angela did not want to leave her house at that point, and they were only able to cover a few rooms. But, tonight, Angela had given in to the charms of Papa Pete and was taking a leisurely cruise in Lake St. Clair on the Consigliere's seventy-two-foot yacht, *Empire State of Mind*. Perhaps they would sleep onboard tonight, which would give GiGi and his men even more time to search. The phone had to be there somewhere. It was the only link to find Stansie and the gardener—and the money. And when they found out where the money was, they would take it all for themselves.

The dim light of the study made the Don's eyes sparkle in the window next to the end table. He put his cigar down, loosened his silk necktie, and drifted off to sleep.

A half-an-hour later, GiGi Rizzo entered the study and carefully woke the Don. "We finally found it. Had it stashed underneath his prissy little bathroom sink."

The Don rubbed his eyes and then focused on GiGi as his bodyguard took an object out of his pocket and showed it to the Don.

In GiGi's hand was a black cell phone. "Do we call tonight?" GiGi said.

"No. We visit Angela tomorrow and have her call for us. Go into our communications room and contact my uncle's yacht, I want to speak with him."

# 25

## Sterling State Park, Michigan,

### *1 Day Ago . . .*

C onrad Cranston emerged from the icy shallows of Lake Erie after one final dive in the water as the sunrise loomed in the distance—beams of orange, red, yellow, and indigo spread across the glass surface. Stansie waited on the shore with a towel, and he shook his long hair by her, spraying drops of water everywhere.

"Someone wants to stay here for a while longer."

He took the towel and started drying his hair. "It's so gorgeous and quiet. I do." Refreshed was an inadequate word for how he felt. After making love last night, he had fallen into a catatonic sleep. When he awoke this morning, he possessed a vibrance unknown to himself, and he had gently woken her up with a long massage, which had led to even better sex than the night before—more intense, with both of them reaching orgasm. Stansie first, and then him.

He took her hand, and they stood, looking at the water. "Did you know that, geologically, Lake Erie is the oldest of the Great Lakes?"

"No," she said. "Am I about to get a history lesson?"

He smirked. "Can't help it. All of our talks have me feeling the pull back to the university campus."

She put her head on his shoulder. "Lay it on me."

"Well, Erie is the shallowest of the Great Lakes. I think the deepest point is just over two hundred feet. But. There are over 1,750 shipwrecks out there," he said, pointing at the water. "Most of them sank in sixty feet of water or less and were probably dynamited to remove them from being a hazard to navigation. You see, Lake Erie has a soft bottom, so when a wreck does settle on the lake bed, large parts disappear ten or more feet into the mud and silt. Some disappear completely, so when you dive for a wreck, sometimes you have to dig a little to even see something. And there's all sorts of stuff that can destroy a wreck that sinks while it's mostly intact."

"Like what?" Stansie said.

"Oh, ice, wind, waves, current—collisions if some of it is still above the water."

Stansie laughed to herself.

"What?" Conrad said.

"You're standing here telling me all about the lake and its shipwrecks. I don't even know how this area was discovered."

"Well, *discovered* is a tricky word. Remember, Native Americans were already living in this area. But, as far as explorers to the new world are concerned, you've come to the right man. Lake Erie was the last Great Lake discovered." He searched his memory. "Think it happened in the late 1600s." He paused as if to verify the date. "Yeah, pretty sure it was then. Anyway, it was the Europeans who figured out just what a treasure trove of resources this area had: lumber, rich farmland, minerals like coal, copper, iron, limestone, and, arguably the most valuable resource of all," he said, waving his arm across his body, "fresh water."

"So, because of these, a lot of people settled here instead of going farther west?"

"Indeed." He gave her a quick peck on the cheek. "Sure you don't want to study history with me?"

"Um, no."

"Because of the resources, industries and massive urban populations took off in the Great Lakes Region. I think there were around three hundred thousand people living in the Great Lakes in 1800. By 1970, around the time my brother Brad was born, the population had exploded to thirty-seven million."

"Okay, I get it, you can stop now. You are definitely heading back to finish your degree."

He looked down at the ground. "Kind of makes you wonder, though, doesn't it?"

"About what?"

"What I could have been had I not gotten into the stuff that I did?"

She pulled his head up by the chin with her palm. "Now, that kind of talk is over. We only go forward from here."

They kissed.

"We're down to our last four water bottles, so it's a good thing we're heading back in a few hours. Don't want to push our luck too much."

It was a welcomed switch of subjects. He paused from his drying off and looked back out at the lake. "No, I suppose not." He turned to her. "But one day we'll be ready, and we won't need water bottles to keep us on track. I believe it. Do you?"

"We'll see," she said, rubbing his cold arm. "Get a shirt on. You've got goosebumps all over your skin."

He did, and they walked back toward the campsite. "I'll make a run to the deli and pick up bagels and coffee, okay?"

"Got it. I'll start breaking down the tent, and then we'll stow everything after you get back."

He gave her a kiss and headed out.

Twenty minutes later, he was back, and they enjoyed their breakfast around a small fire while watching some early morning kayakers enter the water and start to glide through the calm of Lake Erie.

"I'd like to have one of those," Conrad said and took a final sip of his coffee.

"Going to be a kayak man?"

"I was thinking about what you said yesterday about should we live inland or on the water. I'm leaning toward living on the water even more than yesterday. There is just something about being able to walk off of your back deck, trudge across the sand, and then dive in to start the day. Or, put in a kayak and get a workout that way. Hey, we could both get a kayak and work out together."

"I'm liking the idea," she said, looking out as the kayakers cut the lake cleanly with their paddles, "Whatever we do, we have to stay together."

"We can do anything, you know?"

"Are you just saying that?"

Normally, they would be empty, honey-laced words meant to appease or impress or motivate. But, today, they were true. He was moody, and today's mood had him in a place of possibility—hope for the future. He studied Stansie's beautiful face, lit by the sun rising over the water, and thought: *Yes, I am ready to be a father.* "No, I mean it. We have our whole lives in front of us."

"So, the dreamer has become the realist." She squeezed him with one arm. "We'll get back today and talk with Papa and Ciro about our plan. I will even invite mamma, who will stay quiet but have my father's ear later. And Ciro will know this." She gave Conrad a wicked grin, one that meant: We are going to get our way.

259

They hugged. "We really are going to make it, you know?" Stansie said.

"I know," he said, shaking his head enthusiastically 'Yes.' "Okay, let's pack up the tent and get ready for our last hike. They wanted us to wait until around four p.m. to leave, right?"

She shook her head yes.

"And no phone contact either, right?"

"None. We just leave. If they call us, we need to listen because it could mean danger."

"Then it's perfect. We'll go on our hike, come back and shower, go get lunch at the deli, check out of the campground, and then leave right at four. We'll be home for dinner. I bet it's going to be huge." Verbalizing the routine for the day to himself had also become a habit, and it kept him focused and calm. This time he had said it aloud.

"A banquet to celebrate the mission," she joked.

"Okay, okay, I'll stop playing it up. But it still might be pretty bigtime, you know."

"Never lose your sense of romance, Conrad. Oh, and since when have you become so planful with schedules for the day?"

"I guess you're starting to rub off on me."

She gave a nod of approval. "Now, help me with this tent, Mr. Professor Adventure."

Grosse Pointe Shores

Angela Russo sat at a table that had been set for a delicious late lunch in Papa Pete's pool house. She wore a black dress with sandals that covered her recently pedicured feet—one of the many services available on Papa Pete's yacht. They had slept in, and it was now around two in the afternoon.

His housekeeper, Vanni Palazzo, poured ice water into Angela's glass and then filled Papa Pete's, who sat across the table from her.

"It was a wonderful evening, Angie," he said.

"Your company has comforted me during this difficult time, Pietro. I have been a prisoner in my own house, and it was nice to escape last night."

Last evening, they had cruised around Lake St. Clair, sitting on the yacht's top level, which had a jacuzzi, bar, and sunbathing area. After a world-class dinner of steak, shrimp, lobster tail, and the finest red wine that Papa Pete carried on board, they had put on their swimwear and headed to the top level and relaxed in the jacuzzi while some of their favorite jazz musicians—Getz, Coltrane, Sinatra, Davis, Fitzgerald—set the mood. Vanni Palazzo had been onboard and had brought over two large flutes of champagne. She had refilled a second and then a third time.

"I wanted to give you some space to breathe, my dear friend. You have been through entirely too much, and we are working night and day to find out who made the move on Ciro."

She lowered her head, but Papa Pete could still see the outline of her mouth. It frightened him when he saw her clench her teeth and then lift her head to where he could see them straight-on. "I want them found," she snarled. In his fifty years of knowing her, lusting after her, he had never seen her do this. It aroused him, and he felt his massive organ throb against his undershorts. He'd been close to unleashing it on her last night but continued to bide his time.

He took a sip to calm himself. "And we will, my sweet Angie. I swear on the souls of my children."

She relaxed her jaws and began to eat.

Papa Pete saw his opportunity. "We have men posted everywhere. The Don's mansion, your mansion, mine. Everyone is accounted for except for your daughter and her gardener boyfriend, what's his name?"

"Conrad," Angela said.

"Ah, yes, Conrad. A simple German name for a simple man."

"Maybe simple, but sweet, and he has helped turn my daughter's life story from tragedy to triumph."

Papa Pete set down his water glass and leaned forward. "We believe they may be in grave danger, Angie. We need to find them so that we can protect them." He paused, reaching for her hand until he had locked his fingers around her palm. His tone became even more serious. "Do you know where they are?"

Angela Russo gave a knowing grin, the one she had been giving to people for years whenever she was asked a question that dealt specifically with the family business—a business she had never been a part of. "I do not, Pietro. They met with the Don and Ciro a few days ago and then left. My son told me that they would return within a week. That is all I know."

"Have you had any contact with them?"

"None."

"Do you have any way to contact them, so that we could warn them and then arrange an escort to get them back safely."

"No. I assume that my husband and my son were arranging all of that. Why didn't you ask me about this last night?"

"I tried to the other night at your house but saw how distraught you were. I didn't want to push. And because *you* didn't bring it up, I assumed that everything was fine and they would both be home yesterday. When that didn't happen, I decided to get you away from everything so that you could clear your mind and rest. I honestly thought that when we docked the ship today, Stansie and her man would be waiting for us on the pier. When that didn't happen, I decided that I must try and bring it up again during lunch. They may be in danger, Angie." He grasped her other hand and began to massage them both. They were so smooth and cold. "I only ask the following for the safety of your daughter and her boyfriend, Angie. Do you know anything about what they were doing?"

The knowing grin appeared again. "I am so sorry, Pietro. I was not a part of it." A tear appeared in her right eye. It dropped to her cheek. "I just want them back safely."

He believed her and believed that she believed him. Now, he would be able to use her. He leaned back and stretched his arms to the sky—it was the sign for GiGi to enter with the phone—"I want the same thing, dearest. Thinking back to last night, it was almost like old times with us. It made me long for those days when things were much simpler."

She wiped her eyes with a napkin, and Vanni was soon at the table with a fresh one. Many more tears were wiped into the cloth, and, before leaving, Vanni refilled the water glasses and poured them each a glass of Papa Pete's homemade wine, the vintage that he knew Angela loved.

GiGi Rizzo entered the pool house, gave Angela a kiss on the cheek, and then took up position next to Papa Pete.

"Angela, GiGi has come across what we believe to be one of Ciro's phones. Have you ever seen it before?"

Her expression displayed both sadness at the hearing of her deceased son's name and hope at the thought of being able to communicate with her daughter and bring her in safely. "No, where did you find it?"

"It fell out of one of his pockets when...well, one of my men picked it up off of the street. We don't need the police getting their hands on it," GiGi Rizzo answered.

"We don't know where they are," Papa Pete said. The blasted trace had not come in yet. "And we don't know if they are aware of anything that has taken place in the last few days." He took a drink of wine. "What we'd like to do is have you call your daughter on this phone, find out their location, and then tell them to wait there. I will send a security team to them and have them escorted back to your house where they will be safe until we find out who murdered Ciro and Big Joey."

"Should I tell her anything that has happened?"

GiGi and Papa Pete exchanged a glance, one he thought she missed. "No, Angie," Papa Pete said. "If they find that out before we can get to them, then they might do something erratic and perhaps put themselves in more danger. The less they know for now, the better. Plus, their rehab has been so miraculous—a true gift from God—that we dare not chance it now. They could hear the news and take off. It might break them." He dove deep into himself and pulled out his innermost comforting tone, "I will have Father Tony standing by at your house to help you deliver the horrible news when they arrive. We will make it through this together, my sweet Angie. But it must be this way for their safety. You have lost a husband and a son; you will not lose a daughter."

GiGi's cell phone rang, and he moved away to answer it. In ten seconds, he pulled Papa Pete aside and whispered to him, "The phone is in Sterling State Park right now, about an hour south of here." He paused.

"More?" Papa Pete asked.

"There was a third cell phone. We believe it belonged to River Nicky."

Papa Pete's eyes narrowed. "Location?"

"No. He must have destroyed it."

"We'll get it out of them when we catch them. Go let Fabian know. Have my yacht refueled immediately. We may need to use it." He moved away, sporting a charming grin and sat back down across from Angela.

"Business never waits," he said. "Things moved so much slower the last time I took a position like this." He frowned. He toyed with his own cell phone in his hands. "Must be these crazy machines that are driving it, don't you agree?"

Angela nodded.

Vanni filled Angela's wine glass even more. Then, in a sweet voice that would put someone at ease right before having life-altering surgery, she whispered into Angela's ear, "Take some of this to calm yourself. We will have them back at your house this afternoon. Safe and sound." She kissed Angela's cheek and then disappeared into the pool house's kitchen.

Angela took a long drink of the wine, let it sit in her mouth, and then swallowed. "Dial the number for me, Pietro."

And now Papa Pete had one of his own tears escape his right eye. "Of course, Angela."

He dialed the number.

# 26

## Sterling State Park, Michigan

### *1 Day Ago...*

It was half-past two in the afternoon when the cell phone rang. Conrad Cranston and Stansie Russo sat at their site's picnic table drinking water, recovering from their long hike. Conrad was using a pocket knife to chip off a sliver of pea-green paint that had started to peel from the tabletop. *Whoever painted this did a poor job*, Conrad thought. The table's wood was new.

*Probably a rush job before the summer started.*

Sweat dripped from Stansie's forehead and fell on to her phone's screen, which she then wiped with the bottom of her tank top. "Should I answer it?" she asked him.

Conrad looked up from the tabletop and said, "I think you have to."

"I'm putting it on speakerphone," she said, then answered, "Hello?"

"Stansie, my love, it's mamma."

266

He never tired of hearing her mother's calming voice, and he relaxed, knowing that it wasn't Ciro.

"Good afternoon, mamma. Is everything okay?"

"Yes, dear, fine. How are you and Conrad?"

He grinned. Major points for Mama R.

"We're well," Stansie replied. "Did papa tell you when we were coming home?"

"That's what I wanted to talk with you about. There has been an attempt on his life."

Stansie gasped, and Conrad lowered his head. In one statement, his bubble of calm had been replaced with anxiety.

"Don't worry," Stansie's mother quickly said. "Everyone is fine. However, we need to get you both home safely. Papa and Ciro wanted me to make the call. Do you understand me, Stansie?"

"I understand, mamma."

Conrad nodded, his hands shaking.

"Good," Angela Russo said. "We will need to think of a good place to pick you up, someplace public."

"Well, as you know, we are just about an hour south of you at Sterling State Park in Monroe."

"Sterling State Park in Monroe, yes, dear, closer to forty-five minutes with the way your brother drives."

Stansie laughed. "Speed demon."

"I know," Angela said. "The entrance of the park will be perfect. Wait there. We're sending two vehicles with our men. They should be to you around three-thirty."

Conrad gave a thumbs up, feeling more sure about the situation now that a plan was in the works. Details, which had always been a source of limitation to his freedom, suddenly became a source of strength and control.

"What about the green truck?" Stansie asked.

"Leave it at the campsite. Someone else will pick it up later."

Conrad thought he heard murmuring in the background and gave Stansie a puzzled look while raising his shoulders.

She nodded back, seeming to pick up on it too. "Mamma, are you on speakerphone?"

"Yes, my arthritis is kicking in again."

"Who is in the room with you?"

"Oh, just Carlotta. I'm trying to stay out of her way as she cleans the library."

Again, her mother's voice calmed his nerves. Cleaning the library made perfect sense to him.

"Okay, mamma. Three-thirty. We'll be waiting."

"That is good, my child; help is on the way. We can hear all about your adventure over dinner tonight."

"I love you, mamma."

He smiled at Stansie.

There was a pause and then a diminished version of her mamma's voice, "I love you too, Stansie."

*Whoa. What was that all about?*

The phone call ended.

Stansie was shaking as she turned to Conrad.

"Your mom sounded different at the end. I mean, the plan sounds great. She's probably just on edge because of the attempt on your dad, right?"

She tried to say something, but he kept on going, needing to get all of his thoughts out because he was scared shitless. "They'll be here in about an hour." He looked around. "Let's keep our eyes open, though. We don't need anybody sneaking up on us here."

Stansie grabbed his forearm, while shaking her head. "That isn't it." Tears were forming in her eyes.

"What?" Conrad asked. *Have I missed something?*

"Mamma performed beautifully—for whoever is holding her. Conrad, the signal, known only to me, Ciro, and my papa, was if my mamma ever communicated anything directly to any of us, it meant that she and we were in grave danger and to not believe anything she said."

"Oh shit!" he blurted out, losing control. "Sorry, sorry. But you told them we were at Sterling State Park!"

"They knew that already, I'm sure. They're just trying to make it look like they're worried."

"But the only way they would know that is if they got a hold of Ciro's phone or Nico's...oh, God. Stansie, they might be—"

"*Dead.*" She said with a steeliness that proclaimed finality.

*Think it through. Think it through. You've gotta get the two of you out of this.* Nothing but the sight of someone sneaking up behind them and putting a bullet in each of their heads came to him. *The hell with it all!* "Okay, what do we do?"

Stansie was silent for a few moments, and he realized that a new dimension of her had just come alive—a calculating, intense, and powerful force that he had only seen applied to working out, drinking their waters, and their various sexual escapades. Now, he figured he would see it applied to a survival situation that was more common in her father's line of work. He needed her blood to be ice-cold in that area right now, because he was a complete mess.

She spoke. "Okay, we need to split. It will confuse them. We haven't much time, so we'll check out of the park and drive away. A mile down the road, I'll let you out, and it will be your job to reenter the park through the water. You'll have to swim, so here, take this Ziploc bag and put your cell phone in it."

"But shouldn't the phone stay in the park—especially if they are tracking it?" How he came up with a good question, he had no idea.

"You're right. What do you think?"

*Jesus, don't ask me to think anymore right now. Maybe if we had some wings and a six pack of cold ones I could concentrate… Stop it! Get a grip.* He did. "Well, your Ziplock bag gave me an idea. I'll put the phone in the bag and hide it underneath the tank lid in the far men's stall in the bathroom. This way, they'll think we're staying put. I'll still do the swim routine to reenter the park. Then, I'll grab the phone from the toilet tank and hang on to it. I'll hang around the bathroom and turn it off when I see who shows up. This will give us a way to know and recognize who might be tracking us. I'll dash into another bathroom, hide the phone in the same way, and then I'll hit the water and swim down the coast. I'll stay there until midnight and then meet you back up front."

"Right. Our bases are covered. If anyone comes to the front of the park inquiring about us, the park ranger can tell them that we left about an hour ago. I'll drive for a few hours and check into a hotel. I'll pay cash and wait in our room. Then, tonight, at midnight like you say, I'll pick you up at the front of the park, and we'll head back to the hotel and think about our next move." She looked at her watch. "We have to move fast."

He embraced her. "I'm with you. We're ahead of them."

He never felt more uncertain in his life.


Grosse Pointe Shores


"You were magnificent, Angela," Papa Pete said. "We will have them home soon."

She did not make eye contact with him. "I know, Pietro. Thank you for your assistance. What you have done will never be forgotten by me."

His charming smile returned, and he gave her hand one last squeeze. "So, after lunch, let us get you home. Vanni has cooked an entire meal and has already given it to your driver so that you may welcome your family home tonight with no extra stress. And when you are away, I will continue my search for those responsible."

She nodded and continued her meal. Papa Pete took a sip of wine and dug back in too. "You need to come over for lunch more often," he said. "Perhaps, once this is sorted out, I would have the pleasure of hosting you on one of my three-day cruises aboard my yacht?"

"I would enjoy that very much, Pietro."

"So humble and kind. You are one in a million, Angie. And I will personally see that you are taken care of during this time."

Sterling State Park

Conrad took a right out of the park and headed North on Water Works Road. He wore water shoes, swimming trunks, and a white V-neck t-shirt. Right now, the phone was in its Ziplock bag and floating in the tank water underneath the tank lid in the far stall of the southernmost men's room that serviced the southeastern camping sites.

He reached Sandy Creek and walked along the shore until he reached Lake Erie. After looking around and seeing no one, he waded out quietly up to his waist and then dove under. The water was as refreshing as it was this morning, and he began a smooth crawl stroke down the coast toward the beach in front of the southeastern campground where the phone was.

Battle Creek, Michigan

Stansie pulled the green truck into the Econo Lodge parking lot. After paying cash for the room, she drove down to the local grocery store and bought a case of Evian water bottles, crackers, cheese, and energy bars. The provisions would get them by until they could reconnect with her mamma—if she was still alive.

She closed and locked the door and then closed the blinds. Sitting on the double bed, she set an alarm for 10:00 p.m., then she arranged a wake-up call for the same time.

She had a quick bite to eat, and then laid down on the bed and waited—hoping for sleep to come.

Sterling State Park

It was just before 4 p.m. when Conrad saw the two black SUVs pull down the road toward the southeastern campsite. He had the phone in his hand. There was no green truck and no Stansie. Good, everything was going as planned. There were two bathrooms in the campsite, and he was near the southernmost one. The trucks circled a few sites and then stopped at the northernmost bathroom. Six men exited each vehicle. Some of them looked familiar, possibly bumped into them at a party at Don Russo's, or saw them walk by while he was outside mowing the lawn or trimming the hedges. When he thought they had all entered the bathroom, he poked his head out a little further around the concrete edge. Then, another man stepped around one of the vehicles and made eye contact with Conrad.

"Hey!" the man yelled. "I think I've got one of them!"

*Shit!* Conrad ran inside the bathroom and did the only thing he could do, call his older brother, Brad. As he finished the call, he heard the SUVs roar up to just outside the bathroom. Then, there was the loud slamming of doors and what sounded like a horn. He finished the call: "God, I hope this is still your home number. Don't involve the police. Bigtime money."

Then, he turned the phone off, put it in the Ziplock bag, and hid it in the left-most toilet tank. As a sign of surrender, he walked over to the sink and started washing his hands. Then, the door burst open.

* * *

Sterling State Park

At precisely midnight, Stansie Russo pulled her green truck onto the side of the road, just a few yards from the entrance to Sterling State Park. After turning off the lights, she carefully exited the vehicle.

"Conrad? It's me. I'm here, baby."

There was some rustling from the trees behind the rear of the truck, and soon Conrad appeared.

"Oh, baby, we made it. Come and give me a—"

Two men sprang from behind the front of the pickup and grabbed Stansie, putting a cloth doused with chloroform over her mouth and nose. Her eyes shut, and her body went limp.

While she was still conscious, she hadn't seen the chains attached to Conrad's feet, which, now, three men pulled tight and walked up behind him.

"C'mon, we just want to have our own life, okay?" Conrad said.

Two headlight beams could be seen coming down the road, and soon the black SUVs arrived.

"Won't you fellas even listen to me for a second?" Conrad pleaded. His voice was of desperation and filled with terror.

The men spun him around, and Conrad's mouth was gagged, his arms were bound, and he was put in the back of the first SUV. While Stansie was shoved into the second SUV, the pickup truck was cleaned out, wiped, and then pushed into a ditch down the road. Then, the two SUVs took off north for their rendezvous with the yacht *Empire State of Mind*.

The two captives would be joining them on an evening cruise to South Bass Island.

# 27

## Put-in-Bay, South Bass Island, Ohio

## *Present Day*

Allison Shannon listened as Mike Martinson told her about the phones. "Okay, the one phone number belonged to someone who lived in one of those massive mansions out in Grosse Pointe Shores. I dug a little further and found out that many members of the Detroit mafia live out that way. But the particular house where that phone seemed to stay put was owned by Ilario Russo, the Godfather of the Detroit Association. Was your friend's brother involved with the mob?"

Allison asked Brad, and he responded with a look as if someone had just asked him if Conrad Cranston was the President of the United States of America.

"Um, we have no idea what Conrad was involved in."

"Well, the other number is from where you're both at right now: South Bass Island. The signal cut out a day or so ago, but the trace I was able to get had it pinpointed in a house on the southwestern shore of the island, just north of Lighthouse Point."

"Our next port of call," Allison said into the phone. "You just described a guy's place who was seen with Conrad a few days ago. He's got a bo—"

"Boat moored off of his place. I could see it in the satellite photos. Big one by the looks of it. Now, be careful—both of you."

"We will, Mike."

His voice became edgy. "You better take this seriously, Allison. Are you putting two and two together on this? You could have something going on between your missing hiker, someone high up in the mafia, and some guy who has a nice place out on South Bass Island. You said that Conrad was camping at Sterling State Park. Well, call old Mike crazy, but that looks like a pretty nice triangle for transferring product. Plus, your guy said something about money at the end of the message, right?"

"Yeah, a little more complex than we originally thought."

"Hey, wait a minute," Mike said. "You two been following the news lately?"

"Not closely," Allison said.

"Let me bring this up on my computer...let's see...yep. Here it is. Mafia Don Ciro Russo gunned down in downtown Detroit three days ago." He paused. "Oh, shit."

"What?" Allison replied.

"A little four-year-old girl named Nancy Murphy was killed too—shot in front of a hamburger joint. On vacation in Detroit with family. Jesus Christ."

"My God," Allison said. "This is the first I've heard about the girl. We did hear something about the new Don's murder but had no reason to think it was connected."

"Allison, you need to listen to me. These are the kind of people you may run into at that house, and right now it's just you and an illustrator from a small-town press. I'm calling the Detroit FBI Field Office, okay? Do not enter that house without hearing back from me. Got it?"

She paused. Of course, this was the right and prudent thing to do. Set up a surveillance position, watch, and then wait for the Feds to arrive. She looked at Brad, who seemed anxious to find out what the phone conversation was all about, and thought about him and why he had hired her. What if they waited too long, and Conrad was dead or seriously injured by the time they got there? And what about the woman that might be with him? *Dicey. Uncertain.* She'd have Mike make the call, tell Brad what she had just discussed over the phone, and then evaluate the situation with him.

"Go ahead and make the call, Mike. Then get right back to me."

"Got it," Mike said and then hung up.

"What was that all about?" Brad asked.

She turned, and they started walking. "I'll tell you on the way to the boat."

FBI Detroit Field Office

Patrick Bruno sat behind a desk in Terrance Nolan's office with a heap of files and papers taking up the left-hand side and a telephone and his cup of coffee the other side. He was going back through the entire set of correspondence between Nineteen and Nolan, and he was pissed. Nolan had called him this morning and said that he would not be in today—stomach flu, and it was a doozy.

*"Don't worry, I've got the press on the defensive, and if anybody needs to make a call, they'll handle it in D.C. No. No more shit is going to go down today. It's already gone down. With any luck, we'll be turning over in a down period of violence. Questions? For me? No problem. Look, I'll be in tomorrow, and I'll take you to breakfast and tell you whatever you want to know, and then we'll talk about our upcoming meeting with Nineteen. Okay? Okay. What? Your niece? Man, I'm sorry to hear about that. You need time off? No? All right. Well, you call me if you need something. And, Patrick? We're going to get these guys."* And

that was how the phone call had ended. Stomach Flu? Well, Nolan had looked like he'd been hit in the face with a sack of coins yesterday. He just looked...older. Maybe the murder of the little girl was weighing on him more than he had said, and maybe Patrick was right, and Nolan had known about the girl, Debbie Archer, who had been murdered in 2007. He wanted answers now, but, at this point, what would one more day matter?

His phone rang. Should he even bother? After staying up most of last night consoling his wife because of the death of their niece, all he wanted was peace and quiet and coffee. He'd received the report and video this morning. Traces of semen had been found in his niece's mouth, vagina, and anus. One of the sexual partners had overdosed with her and was found ten feet away, facedown in the grass near the park bench. The kid was seventeen. A surveillance camera mounted on a lamppost across the street had recorded most of the incident; the camera had been placed there by local law enforcement after they had received a tip a week ago that the park bench was a drug dealer distribution point. On the video, she had first appeared emerging from the woods at the edge of the frame. She sprinted barefoot to the bench where the kid and an older man were. After a minute of talking, the three-way sexual encounter began. When it was over, the older man helped Patrick's niece and the kid shoot up and then took off. Patrick had watched the video, helplessly, as they both began to overdose, fall over, and eventually stop moving. The phone rang again.

*Fuck it.*

He picked up the receiver and heard a man introduce himself as Mike Martinson.

Fifteen minutes later, he dropped by Nolan's house. No one answered, and he couldn't get Nolan on the phone. Maybe the guy had had enough. He was what, weeks away from retirement, and that might be postponed now? Maybe the little girl had taken it all out of him, and he had taken off for a day. And maybe this was Nolan's way of extending his middle finger at the bureau for trying to extend *him* past his retirement date. Patrick frowned. He'd played the stomach bug card a few times in Nashville when he needed a break. He couldn't really blame Nolan. This was his show now. He could have tried to put together a task force, but he knew what that timetable would've been. Jumping through bureaucratic-ass-covering hoop after bureaucratic-ass-covering hoop until the initiative had been lost and the mission doomed before it even commenced. Not even Nolan's seasoned wizardry of cutting through the red tape could set things in motion fast enough, and Nolan was nowhere to be found. *Screw it all.* He was tired of reacting and had decided to *act* instead.

So, he had asked Maggie Schiff, his preferred choice to be his partner whenever he would meet with Nineteen in the future, if she wanted to go with him on a little trip today. She had accepted, and they were now in a car headed to a house on Lake St. Clair. A fellow agent's brother-in-law, retired cargo pilot Scooter 'Scooty' Daugherty, had a floatplane that was tied up to a dock behind Scooty's lake house.

And since the amount of cash that had been discussed was right, Scooty was fueling up to fly Patrick and Maggie to South Bass Island.

Put-in-Bay, South Bass Island, Ohio

"He's coming here in a what?" Allison said into her cell phone, sitting in the cockpit of Larry's Stingray 25. There was a no-wake rule in the harbor, and Brad was motoring them out to sea where they could turn to port and follow the coastline down to the house where they thought Conrad was being kept.

"A floatplane," said Mike Martinson. "He knows you could get to the house before him, but he wants you to anchor out and wait. He's flying with another agent named Maggie Schiff. They'll land near you and then come over to your boat. Got it? Good. I gave him your number, and he said he'd call you soon. You both take care, you hear?"

The phone call ended, and she said to Brad, "We're going to have company."

He eased the throttle forward as Gibraltar Island started to pass down their starboard side, and she explained the situation to him.

"Let's get close enough so we can take a look with the binoculars," Brad said. "If I see that Conrad is in any danger, then all bets are off. I'm going to try and save him."

Allison went to protest but checked herself. After observing him for the past day, she knew there would be no talking him out of it. It was his brother.

He took his eyes off the water for a few seconds and said, "I just want to say thanks. You've done your job and don't have to do any more. I don't want to put you in any danger because of what my brother might have gotten himself into."

"You won't be alone," she said, and pulled a Glock 22 out of her bag and loaded a fifteen-round clip.

He grinned, shook his head, and then concentrated on the navy water off the bow.

As they passed by Peach Orchard Point, the waves grew in height. Brad opened the throttle, and soon whitecaps were everywhere. She sat down and pulled the binoculars out of her bag and then hung them around her neck. Water sprayed Brad and Allison as the bow hit the waves, and they cleared the remaining land off the port side. As he began to swing *Reminiscing* to the west, it started to rain, and thunder could be heard in the distance. The sky was dark purple in the direction they were heading.

Conrad Cranston felt like his legs would bend at any moment. He was standing in the middle of Nico Colombo's living room with Stansie standing on his shoulders. Only his affinity for westerns had conjured up the memory of watching *Once Upon a Time in the West* where Charles Bronson is placed in a similar situation with a smiling Henry Fonda looking on, waiting for Bronson's legs to give out—which would spell death for the man standing on Bronson's shoulders. Why? Because that man's neck had a noose around it like Stansie's had now. If Conrad could no longer stand, the rope would pull tight, and, as GiGi Rizzo had said more than an hour ago when the torture had begun, *"We'll have ourselves a hangin'!"*

Conrad's arms and feet were spread apart and chained to huge steel rings countersunk into opposite walls. His neck had a shackle around it, and a chain ran straight down where it was padlocked to a ring countersunk in the floor. Stansie's hands were bound behind her back with rope, and the ring from where the noose was hung had held a large chandelier before being removed for the event. He hadn't noticed the rings on the wall when they had stayed here a few days ago, but he had remembered the chandelier. The ring on the floor beneath him had been covered by a rug with a coffee table over it.

They could not communicate with each other, for their mouths were gagged with red handkerchiefs. All they could do was moan in agony or moan in an attempt to encourage each other to keep fighting. His legs felt like they had been dipped in hot oil, and sweat slid all over his body. He didn't know how much longer he could hold out.

Sitting in leather recliners, each with an end table that held a heavy glass ashtray, lit cigar, and a glass of bourbon, were the men witnessing the torture. Stansie had yelled their names before being gagged: Fabian De Luca, GiGi Rizzo, and Nico Colombo. There was another man whom neither recognized who was the quietest of the four, just sipping his drink, smoking his cigar, and watching Conrad's feat of physical strength. On the dining room table, behind the men, were five lines of cocaine, a rubber band, and two loaded syringes.

The previous night, they had been loaded onto a large yacht and then injected with something to knock them out. When he awoke, he was in a familiar darkened place—Nico Colombo's guest bedroom—only this time he was kneeling at the foot of the bed. His feet were bound with heavy rope, and his hands were handcuffed behind his back. On one side of him was GiGi Rizzo, and on the other side was one of the security men from the yacht. They held him as he watched Nico inject Stansie with heroin and then rape her on the bed. His struggle was useless, and his screams could not be heard behind the rag, gagging his mouth. When Nico had finished, Conrad was stood up and carried out of the room. He was given another injection, and when he awoke, he found himself where he was now.

He heard a moan from above. It was the worst sound he had ever heard because he knew that somewhere in the sound was a plea for more heroin—and it broke him. Tears began to stream down his face, mixing with the sweat of his exertion to keep his legs from buckling.

"Oooh, is big dumb gardener crying?" asked Nico Colombo, approaching Conrad.

GiGi Rizzo looked at Conrad and cracked up. "I think he is."

Nico got up close to where he could smell Conrad's rank body odor. All Conrad had on was his underwear. "Still thinkin' about last night, aren't ya," he said, winking. "Waterbeds, if you get in sync, can provide a mind-blowing experience." He motioned with his eyes up at Stansie. "And your girl up there, man, she got *in sync!*"

Conrad lunged at him, coming to within inches of Nico's face. Stansie's feet started to slip, and he had to pull back so she could readjust them in order to stay on his shoulders.

Nico let out a high-pitched laugh.

# 28

Don Fabian De Luca, who until this point had remained seated with his legs crossed and his hands on his recliner's armrest, eased forward and joined his hands together. With a calm smile, he said, "Nico, I hear you are a man who can enjoy his cocaine and not let it dull your senses."

Nico turned away from Conrad, and his smile disappeared. "Well, my Don, I don't know where you heard that, but I assure you that I never mix business with pleasure."

Fabian did not take his eyes off him. GiGi Rizzo casually rose from his chair and began to approach Nico.

Then, Fabian rose. "As you know, I do not partake in our product, Nico. Once you start, it never ends well." He motioned with his right arm across the room as he started to walk. "You have quite a few tissue boxes spread around the house." He watched as Nico's eyes started to count them. The Don tapped his own nose. "Your mucus membranes are damaged, and I'm sure some sores have formed."

GiGi motioned Nico toward the dining room table, and all three men began to walk toward it.

Static from the two handheld radios that Fabian and GiGi carried broke the silence in the room. Fabian brought the radio up to his ear and listened. After thirty seconds, he shook his head and turned the volume almost all the way down. "Turn your volume down, GiGi," he said.

"What was it?" GiGi replied, turning his volume down and then placing his radio on the dining room table.

"A broken transmission from the Captain. I think he said they were diving." He set his radio on the table too. "Anyway, I don't want any interruptions right now. Where was I? Oh, yes. Nico, in my forty years of being in The Association, I also know that when I find something out that my boss should know about, I tell him."

Nico started looking around nervously as he reached the table.

He stopped too late and bumped the edge, turning the five neat and separate lines of cocaine into one wide dusty line. Nico took a step back. "Sorry, Don De Luca."

Fabian went all the way to the other end of the table and stopped, then turned and faced him. GiGi now had one of Nico's arms in his firm grip; GiGi's dagger was in the other.

"Sorry for what?" Fabian asked. "Sorry for jarring the table?" He paused, looking at the three-inch white powder stripe a foot from where Nico and GiGi stood. "Or sorry because you did not tell me immediately, when you found out that I was Don, about the money in an underwater cave a thousand yards off your shore that belongs to me?"

"I—I..."

GiGi sliced Nico's right cheek, and blood began to ooze from the clean line. "Do not speak unless the Don tells you to speak."

The Don exhaled. "Nico, I think you are lying to me. And I do not like to be lied to. So, one more chance to be straight with your Don."

Nico nodded.

"Do you use our product?"

Nico's eyes shifted to GiGi, and then they shifted to the man still sitting in the recliner watching Conrad and Stansie struggle. He looked back at the Don. He nodded.

"Thank you for your honesty, Nico. Your Don appreciates it. Now, I want you to demonstrate for me." Fabian pointed at the table. "Sniff. All of it."

"All of it, my Don?"

"Do it!" yelled GiGi.

"I will do a quarter," Nico said.

GiGi went to slash him with the dagger again, but the Don held up his hand.

"And what, my dear Nico, would you have that could buy yourself out of the other three-quarters? You've already told us where the underwater cave is."

Nico straightened up. "Well, my Don, I guess I'm not the only one with secrets at this table. That man sitting over there—what? Are those Camels he's smoking now instead of that expensive Cuban cigar I put down for him? Fuckin' loser."

The man turned toward him. It was FBI Special Agent Terrance Nolan.

"He's a Fed. I saw you meet with him one night. Swam up to your sea wall and was met by this guy," he said, leaning his head toward GiGi. "You're a rat, Don De Luca, and you too, GiGi." He paused, letting his words take hold. "But now, what you're both wondering is if I have pictures, who I've told, what emergency protocols I have in place if this ever happened, right?"

The FBI agent exhaled in disgust and went back to calmly smoking his cigarette and watching Conrad's knees wiggle.

"So, I believe that I'm the one in charge now, okay?" Nico said. "In fact, I don't think I'm going to sniff any of this precious white powder. I think you are, my Don."

GiGi's right hand dropped the dagger, and his left hand released Nico's arm.

Confused by the move, Nico was too late to react as GiGi stepped behind him and pulled both of his hands behind his back. Nico struggled, but there was a reason that GiGi was the Don's bodyguard—his strength, quickness, and power drove Nico's head to the table and held it there.

Don De Luca took his time rounding the corner of the table and took quiet steps toward the men. "Now, Nico, unfortunately, you have only one option left." He pulled out a dagger of his own. It was sleek and had a ruby at the far end of the pommel. "You are going to tell me if anyone else knows about what you just said, or I am going to insert this dagger into your ear farther and farther until you give me what I want. Although, if you do it now, I won't have to use this." He placed the tip of the blade on the outer rim of Nico's ear and started to make slow circles.

After the third circle, Nico said, "Okay, okay. I didn't tell anyone else; I swear."

"That's a good start," said Fabian. Then he plunged the knife into Nico's left ear.

Nico shrieked in pain but was unable to move due to GiGi's grip.

Fabian withdrew the blade. "I'll ask again. Does anyone else know?"

Nico was crying now. "No. No. I already told you. Why did you do that?"

GiGi looked back at Fabian. They both shook their heads in agreement.

"Because I like to know things for sure," Fabian said. He wiped the dagger clean with Nico's shirt. "You won't be able to hear out of that ear again, but maybe with only one good ear, you will listen better."

GiGi pulled Nico's head off of the table until it was just an inch above the cocaine.

"Now, sniff," Fabian commanded.

Nico drew in a breath and then sniffed the entire amount of cocaine. GiGi released his grip slowly, and Nico began to stumble, grabbing his injured ear.

"Impressive," Fabian said.

GiGi pulled a pair of handcuffs from one of his back pockets and cuffed Nico's hands behind his back.

"Let's take a little walk to the sunroom," GiGi said.

Nico's glazed eyes struggled to focus as he heard the words. "Nooooo!"

Fabian followed. They left their radios on the dining room table.


Conrad had seen nothing but had heard it all. He was breathing heavily now and could no longer stop his legs from shaking. How much longer could he hold out? Not much. Stansie moaned again from above.

*Hang in there, baby. We can make it.*


The floatplane banked hard to the right as seventy-three-year-old Captain Scooty Daugherty struggled to maintain control. Special Agents Patrick Bruno and Maggie Schiff held on from their seats on the back bench. In the co-pilot seat was Scooty's St. Bernard, Sofia, slobbering over the instrument panel and barking.

"Sofia, you old bitch, shut up!" Scooty yelled. Reaching between the seats, he grabbed a handful of dog food and fed the beast. Sofia devoured the brown pellets and then licked his fingers.

"That's my sweetheart," he said, rubbing behind her ears. The dog settled back down, panting and looking out the windows.

The sky was pitch black, and the relentless rain needled the exterior of the plane. The wind had turned the sea below into a churning mess. A lightning bolt shot through the sky, and for a brief second, Patrick could see the island out of his left-side window. "There's South Bass," he said. *We made it*, he thought.

Scooty nosed the plane down. After a few seconds, he said, "I can make out three boats. A big yacht, a peach of a sailboat, and a small cabin cruiser that's gettin' tossed like a tin can down there."

"We're joining up with the tin can at the rendezvous," Patrick said.

"Sucks to be you," Scooty said. After no reply, he said, "Roger that. I'll get you as close as I can. This is going to be a nightmare to land in. You both got your life jackets on?"

They replied yes.

"After I drop you off, I'm buggin' out. Gonna land in Put-in-Bay harbor, tie up to a mooring buoy, and ride this witch out with Sofia and a bottle of Cutty Sark. Look me up tomorrow if you still need a lift back."

Patrick shook Scooty's hand and felt some of Sofia's slobber and fur transfer over.

*This is why I have a cat.*

Scooty flipped a few switches, petted Sofia again, said "Hang on," and immediately took the plane down toward a stretch of water that would be hidden from the yacht, sailboat, and house. Patrick's stomach felt sucked up into his mouth. His eyes darted to Maggie. Her face was emotionless—and white as snow.

"Divers," Brad said from behind his binoculars. He was looking at the giant yacht that had been anchored when they first arrived to scope things out forty-five minutes ago. It had now moved further out to a position approximately one thousand yards offshore and re-anchored five minutes ago.

"How many?" Allison said.

"Two."

Allison had been watching the house but now swiveled her binoculars toward the yacht. They were both wearing wetsuits. Brad was seated behind the helm, and Allison was seated on the port bench. Two more divers appeared at the yacht's rail and then rolled into the water. "That makes four," she said. They held their gaze on the yacht, but no more divers entered the water, and no one else appeared topside.

"I can't see the name of the yacht. Can you?"

"No."

"Wonder what they're up to?"

"Whatever it is, they don't seem too concerned with us. If they were, they would have already sent someone over to check us out." Allison's binoculars were focused back on the house.

"Why in the hell are they diving in this kind of weather anyways?"

"Your brother said to bring a boat. Think he was any of those divers we just saw?"

"I don't think so," Brad said. "His voicemail sounded like he was about to be abducted. None of those divers looked like they were being forced to go overboard. They looked in sync—like a team."

There was another bolt of lightning, followed by a *BOOM* of thunder. "That was close," Brad said.

"You okay?" Allison asked, not breaking her focus from the house at all.

The steady rain wasn't a problem, but he was no fan of being on the water when there was lightning. "I'm fine," he fibbed.

The sound of a propeller buzzing through the storm above caught his attention. He swung his binoculars up. "That's them," Brad said from behind the Stingray's helm. "They're heading for the rendezvous."

Allison still had her binoculars trained on Nico Colombo's house. The waves took the boat up and down with a violent motion, and she had to anticipate the rolls and adjust her body to keep the binoculars level. It looked like her legs were doing a dance with each wave that slammed into the boat. "I still can't see inside the main house," she said. Then, motion from the sunroom caught her eye. "Hey, three guys just entered the sunroom from the house."

The sunroom was one of the first things they had noticed when they had rounded the triangle of land that jutted far out into the water, giving them cover earlier. The furthest point out was directly west of the inland start of the Jane Coates Wildflower Trail. As they had motored by the house, they had seen *Apollonia's Ashes* tied up to a mooring ball fifty yards out to sea from a gigantic deck that extended out over the water. The top of the deck was covered with a bulb of glass, making a huge sunroom. There were massive pilings that extended down into the water to support the deck, and the sides were one giant square of seawall so you couldn't see underneath the deck.

"I'm heading for the rendezvous," Brad said. "Get ready with a line."

"Wait!" Allison shouted. "One of the men just disappeared."

"What do you mean, disappeared?"

"Well, I mean, it looked like he just dropped straight down out of sight."

"That would put him under the deck though, wouldn't it? Doesn't sound possible."

"Well, we'll have to see after we pick up those two Feds."

Brad throttled up, and the Stingray raced back toward the section of coast that had given them cover before.

The captain of *Empire State of Mind* had watched as the floatplane had disappeared and now watched as the small Stingray motored away from the area. "What a pair of dumbasses. Plane better land soon, and that small craft has no business being out here in this weather."

He pushed the button on his radio handset and attempted to give Don Fabian and GiGi an update about the plane and boat, but after three attempts, he put the receiver down and shrugged. He now doubted if anyone had heard his last report. Oh well, he could always blame it on the weather if they called him out on it later. He looked at the chronometer on the bulkhead. It would still be a while before his divers started hauling the cash up from the bottom—getting the dry boxes out of the cave had to be a pain in the ass down there. He was glad to be in the posh air-conditioned and dry flybridge. After pouring himself a fresh cup of coffee, he sat back in his chair and calmly sipped while watching the storm over the lake.

The final few sensory inputs of Nico "River Nicky" Colombo's life were as follows: First: the foul stench as the sliding glass door was opened and he was pushed into the sunroom—Don Fabian and GiGi gagging at the smell as they shut the door quickly behind them. Second: after seeing *Apollonia's Ashes* tossed by the increasing seas, the sound of his own voice, *"Let me swim out and check on her. That mooring ball isn't going to hold."* This followed by the laughter of Don Fabian and GiGi at the ridiculousness of his request. Third: the chafing of the handcuffs against his wrists as he tried to free his hands, then the burn of the heavy rope—rope that he had used many times in the past, taken from his own special deck box—being tightened around both of his legs and finally around his neck before being run through a loop attached to a webbed basket that held an enormous stone weighing around one hundred pounds—his drowning would look like suicide. Fourth: the pain of GiGi Rizzo's strong hands squeezing his arms, positioning of him over the secret trap door. Fifth: the "click" sound of GiGi Rizzo pushing the button, which was on the bottom of Nico's favorite sunchair. Sixth: the brief overwhelming foul odor that escaped the under-deck compartment when the trapdoor opened. Seventh: the cold water engulfing his body. Eighth: the immediate cartwheeling of his body underwater as the stone plummeted to the bottom; it settled at twenty-five feet, kicking up a cloud of silt, with Nico's head a few feet above the stone—his body upended as if he was doing an underwater headstand. Ninth: the sound of the trap door closing with a loud THUNK. Tenth: the feeling of the cocaine coursing through his body and, for a moment, him thinking that he possessed the superpower to break free of his handcuffs, chop the stone in half like his mafioso idol Johnny Judo from Las

Vegas—who blinked twice before every kill—and then ascend to the trap door and get the hell out of there. But the idea lost its appeal after he blinked twice and failed to break free of his handcuffs. His lungs began to burn.

Then, his thoughts overcame his senses. Usually, one would feel alone, ready to die a suffocating death in solitude. However, this was not the case. He knew there were others down here with him. How did he know this? Because he had put them there. For years, he had disposed of the bodies one by one, but because the product had such a hold on him—why not admit it now—he had become inefficient. How many were down here now? The smell in the sunroom told him many, which was why he had stopped going out there—and had not let Stansie or Conrad enter when they had stayed with him. Of course, he had planned to take care of all of the bodies at some point. The entire deck, drowning pool, and sunroom structure was an engineering marvel that his salary from The Association had paid handsomely for. There was an airlock on the far side of the pool where he would, wearing scuba gear, enter from the pool with a body, seal off the pool by securing the inner hatch, and then open the outer hatch to enter Lake Erie and swim with the body to his beloved sailboat. Then, he would load the body, sail away, and then deep-six the unfortunate soul far off shore. If he could only make it to the airlock now... No, that was not going to happen. Had Don Fabian and GiGi made him wear a mask, it would have been too horrific— seeing what was left of those whom he had disposed of. A lover who backtalked, a condescending summer vacationer who thought he owned South Fucking Bass Island, a dealer on the island who started skimming from him, and others. He looked around. Shapes, like huge billowing weeds, hung around him at different intervals. He had mistakenly told Don Fabian about the chamber under the deck and his rope and stone-in-the-basket method as a way to dispose of Conrad and Stansie—even bragged about his secret button on the bottom of his chair. He thought he was helping. Instead, the procedure had become the instrument of his death and the compartment: his grave.

His thoughts subsided, and his senses returned as something cold and clammy touched his shoulder. He started to squirm. The end was near. The cold water felt good up his nose. He opened his mouth and let death in.

# 29

Brad grabbed Patrick's wet hand and pulled him aboard the Stingray, and the men now stood in the stern with Maggie and Allison. Maggie took Patrick's gear bag and brought it below with her own. A line made to a cleat on the Stingray and a cleat on one of the float plane's pontoons kept the boat and plane within twenty yards of each other.

"Is that everyone and everything?" Brad asked.

Maggie had swum over first, carrying a gear bag above her head, and then Patrick had done the same thing.

"We're all set," said a soaked Patrick.

Brad gave Scooty a thumbs up, and the old pilot bent down and uncleated the line from the pontoon and threw it over.

Lightning lit up the sky behind the plane and was followed by thunder so loud that Brad heard ringing in his ears.

"Gettin' outta Dodge!" Scooty yelled.

"Thanks for the lift!" Patrick shouted back.

Scooty gave a salute and then opened the side hatch to enter the plane. Sofia's constant barking could now be heard as Scooty squeezed in and then shut the door. A minute later, the propeller started, and the plane taxied out to sea until it finally lifted into the sky—a small white angular bird against the black backdrop.

"He's heading to Put-in-Bay to ride this thing out," Patrick said.

"Should be fine there—if he makes it," Brad said, watching the small plane dip, then regain altitude, then dip again.

For a moment, they all watched the plane fight the weather until it banked right and headed northeast.

"Okay, situation?" Patrick said.

As Brad pushed the throttle down and started driving the boat back toward their previous surveillance position, Allison debriefed them about the yacht and divers and then the house where they were sure that three people were there, but that one had just disappeared out of view in the sunroom.

"And we're sure that no one who we've seen is Conrad or the woman?" Maggie asked.

"We're sure," said Allison.

"Okay, that yacht is owned by one of the top members in the Detroit Mafia," said Patrick. "We're dealing with serious people here. And that house is owned or at least used by one of their top drug runners. We want to get your brother and the woman out of that house safely if they're still alive. You got the phone call yesterday afternoon, right?"

Brad nodded. They had rounded the bend a few minutes ago, giving them a view of the house, yacht, and sailboat again. Now, Brad slowed the boat as they approached their desired position. He squeezed the helm's wheel, his forearms flexing as adrenaline sped through his frame.

*This is real.*

"Okay, well, we just have to hope that they have done something since arriving here to buy themselves some time," Patrick said.

Maggie had been watching the yacht through her own binoculars. She lowered them and spoke. "There doesn't seem to be anyone paying attention to us right now. Her stern is pointed directly at us, so if anyone is on the flybridge, he or she either can't see us or hasn't seen us. My guess is that all of their men are diving—there might be a crew member or two on the yacht's interior. If someone would have been paying attention to us, then there would be movement."

Allison broke in. "The two remaining guys in the sunroom could have noticed the plane. They're now back inside the main house."

"Then we've got to move now," said Patrick. "They came via the yacht, so as long as we don't let them get to it, we've got time."

"I can bring us right in near shore," said Brad.

Patrick shook his head. "You two have done a helluva job, but we've got to take it from here. I'm not getting either of you hurt. Agent Schiff and I are trained for this."

"No time for that," Brad said. He couldn't believe his assertiveness. He'd never had it his entire life, but maybe it had always been there. "We're not just going to sit here and do nothing. Ms. Shannon is ex-military, and we're on board for everything. My brother and his girlfriend are on borrowed time, and we're going to help them." His voice was gruff, and he felt like there was an animal inside of him, ready to burst out. *Every* muscle now felt tight and alert.

Whether Patrick Bruno sensed this or knew that it would just be a waste of time to talk anymore, he said, "Okay. Then that's the way it is. We'll go for it. I'll gear up, and you drop me off. You three—"

"I'm going with you," Brad said. "I don't care who's in that house. He's my brother."

Patrick eyed Maggie, then said, "Okay. It should be Agent Schiff and I working as a team to clear the house, but we're short on numbers. I need her and you," he said, pointing at Allison, "to suit up, dive, and see what those other divers from the yacht are up to."

"On it," Allison said, but Brad could see her legs shaking. Whatever had her spooked about diving, she would have to overcome it right now. There was no time to talk about it.

Maggie and Allison headed below, and in minutes they were back in the stern with their gear on, crouched low. Both had dive knives strapped to their calves, and both had loaded spear guns in their hands. Maggie had a large dive light that looked like a radar gun, while Allison had a smaller light that had a drawstring around her wrist.

Brad had pointed the bow of *Reminiscing* at the large yacht, hoping that Allison and Maggie could slip into the water unnoticed.

"We'll clear the house and then come out and join you," Patrick said.

"I've got your dive gear out on the bench below," Maggie replied.

"And yours is too, along with my Glock and extra cartridges," Allison added, looking at Brad. "Good luck."

Then, Maggie said to Brad, "I put my bulletproof vest by the Glock. Might be a little snug, but you've got an ordinary build."

*Just like everything about me.* "Thanks," he said.

Allison and Maggie crept down onto the swim step, put on their masks, and slid into the churning water.

Brad watched them disappear beneath the surface and then followed the trail of bubbles heading away from the boat. "They're clear," he said to Patrick.

"Let's gear up," Patrick said.

They headed below, and Brad put the bulletproof vest on. It fit fine. He grabbed the Glock and extra cartridges while Patrick pulled his own vest over his head and strapped it tight. Then, he holstered his Glock and slung a strap with a Heckler and Koch MP5 submachine gun on the end over his shoulder. "Let's go," Patrick said.

They emerged topside, and Brad nudged the throttle forward while performing a turn to port. The moment they were aimed at the desired point of land, he steadied up on that course and pushed the throttle down. The Stingray sped toward the beach.

"Who in the hell are they?" Nolan said, now standing next to GiGi Rizzo and Fabian De Luca in the dining room. "You said no one knew about this place." His tone was firm with the slightest hedge toward annoyance.

Both Fabian and GiGi picked up their radios and tried to contact *Empire State of Mind*'s Captain. They heard nothing in return.

"Calm down," GiGi said. "You'll still get your cut. That's what you're here for, isn't it? Retirement pay for helping us get Don Fabian to the top rung."

"I'm here to stay alive so that I can enjoy that bonus," Nolan said. "You're the security, go take care of the problem outside."

GiGi began reaching inside his linen sport coat.

"Stop," Fabian said. "Terrance is right. Why don't you go outside and see what is going on?" He motioned to Nolan and himself. "We'll finish up with these two, and when you return, it will be time to go."

GiGi pulled his hand away from his jacket and regained his composure. He took a pair of binoculars from a drawer and headed toward the sunroom—his left hand pinching his nose closed.

Fabian and Nolan moved around in front of Conrad Cranston, whose entire body was shaking now. His eyes were closed, and he was grunting hard through the rag in his mouth.

Fabian looked up at Stansie, who was crying—legs shuddering too. "You two have both lasted a lot longer than I thought you would." He eyed Nolan. "Right, Terrance?"

Nolan did not pander to the man's entertainment. "Makes no difference to me," he said. "Let's just make it quick."

"You disappoint me, Terrance. Here are two drug addicts struggling for life, and you want to make it easy on them. The expensive watch around your wrist that I gave you as a present tells me it *is* time for you to retire, my friend."

Nolan just shrugged.

"Okay, we'll end it," Fabian said. "But not this way." He walked over to the wall cleat where Stansie's noose chain was secured to. Carefully, he unwound it and then slowly lowered Stansie to the floor. Conrad's knees gave out, and his body hung from his arms still held to the wall by their own chains.

Fabian walked over to Stansie and knelt down. He began to stroke her hair. "You should have been my Leo's wife," he said.

Her eyes narrowed at him with hate, and she shouted some obscenity, but it was distorted by the rag.

"Ah, your demeanor and speech could never rise to the stateliness of your family name. You still can't escape the street. But I should tell you now before the end that it was I who ordered Ciro's death." He paused, seeing the surprise in her eyes. "Yes, Ciro is dead, and Silvio, and your father, and Giuseppe." He grabbed her hair and twisted her head so that it was facing the water. "That money out there beneath the waves is *mine*. Your father became too greedy, as did his consigliere. Now, I will distribute it to the members of The Association who earned it." He took off her rag.

*Air!* She took in deep breaths while she thought. She needed to buy time by playing dumb. Of course, she had known they were dead when her mother had called. She also wanted more information. *How to do it? Play along with his game. Your hands are almost free.* "You're lying. My mamma told me on the phone that everything was fine."

Fabian laughed. "And who do you think was in the room with her when she made that call? Yes, you see it now, don't you? And when I return to Detroit with The Association's money, my uncle will carefully take care of your mamma."

He was back to stroking her hair. "She's been through too much. Better for her to not suffer anymore." He tied the rag over her mouth again.

Stansie writhed on the ground, yelling into the rag.

Fabian took a step back and observed. "My God, what they said really is true. You do have childish temper tantrums. It is one thing to hear about them but another to see them up close." He let her roll, struggle, and cry for another minute but apparently decided he had seen enough and held his hand over her nose and mouth until she stopped. "What I can't figure out, though, is why you took off in the truck and left your boyfriend at the park? I asked my uncle and GiGi, and they said that your mother didn't give a thing away." He pulled back his hand, and she struggled to breathe in through her nose. He untied the rag.

"We freaked out," she finally said. She was crying now—because of what she had endured and because she had to sell it. "We had a taste of freedom and didn't want to go back. We didn't think anyone cared about us."

"No one does," Fabian said and tied the rag around her mouth once again.

Conrad had heard it all. If they could get out of this, then they would tell everything. The entire Association had been deceived and deserved the truth. Thank God she was playing along. She had just told him the exact thing he had said when the men had picked him up in the park bathroom. They just wanted to be free and didn't care about the family anymore. *Stick with it, Stansie.*

For the first time, he felt real hope.

*We're going to get out of this.*

With Nolan's help, Fabian picked her up and laid her on the dining room table. "Another fix, my dear?" He began wrapping the rubber band around her arm.

Stansie made a muffled noise again.

"I changed my mind. Get rid of that rag," he ordered Nolan.

Nolan untied it, and Stansie gasped for air. After a few breaths, she said, "Fabian, no, please. No more. Let Conrad and I go. We will never come after you in vengeance. We just want a quiet life away together. Please?"

Fabian regarded her for a moment. Then, he heard Conrad struggle to break free of the chains. "Hmmm. I'm sorry, my dear, but that cannot happen." And with that, he picked up the loaded syringes. "Now, here is how it works. One of these syringes has fentanyl in it, and one has heroin in it. One of you will die in a few seconds, and one of you will become a heroin addict. The dead one will be buried. The addict will be dropped off in a small town in Ohio where the overdose rate is skyrocketing, which means the product is available. You'll be given another dose and one thousand dollars in cash." He paused. "And we will never see you again. Of course, you'll be under surveillance until you overdose. Don't want you trying to carry out some wild idea of retribution while you're still alive."

Nolan just looked at the ground.

"And so, Stansie, which syringe will it be? Fentanyl or heroin?"

Caught up in his grand proclamation of punishment, Don Fabian De Luca had not seen Stansie Russo's hands slipping out of the rope that bound them behind her back, a task she had been working on for three hours now. At last, her fingernail found the right angle, and she was free of the ropes. She remained motionless as if they were still bound.

"Conrad, I love you," she said.

All he could do was yell into his rag.

"Touching," Don Fabian said, "but wrong." His eyes hardened, and he looked directly into hers. "How could you love anything like *that*?"

Suddenly, her hands whipped out from behind her back, and in one movement, she tore the syringes away from Fabian and then stabbed them into his back and pushed the plungers in.

Fabian turned toward her, his eyes wide open. He went to speak, but his body began to convulse as if a million tiny joysticks were controlling separate movements all at once. Then, his eyes rolled up inside of his head, and he fell straight to the side, the force of his head shearing off the edge of the dining room tabletop as he went down.

Nolan stood back in horror as Stansie got to her feet, holding Fabian's dagger in one hand and his revolver in the other. Nolan's Glock was still in the holster by his side.

"Where are the keys to unlock him?" she snarled at Nolan.

He pointed to Fabian's pants pockets.

"Get them out, unlock Conrad, and take his rag off."

Nolan did as he was told, and soon Conrad was a crumpled heap in the middle of the floor, breathing heavily.

"I'm going to get you out of here, baby."

She stood up; her gun was still leveled at Nolan. "Any last words, you scumbag?"

Then, bullets tore through the living room windows, and the two dove for cover.


GiGi Rizzo opened up on Patrick and Brad as they scampered for cover behind the back wall of the attached garage.

"Brad, fire a few shots and then get behind me. I'm going to come after him with this," Patrick said, pointing to the MP5.

The firing stopped, and Brad took a breath.

"Now," Patrick commanded.

Brad came out from behind the protective wall, fired four shots in rapid succession, and slid back behind Patrick.

Patrick then swung around him and took his best aim at where GiGi had been shooting from and let the MP5 loose. Bullets shattered glass and ripped into the siding of the house. Patrick moved farther out and shredded the entire side of the sunroom's glass. He heard a loud shout of pain and stopped.

"Brad, let's move!"

They crept along the wall until they were at the steps that led up to the deck and destroyed sunroom. Patrick held up his weapon and fired into the opening. Then, he listened. No sound.

"Okay, we're going in. I'll go first. Cover me."

And up the stairs they went, a grotesque smell hitting them as they reached the top.

Patrick saw bloody legs laying on the deck about ten feet in front of him. He moved to the man, whose legs were bleeding out and turning the deck into a massive pool of blood. The man was in shock but still held a dagger in his hand. The man's gun was on the ground, out of his reach. Patrick closed the distance while Brad covered the entrance into the house, both of them gagging at the disgusting odor.

When Patrick arrived at the man, he looked down into the face of his childhood friend, GiGi Rizzo. In addition to the blood spurting out of his legs, there was a wet spot of blood spreading on the portion of his shirt covering his stomach. He had seconds to live.

"I'm sad to see you go this way," Patrick said.

GiGi looked up at him in disgust. "Fuck you. You'll never stop us." His chest stopped moving, his dead eyes fixed on Patrick.

"He's right," came a voice from behind him.

Patrick felt sick to his stomach as he turned away from the body.

Terrance Nolan was standing in the doorway that led into the house. He had Brad's arm twisted behind his back and was aiming his Glock at Brad's head.

# 30

llison Shannon and Maggie Schiff swam side by side with their dive lights and spear guns trained on the water in front of them.

Maggie checked her underwater compass and adjusted course. Allison followed.

*She's a seasoned diver*, Allison thought. *Smooth and comfortable in the water—just like I used to be.* She kept abreast of Schiff—she was still in good shape—but her strokes were choppy, and she could not find a rhythm. It had been so long since she had been scuba diving that she was taking larger breaths than normal, using up more of her air. She tried to relax and guide off Schiff's even kicks. After a dozen more, she started to relax.

*What were the divers from the yacht diving for?* None had come up while they were still watching on the surface. Then she remembered her conversation with Brad about Conrad's voicemail. Bigtime money. Yeah, and about Brad. When she looked at him for the last time before jumping in, she knew that there was something between them. The question now was: Would they survive to find out what it was? She checked her depth gauge. Thirty feet.

Maggie slowed and then abruptly stopped. She grabbed Allison's arm and motioned for her to turn off her light. They did so simultaneously and were now surrounded on three sides by darkness. She knew the storm was raging on the surface, but it was quiet down here.

Approximately twenty-five yards ahead of them and about ten feet deeper was the entrance to an underwater cave. Two divers were stationed as sentries on either side of the opening, their dive lights clipped to metal rings that had been driven into the rock with pitons. They hadn't noticed Maggie or Allison because their attention was on the interior of the cave.

Just outside the mouth was a growing stack of dry boxes.

*What in the hell was in those? Money?*

They watched for a minute, and soon a diver emerged from the cave with another dry box. He placed it on the stack and then headed back inside. Moments later, a second diver came out with a box and placed it on the pile and then returned to the darkness of the cave.

Maggie and Allison each had a dive slate, and so they turned around with their backs to the cave. Allison aimed her smaller light at the sand and held it an inch above the lake floor. She turned it on and quickly wrote on her dive slate:

Watch for a little bit longer?  See if something else happens?

Maggie wrote on her slate:

Okay.  Keep an eye out for more divers.

Allison turned off her light, and they turned around to watch the cave entrance again.

"Drop the MP5 and kick it away, Patrick," Terrance Nolan said.

"Compromised yourself, didn't you?" Patrick said. He did not let go of his weapon.

Nolan smacked Brad across the back of the head with his Glock. "Drop the MP5 and push it away."

Patrick set the weapon down and gave it a kick.

Nolan moved further into the ruined sunroom. "Compromised myself? You've got a lot of nerve. Why don't you go look inside the dining room and see who is dead on the floor?"

Patrick took a step.

"No, no. Stop. I'll save you the walk. It's Don Fabian De Luca." He paused, letting the words find their mark. "Yeah, this was a game played today at the highest stakes, Patrick. And you're showing up with your chips *after* it's been played."

"So, why do you have a gun aimed at an innocent guy's head right now then? And why have me unarmed? There could be more of these guys around."

"There won't be. This was a private trip down here today for me to collect some hard-earned retirement money, which I still intend to do."

Patrick shook his head. "You're no better than them."

"And neither are you!" Nolan exploded. "That's the part of this job that you don't understand. And now that you're here, you know what I've got to do."

Brad looked at Patrick's eyes. The pupils looked black.

"Where are Conrad Cranston and the woman?" Patrick asked.

"No idea. They took off just before you put the lead to GiGi Rizzo here. Everything cleared up now?" Nolan said, patronizing him. "Well, then it's time for me to collect my money and head out." He pushed Brad a few feet away. "Kneel and interlock your fingers on top of your head."

Brad did so.

"Terrance, let him go. He was just here to get his brother."

"Oh, that was *his* brother in there? Strong guy, took a lot of punishment and didn't give in. But he must have been stupid to put himself in that position in the first place."

Patrick pleaded. "Just let him go."

Nolan looked down at the kneeling Brad and then back over at Patrick. "Oh, you thought I was going to shoot him execution-style? You have too much of an imagination, Patrick—probably how you got down here. You've got good investigative instincts, and, unfortunately, you would have found out in time that they don't serve you well in this job. They destroy you. Because you keep finding out how the whole system really works. No, not a healthy thing for you at all. I'm going to do you a favor today by ending your pain prematurely."

Without another word, Nolan raised his Glock and shot a single round into Patrick's forehead.

His head exploded, and his body fell backward, eventually landing in a pool lounger.

Nolan watched for a full minute, lost in his thoughts.

Brad weighed his options. The doorway was six feet away. Could he make it? No, Nolan would shoot him by the time he made it there. The stairs going down the deck? They were three feet away. If he dove? It was his best chance. He started to part his hands.

Nolan swiveled the gun at him. There were tears in his eyes. "I'm sorry for you too, sir. But this is the only way—"

Nolan's speech was interrupted by a sound from the roof. Before he could turn, a blur of a huge human being leaped down from above.

It was Conrad.

His hit drove Nolan down with such a force that Nolan's head broke through a deck board, exposing a pool of water below. Nolan's gun dropped, and Brad scrambled to pick it up. He reached it and stood, aiming the gun at Nolan. But he paused as he saw his brother put a chain around Nolan's neck and begin to strangle him. Conrad's knees dug into Nolan's back, and Nolan's neck arched, his eyes now looking at the sky. Then, his face turned blue, and Conrad pulled the chain even tighter.

After the last few twitches of Nolan's legs, Conrad removed the chain, and Nolan's head smacked the deck. "Got you," was all he said.

Before Brad could get out a word, Conrad stood and slammed his foot through three other deck boards. Then, he stuffed Nolan's body down underneath the deck and watched it float face down on the surface.

Brad threw Nolan's Glock to Conrad and picked up Patrick's MP5. Then, he embraced Conrad, who began to sob into his brother's shoulder.

"Where is she?" Brad asked. "Is she okay?"

Conrad couldn't speak. He just motioned for Brad to follow him inside.

They reached the door to Nico Colombo's master bedroom, and Conrad opened it. On the bed was the lifeless body of the woman in the photographs.

Conrad approached her and sat down on the edge of the bed. He then began to gently stroke her silk locks of black hair and regained his composure for a moment. "I had just been freed when the guns went off outside. Nolan had time to get out his gun, and, as Stansie dove to the floor by me, he shot her. We made it in here. She was still alive, but he had hit her in the chest, and she died in my arms. Conrad's eyes filled again. "She was pregnant."

"Oh, no," said Brad. He reached out his hand and put it on his younger brother's shoulder. "I'm sorry, Conrad." He wanted to apologize. *If we could have only gotten here quicker. If we hadn't shot when we did.* It was pointless. Nothing could change the past, and nothing was going to bring her back to his brother. "Who was she?" Brad asked.

Conrad told him and then turned to him. "You came after me. That's all I could have ever asked for."

"I didn't come alone."

"Who else?"

"Another FBI special agent and a private investigator."

Conrad looked around. "Where are they?"

Brad motioned with his head toward the water. "Scuba diving to see what the divers off the yacht are interested in."

Then, as if Conrad was in a confessional booth with too heavy a burden to carry, he told his brother everything that had happened since the abduction.

Brad processed it and then said, "So, Fabian's uncle, what did you call him...Papa Pete, is going to kill Stansie's mother?"

A nod from Conrad.

"And millions of dollars are secured in fifty dry boxes that you helped hide deep in a cave out there?"

Another nod from Conrad.

"And these guys diving from the yacht are just as dangerous as the ones we fought in here?"

"More dangerous. That's Papa Pete's yacht that they're diving from. All I ever heard from Stansie and Ciro was that his bodyguards and crew are like animals."

"Then we've got to go down and bring Allison and Maggie up. Then Maggie can call in some more help."

And it was at that moment when Brad observed a change in Conrad that only a brother who had known him all of his life could see: drying of the eyes, gritting of the teeth, a stretch of the neck, and clenching and unclenching of his fists—Brad watched Conrad's pain turn into rage.

"How many divers from the yacht?"

"Four."

Conrad bent over and gave Stansie a kiss on the forehead. "I'll be back to get you soon." He stood up. "I see you've got your wetsuit on. Where's the rest of your dive gear?"

"On the boat."

"Let's go. It's time to destroy."

# 31

The stack of dry boxes outside of the cave had grown to be enormous. *It'll take hours to get these up*, Allison Shannon thought. The two sentry divers were still positioned outside of the cave entrance. She wondered how Brad and Patrick were doing at the house.

Then, a light illuminated her from behind. She turned and saw two divers heading their way. The light went out. Maggie turned with her, and they readied their spearguns. Then, the light came on again, and she could see that one of the divers was Brad and the other larger one...was not Patrick.

Brad gave them the okay sign and then extinguished the light. Moments later, the four knelt in a circle on the bottom. Taking turns with the dive slate, they updated each other. Maggie's head sunk at the news of Patrick, and Allison could see the pain in Conrad's eyes behind his mask. But she could also see a fierceness there too and a raw determination in Brad's eyes when the dive light had come on for a moment while he wrote on the slate.

Now, the lights were off, and the group turned toward the cave. One of the sentries had unclipped his dive light from the ring on the side of the cave and aimed it in the direction of the group. The light found nothing; the group had dispersed moments before.

Conrad and Brad took out their dive knives and kicked around behind the cave entrance, while Maggie and Allison positioned themselves between the stack of dry boxes and the yacht. Conrad and Brad would kill the sentries, and Allison and Maggie would take out the two other divers as they exited the cave to deposit the dry boxes.

They knelt on the lake floor and waited.

What they didn't know, however, was that while they were making their plan, one of the divers had left the cave, passed over the stack of dry boxes, and headed for the surface.

The captain of *Empire State of Mind* leaned over the starboard gunwale and listened to a diver who was treading water at the surface.

"Boxes are all out of the cave," the diver said. "Drop the airlift bags to me. We'll float them to the surface and then kick along with them until we reach the swim platform."

The captain gave a thumbs up and then threw over four air lift bags. Then he stood and turned around, facing two divers who had just finished gearing up. "Okay, we're ready to start the transfer. Go down and join the other four. Use the bags and bring the boxes to the stern where I'll collect them." He looked back toward shore. The rain and wind were so fierce that he had trouble even making out the shoreline, let alone any of the residences. "Haven't heard anything from the house in a while. Earlier, I thought I heard gu—ah, forget it. Must just be enjoying staying dry while we're out in this shit." There had been a finger or two of Wild Turkey in his coffee. He paused, eyeing the men. "Don't tell the boss I said that. Let's just get the boxes recovered. Remember, it's only me up here, so you're going to have to help push the boxes up onto the swim platform for me before you take the airlift bags back down. Got it?"

"What about that small powerboat over there?" one of the divers said.

The captain turned around to see the Stingray bobbing at anchor. "Hey, when did that little sonofabitch return?" Earlier, he had put his coffee cup down after a few gulps and taken a little snooze, but he didn't think that it had been long enough for that boat to return.

He turned around, and both divers shrugged.

*Don't get paranoid.* He took one last look at the small cabin cruiser, saw nothing move, and said, "Nothing to worry about. They're anchored and are probably riding this thing out in the cabin. I think it was a guy and a lady friend, so who knows, maybe they're boppin' down below to the rhythm of the rocking seas."

The divers laughed.

"Okay, get in there," he said, motioning to the dark water below.

The divers gave the okay sign, put their regulators in their mouths, and moved past him to the gunwale.

The captain slid over and called down to the diver treading water on the surface. "Here they come! Let's make this quick!"

And with that, the two divers jumped in. Seconds later, they surfaced next to the other diver. Then, one by one, they submerged.

Brad and Conrad pulled their way across the top of the cave until they were directly above the two sentries. Brad held his dive knife in his right hand, his heart racing.

**Watch me take my guy out, and when the other sentry goes after me, you surprise him from behind,** Conrad had written on the dive slate.

Brad had wanted the four of them to get out of there, but Conrad's rage had dominated the planning session. After writing that he would go it alone if he had to, they had decided to stay with him.

Brad controlled his breathing and waited. He could see the light reflect off of Conrad's mask's faceplate, making it look like a mirror that he could not see behind. To the left of Conrad's mask, the light glinted off Conrad's stainless-steel blade. Brad continued to focus on his breathing. Then, Conrad started to move.

In a burst of speed, Conrad kicked over the edge and got behind the sentry on the right. Using the serrated part of his knife, he drew it fast and deep across the man's throat. Blood billowed from the wound, and all the man could do was grab his own throat with both of his hands as he died.

The other sentry pulled out his own dive knife and went after Conrad, but Brad grabbed him and ripped his knife across the man's throat. The man spit out his regulator and died like the first man with his hands around his throat trying to stop the bleeding.

The water became warm around him from the man's blood, and Brad's hands shook. He'd just killed someone. Conrad was at his side and looked him in the eye as if to say, *"You did fine."*

Quickly, they pulled each man to the side of the cave and then took their positions as sentries. They had thought about turning off the lights clipped to the cave entrance, but decided against it because it might tip off the divers who would be exiting the cave. When the two men did come out of the cave, Conrad and Brad would each take a man. If either man got away and tried to make an effort to reach the boat, Allison and Maggie would unload on him with their spearguns.

The brothers waited, each with his knife in hand.

Allison had watched the brothers take out the sentries. Now, all they had to do was take care of the other two divers in the cave. It was four on two. Allison's anxiety subsided.

*We're going to get this done.*

From deep within the cave, a light started to grow brighter and brighter as one of the divers approached the cave opening. She watched as Conrad drew back his knife.

Then, the water around them started to become lighter and lighter, and before her brain processed what had happened, she watched as Maggie bent over next to her—a spear had entered her from behind and was sticking out through her chest. Blood escaped from the wound, and, on instinct, Allison turned and fired her spear directly behind her.

It hit a diver square in the chest, and he screamed bubbles of air as he grabbed the spear and sunk to the lake floor.

There were two other divers next to him!

She dropped her empty gun and pulled out her dive knife. One of the divers aimed his spear gun at her. Just before he shot, she kicked to the left. The spear sped by, missing her right shoulder by inches, and continued into the open water. Both remaining divers dropped their empty guns and pulled out their knives. She kicked hard toward the cave opening, but one of the divers was fast and grabbed her ankle, making her head snap back with the force of being stopped. She turned around and saw the other man closing in and drawing back his knife.

Conrad saw Maggie get hit and assessed the situation immediately. He motioned to Brad to take the diver coming out of the cave and then bolted toward Allison.

Allison kicked and struggled, but now the men were on top of her, ready to stab. She thought of Keller and of the explosion and her long road to recovery. She thought of Brad and having feelings for someone again after so many years of emptiness inside her.

She felt the strength of the man who was now holding her leg with both hands and then saw the flash of the knife above her.

Conrad Cranston hit the diver holding the knife at full kicking force, and the man tumbled away from Allison.

Seeing his partner in trouble, the other man let go of Allison's leg and rose to help.

Conrad's mask had come up over his nose and had filled with water. Just as he was clearing it, he felt a sharp pain as the diver he had knocked over plunged his knife into Conrad's stomach. Then, he felt another burning ache as the other diver stabbed his knife into Conrad's back. His strength started to give out, and he made one last powerful swing with his own knife. It caught the diver, who was in front of him, in the neck, and with the last reserves of his energy, Conrad grabbed the man's hair with his other hand and sawed back and forth with the serrated edge of the knife until the water around them was a mess of flesh and blood. But the effort had left him exposed, and the diver behind him took his knife out of Conrad's back...

Brad had killed the diver that had come out of the cave and was now kicking as fast as he could with his dive light aimed at the mass of bodies colliding near the lake bottom. He was within half a dozen kicks of reaching them when, through the haze of blood, he saw an arm reaching back with a knife ready to swing down on Conrad.

Brad reached out with his hands but watched in horror as the knife entered Conrad's neck. Brad's scream sent a balloon full of bubbles toward the surface, then he took his own knife and went for the diver's neck, missed, but cut the air hose instead. The diver sucked in water and immediately tried to surface, but Brad held on to the diver's right leg...and was then joined by Allison, who held the diver's left leg.

The diver made a final attempt to swing his knife at his assailants but missed. His motion then became erratic as more and more water filled his lungs. His movements lessened and finally stopped. Brad and Allison let go and watched the lifeless body sink away.

Brad swam down to Conrad. *I can't lose him now.* Blood from the wounds in Conrad's chest, back, and neck leaked out and spread into rising clouds like three separate oil leaks from a sunken ship. Brad looked into Conrad's eyes and saw them blink once; a few bubbles rose from his brother's regulator as Conrad took his final breaths.

*He's gone, and I never told him how I felt about him or what he meant to me.*

Then, Allison was next to him, holding him. Looking around, they became overwhelmed by emotion and embraced each other—breath in, bubbles out, breath in, bubbles out...rising to the surface.

The sound of the yacht's motor broke their trance, and they kicked toward the sound.

# 32

The captain of *Empire State of Mind* had just finished raising the anchor and was in the flybridge ready to get the yacht out of there. No one had come up from beneath the surface. Plus, the rain had let up, and on the shore were police with megaphones ordering him to come ashore. *The hell with that.* He had stolen a glance at Nico Colombo's house and seen the shattered sunroom. Whatever had gone wrong there or underwater was no longer his issue. He needed to get the yacht back to Detroit. That was what Papa Pete would want him to do, and Papa Pete would know *what to do* once he arrived.

He was the only one left on board, but he could manage the luxury yacht with ease; everything about the yacht had been constructed so that, if needed, someone could operate her alone. Automation was the way of the future— different from when he had started as a sailor long ago, but those days were never coming back.

He took one look around and then pushed the throttle forward.

At that very moment, two divers emerged from the water and climbed aboard the swim platform as the yacht began to race away from the island.

✳ ✳ ✳

Allison and Brad removed their dive gear and stepped into the stern, only wearing their wetsuits. Each had a dive knife out, ready to use. Thunder erupted above, and in seconds they were in another all-out downpour as waves smashed against the sides of the hull and sent buckets of cold lake water over the side and into the stern.

"Do you think anyone else is aboard besides the person driving the boat?" Brad asked.

"Can't be many if there are," Allison said. "Be ready."

"What's the best way up to the flybridge?" Brad asked.

She looked up at the flybridge two levels above the main deck. There was an exterior ladder, exposed to the weather, that led up to a closed hatch. There was bound to be an interior ladder as well. *Should we split up or both approach from the exterior ladder?* The boat hit a huge trough, and they were knocked to the deck.

"I say we split up. I'll take the exterior ladder. You head inside the cabin and come up the interior ladder. Yell if you are in trouble."

"Okay," said Brad, and they took off in opposite directions.

She placed her knife back in its sheath and held on tightly to the ladder's steel handrails as she ascended. Rain pelted her wetsuit, and the wind lashed her wet hair against her face. She continued on.

Near the top of the ladder, she could see the man steering the boat. He was trying to use a cell phone but kept swearing because he had no reception. Then, it slipped out of his hand and slid across the deck.

*Is he armed?* She couldn't tell.

Brad carefully made his way through the yacht's salon. Christ, the luxury was everywhere. Massive 4K TV, Bose speakers, leather couch and recliners, card table with poker chips and cards strewn all over the deck around it, a wet bar, and an enormous galley. Then, he saw six sets of men's clothes laid out neatly on a bench. He stopped looking and made his way to a spiral ladder on the other side of the galley. He looked above and could hear a man shouting like he was trying to hail someone on the yacht's VHF or talk to someone on a cell phone. Then, he heard a clank as something fell to the deck, followed by "Fuck!"

He started to climb the spiral ladder.

From the porthole in the flybridge's aft hatch, Allison could see the top of Brad's head rising through the hole in the deck. She decided to make her move. Drawing her knife, she slowly opened the hatch. When there was enough room for her to enter, she charged the man driving the boat.

Looking into his rearview mirror, the man saw her, and at the last second pulled a revolver out from his waistband, turned, and shot.

Allison felt the bullet enter her abdomen and got thrown off balance.

The man was lining up another shot when Brad leaped from the top rung of the ladder and knocked the gun out of his hand. They fell to the floor, and the man wrapped his hands around Brad's neck and squeezed.

Allison started to feel lightheaded as she stood up. Blood was squirting out the hole in her wetsuit, and with no one steering the boat, it turned and hit a huge wave, knocking her to the deck again.

She shook her head and tried to focus her vision. The man was still on top of Brad strangling him. She saw the revolver a few feet away. Her body was starting to feel warm all over like it was time to take a long winter's nap underneath a dozen blankets and wake up hours later to a warm meal and wine by the fire. She took a desperate breath and dove for the gun.

The man saw her and released his grip on Brad. As he went to jump on her, she aimed the gun and pulled the trigger as many times as she could.

The man grabbed his chest and fell back to the deck. The gun dropped from her hand.

Brad regained his breath and crawled over to Allison, immediately applying pressure to her wound. "Allison, can you hear me? You're going to be okay."

She could hear him, his voice sounding better than anything she had ever heard. She managed a smile as she looked up at his dripping face, and then she saw and heard nothing.

# 33

## Grosse Pointe Shores, Michigan

### *1 Month Later . . .*

In a darkened corner of the spacious basement in Giancarlo Abruzzi's home, Father Tony sat in a red leather chair next to one of Giancarlo's soldiers, who was also seated. Behind them was an impressive floor-to-ceiling cabinet built out of pine. The room was paneled in dark maple with ornate lighting fixtures spaced evenly at a height of five feet off of the space's soft black carpeting.

From behind a large desk, Giancarlo sat and watched as Father Tony finished a sip of wine and then patted his lips with a white handkerchief. *That will be your last taste of the blood of Christ*, Giancarlo thought. Blood in, blood out. It's part of the business—a way of life. *Time to join your God.* The Association could deal with an attack from the outside, but an attack from within meant that everyone in on it was history.

Grasping his rosary, Father Tony sniffed the air. "I smell lime, my son," he said to Giancarlo.

The soldier seated next to him gave Father Tony a rather hard pat on the old priest's shoulder. "Keeps the basement smelling fresh, you know?" he said.

Giancarlo remained quiet. *Let him think some more.*

Father Tony kissed his rosary and nodded in approval. "I shall have to buy some and spread it around the musty corners of my church then."

*It never was your church*, Giancarlo thought. It is and always would be *God's* church. At least now, no one would ever again have to experience the old priest's rock soup—a recipe of water, vegetables, and rocks, used for their minerals, that had been passed down to Father Tony from his family and their origins on the west coast of Italy in the early 1900's. The soup had been a staple at St. Anthony's, but Giancarlo and most of the poor hated it. If the priest had been "in the life," then there would have been an option to put him on the shelf, or excommunicate him from The Association by letting him live. But, since the good father was not a made member, there only remained one way for him to be permanently separated.

Father Tony looked around, hoping for words of affirmation.

Giancarlo took a puff from his cigar...and waited.

The room was quiet, and seeming to sense that the pleasantries were over, Father Tony set down his wine and began. "I have no idea what is going on, my dearest Giancarlo. I brought a fresh stack of holy cards—the kind Don Gallo would approve of," he said, placing the stack on the table. Then, he set six new decks of playing cards next to the stack. "Bicycle red and bicycle blue," Father Tony said. "I know your love of cards." He put a chubby palm on top of the decks. "And, these are the only true playing cards, right?"

Giancarlo continued to stare at him, showing no signs of thanks or even acknowledgment.

The priest's voice began to shake. "I have prayed every night. I—"

Giancarlo raised his hand, and Father Tony immediately stopped speaking.

The soldier seated next to the priest rose and walked over to the corner of the room off to Father Tony's right. There, he turned on a lamp.

Giancarlo spoke, "I have plenty of lime if you need to borrow some for the church. Look."

Father Tony turned his head toward the corner where the light had just come on.

Leaning against the wall was a rectangular section of carpeting that had been removed from the floor. Giancarlo could see the confusion in Father Tony's eyes, like, *"How is that carpeting staying so stiff and retaining the shape of a perfect rectangle?"* The answer was, of course, that the section of carpet was affixed to a heavy wooden frame; it was a hatch cover. Perhaps aware of this now, or perhaps not, Father Tony's eyes focused on the section of floor that the rectangle of black carpeting had covered. What should have been the bare floor seemed to be covered in a layer of lime dust...but, in the middle, a *hand* was sticking up out of the ground.

Father Tony shrieked and turned around, burying his head in his chubby hands.

The soldier turned the light off and sat back down next to the frantic priest.

*He knows whose hand that is by the rings on the fingers. Good. They say all of the tough guys are in the cemetery. Well this basement is no cemetery, and that hand belongs to no tough guy.* Giancarlo waited, and eventually Father Tony's head rose, tears streaming down his face. "I swear on my life that I had nothing to do with—"

He never got another word out. Giancarlo placed his hand over a simple silver bell on his desk and pushed down, ringing it.

The doors to the wooden cabinet burst open, and the soldier who had been waiting inside shot Father Tony in the back of the head.

Giancarlo calmly smoked his cigar, watching the smoke lift toward the ceiling.

* * *

Angela Russo sat behind an immaculately set table for two. She had on a cream-colored gown with a scarlet scarf. Her lipstick color was scarlet, and she wore matching heels. A fresh fire roared in her dining room's fireplace, and a special bottle of red that she had chosen from her cellar for the occasion rested on the table. Sinatra's album *In the Wee Small Hours* had just started to play, and she took her seat and waited for her guest.

Two minutes later, Pietro "Papa Pete" De Luca was escorted in through the large mahogany doors that led to the dining room. *He looks good*, she thought. Black suit, gray tie, gold watch, gold pinkie ring, gold-rimmed glasses, and his thin hair was combed in a way to make him appear as youthful as possible. His smile was welcoming and magnetic.

She stood, and he embraced her, kissing both of her cheeks and then her hand. There were no words. She inclined her head thanks, and motioned to the seat at the end of the table. He moved with the purpose of a much younger man and took his seat.

A waiter entered through the doors and opened the wine. He poured a small amount in Papa Pete's glass and waited as the old man swirled the liquid, then tipped the glass back, and finally let the liquid enter his mouth. After a few seconds, he swallowed and nodded his approval with a smile.

"I thought you might like that particular bottle," she said.

"You know my tastes. You've always known them."

The waiter poured them both a glass and exited, closing the doors shut behind him.

"This has been a most heart-breaking month, Angie," he said. "I struggle to make sense of it all. Fabian? An FBI informant? He has betrayed us all." He took off his glasses and wiped his eyes.

She took a sip and watched him regain his composure. After all of the funerals, her housekeeper, Carlotta, had delivered an envelope addressed to her. It was from a man named Brad Cranston, the brother of Stansie's lover. As she read the letter by the pool, her blood boiled. Until that point, she had thought that Fabian had been using his uncle, but she now had proof that he was a part of it from the beginning and intended to have her murdered. She had immediately summoned the new Don, Salvatore "Street Sal" Gallo, to her home and had him read the letter. He had left without a word but returned later that night.

"It is true, Angela," he had said. And over brandy in the library between just the two of them, it had been decided that Brad Cranston and Allison Shannon would never be touched. The person who would be *touched* would be Pietro De Luca. The Association's millions off the coast of South Bass Island? The Feds had seized it. Don Gallo had explained that it was a major setback but not fatal. He knew the streets, and there would always be people in them, which meant an unlimited supply of customers. The discovery of River Nicky's underwater graveyard had sent shivers all across South Bass Island, and it would be some time before Don Gallo would be able to find a reliable runner from Canada to Detroit, but time was on his side.

"I had no idea that my yacht was even down there, Angie," Papa Pete said. "As an old man, I have been taken advantage of because of my kind heart." He gave a smooth laugh. "I believe they call it elder abuse or something nowadays."

She humored him and laughed along, knowing she had the advantage. He wanted what all men want: to share a tasty dinner and a wonderful bottle of wine with someone irresistible, engage in pleasant but not too deep of a conversation, and end the evening with great sex by the fire. Because of this, she knew he would have his guard down and his rumored enormous penis up.

"I don't know about you, but I just want things to settle down for us now in our twilight years. You and I have earned them. You lost your son and daughter, and I lost my nephew. And, now," he began to cry, "I hear that Leo is missing. Oh, when will it stop?"

She reached over and gave his hand a loving squeeze. "Where could he be?"

The truth was that Don Gallo's new Underboss, Roman Abruzzi, had garroted Leo De Luca last night at a poker game in Giancarlo Abruzzi's basement, and Leo was now buried in a corner of the basement with a sack of lime on top of him.

"I do not know," Papa Pete said. "He is so young, so much potential. We must find him together."

She shook her head yes, and she could see that it relaxed him. He put his handkerchief back in his suit's breast pocket and then took another sip of wine.

"I'm hungry," she said. "And you?"

"A meal with you is all I need, dear."

She gave a fatal grin and rang a bell on the table.

"More wine?" she asked.

"I have just what I need for now," he said.

Half-a-minute passed, and the heavy doors opened. Papa Pete closed his eyes, assuredly ready to breathe in the heavenly scent of whatever Carlotta had cooked for their wonderful dinner.

He sniffed. She knew that he smelled nothing. With a confused expression, he opened his eyes and saw Don Gallo and Roman Abruzzi enter. She imagined his warm, athletic sweat—like in warm-ups, when a player feels the best he's going to feel all night—brought on by the possibility of making love to her, turn to a cold sweat of fear.

"Godfather, I did not know you would be joining us tonight. I am honored, of course."

"Angela invited us. I hope you don't mind?" Don Gallo said.

"Of course not," said Papa Pete. "Only, I do not see two other place settings."

The Don and his underboss reached the table.

"That is true," the Don said.

Gently, Don Gallo took Papa Pete's left arm, while Roman Abruzzi took Papa Pete's right. Then, Don Gallo nodded, and they squeezed harder, raising him up.

"I—I don't understand," Papa Pete said. "Angie, what is going on?"

Angela Russo took a long sip of wine and then stood. *You're about to find out, darling.*

The two men walked Papa Pete to the fire, and it was then that Papa Pete noticed that the protective screen that usually ran across the front had been pulled back. The old mafioso struggled to break free, but it was useless. The new, young power of The Association now controlled his old and suddenly tired body. Then, in desperation, he called out for his bodyguard and driver, Marcello Mantegna.

"Marcello, Aldo, and Vanni have all gone for a swim in Lake St. Clair, Pietro," Roman Abruzzi said.

"No! No! I had nothing to do with any of this! Angie, please!"

But Angela Russo did not hear Papa Pete. She was too busy concentrating on warming the poker in the fire. When the tip glowed orange, she undid his pants and let them drop to the floor. The rumors were true, and she sensed that he had popped a Viagra pill before arriving. Angela raised her eyes and bore them into his. "Stansie was pregnant—my first grandchild."

His eyes became wet.

"I haven't silenced you because I want to hear your scream," she whispered. "My daughter had a chance at life again, away from all of this, and you took it from her. I will always mourn my son, but he was a part of the life. She was not."

"When did you know?" he asked.

"When you asked me to call my daughter, I knew something was wrong, but I didn't think it was you. Now, I do."

"How?" he yelled.

She ignored him, setting the poker in the fire once more. Then, she grabbed his face with both of her hands and gave him a long kiss on the lips.

Papa Pete sobbed.

She picked the poker back up and, without hesitation, proceeded to stab it into his genitals. The screams were loud at first but then subsided when he passed out due to pain. This changed when Don Gallo and Roman Abruzzi stuck his head in the fire and held it there.

Angela watched and then returned to the dinner table and finished her wine.

# EPILOGUE

## Baxter Peak, Katahdin, Maine

### *1 Year Later...*

Brad Cranston and Allison Shannon climbed the last few feet of Mount Katahdin, named 'Baxter Peak' in Maine's Baxter State Park. He felt strong and warm, as the sun was out and there were few clouds in the sky. The peak not only symbolized the top of the mountain but also the emotional end of their six-month thru-hike of the Appalachian Trail, one they had dedicated to the memories of Conrad, Stansie, Keller, Patrick, and Maggie.

Brad's legs had become iron, and Allison's injury had only gotten better with each mile. As he took a step closer to the summit, he remembered that at the start of the hike, they were only averaging eight to ten miles a day. They had eventually worked up to twelve to sixteen miles, and, like most hikers who completed a thru-hike, they had a few twenty- to twenty-five-mile days along the way. Of course, the real reason he was recalling these numbers was to prolong the real feelings that were ready to escape at any second.

Perhaps the hardest day of the hike had been the first day as they departed Amicalola Falls Lodge after a hearty breakfast and stood in front of the stone archway, where he was supposed to stand with Conrad so many years ago. It was then that another memory came back to him: one of his brother and him helping their mother clean their house on Saturday mornings, Streisand's *Guilty* record playing as they scrubbed toilets, swept the floor, and dashed Ajax in the tub before scrubbing. It had been a simple start to life. His tears had been earned and were plentiful before composing himself enough to have his picture taken with Allison, right before they took their first steps.

They were engaged to be married, happy, but changed in a way that only those who have had to face their own mortality in such a terrifying manner could understand. Now, here, feet from the peak, he felt full and empty at the same time. His mouth became dry, and his feet stopped. He tried to move them, but the memories coursing through his brain had become more powerful than the muscles in his two powerful engines. The mind *was* stronger than the body. He looked to Allison, and she responded, taking his arm, and pulling him the final feet up to the legendary sign, painted brown with the white letters KATAHDIN written across the top, held up by four wooden posts.

There were other hikers on the mountain, but they were a hundred yards or more away from them. Brad Cranston, trail name Patrick Conrad, and Allison Shannon, trail name Maggie Stansie Keller, were the only two people at the peak.

They looked at each other and then leaned over and kissed the sign. People start, quit, or finish the hike for many reasons just like they start, quit, or finish things in life. For Brad and Allison, they had started to honor memories. And they had now finished what they started. He held on to the moment and then let it go.

As they descended the mountain, Brad's thoughts turned to their next hike. It wouldn't be as personal as this one, but it would hit closer to home—geographically. As of right now, the Michigan Iron Belle Trail was over seventy percent connected.  Planned to run from Belle Isle State Park in Detroit to Ironwood in the Upper Peninsula, the trail would be over two thousand miles long—approximately 1,204 miles of hiking trail and 828 miles of biking trail crossing forty-eight counties and 240 townships.  When completed, it would be the longest state-designated trail in the United States, and they planned to be among the first to hike it.  Being together outdoors for the past six months without any distractions had been revealing.  When you stripped away the false sense of connectedness that technology provided, you arrived or returned to the essence of life: to genuinely connect with another human being, to have a conversation, to enjoy the beauty and wonderment that the earth has to offer, and to find peace and harmony amongst nature with the only baggage being what you can carry on your back—the mental baggage lightening with each footstep from Georgia to Maine.

And here, on Mount Katahdin, Brad thought, if Conrad had just *shown up* for the hike, he might have discovered these things too.

# AUTHOR'S NOTE

Thank you for reading or listening to *The Hike*. As an independent author, my success greatly depends on reviews and referrals. If you enjoyed the book, it would help me out if you left a quick review and then passed on the recommendation. If you would like more information on upcoming books and discounts, please sign-up for my email list through my website (landonbeachbooks.com) or follow Landon Beach Books on Facebook, Twitter, or Instagram.

As with my other books, *The Hike* took a great deal of research in order to bring the novel to life. A few works that stood out were: *Five Families* by Selwyn Raab, *Gotti's Rules* by George Anastasia, *Deal With The Devil* by Peter Lance, *Murder Machine* by Gene Mustain and Jerry Capeci, *Mob Boss: The Life of Little Al D'Arco, the Man Who Brought Down the Mafia* by Jerry Capeci and Tom Robbins, *Great Lakes Crime* by Frederick Stonehouse, *The 100 Best Great Lakes Shipwrecks, Volume I* by Cris Kohl, *Islands: Great Lakes Stories* by Gerry Volgenau, *I Henry IV* by William Shakespeare, *You Can't Go Home Again* by Thomas Wolfe, "The Man He Killed" by Thomas Hardy, and the documentary *Detroit Mob Confidential*, directed by Alan Bradley and featuring Scott M. Burnstein.

*The Hike.* Every family has at least one outcast, and I have always wanted to tell a tale about one of these so-called troublemakers. I have found that many of them are misunderstood or become estranged due to either asserting independence or just plain old screwing up—repeatedly. However, the story eluded me until a few years ago when, on a walk around my neighborhood, Conrad Cranston popped into my mind and would not leave until I had told his account. Additionally, I wanted to tell a story that involved organized crime in some way. Looking back, I suppose the seed was planted the first time I watched Francis Ford Coppola's masterpiece *The Godfather*. My other novels are centered around the Great Lakes, and, in terms of fiction, I believe that this geographical area—particularly, my beloved home state of Michigan—has never gotten its due. Certainly, there is no mafia novel that I know of that showcases Detroit. Is there a crime organization called "The Association" in the motor city? No. My works are all fiction and purely meant for entertainment. However, a lot of material in *The Hike* comes from real life examples, which is both scary and intriguing. I sometimes wonder what a being from outer space, observing us for a year or so without our knowledge, would think. The older I get, the grayer the areas of life become.

Next up, The Great Lakes Saga finale: *The Bay*.

Many thanks to MB and EL, who both provided helpful comments on early drafts of the manuscript. A huge thanks to my developmental editor, my copy editor, and all of my advanced readers (especially APH, BB, DB, JBx2, RB, KF, CG, JG, JH, KL, CM, MM, DM, RR, and JS); the book is immeasurably better because of your hard work and collaboration. To my fans: Thank you for your support and friendship. I always have you in mind when I sit down to write. Finally, my eternal appreciation to my wife and two girls. It has been a rough year, and the three of you are the reason I made it through.

Happy Beach Reading!

L.B.

If you enjoyed *The Hike*, expand your adventure with *The Wreck,* the first book in The Great Lakes saga. Here is an excerpt to start the journey.

# THE WRECK

Landon Beach

# PROLOGUE

## LAKE HURON, MICHIGAN
## SUMMER 2007

The Hunter 49's motor cut, and the luxury yacht glided with no running lights on. Cloud cover hid the moon and stars; the water looked black. A man in a full wetsuit moved forward in the cockpit and after verifying the latitude and longitude, pushed the GPS monitor's "off" button. The LCD color display vanished.

Waves beat against the hull, heavier seas than had been predicted. He would have to be efficient or he'd need to reposition the boat over the scuttle site again. The chronometer above the navigation station read 0030. This should have been finished 30 minutes ago. Not only had the boat been in the wrong slip, forcing him to search the marina in the dark, the owner—details apparently escaped that arrogant prick—had not filled the fuel tank.

He headed below and opened the aft stateroom door. The woman's naked corpse lay strapped to the berth, the nipples of her large breasts pointing at the overhead. A careful lift of the port-side bench revealed black wiring connecting a series of three explosive charges. After similar checks of the wiring and charges in the gutted-out galley and v-berth, he smiled to himself and went topside with a pair of night vision goggles.

A scan of the horizon. Nothing.

He closed and locked the aft hatch cover. Moving swiftly—but never rushing—he donned a mask and fins, then pulled a remote detonation device from the pocket of his wetsuit. Two of the four buttons were for the explosives he had attached to the outside of the hull underwater, which would sink the boat. The bottom two were for the explosives he had just checked on the interior.

He looked back at the cockpit and for a moment rubbed his left hand on the smooth fiberglass hull. What a waste of a beautiful boat. How much had the owner paid for it? Three...Four-hundred thousand? Some people did live differently. With the night vision goggles hanging on his neck and the remote for the explosives in his right hand, he slipped into the water and began to kick.

Fifty yards away he began to tread water and looked back at the yacht. It listed to starboard, then to port, as whitecaps pushed against the hull. He pressed the top two buttons on the remote. The yacht lifted and then began to lower into the water; the heaving sea had less and less effect as more of the boat submerged. In under a minute, the yacht was gone. He held his fingers on the bottom two buttons but did not push them. The water was deep, and it would take three to four minutes for the boat to reach the lake bed.

At four minutes, he pushed the bottom two buttons, shut the remote, and zipped it back into his wetsuit pocket. He treaded water for half an hour. Nothing surfaced.

He swam for five minutes, stopped, scanned the area with his night vision goggles, and swam again.

After an hour of this, he pulled the goggles over his head and let them sink to the bottom. He continued his long swim to shore.

# 1

## HAMPSTEAD, MICHIGAN
## SUMMER 2008

The sand felt cool under Nate Martin's feet as he walked hand-in-hand with his wife down to the water. A bonfire crackled away on their beach behind them—the sun had set 30 minutes ago and an orange glow still hung on the horizon. The Martins' boat, *Speculation*, bobbed gently in her mooring about twenty yards offshore.

They parted hands and Nate stopped to pick up a piece of driftwood and toss it back toward the fire. Brooke Martin continued on and dipped her right foot into the water, the wind brushing her auburn hair against her cheek.

"Too cold for me," she said.

Nate took a gulp of beer before walking ankle deep into the water beside her.

"Not bad, but colder than when I put the boat in," Nate said.

"Glad I didn't have to help," Brooke said and then took a sip from her plastic cup of wine.

"Not up for a swim?" Nate joked.

"No way," Brooke said.

They started to walk parallel to the water, with Nate's feet still in and Brooke's squishing into the wet sand just out of reach of the lapping waves.

Four zigzagging jet skis sliced through the water off the Martins' beach. Two were driven by women in bikinis and the other two by men. They weren't wearing life jackets, which usually meant these were summer folk who spent June, July, and August in one of the beach castles smoking weed in mass quantities. These four were probably already baked.

One girl cut a turn too close and flew off.

"Crazies," Nate said.

She resurfaced and climbed back aboard. Her bikini bottom was really a thong and her butt cheeks slapped against the rubber seat as the jet ski started and took off.

"Should they be riding those things this late?" Brooke asked.

"No," said Nate, "but who is going to stop them?"

They continued to walk as the sound of the jet skis faded. A quarter mile later, they reached the stretch where the larger homes began. The floodlights on the estates' back decks illuminated the beach like a stage. The Martins turned around.

When they arrived at their beach, Nate placed a new log on the fire and sat down in his lawn chair. Brooke sat down but then rose, moving her chair a few feet further away from the heat.

"What are your plans for tomorrow?" Nate said.

"I think I'll lay out. I looked at the weather report and we're in for a few good days until rain arrives," Brooke said, "then I'll probably go to the bookstore." Her voice trailed off. She gathered her thoughts for a moment. "We need to make love the next four nights."

"Okay," Nate said.

"You could work up a little enthusiasm," Brooke said.

He had sounded matter-of-fact. "Sorry. It's just that scheduled sex sometimes takes the excitement out of it. We're on vacation. We should just let it happen."

"So, you get to have your strict workout regime everyday, but when I mention a specific time that we need to make love in order to give us the best chance at conceiving, it's suddenly 'We're on vacation'?"

She had a point. He thought about trying to angle in with a comment about her obsessive need to clean the house the moment they had arrived earlier today, but as he thought of it the vision of his freshly cut and edged grass entered his mind. If they really were on vacation, as he had put it, then the lawn being manicured wouldn't be so important to him. Damn.

"What is your plan for tomorrow?" She said.

A switch of topics, but he knew she was circling. "I'm going to get up, take my run, and then hit the hardware store for a new lock for the boat."

"What happened to the lock you keep in the garage?"

"It broke today," Nate shrugged.

"How does a lock break?"

"I put the key in, and when I turned it, it broke off in the lock."

"You mean our boat is moored out there right now without a lock?" Brooke asked, while shifting her gaze to the white hull reflecting the growing moonlight.

"Yep."

"Do you think someone would steal it?"

"Nah. The keys are in the house. If someone wanted to steal a boat worth anything, they'd go down to Shelby's Marina and try and take Shaw's *Triumph*." Leonard Shaw was a Baltimore businessman who had grown up in Michigan and now summered in the largest beach mansion in Hampstead. Once his two-hundred foot custom-built yacht was completed, he'd hired a dredging crew to carve out a separate berth in the marina to dock the boat. With the dredging crew working mostly at night, locals and vacationers complained of the noise and threatened to pull their boats out of Shelby's. Nate was glad he had avoided the hassle by keeping *Speculation* moored off of his beach.

Brooke swiveled her eyes between Nate and the boat. "Why didn't you get a new lock today?"

He moved behind her and started to kiss the back of her neck. *We're on vacation, relax, baby.* "Is that a hint? Do you want me to swim out and sleep on board tonight?"

"Of course not," Brooke whispered back, enjoying the foreplay. "Are you trying to get a head start on tomorrow night?"

"No. Just trying to enjoy *tonight*," Nate said. "Can we concentrate on that?"

She leaned her head back and he kissed her lips.

Ten minutes later, the fire started to die with two empty lawn chairs sitting in front of it.

# 2

S un rays peeked around the edges of the horizontal blinds in the Martins' bedroom window. Nate opened his eyes and looked at his watch, eight o'clock. He was normally up by six. Brooke was snoring, and he eased out of bed and lifted one strip of the blinds. *Speculation* was in her mooring. He smiled and dropped the blind back into place.

After putting on a pair of shorts and a tank top, he grabbed a pair of socks and his running shoes and exited the bedroom. The hallway was dark as he made his way to the kitchen. He pressed "start" on the coffee pot, and the coffee he had prepared the night before began to brew as he put on his shoes.

The past year had been a revolving door of pain, uncertainty, and disappointment. They had been trying to conceive for six months when his father died. Only last month had it felt right to try again. He hadn't been himself in the classroom either. His ninth grade physical science lessons at W. M. Breech High School had wandered aimlessly, his tests were rote memorization, and the usual passion he brought to each day had been missing; his students let him know they knew it.

His mother had lasted in the beach house until Christmas. The original plan had been for Nate and his older sister, Marie, to share ownership when their parents were unable to handle the upkeep, but Nate had bought Marie's half and the house was now his and Brooke's. His mother had left in January to move in with his sister in St. Petersburg.

He pushed the brass button on the doorknob and closed the door behind him. After wiggling the knob to make sure it was locked, he hopped off the small porch onto the stone walkway, went past the garage, and followed the dirt driveway until he was parallel with their mailbox. After stretching, he looked at his watch and started to jog down Sandyhook Road.

Each lakeside house had some sort of identifying marker next to its mailbox. A red and white striped lighthouse carved out of wood. A miniature of the house painted on a three foot by three foot board. A post. A bench. Something with the owner's name and the year the house had been built on the marker. This five miles of beach, once sparsely populated with neighbors in similarly sized residences, was now dominated by beach mansions that looked more like hotels than houses. The lots were owned by lawyers, congressmen, real-estate tycoons, government contractors, Detroit businessmen (of the few businesses that remained), and a few others who had money. Some were migrants from the already overcrowded western shore of Michigan. White collar Chicago money had run north and was moving around the Great Lakes shoreline like a child connecting the dots to make a picture of a left-handed mitten.

The sun flickered in and out of Nate's face as he ran under the oak trees spanning the road. He thought of the advice his father had given him when he was searching for his first teaching job: "Make sure that you buy a house east of the school so that when you go into work you'll be driving west, and when you come home from work you'll be driving east. That way, you'll never be driving into the sun. Just a simple stress reliever that most people don't take into consideration—that is, until they rear-end someone for the first time." As with all of Nate's father's advice, it had sounded too simple but ended up being right.

Last June his father had been diagnosed with stomach cancer. Three months later, on an overcast September day, Nate had buried him.

Brooke heard the back door close and rose from bed. She turned off their box fan and opened the bedroom blinds. The entire beach was motionless, and their boat was still moored, surrounded by flat water. The aroma of coffee drifted into the bedroom as she put on her robe.

By the time she reached the kitchen, Nate had already filled his mug and was headed down to the water. She poured herself a cup and started a bacon and eggs breakfast.

The sand parted with each step as Nate walked toward the water. Bordering both sides of the Martins' property was a wooden fence; the spindles were flat, painted red, and held together by wire with a metal rod driven into the ground every fifteen feet or so. The fence was not only a "beachy" way to mark property lines but served its primary purpose of trapping sand. Nate took off his shoes and set his mug down by the end of the northern fence line. He began to walk south.

The water ran over his ankles and then receded. It was cool and felt good on his tired feet. The beach looked abandoned. No more than twenty yards from where he started, Nate stepped down with his right foot and felt something sharp. He stood, balancing on his left leg as he inspected the bottom of his right foot. No apparent cut. No bleeding. He rubbed in circles and the pain went away. As he stepped back down onto the wet sand, he saw something sparkle in the place he had stepped before. Glass? A toy left behind by some toddler? As Nate picked the object up, he saw that it was neither. He submerged the object, wiping the wet sand off it, and then dried it with the bottom of his tank top. He held the object a foot in front of his face and studied it. In his hand was a gold coin.

* * *

Brooke saw Nate returning from the water. Assuming that he was coming in to complete his morning routine of running three miles, taking a walk to the water with his coffee, and now eating breakfast and reading the newspaper, she rose to unlock the sliding glass door from the deck. However, he walked right by the deck and headed for the garage. She unlocked the door anyway and refilled her cup. She took a seat at the worn kitchen table, which she wanted to replace but didn't as it had been in the family since Nate was a child. She had plans to redo many parts of the house, but Nate was adamant that the table remained and that the bedroom he stayed in as a boy not be changed. When his father was alive, Nate would have coffee with him in the morning and read the paper at this table. Brooke would still be sleeping and his mother would be cooking breakfast. He had remarked to her that at times he still felt like a visitor, expecting his father to pull up a chair and start a conversation with him about the old days and family stories he'd heard over and over again.

Brooke finished the paper, breakfast, and her cup of coffee and Nate had not come in yet. What was he doing? His bacon, eggs, and toast were cold. She grabbed the coffee pot and headed to the garage.

Nate heard the garage door open as he stared at the coin through a magnifying glass, mesmerized by it.

His wooden writing desk sat in the middle of black carpeting that covered one-quarter of the garage's concrete floor. Two bookcases that he had constructed from odds-and-ends left over from the addition that his parents had done a few years ago rested against the wall behind the desk. Favorite authors had taken up permanent residence on the top two shelves of the first bookcase, and the remaining three shelves were full of paperbacks, read according to his mood at the time he had purchased them. On the top shelf of the second bookcase rested a pair of fins and a mask that he used when cleaning off the bottom of his boat. His father's dive knife was next to the mask.

The shelf below the diving gear contained books that Nate had almost worn the covers off: a Marine Biology desk reference set, half-a-dozen books by Dr. Robert D. Ballard from the Woods Hole Oceanographic Institute, a few by Jacques Cousteau, and five years' worth of magazines from his National Geographic subscription.

The bottom shelves contained books about Great Lakes ports, navigation rules and aids, and boating regulations. Next to one of the rows of books were rolled up charts and a navigation kit. Nate had taught himself how to navigate and routinely took *Speculation* out overnight.

Brooke arrived at Nate's desk and refilled his coffee mug. "Are we rich?" She asked looking at the coin.

"Very funny," Nate said, "I found this on our beach this morning."

"Is that gold?" Brooke asked, more serious now that she had a better look at the coin.

"Maybe. I don't recognize any of these marks or the language that is engraved on it." He put the coin and magnifying glass down and pointed to the bookshelf. "Hand me that book."

Brooke reached up to the top shelf and grabbed a heavy, hardcover book. She looked at the title—*The Golden Age of Piracy*—and tried to hide a grin.

Nate knew her expression meant: *only you would have a book like this, Nate.* "Thanks," he said, laughing at himself with her. "I'm glad to see that I'm still a cheap source of entertainment for you."

She giggled back, and then kissed him on the cheek.

Nate began to leaf through the book.

Brooke set the coffee pot down and picked up the coin and magnifying glass.

After checking the appropriate pages, he closed the book and looked up at Brooke. "Nothing in here that resembles the markings on this coin." He took a drink of his coffee.

Brooke passed the coin and magnifying glass back to Nate. "I can't make out anything on it either." She picked up the coffee pot. "Well, I'm going in to take a shower and then head out to do a little shopping. Your breakfast is cold, but it's on the table if you still want it," she said. "I looked down the beach this morning and I think the Gibsons are up."

Nate was once more absorbed in the mystery of the coin and only grunted in reply.

"I wonder if anyone will make us an offer on our place this summer," Brooke wondered aloud.

A few Hampstead locals had hung on to their homes, repeatedly declining offers that were made for their property. In some cases, it was enough money to bankroll them for a decade. The ink on the paperwork transferring ownership of the house from his mother to Brooke and him hadn't even dried yet when they had been approached. It was over Easter weekend, and they were at the beach house furnishing it with some of their own things. The doorbell had rung, and after five minutes of polite conversation, Nate and Brooke had said no; the prospective buyer and his trophy wife had stormed off.

Some of the mansion owners had even tried to sue the cottage owners, claiming that the cottages detracted from the beachfront's beauty. They wanted the locals out. Most of the locals wanted the castles bulldozed.

Nate set the coin and magnifying glass aside for a moment. "You think that the local kids have all the lawn jobs sewn up yet?" His father had once told him of an unofficial lottery held at the town barbershop to determine who would be allowed to apply for the summer mansion mowing jobs. It had been one of their last conversations.

"Probably," said Brooke. "I've felt stares at the dime store from Judge Hopkins and Sheriff Walker. I know they're wishing we would just sell our cottage already."

"How wrong is that?" Nate said. "The town leaders turning on the townspeople."

"What do they gain by us selling?"

"New mansions mean more opportunities for their sons or daughters to mow a summer resident's lawn," Nate said. "And if their kid does a good job, then maybe, just maybe, they'll get invited out for a summer party."

"Funny how some people get fooled into thinking they're moving up in the world," she said.

"If they only knew that they look like the person who walks behind a horse and picks up its droppings."

He couldn't help but laugh at the scene he was now picturing.

"What?" Brooke said.

He continued to laugh.

"Naaayyyyte," she said, poking him with her finger.

He gathered himself. "I started to envision some of the people we know who want to break into that circle walking behind the Budweiser Clydesdales at the Fourth of the July parade picking up piles of shit and waving to the crowd. Agree?"

"One hundred percent. Oh, the pictures you paint, Mr. Martin," Brooke said.

"You're the only one that can see the pictures I describe, sweetie."

"When are we getting our internet connection?" Nate said.

"They can't make it out until next week."

"Damned cable company. We're supposed to have cell phone reception out here next summer too. I'll believe it when I see it."

She kissed him and then left the garage.

He picked up the coin again and then looked out the window at the spot on the beach where he had found it. Where had it come from? Were there more? He put the magnifying glass and coin in the top drawer of his desk and reshelved the book. He stood with his hand resting on the dive gear for a moment. *Let's have a look.*

He entered the house through the sliding glass door and could hear the shower running as he walked down the hallway and grabbed a towel from the linen closet. He exited the house and as he stepped off the deck, he noticed that the blinds were now open on the lakeside windows of a house two down from them. No doubt the owner had his binoculars out and was watching to see what Nate was up to. The man spent more time prying into other people's lives than living his own. The beach mansion owners had one complaint that held weight: the locals were nosey.

Nate passed by the stack of unused wood in the sand and made his way to the water. The lake was placid and the sun had risen far enough to see the sandy bottom. He positioned himself at the approximate point where he had found the coin. He looked back toward the house to make sure it had been found on his property. It had.

After strapping the knife to his right calf, he pulled the mask down past his face so that it hung by its strap around his neck and rested on his upper chest. He entered the water holding the fins above the surface and probed the bottom with his toes for more coins as he walked out up to his waist. Feeling none, he put his fins on and pulled the mask over his head. He spit into the faceplate, rubbing warm saliva all over, and then dipped the mask into the cold water. After securing it to his face, Nate verified his alignment with the spot on the beach where he'd found the coin and dove under.

The water's temperature was probably in the high fifties, and Nate kicked to warm his body, seeing nothing on the bottom at first. Then, his own anchor auger, wire, and buoy appeared. He surfaced next to *Speculation*, took a deep breath, and dove to the bottom to test the auger. Holding onto the steel pole, he pulled from side to side, then up and down. Neither motion moved the mooring. He checked the wire which ran through the auger's eye to the buoy and back to the eye: they were secure.

A few summers back, he had applied for a job as a navigator on a yacht out of Shelby's. The local paper had advertised that a crew was needed for the vessel's summer voyage up Lake Huron to Mackinac Island, down Lake Michigan to Chicago, and then back to Hampstead. Perhaps "applied" was too strong a word. Thinking that mailing an item like a resume would be too formal, he had shown up at Shelby's to inquire about the job. The marina owner, Kevin Shelby, had finally opened his office door after Nate's third stream of knocking. Shelby had a cigarette and cup of coffee in one hand and was running the other hand through his greasy hair. There had been an open bottle of Baileys on his small desk.

After hearing Nate out, Shelby had said, "Fuck if I know. I've never even heard about the cruise, you sure you've got the right marina?"

And that was the end of his career as a navigator—and possibly berthing his boat there.

Nate swam under *Speculation* and after seeing that the hull was fine, he surfaced and kicked further out until the water was approximately ten feet deep. He took a deep breath and dove.

He traced the bottom and swam in a zigzag pattern out to a depth of twenty-five feet. Odds-and-ends were scattered across the sand: rocks, a tire, a rusted can but no coins. He surfaced. The sun hid behind a cloud making the water darker as Nate treaded. A breeze had started and *Speculation* wandered around her mooring. Where did the coin come from? Nate rotated in a slow circle watching the waves and hearing the distant cry of a seagull.

The sun came out from behind the cloud and the khaki colored bottom illuminated under his black fins. He dove and kicked back toward shore while hugging the lake bed. Had he hoped to find something? Sure. Did he really think that he would? No. At least he knew the boat wasn't going anywhere.

As he dried off on the beach, Brooke emerged from the house.

# ABOUT THE AUTHOR

Landon Beach lives in the Sunshine State with his wife, two children, and their golden retriever. He previously served as a Naval Officer and is currently an educator by day and an author by night. Find out more at landonbeachbooks.com.

Made in United States
North Haven, CT
18 November 2022